DANGEROUS VISIONS

DANGEROUS VISIONS

Copyright © 2020 by Liz Hartley

Published by Rainy Valley Press, Salem, Oregon.

Library of Congress Control Number: 2020922536

ISBN e-book: 978-0-9974387-8-9

ISBN trade paperback: 978-0-9974387-9-6

This is a work of fiction. Names, characters, places, and incidents are the product of the author's imagination or are used fictitiously. Any resemblance to actual persons, living or dead, business establishments, events or locales, is entirely coincidental.

Cover design by Kim Killion of Killion Publishing.
https://thekilliongroupinc.com/

DANGEROUS VISIONS

AN EDEN BEACH CRIME NOVEL

LIZ HARTLEY

RAINY VALLEY PRESS: SALEM, OREGON

For Devon Monk, my dear, generous-hearted friend.
I would never have dared this without you.
Thank you.

"Intuition is...like a crystal through which one can see with uncanny interior vision."

Clarissa Pinkola Estés
  Women Who Run With the Wolves

ONE

STACIE SHIVERED SLIGHTLY IN THE FOGGY FEBRUARY dampness. Flipping up the collar of her navy blue pea coat, she shrugged the jacket closer around her. She watched the koi scrolling through the pond next to the interpretative center of the Lillian Becker Botanical Preserve, where she volunteered, as she waited for her group. Today, a hand-spinning group from Costa Mesa wanted a tour focused on dyeing plants. She'd researched the topic herself and was looking forward to sharing what she'd learned.

The thick fog blurred and softened the colors and shapes of the bougainvillea, yucca, and even the ground-hugging succulents. The path behind her disappeared into gray folds of drifting mist. The stone wall of the interpretive center, twenty feet away on the other side of the pond, was ghostly. Even the sound of trickling water falling into the pond was muffled.

It would have been warmer to wait inside, but Stacie loved the way fog made the familiar strange, mysterious. Anything could happen. Sherlock Holmes could appear.

Stacie smiled at the thought. *That's what I need,* she thought, *a deer stalker cap to keep my ears warm.*

Absently, she pulled the chain at her neck, drawing her pendant from inside her soft, teal-colored turtleneck sweater. The deep violet amethyst crystal, an old, family heirloom, had been broken at one time. It was now wrapped with gold bands and capped on the base where the bail connected to the chain. Her great aunt Amelia had worn it before her, and had given it to Stacie when she had graduated from Orange Coast Community College with her certificate in accounting. She always wore it, its perfect termination lying just next to her heart.

After all, it was said to be magic.

Magic, thought Stacie, as she idly ran the pendant, warm from her body, along the sturdy gold cable chain. Her smile faded. *Some kind of magic.*

Family legend had it that the crystal would announce the wearer's true love. But even though Stacie had been born on Valentine's Day, love had eluded her.

Anything like a normal life had eluded her.

She watched one white koi, curling in and around the other jewel-colored fish. *You can try to blend in,* she thought, *but, sooner or later, they'll see you're not really like them at all.*

Amelia had called it a gift. For Stacie, it had been a curse. No matter how she had tried to suppress it or deny it, somehow it had always come out and left Stacie standing alone, smarting, among the shards of broken relationships, broken friendships.

It wasn't that she didn't have friends. She did. Good ones. But after the disaster with Drew, her otherness was a constant, hard kernel of ache, a stone under her heart she could actually feel.

Even her own mother had called her a freak. Her and Amelia.

Yes, well. Pamela, thought Stacie bitterly. *To know her is to despise her.*

If it hadn't been for her dad...

She shook herself mentally and took a deep breath of damp air. *Enough*, she told herself. *I've got a sweet little home, work I enjoy, and I live in the most beautiful spot on the South Coast. I even have a dog. So. Just. Stop.*

Stacie didn't often feel sorry for herself, but she had just turned twenty-nine. Sometimes—no, all the time—she just wanted to be like everyone else. To talk to people without being afraid of what she might unwittingly say. To fall in love, have a family.

Love, she thought, feeling a familiar flicker of resentment. It had never happened for Amelia. It would never happen for her. Magic crystal or no.

But the hope of love, she'd found, didn't die easily.

Her thoughts spiraled, like the koi, back to the man she'd met at the South Coast Heritage Park the previous Wednesday. Early in the morning, with few other hikers around, she could walk, meditate, clear her mind. Even when it was foggy at the coast, it might be clear at the top of the canyon. Wednesday had been just such a morning, with the sun turning the grasses golden, and mockingbirds mimicking every bird in the area and even a few car alarms. Her pea coat draped over one arm, her daypack slung over the other shoulder, Stacie was headed back to the parking lot after a peaceful walk.

As she rounded the curve at the bottom of a hill, she was surprised to find a photographer waiting patiently for a shot. He knelt at the side of the path, his camera mounted on a shortened tripod. His attention was riveted on something in the grass. Stacie stopped to wait.

She hadn't seen him on the trails before, and she studied him as she waited. Worn, tan boots toed into the dirt and gravel of the trail, his legs in faded blue jeans were folded, his butt settled firmly on his heels. The leather elbows of the battered, camel-colored corduroy jacket were scratched and rough. The collar of a faded royal blue flannel shirt poked out untidily next to his right cheek.

Obviously he was outside a lot. His dark, curly hair had been shaped in what she thought of as a military cut, but he was at least a couple weeks past a haircut, which softened the look. His face in profile was strong, all planes and angles, a bit of stubble over tanned olive skin. *No shave this morning, but not unshaven for days,* she thought. His hand on the cable release was square, nails trimmed.

Precise, neat, not a slob, but not a slave to fashion.

The morning breeze, warming as the sun rose, flipped the shirt collar against his cheek. He might have been a boulder on the hillside for all the notice he took. She smiled. The quiet patience of this man waiting for the perfect shot made her content to simply wait with him, the sun on her face, its warmth penetrating her shirt. The amethyst crystal, hidden just next to her heart, warmed as well.

She was so focused on her study of him, she started slightly when the shutter clicked. The stranger smiled as he rose smoothly and gracefully to his feet. There was a flash of movement in the grass. When he turned, he was startled to find her watching.

Stacie was startled, too, by the intense blue of his eyes. It was as if a piece of evening sky had fallen into them. The blue was brilliant against the warm tones of his skin.

"Looks like you got your shot," she said, surprised to see

4

a mask of neutrality slide over his face. It was as if he were embarrassed to find her watching, seeing him vulnerable, wrapped in the joy of the camera and the subject.

"I did," he said, and in one quick glance, she realized, he had examined her as thoroughly as she had taken minutes to examine him. "Thanks for giving me the space."

"May I see?" she asked.

Then he smiled fully. "It's not digital," he said. "It's an old single-lens reflex. You'd have to wait until I print it."

"That makes you almost a dinosaur, doesn't it?" She smiled back and stepped down the trail. He was about six feet tall or slightly over, and as she got closer, she found herself looking up. "Black and white?"

He nodded, bending to lift the camera affixed to the tripod. When he looked back up at her, hands automatically adjusting the legs of the tripod, he asked, "Are you a photographer?"

Stacie laughed. "No," she said. "I took a class once. Too... I don't know. Unimaginative. I was no good at it. I'm a book-keeper," she cut the air at a diagonal with her hand, "tax preparer. Numbers I can handle. Anything to do with art, I'm at a loss."

He smiled at her. "Maybe you just never found the right art," he said. "I'm sure you're good at something."

If you only knew, she thought with a pang. For years she'd wished she could meet someone who'd accept her for who she was. But every time, her wretched gift had made itself known, and it had been a disaster.

But not today. Today, she would let the past lie. It was her birthday. The sun was warm, and so was the stranger's voice. Rather than think about what would never be, Stacie was content to simply stand on the hillside and talk.

"Do you sell your work?"

He hesitated, then shrugged, glancing down to remove a filter. "I've participated in a few shows," he said, "and sold a couple."

Before she could ask anything more, he gestured with his head to the path behind her. "What's up ahead?"

"Your first time up here?"

He shook his head. "I've been to the park before, but I usually hike out of the Live Oak Canyon parking lot."

Stacie raised an eyebrow.

"Don't you have to dodge mountain bikers?"

He grinned. "Sometimes. But usually not this early." He pointed up the trail. "Is there really a lake up there?"

"Normally," she told him. "But the drought has been very hard on it. It's not much more than a puddle right now." She pulled her daypack forward, unzipped a pocket and unfolded her tattered map of the park. "For some interesting images, you might try these areas." She pointed out a couple paths, giving him a short synopsis of what he might see on each.

"You must come up here a lot," he said.

"I'm up here most mornings," she agreed, then winced inwardly. *I shouldn't have said that*, she thought, *telling a stranger my habits*.

Stacie was not generally secretive, trusting in the basic goodness of people. But she was alone, and she had seen no one else on the trail that morning.

As she talked about one of the trails, she casually put her pea coat back on and slipped a hand into her pocket to hold the quartz crystal she always kept with her. She'd found it at a gem show in Pasadena when she was just twelve. Clear and colorless as pure water, nestled in a spray of tourmaline crystals, the crystal had called to her so strongly it had practically stuck to her hand. Her great aunt had bought it for her and

6

told her to carry it always. "It will protect you," Aunt Amelia had said.

She'd been right. Like an amplifier, the stone augmented Stacie's natural intuitive gifts. Over the years, she'd learned to read the crystal's signals.

The touch of the stone confirmed her sense that there was nothing in this man to fear. She sensed only calm happiness, though it was underlain by sadness, caution, a touch of bitterness and, oddly, she thought, confusion. There was strength and sureness there. Trustworthiness. Safety.

"Anything in particular you're looking for?" she asked him.

"Not really," he said, lifting the strap on his camera bag over his shoulder. "Anything with a strong pattern. Lots of contrast. Close-ups, usually."

"Ah. Then maybe you would like the lake. All that cracked mud. But I'd also recommend heading up here," said Stacie, moving closer to the stranger's shoulder and pointing to an area of the map. "The bark on the sycamores is always fascinating, and there's a stand of scrub oak that casts some great shadows this time of day." She mentioned a few other plants that might give him what he wanted and told him where to find them.

He was surprised. "You really know your plants for a bookkeeper," he mimicked her slash through the air, "tax preparer."

Stacie laughed. "I love plants, particularly California natives, though they've been outnumbered by imports. Our climate is so good for so many plants."

They talked a while more about the park, the plants, the weather. Gradually, the guarded look fell from his face. She even made him laugh. His voice was warm, baritone. His laugh was a throaty chuckle. When Stacie spoke, there was

7

focused attention in those sharp, blue eyes. She could have talked to him all day.

She had to go, though. She had a shop to open.

They exchanged good-byes, and he headed up the trail, taking Stacie's map with him. It wasn't until she got back to her car that Stacie realized she hadn't asked his name.

But she'd thought about him since then—many, many times.

Now, as she stood in the dense fog, waiting for the hand-spinners, a baritone voice behind her said, "Well, hello!"

Slipping her pendant into her sweater, she turned, her smile already in place. Her memories of the stranger were so strong, she expected to see him there.

The man standing behind her—far too close to her—was not the dark-haired photographer.

He was about her age. His straight, blond hair folded over the collar of his camo jacket and fell across his forehead to light, ice blue eyes under dark blond brows. A straight nose, angular lips. Some would say he was strikingly handsome, but there was something in his eyes. Or rather, something *not* in his eyes. Stacie wondered if she would have noticed if she hadn't been remembering the dark-haired stranger in the Heritage Park.

Stacie's smile slipped as a sudden headache hit her between the eyes, as if she'd eaten ice cream too fast. She had a sudden sense of vertigo. She stepped back instinctively to create more space between them. Her boot heel knocked against the rocks at the side of the koi pond. Her hand went immediately into her jacket pocket to hold the quartz crystal.

Her heart kicked into a racing beat at the touch. The crystal was ice cold, the edges between the faces like razors slicing her hand. She felt blood running over her fingers.

There was no doubt what it meant.

Danger. *Extreme* danger.

Adrenaline surged through her.

She saw him register the change in her face.

"Guess you were expecting someone else," he said, his smile cooling, but still firmly in place.

"Yes," Stacie managed to reply calmly. "My tour group." *Please, please, please,* her mind chanted. *Don't let him be part of it.*

The stranger laughed, a forced sound. "I guess I should have known," he gestured at her jacket.

Stacie flinched. Every instinct made her desperate to step away from his hand, but the pond behind her barred her escape.

"Your name tag. Stacie," he read. He gave her the creeps looking pointedly at her chest. She was devoutly glad her last name was not printed there. Cappella was not a common name. The Internet would lead him right to her. "Do you often lead groups here?"

"No," she lied. "I'm just filling in."

"Lucky for me," he said. He put out his hand. "My name's Troy."

No, it's not, thought Stacie.

She cringed at the thought of touching him, but he had her trapped. She had to pass him to get to the path. She was afraid to take her hand out of her pocket in case she truly was bleeding, afraid to let go of the crystal. As if it could help her.

Cursing the cultural training that indoctrinated women to be "nice," and praying for her garden group to arrive, she reluctantly let go of the stone and put out her hand. It wasn't bleeding.

His grip was hard, warm, and slightly damp. He held her hand too long, pulling her subtly, but strongly toward him. Stacie pulled back, trying to release her hand.

9

"Careful," he said. "Don't fall in." His smile was triumphant.

The door to the interpretive center burst open, and the air was filled with the sound of fifteen or more chattering women.

Stacie almost sobbed with relief. She tugged her hand free, not caring how rude it was. "My group," she said. "Excuse me." She stepped unwillingly toward him, steeling herself to shove past him if he tried to stop her.

He looked amused and stepped back, clearing her path.

"Perhaps we can take a tour together some day," he said, as she passed him. "I'm sure there's *lots* you could show me." His slippery, insinuating tone turned her stomach.

Stacie glanced back as she moved away. "I don't think so," she said firmly. She hurried down the path, anxious to get away.

"Then perhaps we can meet for coffee some time," he called to her.

"Good morning!" Stacie walked quickly to her group, pretending not to hear him. The women's voices rose in pleasure as they saw and surrounded her.

As she began to tell them what they would be seeing this morning—or not seeing, given the fog, she joked—she felt Troy watching her. She tucked her hands into her pockets, wiping her right one on the handkerchief there. She clutched the crystal. The feel of razors was still there, but not the sense of bleeding.

She and her group moved away. When she was sure it would not be obvious, Stacie glanced back. Troy was gone.

Gradually, her erratic heartbeat slowed, became more regular. The sharpness of the crystal slowly faded until it was as it always was.

It took a long time, though, for Stacie to stop shaking.

TWO

J ACQUI R UNION, TALL AND THIN, IN A RED-CHECKED SHIRT and jeans, was scrubbing the windows of her Windrift Bookstore with a long-handled brush a few mornings later when Stacie stopped.

"Not again," said Stacie, as she walked up.

Jacqui looked over, blue eyes half hidden behind oversized lenses in bright red frames. "These people are really beginning to piss me off," she said.

Stacie glanced at the big window on the other side of the front door and saw brown smears all over it. Brown lumps lay on the sidewalk below.

"Oh, no. Not the..."

"Yes. The dog shit again."

Stacie's shop, the bookstore, Matt Harrelson, the acupuncturist on Mockingbird, and the psychic on the Coast Highway had all been regularly vandalized ever since a fanatical religious group had moved into the area.

"But that's not the worst," Jacqui continued.

"There's worse?"

Jacqui nodded, rested the brush on the ground and

leaned on the handle. An early walker went by. Jacqui waited until he was out of earshot and spoke in a lower voice.

"Our books on sexuality always tend to wander around the store. We've got a group of middle school kids whose parents must carefully control their Internet access so they can't get their sex that way. They come in on their way home, pluck the books off the shelves, then go hide in the graphic novel section thinking we don't suspect. We usually find the books there after they leave. But yesterday, Neal found a couple of the books in the sports section. When he opened them, he found pages had been razored out. Then Jaz checked her YA titles dealing with gender identity. Three of them had been vandalized, too."

Stacie felt sick. Most of the small businesses in town, like Jacqui's and hers, were labors of love. They survived on grit and small margins. This kind of willful destruction could cost them what little profit they made.

Jacqui wasn't done, however.

"Then this morning, just before I came out here," she gestured at the windows, "Sandy found four of our books on Wicca and Tarot had been marked up with things like 'Witches shall burn!' Stupid, childish stuff."

"Oh, Jacqui. I'm so sorry."

"Probably wouldn't hurt to check your own book stock."

"I will. As soon as I get to my store."

Jacqui gave her a lopsided smile. "Takes me back to the '70s. When we put Neil Sheehan's *Pentagon Papers* in the window not long after David Rueben's *Everything You Always Wanted to Know About Sex*... Oh, my! You'd have thought we were trying to bring down the country, if not civilization." She threw up her hands in mock horror. "The picketers! The nasty op-eds!" She laughed. "Exciting times. But this." She shook her head. "At least in the '70s they bought the books before they burned them in the park."

"The police have got to catch these people. This can't go on," said Stacie.

"I want so bad to catch these bastards on film. Neal knows someone who can wire up security cameras out here." Jacqui gave a shudder. "My hippie heart cringes at the thought of acting like Big Brother, but the business owner in me says I have to do what I can to stop this."

"Security cameras might not be a bad idea," said Stacie.

"Anyway, enough bad news. What brings you by so early?"

"Tax season is warming up. I'm looking for something to read that will slow my brain down before I go to bed. Otherwise I dream in debits and credits."

Jacqui smiled. "Go on in. I'll be done in a minute. I may have a suggestion or two."

Because she thought she should, Stacie went to the business section first, but her heart wasn't in it. Nothing literary that would demand a lot of thought. Ditto thrillers. *Nothing that will keep me reading all night*, she thought. The humor books didn't strike her as humorous. Travel would only make her long to get away. Right now romance just depressed her. It wasn't long before she ended up in the fantasy and science fiction alcove. *A good sword and sorcery*, she thought. *No deep thought required, and nothing to do with numbers*.

She was reading spine titles when she got a sharp pain in her forehead. Fear seized her, and she spun around. Troy blocked the alcove opening behind her.

"Well, this is a surprise," he said with a triumphant smile. "Oh, not really. I lie. I saw your car outside. Cute little Honda? Such a girl car."

Anger churned with horror in Stacie's stomach. Two days

earlier he'd cornered her in a greenhouse at her favorite nursery. Fortunately, one of the gardeners had walked in, and Stacie had called to him. Troy had stormed off.

Stacie had thought—she'd hoped—it had been a coincidence. Now she knew it wasn't.

"You're following me," she managed to say.

"I can't help it. I guess it's in our stars or something. We're just destined to be together." Another wolfish smile. "It's pointless to resist."

"I'm not interested." She tried to keep her voice from shaking. The less she said, the better.

"Fantasy," he read from the sign at the top of the shelving. "Perfect. I'm all about fantasy. What's yours?" He stepped closer and reached toward her. "I like your hair down. More womanly."

Stacie flinched away. "Get away from me!" Her voice sounded faint and weak, even to her.

Troy smiled. "Oh, I don't think so. I think we're going to be *good* friends." His hand got closer.

Stacie took a quick deep breath. Could she bring herself to shout for help? she wondered.

"Stacie?"

Troy spun around. Jacqui was standing behind him, books in her hand. Stacie knew the bookstore owner had assessed the situation immediately.

"I found those books you wanted." Jacqui shouldered by Troy, putting herself between him and Stacie, but she didn't turn her back on Troy. "Neal!" she called toward the front of the store, her voice loud in the small space. "Can you give us a hand here?" She kept her eyes on Troy. "Bring your phone."

Troy stepped back as if slapped, rage suffusing his face. With a last look at Stacie, he turned and left.

Jacqui turned back to Stacie who was blinking back tears. "Did he touch you?"

Stacie shook her head. She couldn't speak with her heart blocking her throat.

"You need to sit down." Jacqui took her elbow.

"Jacqui? What's up?" asked Neal, coming around the shelves.

"Follow the blond guy. See if you can get a car description or a plate number."

Neal nodded and took off.

"Come with me," said Jacqui, leading Stacie to the bookstore's stockroom. There were several comfortable chairs there for staff during breaks. Stacie collapsed into one of them. She was angry and frightened, but didn't know which emotion was stronger.

Jacqui fussed with a hot pot and mug and brought Stacie a cup of tea. "Here." She put it into Stacie's hand. "My English mother-in-law swore by sweet, hot tea in times of crisis."

Stacie took it gratefully and tried a smile. "My not-so-English aunt did, too."

Jacqui sat down next to her. After giving Stacie a few more minutes to calm down and sip her tea, she asked, "Do you know that guy?"

"No," said Stacie. She told Jacqui how she'd had the misfortune to meet Troy.

"And now he's threatening you."

Stacie shook her head. "Not in so many words. It's creepy innuendo."

"But he's following you."

"He must be. I decided to come here at the last minute. Same thing with the nursery. It was an impulse stop."

"Following you and trying to touch you or force a date," said Jacqui, brusquely, "is threatening in my book."

"It's all just so...so slimy, the way he says things." Stacie shivered. "It makes you feel dirty."

"It isn't you," Jacqui told her. "It's him."

"I know. But it helps to hear it anyway. Thanks, Jacqui."

Neal stuck his head in the back room.

"Sorry, Jacqui. I lost him. Was he shoplifting?"

"No. He was harassing Stacie."

"Turd," said Neal. "I'll let you know if he tries to come back." The front door chimed, and Neal ducked back out.

Stacie finished her tea and got up. "Now I better go get *my* store open."

"Take these," Jacqui said, handing Stacie the books she'd been carrying. "Terry Pratchett. They'll make you laugh and help you sleep."

"I've never read him."

"You're in for a treat."

"Thanks," said Stacie, reaching into her purse.

Jacqui shook her head and laid a hand on Stacie's. "A gift."

"Oh, no, I can't..."

"Yes, you can." Jacqui gently pushed the books toward Stacie. She gave Stacie a half smile. "Women on the barricades need to stick together."

Stacie managed to smile in response.

"I don't like the thought of you being at the store alone, though," said Jacqui.

"Mir's coming in this morning."

"That might not be enough to stop someone like this. Do you still have that monster dog?"

"Bananas? Yes, but," Stacie chuckled weakly, "he's hardly protection."

"That creep doesn't know that," Jacqui told her. "It might not be a bad idea to bring the dog to work with you."

Stacie nodded slowly. Jacqui was right. Bananas was a huge, black poodle and gorilla mix. He looked like a menace. Having him nearby *would* give her peace of mind. "Yes. A good idea."

"I'll have Neal walk you to your car."

"It's not really necessary. I'm just a block down on Canyon." Then she remembered Troy had said he knew where she was parked. "But thank you. I appreciate that."

"No chances," said Jacqui. "Stay smart. Maybe if he sees you're protecting yourself, he'll go somewhere else."

"I don't like the idea of him targeting anyone else, either," said Stacie.

"No. But he's targeting you, now. You have to take care of yourself."

Troy didn't make an appearance as Neal walked Stacie to her car. But Troy had been there. A red rose was tucked under her windshield wiper.

Suddenly frightened again, Stacie looked around. He was nearby. She knew it.

"From him, you think?" Neal nodded at the rose.

"Without a doubt."

Hating to even touch it, Stacie pulled the rose out and tossed it into the street.

"Thanks, Neal," she said. He stepped back and headed toward the bookstore.

With another quick look around, Stacie got in the car, locked the doors, and carefully pulled into traffic.

She glanced into her side-view mirror. It gave her a great deal of satisfaction to see the rose had been smashed flat in the street.

. . .

TWENTY MINUTES LATER, Stacie pulled into the public parking lot across the street from her store. She had taken Jacqui's advice and detoured home to get her dog. As she leashed Bananas up, she was delighted to see her friend Colin in front of her shop, but dismayed to realize he was scrubbing the siding with an old-fashioned push broom.

Colin turned as she walked up. "Sorry, Stacie. I saw him throwing eggs, but I couldn't get over here fast enough." Colin lived in an upstairs apartment on the far side of the parking lot. "I didn't even get a plate number when he drove off."

Stacie sighed. "Jacqui got hit this morning, too. Dog doodoo. I guess this could have been worse."

"Oh, ugh, yes." He looked down at Bananas. "You really have to stop feeding him," he told Stacie. "I swear he gets bigger every time I see him." Colin patted the curly head and gave him a scratch behind the ears.

"It's the mutant genes," she said. "I'm sure he was part of some kind of a military experiment somewhere. Like Einstein in Dean Koontz's *Watchers*."

The dog nudged Colin's belt buckle to request more scratching.

"Bananas, you've gotten enough attention. Sit."

With a sigh, Bananas sat. Stacie slid her fingers into the fur at the back of his neck and massaged his ears.

"You didn't have to do this," said Stacie, pointing at the broom.

"Of course, I did. What are good neighbors for?"

"In other words, you're hoping this bag," she lifted it, "contains coffee cake."

Wiry and compact, with the muscular shoulders of a powerful batter, which he was, Colin could eat his weight in carbohydrates and never gain an ounce. It was a source of wonder to the women business owners on the street.

"A calumny!" said Colin, hand to heart. "I never." He paused. "Does it?"

Stacie laughed. "Of course. And you're welcome. Come on in."

"I'm almost done here," he told her, nodding at the siding. "Give me a few more minutes."

As she unlocked the door, the hose bib squealed, and a spray of water hit the side of the store.

When Colin finally came in, Stacie was lifting a plastic bin full of malachite touchstones from their spot under the front window.

"All done," said Colin. He looked Stacie over, taking in her mid-calf-length brown skirt, forest green silk shirt, and patterned scarf in rusty oranges and browns. Her shirt sleeves were rolled up, and everything was protected by a chef's apron. A clip allowed her auburn hair to waterfall down to her shoulders. "You're all dressed up today."

"Tax season. I have clients this afternoon."

"So early? It's not even March yet."

"Early works for me. Soon enough I'll be here mornings, nights, weekends..." She shrugged. "But what brings you out so early you saw our vandal?" she asked.

"Blocked," he said. "I have an awful project that I should have said no to, but money talks, you know, and I said yes, hoping to get friendlier than I have been recently with bills larger than a five, and now I regret it, and it's crunch time, and I'm *blocked*!" He gave her what was supposed to be a pitiable look. "I was hoping that talking with a sensible person for a while would help free the creative juices. You're laughing at me."

She was.

"So, what you're saying is that, besides mooching breakfast, you're essentially procrastinating."

He heaved a sigh. "Busted," he said.

"I'm happy to enable you," she smiled at him, "but you'll have to earn it. I'm grateful for the help with the clean-up out front, but I could use some help here, too. I'm getting a late start."

Colin's face went from bright to crestfallen. "Bait and switch," he told her with an offended look. "Instead of friendship, I get indentured servitude."

"Absolutely. Do you want the coffee cake and conversation or not?"

"You drive a hard bargain."

Stacie handed him the bin full of stones. "I do. These need to be washed. Gently. The detergent is on the counter next to the sink."

"Stacie?"

"Hmm?"

"Why am I washing rocks?"

"Because you want coffee cake?"

He gave her a look.

"They need their energy shampooed."

"It's really penance, isn't it?" he said with another look.

She laughed. "No, really. When people choose a touchstone, they're actually responding, very subtly, to its energy. If too many people handle the stone, it muddies the energy and makes it difficult for someone to choose the stone that is right for them at that moment. Sometimes the energy of a particularly tense or disturbed customer can actually rub off onto the stone which then passes that dark energy onto the next person who handles it."

"Really." There was a world of doubt in Colin's tone.

"Really."

"So you wash them? You don't bathe them in the light of a full moon, or in dew collected on the Equinox or during an eclipse? Oh, and chant. Isn't chanting mandatory? And dancing?"

Stacie laughed again. "No. No chanting, no dancing. For the most part cool, clean water is enough to clear them." She didn't add that she *did* purify certain crystals, like her quartz, in moonlight. That was probably too woo-woo for Colin. It was almost too woo-woo for her. But her aunt had insisted.

"Can *you* tell when a stone's energy has gotten dark?" he asked.

"Yes," she said. "But then most people can. They just don't know they can. They simply don't hold onto the stone after they pick it up."

Colin was one of the few people who knew about Stacie's gift. He'd taken to dropping into the shop not long after she opened it for the same reason he was here today. He'd get blocked or bored with his work as a graphic artist, wander through the neighborhood shops, chatting—and eating—until something sparked. Then he'd hurry away to his apartment to get back to work.

One day he'd bounced in while Stacie was unpacking some new fountains, which had arrived in a number of pieces with few instructions. He'd recently confided to her that he was in love with Peter, the man he'd been seeing. Stacie had had doubts Peter returned Colin's feelings fully, but had hoped she was wrong.

Instead of helping assemble fountains, as he'd volunteered to do, Colin had just sat on the floor across from her with a piece of curved copper tubing in his hand and stars in his eyes.

"I hadn't dreamed this would happen," he said. "He was so reluctant to commit. So when he told me he'd found a

21

house that would be perfect for us, well, I just hopped to the bank quick as a bunny to see if I could get a loan, he can't of course, because of the bankruptcy, and can you believe it, I could, and add that to our savings, and we can just *squeak* in."

"Won't the mortgage be a killer?" Stacie asked. She was half listening, trying to puzzle out the confused drawings on the instruction sheet. "Not to mention the taxes."

"Oh, we've penciled it out. It will be tight, but between our incomes, we should be fine."

"You've remembered the mortgage insurance?" she asked, the tax preparer side of her brain in gear.

"Yes, we did, though we'll have to go a year or two without health insurance in order to pay for that and a few small remodels."

Her eyes moving back and forth between the diagrams and the pump and the tubing in her hands, Stacie said, "Colin, is that a good idea? Especially since Peter's been diagnosed? The meds must be horribly expensive, even if he can get assistance." The tubing slipped into the pump, and Stacie felt a surge of success.

Colin had gone silent.

She looked up into his white and stricken face and knew immediately what she'd done.

"You're wrong," he said in a strangled voice. "That was just pneumonia. He's been tested. He told me. He's fine."

"Perhaps he was," Stacie told him as gently as she could. "At one time. But maybe you should go together to get tested. Just to be sure."

"I can't do that," said Colin. He set the tubing on the floor as if it were glass and stood up. "A relationship is nothing without trust."

"It's nothing if it's built on a lie, either, Colin," she said quietly.

"He's not lying. He can't be lying." With that, Colin had walked out the door.

Stacie hadn't slept for days. She and Colin had become good friends. Now she knew she'd never see him again. Worse, she was afraid he wouldn't believe her until it was too late.

She was wrong. Colin was back several weeks later, heartbroken. They'd sat in the kitchen with tea and the bag of bagels he'd brought.

"He wouldn't get tested," he told her, tears in his voice. Unusually for Colin, he was shredding a bagel, not eating it. "I told him we'd go together, so there would be no doubts. He said..." Her friend choked up. "He said I was calling him a liar. He insisted I apologize."

That rotten bastard, thought Stacie angrily.

"And somehow, somehow *then*, I knew. I just *knew* he *was* lying. Because, see, we'd never really talked about it. He'd never asked *me*. He'd just volunteered that he'd been tested." Colin reached for a tissue and blew his nose.

"So I said... I said if he wasn't willing to address my concerns, then maybe I wasn't important enough to him. Then, the little shit, he said I wasn't! And he walked *out*!" Colin's pain had gone to anger.

"Oh, Colin. I'm so sorry."

"I lost the deposit on the house, of course. He hadn't even helped pay for *that*."

Stacie was glad the deal hadn't closed. That would have been a bigger mess.

"*That*, my dear, that wasn't even the worst! I was telling a friend of mine all the gory details a few days later, and she said

23

she was so glad we'd broken up. That everyone knew Peter had been diagnosed last fall. Last fall! And no one told me! Peter was up to his ears in debt paying for the drugs because he'd *already* let his insurance lapse, can you believe how stupid? *That* was why he'd gone bankrupt, though that wasn't what he told *me*, the ass. Now I suspect he was lying about how much he had in savings. When I said thank you *so* very much for telling me, super sarcastic, you know, she said we didn't want to break your heart. Break my heart! I couldn't believe it."

Stacie tried not to smile at his indignation. His heart, she could see, was mending.

"Colin. You did go get tested yourself, didn't you?" she asked him then, taking his hands.

"Yes, my dear, I did. I dodged the bullet, *don't* ask me how. But Stacie," he said, and she saw it coming. "Stacie. How did *you* know?"

He'd put everything on the line because of a doubt she'd planted, intentionally or not, and lost someone he'd cared about, even though the loss had not been so great.

It was her turn to risk it all, risk a friendship she'd come to treasure dearly.

"Sometimes," she told him, "I don't know how, and I never know when, sometimes, I just know things."

"Second Sight," he said without batting an eye.

"Yes," she said, startled.

"I thought so. I thought that's what it had to be. Have you always had it?"

"Yes. As long as I can remember."

"Was it, like, a lightning strike or something?"

Stacie laughed. "No. No lightning strike."

"Oh. Wait. Someone told me your grandmother had a tea shop here. She used to tell fortunes?"

Stacie sighed inwardly. She'd never outrun her aunt's shadow.

"Yes. My great aunt—not my grandmother—had it, too. It kind of runs in the family."

"Well, I'm grateful. It saved me from a terrible mistake," Colin had told her, and that had been that.

Now Colin was asking her, "So, what stone do I need to restore my creative juices?"

"Which stone do you think will help?"

"Well, I read online..."

"Yes, you did, I'm sure," she said. "Certain stones will make you smarter, or more eloquent, or purify your blood, or find you true love." She saw something flicker in Colin's eyes. *Ah*, she thought. *That's what this creative block is really about.* "Some of the things you read online are right on the money, though not everything is. For the most part, I think a personal choice is more accurate."

"Can *you* tell what stone someone needs?" he asked curiously.

"Sometimes, yes. But it doesn't mean they'll take my advice. A lot of times, they don't like the stone I recommend. Or they want the one the Internet said would heal something or protect against something. In the end, I have to respect that." She shrugged. "My best sellers are obsidian—Apache tears—malachite," she pointed to the bin in his hands, "and pyrite. Not one of them gives me so much as a tingle. Maybe those customers simply sense something I can't."

"So for creativity I'm on my own?"

Actually, Stacie knew what stone was best for him, but she really did believe it was better if he found it himself.

"Pretty much," she said. "So while you're washing those stones, you can see which one talks to you."

"That's a hint, isn't it?"

25

"Only if you want coffee cake."

"You're a hard woman," he told her, and headed toward the kitchen.

"And no filching pieces of that cake!" she called after him.

"I can't hear you!"

Stacie grinned as Colin turned the water on.

They worked companionably, Colin going back and forth with the stones, and Stacie cleaning cases and straightening shelves.

As he carried the last batch of stones to the window, Colin stopped suddenly next to a case in the middle of the store.

"Oooh," he said. "Now that's gorgeous. I haven't seen that before."

Bingo, thought Stacie.

She opened the case and pulled out a bead. It was about an inch-and-a-half long, oval, with sharp-edged lines of white, gray, black, and yellow on either side of an arrow-shaped patch of maroon. She handed it to Colin.

"I like this," he said, rolling it in his hand. "Is that all it is?" He nodded at the price tag.

"Yes," she told him.

"I don't suppose it's good for my creativity."

"Actually, it's an agate. Most agates are great for creativity."

"Seriously? You're not just humoring me?"

"Nope. I told you. Most people know what stone's right for them."

"Hunh. You mean I washed all those stones, and the one I wanted was in this case, and I never even had to touch it?"

"Yeah. Pretty sneaky on my part, don't you think?"

"Oh, definitely. I definitely think I've earned more than one piece of coffee cake."

Bananas, sensing food, followed them into the kitchen, positioning himself next to the counter where a large glass jar full of Milk Bones was sitting.

"Nope," Stacie told him. "You already had your limit." She pulled a bag of carrots from the refrigerator. "Here. Have a cigar." Bananas took it from her gently and, holding it out of the side of his mouth, headed toward the sliding door that led onto a small patio and garden.

"He looks like a Mafia don with a stogie," said Colin. "You don't usually bring him in." Colin looked at her questioningly.

So while Stacie made tea, she told him about Troy and the episodes at the bookstore and nursery.

"You have to report it," said Colin.

"There's really nothing to report."

"But Stacie. He could be dangerous. You really should tell the police."

"Colin, they already think I'm a crank."

"Well, have you at least made notes of it in your vandalism log?"

"No," she said. "But that's probably a good idea."

As she poured hot water into the pot, Colin asked, "You don't think it's him, do you? The one throwing the eggs and doing the dog shit?"

"Doesn't make sense. That jerk's targeting other people, not just me."

"You have a point." Colin frowned.

Stacie put the pot of Earl Grey tea on the table between them, then set a large piece of coffee cake on a plate for Colin. She was ready for a change of subject.

"So, why are you in such hot pursuit of cash?" Stacie asked, smiling. "You're usually pretty cavalier about money."

27

"Umm," he said, chewed and swallowed. "That was before I got a rent increase."

"Ah," she said. "Not surprising. Property taxes just went up. Significantly. I know. I just got two tax bills. I'm afraid things are going to get tighter for all of us around here."

"But I've been there more than five years!" Colin was indignant. "That should earn me some kind of consideration."

"Colin, we're just a couple blocks from the beach..."

"I have a view of the parking lot!"

"True. But your landlord could probably get double or triple for that space during the summer if he turned it into a vacation rental." She sighed. "Heaven knows, I've thought about doing that with the apartment upstairs," she gestured toward the ceiling, "and working from home. It would certainly help pay for things."

"I'm going to have to raise my rates, and people are still whining about the last one—three years ago!"

"I know. I'm probably going to have to raise my fees, too. And prices in the shop."

"But Mir said you gave her a raise."

"Of course! She earns every cent."

"At least you could earn more money if you got a CPA," said Colin. "Surely you could pass the test."

"I planned to get a CPA, once," Stacie told him. "But... Well, there's a long complicated story about why that's probably not going to happen." She shrugged. "I'm sure things will work out." She smiled at him. "I guess I have a cavalier attitude toward money, too."

Colin snorted. "I doubt that. You're like the Inquisition when you do my taxes."

They sat quietly for a moment while Colin demolished his coffee cake.

"So..." said Colin, wiping the icing from his fingers.

She raised an eyebrow. "Yes?"

"Well, it's just that...if it's not the CPA... Look, Stacie. You've got this great ability, you could probably make a ton of money doing some kind of...of psychic readings or something. People would pay simply *scads*..."

"No," said Stacie flatly.

"But your aunt..."

"No."

"But..."

"No. For several reasons. First, I have no control over it. I can't will my intuition to come." Actually, Stacie had spent her life willing it *not* to come. "Second, it's always a disaster. My aunt was always getting threats. And look what could have happened when I told you about Peter. I could have lost your friendship forever."

"But you didn't."

"Yes. Well. I haven't been so lucky in the past."

"Oh, girlfriend. You've been holding out." Colin, always eager for gossip, leaned forward, elbows on the table. "Do tell. What happened?"

Stacie paused. She'd never really talked about it, any of it. To anyone.

"Lips sealed," said Colin, reading her hesitation.

Stacie stalled, reaching out to feel the teapot. "Warm it up?"

"Please."

She topped up their cups, then cut two more slices of coffee cake and served them.

Into her unwilling silence, Colin asked quietly, "It's bad, isn't it?"

"Now who's got Second Sight?" she asked him.

Colin smiled slightly, but didn't say anything.

Why not? she thought. Maybe it was time to cauterize the wound.

"We were talking about the CPA."

Colin nodded.

"When I got out of school, I went to work for Stanley, McConnell, and Walleram with that in mind."

"Wow! I knew you were good but..."

Stacie took a forkful of cake and a sip of tea. "But then..."

Then, she thought.

"While I was there, I started dating one of their CPAs, a guy named Drew. He was nice. Steady. Rising in the company. Judd Walleram was grooming him for a partnership. We got along well. We'd started talking about moving in together. Started nibbling at the edges of the conversations you have when you're talking about getting married. Like kids." Stacie paused and rubbed her temples. This was an ugly, humiliating memory.

"Did he know about the Sight?"

"No. I hadn't figured out how to tell him about it. He'd been hinting that maybe I shouldn't see my Aunt Amelia so much because of the tea room and the rumors he'd heard about her telling fortunes. I guess I was hoping that either my abilities would just go away. Or if it happened after we were married, he would just accept it."

Stupid, she thought.

"But he found out."

"Oh, yeah. Big time." She took a deep breath, then blew it out.

"Drew had a lot of big clients. One of them was State Senator Elijah Michaels."

"Wait. I remember this."

"I'm sure you do." She shook her head. "Walleram had given Drew the Michaels account to show his faith in him. It was part of his move toward partnership. Later, I realized there were darker reasons for shifting Michaels to Drew, but at the beginning, I just thought it was a great opportunity. They assigned me to help Drew with the preliminary work on his clients, so he'd have time to take on more clients, and, of course, make more money for the firm. I did the piddling stuff, like check changes in addresses, dependents, made sure all the necessary supporting documents were there. I looked for anything glaring that was missing." She quirked a small smile at Colin. "Learning to be an Inquisitor.

"Anyway, that's what I was doing when I met with Michaels. But when I asked him—in front of his wife—if the new property in Temecula was a vacation home or a rental, there was dead silence. When I looked up, he looked like he wanted to kill me. His wife looked like she wanted to kill *him*. I suddenly realized the property wasn't documented anywhere in his paperwork."

"Oh, my. What did you do?"

"Apologized like anything. Said I had momentarily confused him with another client."

"He didn't believe you."

"No. Neither did she. She hired a private detective, found out he *did* have a house in Temecula. He was keeping a girlfriend in it. She started divorce proceedings. It was all over the papers. Privately, he accused Drew and me of trying to blackmail him. I swore up and down that it was a simple mistake, but of course, the partners knew it wasn't, not when the news hit about the private eye. And none of Drew's other clients had houses in Temecula. Drew tried to dump it all on me, but the partners cut us both loose."

"No more wedding plans."

"He threatened to sue me. Sue my aunt for depriving him of his livelihood."

"Did he? Sue?"

She shook her head. "Packed up and left. I heard through the grapevine that the partners offered him a reference as long as he didn't practice in California. He decided to cut his losses."

"So why didn't you go on and get your CPA and work somewhere else?"

"I was the little fish. Not a CPA. Not partnership material. And let's face it. I'm a woman. SM&W didn't offer *me* a reference. Judd Walleram and Michaels had been good friends. It came out—again through the grapevine—that Walleram had hoped for some kind of political favor from Michaels." She held up a hand. "No, I don't know what it was, before you even ask, bless your gossip-loving heart." She smiled.

"I'll get it out of you another time."

"No, you won't. Because I really don't know. But that's why Judd had shifted Michaels to Drew. He wanted to avoid any appearance of blackmail, bribery, whatever. Appoint your accountant to a plummy job, and people wonder what he knows.

"Anyway, getting rid of me, and burying any hope I had of a career, was Walleram's revenge for Michaels threatening to sue SM&W. That, and losing his political future, really pissed Judd off."

"So you couldn't get another job at a CPA firm."

"No, not around here." Stacie shook her head. "That's why I work on my own."

"But Stacie, you *are* working on your own. You don't need a reference from them anymore."

"I need them not actively trying to destroy me." She sighed. "Not that anything stops them."

"What do you mean?"

"I told you. Judd Walleram wanted something from Michaels. It must have been something big. After the fiasco, he wasn't going to get it, especially after Michaels lost his seat in the scandal. Walleram can't do anything to me legally. It was an honest, though embarrassing, mistake. So he tries to destroy my business whenever he can. I've had a lot of years of people making appointments, then cancelling them after *someone* told them I was incompetent."

"He told people that?"

"Probably not in so many words, and quite likely not him personally. There are laws against slander. But yeah, essentially."

"But that was a lot of years ago. Surely he's moved on by now."

"You'd think. But just a couple weeks ago, the same thing happened. A new client called, I scheduled her, then she called back to cancel. When I offered to reschedule, she said she was going with someone more 'discreet.'"

"That son of a bitch."

"Pretty much. So that's why I don't bother trying to get a CPA. Because, what's the point?"

"And why you're not interested in advertising your ability."

"Exactly. And why I wish it would just go away. I never understood how Amelia could take it all so in stride."

"Did she know what was going to happen? With you and Drew?"

Stacie shook her head. "No. She'd been lukewarm about Drew. She told me later she'd known there would be a big blow up of some kind, but didn't know what it would be. Like I said. This thing is unpredictable. Even Amelia couldn't always read it right."

Colin lifted the last piece of coffee cake.

"Well. That explains why two such catches as we," he pointed at her, then at himself, "are singletons. I always make lousy choices. And you, your sight is hooked to your mouth so you blab the wrong things at the wrong time." He popped the cake in his mouth.

And Stacie *knew*.

"You don't always make the wrong choice," she said. "This time, you're making the right choice. You just have to have the courage to reach out."

Colin almost choked. He swallowed hard. Stared at her. His mouth opened, then closed.

"You're sure," he finally said. A statement, not a question. She nodded.

"But how do you..."

"I just do."

"But he's so...so amazing. He's not like me at all. I'm sure he thinks I'm just a flake."

"I think you'll be surprised."

"I just can't...imagine..."

"He sees you, Colin." Stacie leaned forward and put her hand on his. "He *sees* you. He knows you are smart, funny, kind, courageous..."

"Killingly attractive. Don't forget that," Colin interjected. "Courageous might be pushing it a bit."

"Gay man. Playing in the minor leagues. Focused on the majors. You tell me it doesn't take courage to negotiate all that machismo."

Colin suddenly looked a bit older.

"That's not courage," he said. "That's just life. Matt's the one who's courageous. He's on the front lines, fighting for LGBTQ rights."

"Ah. Matt Harrelson."

"You didn't know?"

"No. I just knew there was someone. Someone right. Not who."

Into the silence between them, the clock behind the sales counter chimed eleven.

"Now, I have to get to work." Stacie squeezed his hand and stood up, gesturing at the empty cake plate. "I'm going to have to explain that to Mir," she said. She picked up the dishes and put them in the sink.

Colin was staring at her.

"You're sure," he said again.

"Yes, Colin. I'm sure." She smiled. "But I'm also sure he's yours to lose. Don't rush your fences."

"No," he said, looking stunned. "No, I won't." Then he smiled in sheer delight. "Do you know how happy you've made me?"

Stacie's hand happened to be in her pocket, holding her crystal.

"Yes, Colin. I do. Now, go home so I can open this store."

Colin jumped up and kissed her on the cheek. "I'm going to fly," he said, and practically danced to the front door.

THREE

Stacie smiled as she closed the door after Colin. It was so rare that her gift gave her *good* news to share. She flipped the sign in the window, turned on the fountain, and headed back to the kitchen. Bananas was lying in the middle of the floor.

"Up, lazy bones. You're blocking traffic." Bananas snuffled, surged reluctantly to his feet and went out the open sliding door to the patio to drop in a sun puddle. Stacie went into the kitchen to make another mug of tea.

The converted bungalow had been built it in the 1920s by her great grandfather, Michel Travers, for his mother-in-law, Anastasia. Though Anastasia had lived with Stacie's great grandparents when they first immigrated to the US, Michel was always uneasy with her gift of prophesy, thinking it was a way to control people. So he'd built her a home of her own. Amelia had made it into the Crystal Tea Room. After Amelia died, Stacie turned it into The Bell, Book and Crystal. Her aunt's customers had been disappointed when Stacie didn't continue doing readings, like Amelia. Stacie told them she didn't have the gift.

Some gift.

She hadn't told Colin the worst. Stacie could hardly bear to think about it, much less talk about it.

She cupped her hands around the mug's comforting warmth.

Stacie had been eight. Waking with a queasy feeling about her dad one morning, she'd tried to stop him from going to work. He hadn't laughed, exactly, but he'd smiled, and Stacie knew, young as she was, that he thought she was mimicking Amelia. He'd hugged her, told her he would be careful, and left the house. She'd been so worried, she'd called him, minutes after he got to his office, to be sure he hadn't had an accident.

"Nope. Safe and sound, little one. I love you. I'll see you tonight," he'd said.

It was the last time she'd spoken to him. It hadn't been a car accident. It had been a heart attack later that morning.

Amelia had tried to explain to the heartbroken eight-year-old that she could not have prevented it, but Stacie, convinced her father's death was her fault, had felt guilty for years. Illogical as it was, she was still angry. If the Sight couldn't save the person she loved most in the world, she thought, it was no good to her.

As Stacie got older, Amelia tried to make her understand that her gift carried a responsibility, an obligation to help others, even if it failed to work for her. But Stacie continued to want no part of it. She saw the havoc it brought to Amelia's life. Her refusal to learn more about using the Sight was the only point of contention between her and her aunt.

Stacie took a deep breath. The morning light falling through the windows, the quiet trickle of water in the fountain, the wind chime tones—light and delicate to deep and sonorous—it all soothed her. She might not want anything to do with Second Sight, but she loved spending time in her shop among the crystals, the touchstones, the metaphysical possibilities of Tarot and runes.

"The only thing missing in this shop is a cat," she told Bananas, as he wandered in and folded down near the chairs in the corner. He gazed at her sorrowfully with large brown eyes.

She laughed. "Oh, don't look so offended. I was joking." He thumped his tail on the floor, then dropped his big head onto his paws.

Stacie flipped on the CD player, filling the store with Native American flute music. She closed the sliding door, took her tea and sat down near the dog, scratching his ears first. He sighed. She opened the galley proof of a new book a publisher had sent her.

Forty minutes later, Stacie knew she didn't want to carry the book. It contained too much wrong, and possibly danger-ous, information on herbs. She was heading to the kitchen to recycle it, when the front door shot open, and a short, busty woman in her mid-sixties barged in. She was dressed and made up as if she were in her thirties and was riding a wave of cloying perfume. Stacie didn't have to reach for the crystal in her pocket to know this woman was trouble.

The woman's flushed face said she was perpetually angry. *That can't be good for someone with a heart that bad.* The downturned corners of her mouth told Stacie she was always disappointed. In fact, she *expected* to be disappointed.

A silky kimono-style jacket covered with dragons flapped around her as she marched into the shop.

"Good morning," said Stacie.

"I'm just looking," snapped the woman.

Whatever you're looking for, thought Stacie, *I don't have it.* "Please take your time," she said mildly.

Stacie did not often see auras, but the roiling, dusky red, slightly opaque storm cloud surrounding this woman would be hard to miss. Stacie half expected to see lightning shooting out of her head.

Thinking about auras brought her aunt to mind again. Aunt Me had been a plain woman, middling height, faded red hair streaked with gray, wire-rimmed glasses magnifying sea-blue eyes in a plump face. Most people would look through or past her. But Amelia had been wrapped in a glorious aura. As a baby, Stacie always stopped crying when Amelia held her. She would laugh and bat at the air around her aunt. One day, when she'd been about three, Stacie had exclaimed, "Colors!"

Her mother, Pamela, had been angry, but Aunt Me had simply hugged Stacie and winked. "That's because I'm magic," she'd said.

And she was, thought Stacie with love and sadness. She'd been Stacie's guardian angel from the first moment she'd held Stacie to the moment she'd died several years before. There wasn't a day that passed that Stacie didn't miss her.

The angry woman suddenly made a determined bee-line across the room. Stacie stepped back as the edge of the aura hit her, snapping her out of her reverie.

"Where is your consultation room?"

Stacie looked at the woman dumbly. "I'm sorry?"

"I'm not going to discuss my private matters here in this...this...place," she said, waving her hand dismissively around the store. She looked back at Stacie, mouth tight. "I want to talk to you in private."

"I'm sorry," Stacie said again. "I'm afraid I'm not follow-ing." But she knew perfectly well what the woman was talking about. Her irritation rose.

"A treatment room. A consulting room. A place of

privacy," the woman said as if speaking to a four-year-old. "I want to talk about a healing."

"Ma'am, I'm not sure…"

The woman opened her hand to reveal two touchstones she'd picked out of the bins: a moss agate and an apache tear. "What do these do?" she demanded.

"People hold touchstones during meditation as a way to concentrate their attention…"

"I don't care about that," the woman interrupted. "What do they *do*? What will they cure?"

"Some people believe that certain stones have beneficial properties..." Stacie started to say, but the woman ran right over her.

"Which ones do you use in your healing? Do I have to buy them? I don't want to buy something before I know it will work."

"Ma'am, I'm afraid…"

"Yes, I know I didn't make an appointment, but it's not like going to a real doctor, is it? I'm sure you people must be able to take walk-ins." The woman looked around disdainfully. "It's not like you're busy."

Stacie took a deep breath and tried to center.

"Ma'am, you've made a mistake," she said with determination. "I'm not a medical person."

"Of course you're not, that's obvious." The woman looked her up and down. "I want a crystal healing. I've tried a lot of different things, I'll tell you that right up front. I'm not a pushover. I'm very skeptical.

"Now, where is your treatment room? I'd like to get started. I have a busy day." The woman gawked around. "Upstairs?" she said, turning toward the door opposite the sales counter that led to the second floor. It was clearly marked "Employees Only." As all Stacie's clients' financial records were up there, the door was also locked.

"There's no treatment room, Ma'am," Stacie said firmly, stopping the woman in her tracks. "There's no healer here. You've made a mistake."

"You're not the owner?"

"I'm the store owner," said Stacie, "but I'm not a healer." *And if I were, I wouldn't come near you*, she thought.

"That's not what I was told," the woman answered forcefully. "I was told that you healed a young woman of terrible acne. Another man's cancer went into remission." The woman stared at Stacie belligerently, her face mottling with purple. "Don't worry. I expect to pay for it. If it's reasonable. And if it *works*."

Mir, thought Stacie. *But cancer cure? Oh*, she thought, remembering. She sighed to herself.

"Well, Ma'am," she said, as politely as she could, "You misunderstood. I can't heal anyone. Not with crystals or anything else." She gestured to the shop's displays. "I simply sell crystals and stones, things people find useful in meditation. If you're feeling ill, you should see your family doctor." *Especially with that heart*, she almost said aloud. This woman was a beat away from a heart attack. Stacie just hoped it wouldn't happen right now.

"You're trying to get the price up, aren't you?"

"What?" Stacie blinked at the sudden change in subject.

"You're hoping I'll say, 'I'll pay anything,' then you'll pretend to be reluctant and set some high price." The woman was working herself into a fit, thought Stacie. She was almost panting. "You're hoping I'll be so desperate I'll agree to it! Well, you can't pull that on me! I'm not some fool you can trick like that!"

41

"Ma'am, I've explained that I'm not a healer. Now I'll have to ask you to leave," said Stacie, an edge to her voice.

"I will. But you haven't heard the last of this." The woman whirled, just as a small, slender woman in her mid-twenties entered the shop. Her cork-screwed, dark blond hair was a pink-streaked cloud around the almond-colored skin of her elfin face.

Mir.

The flushed woman stopped short and stared. She glanced back at Stacie. "Well. I see what kind of customers you *prefer*," she said. She held her hand out, turned it over, and dropped the touchstones to the floor. She pushed past Mir and went out the door.

"What was that about?" asked Mir, waving her hand in front of her. "And what was that perfume?"

Stacie blew out a breath and shook her head. "She wanted a healing. Mir. Please. You have to stop telling people the touchstones cleared up your acne."

"But it's true!"

"No, Mir, you just outgrew it."

"But, Stacie, really…"

Stacie shook her head. "Mir, you're really not helping me or the shop. It's a small town. These things get around, often in ways you don't intend. So, please? For me?"

"Got it," said Mir. "Lips are zipped." She drew her hand across her mouth. "Promise."

"Thanks," Stacie laughed. "Now, would you prop the front door open, please?"

Stacie opened the sliding glass door again. Fresh air from the ocean a few blocks away began to blow the perfume away. Bananas lifted his head and sneezed. Both women laughed. The dog lurched to his feet and crossed to Mir to have his ears scratched.

Stacie picked up a striker and tapped a large, bowl-shaped, bronze meditation bell. She paused, tapped it again, harder, then once more. The heavy atmosphere began to dissipate as the rich tone filled the room.

"I'm not sure, but you may need an exorcist," said Mir.

Stacie chuckled. "I'll look into it." Reluctant to touch the stones that lay on the floor, Stacie fetched a plastic basin and broom from kitchen and swept them up.

"I'm going to have to clear all the touchstones again," she sighed. "Colin just washed them this morning."

"If Colin was here, there's no need to ask if there's anything to eat, is there?" asked Mir.

"Normally, I'd say none whatsoever." Stacie flashed her eyebrows up and down conspiratorially. "But I bought two this morning and hid one."

"Oh, you clever woman," Mir laughed. "Tea?"

"Not for me. I still have some. But you should probably get some while you can. I have to head upstairs soon."

"Glad you bought an extra coffee cake," said Mir. "I didn't get breakfast."

"I will take a slice of that. Colin ate almost all of the first one this morning."

Bananas followed them to the kitchen, hoping for another treat.

Even if Stacie had looked out the front window, she would not have seen the watcher across the street.

FOUR

His chair squeaked as Ben Robard leaned back, shut his eyes against the grisly report on his monitor and rubbed the bridge of his nose. The computer hummed next to him.

Another one. The fourth discovered in the county in the last year. The previous three bodies had been buried a long while, discovered as the result of renewed building as the economy had improved. The latest one, however, had died within the last month. The only reason they'd found her was because a couple had their car break down on a fire road in the hills where they weren't supposed to be. The guy had been trying to climb high enough to get cell reception and literally stepped into the soft soil of the shallow grave.

The guy's going to have nightmares for months, thought Ben. *If not years*.

He sighed. Maybe this girl's death wasn't connected to the others. Maybe none of them were connected.

Because the killings were all somewhat different, up until now, the different police departments had treated them individually. But with this one, he'd heard muttering about a serial killer.

He hoped not.

Not my case, he reminded himself, selfishly glad he worked Fraud. He wasn't sure he'd have been able to handle the murders of young women, especially raped and mutilated young women. He couldn't avoid hearing about it, though. The whole department was talking about it in hushed tones.

What did this to a man? he wondered. *Why would he pick out women at random and kill them?* He'd seen things in Iraq, incidents that would haunt him forever, that he had not understood, the war notwithstanding. But this kind of thing was truly incomprehensible.

He wondered again if he'd made the right choice, joining the police department after the Army. After the World Trade Tower attacks in 2001, and against his parents' counsel, he'd dropped out of college, married his high school sweetheart, Dania, and gone off to Iraq. He'd been an MP, and had the skills and the training, so joining Eden Beach PD had made sense.

He could never decide if he regretted joining the military. He knew he regretted marrying Dania. That mistake had been crystal clear when he'd come home on leave to find her pregnant by someone else. Their divorce had been as quick as their marriage had been.

But joining the Army. That had felt right. It was black and white, right? Good guys, bad guys. Right, wrong. Moral, immoral.

Except it hadn't been. Maybe it was boredom. Maybe it was because they were there due to an attack on US citizens. Maybe it was racial or religious. But Ben had first been shocked, then appalled, then confused by the actions of some of his fellow soldiers. One guy in particular left Ben shaking his head. He made crude remarks about the women in their unit. He joked about Ben's parentage due to his olive coloring. He picked up anything he fancied when they raided homes of suspected insurgents. But then he'd saved Ben's life one night without thought of the risk to himself.

Ben had been spat upon by one woman, yet been blessed by another whose child he'd carried to a hospital. He'd heard of translators who'd been shot as traitors after being denied a visa for the US. One of Ben's buddies, whose legs had been blown off by a mine, had begged Ben not to call for medics, begged Ben to let him die. Ben didn't grant the request, sure it was born of shock. Later, his buddy had killed himself.

By the time he'd been discharged, Ben's sense of right and wrong had been upended. He'd moved home and lived in his folks' guest quarters in Sycamore Canyon for a while. He'd talked for hours to his dad, but his dad had never served. He'd been sympathetic, but didn't really understand.

His mom, bless her woo-woo heart, insisted on doing curative massage on him and urged him to read Deepak Chopra. Ben had agreed to the massage but resisted the Chopra. Fortunately his dad had pointed him to the local vet group that met at the hospital, and Ben had met Tucker Hayes. Tucker had saved his sanity.

Tucker was a balding, bearded, pony-tailed, and paunchy Vietnam vet. He had a loud laugh and a soft spot for kittens. Tucker had been there. Only nineteen when he was shipped overseas, he'd had friends killed in front of him. He'd shot a twelve-year-old boy who'd pulled the pin on a grenade, then charged Tucker and three others.

Tucker had almost killed himself with drugs and alcohol after that, he'd told Ben. Then a friend had dragged Tucker to a pottery workshop at the VFW in Costa Mesa. It had been his salvation. Throwing pots gave Tucker a way to prove to himself that his hands were peaceful, that he wasn't a killer. He was simply a human being with a hard past.

It hadn't hurt that he'd fallen in love with the teacher, Maureen. They'd quickly become inseparable, eventually marrying.

Tucker had helped Ben see that's what he was, too. Damaged, yes. Destroyed or worthless, no. It was after meeting Tucker that Ben had remembered the camera he'd had as a teenager, remembered the magic of looking at the world through a lens. He'd found his old single-lens reflex and lenses in his folks' garage, had the gear cleaned and taken a few classes at Orange Coast Community College. Now he worked as a detective solely to support his days off when he could travel along the coast, run up to the mountains, camp in the desert and take pictures. Looking through the viewfinder or swimming in the morning beyond the ocean breakers, that was when he found peace, when the world felt right. Those were the times, he sometimes thought, that allowed him to function as a police officer.

Then something like this came along.

He found himself thinking of the lovely redhead he'd run into at the South Coast Heritage Park. Her dark auburn hair, falling below her shoulders, had been tousled by the same wind that had put a blush into her cheeks. She'd startled him on the trail, standing a short distance away, patiently waiting for him to finish his shot. Most people wouldn't have been so considerate. Her smile had been slow and deep, sincere, her laugh infectious. But what had really mesmerized him were her jade-green eyes. Open. Honest.

Ben had been surprised by his desire to keep talking to her, to hike with her, to have her show him the trails she'd described. He never wanted that. Time with his camera was *his* time. Time to find himself again. It was odd that being near her hadn't disturbed the sense of calm that came over him when he was working with the camera. She'd felt whole. Stable. Real.

He remembered her delicate fragrance when she'd come close to show him trails on her battered map. Her fingers were long and slender. Ben had been shocked by the sense that he already knew how those fingers would feel on his face.

Ben smiled as he remembered the way she swung her pack to her shoulder, the sway of her hips as she walked confidently down the hill. It was only as she went out of sight that he realized he hadn't asked her name. He'd felt so comfortable talking to her, he'd actually forgotten they'd just met.

She had given him the same sense of peace as the ocean. As the camera.

He wished he knew who she was. Someone should tell her not to walk the hills alone. Not with a killer somewhere in the county.

His smile faded.

"Headache, Robard?"

Ben opened his eyes and dropped his hand. His partner, Lauren Cruz, was leaning on his cubicle wall.

Ben jerked his head toward the computer monitor.

"Ah," she said, her look grim. "Yeah. Breckenridge and Danner went up to Mission Viejo this morning."

Ben frowned at her in puzzlement.

"As many as three of their open cases from up to five years ago might be connected."

"Three?" he said incredulously. "Here in Eden Beach?"

Cruz nodded.

The light went on for Ben. "That girl they found up in Swallowtail Canyon, when they broke ground for the new home?" Ben had been a new detective at the time.

Cruz nodded. "That's one of them."

"That would make seven in the county. And over years?"

Cruz nodded again.

"Any idea what makes them think the killings are connected?"

Cruz shrugged. "I gather there was some kind of forensic evidence found on the latest body that's ringing bells."

"So, we really may be talking serial killer. It's not just shop gossip."

"Yeah. It's possible. In fact, though Mike hasn't said as much, I get the feeling he thinks it's probable."

Ben felt sick. His mind went again to the woman in the Heritage Park. *Shit*, he thought, *Why didn't I get her name?*

"I wonder how many more there are," he said.

"I'm sure that's the question keeping all the crimes-against-persons guys awake right now," she said. "Brecken-ridge said everyone in Orange County is pooling their open homicides of young women, looking for commonalities. He said a couple cops were even coming up from San Diego."

"Jeez."

"Yep. Department tom-toms are saying there's discussion about bringing in a profiler from LA."

Ben closed his eyes, sighed and shook his head. He wasn't sure he wanted to be around during this investigation. In the back of his mind rose the preposterous idea he'd been having for a couple weeks now. He pushed it aside to listen to Cruz.

"Which," she was saying, "really makes this complaint such small potatoes."

"Complaint?"

She sighed and dropped into the chair next to Ben's desk. A small, attractive woman nearing forty, Cruz had short, dark hair, and a deep voice for someone her size. She usually trailed the scent of cigarettes, something Ben found comforting somehow, a reminder of his days in the Army. The good ones.

"You know Councilman Andrew Byers?" she asked.

"Not personally, no, I'm glad to say," said Ben. The long-serving councilman, now rumored to be planning a run for mayor, was widely considered to be an ignorant, as well as arrogant, prick. "What's he complaining about?"

"Not him," said Cruz, "his wife. Who happens to be my husband's Aunt Celia. So she came to me, and the lieutenant says it's my problem."

Ben raised an eyebrow and gave her a lopsided smile. "And now you're making it mine."

She grinned. "That's why you made detective, Robard," she said. "Nothing gets past you."

"So what's this problem?"

"I'll explain while we drive," she said, standing up.

"That depends on who's driving," said Ben, trying not to grin.

Cruz gave him a look that said *Seriously?* and dangled the keys in front of him.

He did grin then and followed her out to the car. By the time they'd crossed the lot, she'd given him the gist of the situation.

Ben was incredulous. He leaned on the top of the car and looked across at Cruz.

"Wait," he said. "I can't believe I'm getting this right. Your aunt…"

"Husband's aunt."

"…husband's aunt, Celia, went to a woman who claims to be a crystal healer. Now she's charging fraud because the woman wouldn't use *rocks* to heal her?" He spread his hands in a *What?* gesture.

"That's it pretty much in a nutshell."

"Eden Beach has gotten this weird?"

"Eden Beach has always been this weird," she said.

"There's a possible serial killer out there somewhere murdering women and hiding their bodies, and we have to waste time on *this*?" Ben's voice rose.

"Ben, I'm not thrilled about it either. Unfortunately, Celia's the wife of an influential—and loud-mouthed—councilman. And unfortunately she's an aunt—only by marriage and only under protest—of a detective in the Fraud division. The lieutenant was adamant. I have to make this go away. You're my partner. We don't have a choice."

"What does Byers say about his wife's complaint?"

"Don't know. Not going to ask," said Cruz. "Get in the car. The sooner we get over there, the sooner this will be done."

As he yanked open the door and dropped into the passenger seat, he clearly heard her say, "I hope."

It didn't improve his mood.

FIVE

"I'M GOING TO DIE. I'M HONESTLY GOING TO DIE," MOANED Colin, clinging to the handrail as they descended the stairs. Today he was wearing poison-green spandex stretch pants, a white tank and purple hoodie. His thinning sandy hair was damp from the workout. "That woman is a fiend. An absolute fiend!"

Stacie laughed. She was a bit wobbly, too. Their yoga instructor had seemed determined to help them build thighs of steel in one session. "Just keep your mind focused on food," she told him.

"I don't suppose I could convince you to go on ahead, bring the car down and drive me back, could I?"

"You could not," she said, grinning.

"Thought as much." He sighed dramatically and continued limping down the stairs.

"Anyway. Why are you complaining? Aren't you the star slugger, the prize speed demon for the Canyon Blue Jays? 'Galloping Gates,' isn't that what *The Record* called you?"

Colin held up a hand. "It was 'Goin' Gates' and please, don't remind me. Baseball uses a whole different set of muscles. None of these," he gestured to his legs, "are any of them."

They stepped outside into bright sunlight. Colin squinted up. "Well, that's a nice surprise," he said.

"It is," said Stacie, pulling sunglasses from her bag. She zipped up her gray hoodie. The sun might be out, but it was still chilly this early in the day.

"Oh, now that is just the limit," said Colin. "First, Mir manages to get out of that torture session, and now you are disgustingly prepared for sunlight even though we were socked in with fog this morning."

"Grouchy, grouchy," said Stacie. "You need tea and sugar."

"It's Mir's turn today, right?" asked Colin hopefully as they walked slowly away from the beach toward Glen Eden Avenue.

"Nope. You'll have to make do with Entenmann's," said Stacie. Mir always stopped by Christakos', the Greek bakery on Hennessey and brought something delectable. Stacie and Colin shopped at Ralphs.

"You know I do this only for the snacks, don't you?"

Stacie smiled. "Not for friendship?"

"My dear. I'm sure death-by-yoga is not required in any friendship contract."

"Whine, whine, whine."

"Ah!" He held up a finger, like an attorney making a point. "Whining *is* allowed in a friendship contract," he said. "I checked."

Stacie laughed. "I'll remember that when it's my turn."

They limped along for a half block, both of them feeling every aching muscle.

"So. You seen your stalker lately?" asked Colin finally.

"Don't even joke about that," said Stacie sharply. She

shivered involuntarily. "No. I haven't seen him. Not since he popped up at Del Mundo when we were having coffee."

After the incident at the bookstore, Stacie hadn't seen Troy for days. She went everywhere with Bananas now, and she'd begun to hope the dog had scared him off.

Then she'd arranged to meet Colin at their favorite coffee shop, Del Mundo, to discuss a client who was resisting paying him. Colin was just giving Stacie the outlines of the situation when a headache stabbed her just above and between her eyes. As she put a hand up to her forehead, the air pressure changed deep in her ears. The noise in the café blurred and faded. She thought she was going to faint.

Suddenly, Troy was there between Colin and her.

His smile was wolf-like, his almost-colorless eyes were icy. Her blood went cold, sluggish. Violence flashed in the darkness around him.

Colin had stopped speaking.

"Anastasia," Troy had said in the voice she'd come to hate. "You should have told me you had a," he glanced disparagingly at Colin before locking his eyes on hers again, "a *boyfriend*. You shouldn't have let me make a fool of myself."

Colin, startled, started to put his hand out to introduce himself, but Stacie's hand shot out and gripped his fingers in hers. For once, Colin held his tongue.

"I've told you, several times, to leave me alone. I'm not interested in seeing you," she said. Her blood was roaring so loudly in her ears, she could barely hear her own voice. "My friend and I are having a private conversation. Don't bother me again. Or I'll call the police."

Troy's eyes went almost white. Then he smiled, a horrible sight that chilled her even more. "Oh, I don't give up easily,

Anastasia. I'll just have to put myself out a little more. It'll be worth the wait. I promise you that."

The hair on Stacie's neck actually stood up. *It's not a figure of speech*, she thought in some functioning part of her mind.

"Who, or rather what, in the name of *hell* was that?" Colin asked as Troy walked out Del Mundo's door. "I'm thinking I should get that bat I broke and drive it through his heart."

Sound crashed in on Stacie again. She gulped and realized she'd been holding her breath. The sharp scent of roasting coffee smelled suddenly bitter. She was gripping Colin's hand so hard her fingers and his were bloodless.

"Stacie?" said Colin, not joking now. "What's going on? You're white. Your hand is freezing." Then his eyes went wide. "Oh, my God! It's him, isn't it? The guy from the Becker. And the bookstore. Oh, Stacie!"

For a few moments, she simply clung to her friend, her heart hammering so hard she felt the artery in her neck pulsing.

"Yes. That's him," she said, when her breathing finally steadied.

"You have to call the police," Colin told her. "He's stalking you." It sounded preposterous when it was said out loud, but Colin didn't laugh. "Really, Stacie. He might be dangerous."

There was no maybe about it. Troy *was* dangerous.

But she still hadn't called.

"I haven't seen him," Stacie said again as she and Colin walked to her shop, "and I don't want to see him. So don't mention him. It feels too much like conjuring the devil."

"Whoa! That's crediting him with an awful lot of power, isn't it?" asked Colin.

Stacie didn't think so, but didn't say so aloud.

"If you haven't seen him since Del Mundo's, maybe he's given up," said Colin.

"No," said Stacie grimly. "He hasn't. He's still around."

"How do you know? Oh. Of course. The way you knew about Peter." Colin linked his arm through hers. "I wish you'd call the police."

Stacie snorted. "And tell them what? That I think some creepy guy is following me even when I can't see him?" *And that he makes my crystal go all wonky*. She shook her head. "That would get their attention. And not in a good way. I'm pretty sure Troy is not even his real name. So what could they do?" She waved her hands in front of her. "Anyway, Colin. I really don't want to talk about him. Just the thought makes my skin crawl."

Colin nodded and stopped as they reached the corner of Glen Eden. He ran a hand down a thigh and changed the subject as they crossed the street. "Mir was smart to dodge this class. You said there was an estate sale?"

"Yes," said Stacie. "Supposed to be heavy on jewelry. She said something about looking for mid-century pieces."

Mir bought old costume jewelry and recombined and refashioned it. She was slowly building an online business for her remarkably striking pieces. She'd even placed pieces in some of the funky dress shops in Eden Beach and other coastal towns nearby.

"I wish her luck," said Colin, then almost ran into Stacie who had stopped in the middle of the sidewalk her hand over her mouth.

Colin looked down the block to The Bell, Book and Crystal. "Oh, for God's sake."

"Yes," said Stacie tightly. "I suspect that's exactly what it's for."

In front of her pretty, light blue cottage with the yellow shutters and white picket fence, there was another line of pickets, these not so attractive or welcome. Marching in front of her store were about a dozen men and women with signs.

"When the hell did they start this?"

"Must be a new thing." *Like I need more crap raining down*, thought Stacie.

She took a deep breath. "You don't have to come with me," she said to Colin.

"Are you kidding?" he said. "One of those signs says 'Death to faggots.' Of course I have to come with you." Colin's tone was light, but there was no humor in his eyes.

Stacie looked at him for a moment, then leaned over and kissed him on the cheek. As she moved down the block toward her store, Colin drew his phone out of his pocket and started recording a video.

"Excuse me!" Stacie began working her way through the crowd blocking the narrow sidewalk. "Let me by, please."

Someone tried to push a flyer into her hand. Stacie snatched her hand away.

"Evil walks among us," someone shouted in her face. Stacie marched on.

Behind her, Colin was creating a stir, pushing his phone into everyone's face as he passed.

"What are you doing?"

"Sodomite!"

"You can't take my picture! Stop that right now!"

As Stacie turned up the front walk, the voices changed.

"It's the witch!"

"Go back to hell, bride of Satan!"

With shaking hands, Stacie unlocked the shop door. With one last shot of the group shouting, Colin dodged in behind her.

"Well. No doubt about that group. They're definitely from that obnoxious, so-called church that moved into the old Computers 'n' More building," said Colin, anger obvious in his voice. "I'd like to send *them* back to hell."

"I have to call Mir. Warn her," said Stacie.

"Let me send her a text." He waved his phone. "I'm already halfway there."

"Thanks." She flicked on the fountain. The sudden rush of trickling water obscured some of the shouting from outside, but it didn't sooth her agitation.

Stacie went to the kitchen to put the kettle on, then leaned on the counter trying to bring her pounding heart under control.

This has got to stop. First eggs, then dog poop, now picketers. Then what? she thought, remembering the destruction at Windrift. *When do they start breaking windows? Or worse.* Between this, discovering that Judd Walleram's poison was still spreading through town, and the tax bills, not to mention the dangerous creep following her, how much more was she expected to take?

She closed her eyes. Anger burned around her fear. *Yes. Let's not forget that*, she thought, though she wished she could.

She took a deep breath and scrubbed her face with her hands. *One thing at a time*, she thought as she went to let Bananas in from the patio. She'd dropped him off earlier since she couldn't take him to yoga class.

"Why didn't you put a stop to all that?" she asked the dog, nodding at the front of the store. "Some help you are." Bananas wagged his tail and smiled a toothy grin. "For that you expect a biscuit?" He wagged harder. Stacie shook her head, got him a treat and sent him back out to the patio.

"Mir said she'd have Ace bring her to the store," Colin

reported, coming into the kitchen. Ace wasn't big but he was multi-pierced and tattooed. Hopefully, he'd be an intimidating sight to the narrow-minded group outside.

"Did you call the police?" he asked.

She shook her head. "I doubt they can do anything," she said. "Right to free speech? Right to protest?"

"Freedom of pseudo-religion?" Colin chimed in. "You should still report it. They were pretty threatening."

"Maybe you're right," she said.

"Something else to add to your log, too," said Colin.

"I'm going to need a new notebook, if this keeps up," she said bitterly, then sighed. "You're right. I'll call the police later and talk to Detective Meissner." *For whatever good it will do*, she thought

"I sent you the video I took," said Colin. "Send that along to her as well."

"Thanks."

As she kicked off her shoes by the back door in the kitchen, Stacie slipped a hand into her hoodie pocket, folding the crystal into her palm. Checking her crystal had become a frequent thing. She was constantly afraid Troy would sneak up on her when she was alone, even with Bananas, the Mighty Guard Dog, next to her. She was particularly spooked by Colin bringing him up this morning.

The crystal was calm. Only the light joy she felt when Colin was around. He always made her smile.

"Stacie, could he be part of that group of religious phonies out there? The stalker?"

She shook her head. "No. They just throw eggs and dog doodoo. Childish, spiteful acts. Like the name calling." She waved a hand toward the front of the store.

Troy, she thought, *is quite likely crazy*. She just barely managed to not say that aloud to Colin.

Stacie padded over to the counter, pulled out a knife and slit the cellophane on the Entenmann's. "But frankly, I'm getting really, really tired of it. All of it," she said. "Almost anyone in town who has some kind of," she put the knife down and made air quotes, "'alternative' business, service or product has been having this kind of thing happen." She picked up the knife, sliced up the coffee cake and set it out on a plate.

"Yeah. I helped Matt clean graffiti off his walls last weekend."

"How's that going?" Stacie asked casually.

The brilliant smile that lit Colin's face was his only response.

"I'm glad," she said.

Bananas nudged Stacie. She looked down. "You're as bad as Colin. You both look pitiable when food is around. "

"Oh, that hurts," said her friend, hand to his heart.

She smiled. "Would you give him a biscuit? That's his two for the morning. I swear he can count."

"Anyway," she said, as Colin opened the jar and gave the dog his treat, "I'm hoping that when that group moves on—or splinters—this will stop. Outside," she said to the big curly-haired dog as he dropped his treat on the kitchen floor. "Share the crumbs with the birds." After a look to confirm she was serious, Bananas picked it up delicately and trotted back to the patio, where he dropped to the flagstones and began to crunch.

"The police think the same thing," she went on. "Unless they can catch whoever's throwing eggs or scrawling graffiti while they're doing it, we're pretty much helpless." Her jaw tightened.

There was a knock at the front door. Stacie looked up and smiled. "Mir. She's early. Must not have been anything worthwhile at the sale." She cocked an ear. "And no shouting. Ace must have scared them quiet."

"Stace, really, about the other thing..." Colin started to say.

Stacie held up her hand. "Colin, I really, really don't want to talk about it. Please. Just do me a favor and go let Mir in."

She knew he would pick up the subject again, later, but for now, he went out front to let their friend in.

What Stacie didn't say, couldn't say, even to Colin, was that the shop felt safe, protected, unless she brought Troy into the space by talking about him. She wanted to keep feeling that way. Yes, it was probably a dumb thing to think. And yes, it was probably superstitious stuff about conjuring the devil. But she'd grown up trusting—had been taught to trust —her intuition. It had never let her down. As long as she listened to it.

She heard voices out front as she pulled the cozy over the tea pot. She frowned. A man and a woman, but not Mir and Ace. She sighed. Early customers who'd braved the gauntlet. It was too much to hope the picketers had left. Her tea would be cold by time she could join her friends.

"Stace..." Colin called from the front, an odd tone in his voice.

She paused, hand on the pot, then went out into the shop.

She glanced at Colin, then looked past him. She just had time to see the woman putting away a badge.

"It's not Mir," said Colin.

TROY

Be calm. Think.

That's what the shrinks always said. Said his anger got him into trouble.

Pissed him off. Anger didn't get him into trouble. It was the assholes who messed with him. Dissed him. Acted like he was nothing. Less than nothing.

Even his beautiful Anastasia. Wouldn't even shake his hand that day. Almost fell in the fish pond when she pulled away. Too bad she didn't. Would have been fun to see her wet.

Yeah. He'd have to find a house with a pool where they could get wet together. Then he'd take her on the cement. Hard under her. Hard in her.

Yeah. She'd like that. He'd make her like that.

Look at her. Playing hard to get. Flaunting that perv in front of him. Acting all superior. Telling him to go away in front of the little creep. But he saw her. Looking around. Looking for him. Making sure he saw what she was doing. Teasing him.

Fine. Let her have her little game. But soon. Soon.

He knew he had her hooked. She could feel his vibe. He

could tell. Women loved that edgy shit. Loved it when he scared them. Made them hot. Made him hard. They'd do anything so he wouldn't hurt them.

He hurt them anyway. Made them pay. Stupid women. Always act like they want it, then act like they don't. He didn't like being jacked around.

Anastasia. Sexy. Like his mother's name, Angelina.

Angelina.

Why do women always have stupid names, like McKenzie or Brittany? Stacie's a stupid name, too.

Like Angie. Or Ang. Like those losers she was always fucking called her. Like she was some two-dollar whore giving blow jobs in a back seat.

Anastasia. That's what he'd call her. Like the name on the brass plate on the front of that building, telling who lived there, when it was built, blah, blah, blah. Like anyone gives a crap. A real woman's name. Sexy. Made him hard just saying it to himself. Angelina.

When he got her alone, he'd make her use Anastasia. Make her say it over and over.

And she'd call him Troy. Troy, baby. He could hear it on her lips. Anything you say, Troy, baby.

They all said it in the end.

First, he had to get her alone.

Pissed him off all over again. She hadn't been alone since that first day. Always someone hanging around. Like the faggot. Or that bitch with the big hair and little tits. Now she always had that big fucking dog with her.

He'd waited for her one night. But the old hag next door must have seen him when she looked out her window. Had to be her who called the cops.

She'd better watch herself.

Women. Always thought they were too good for him. Acting like he was slime.

Even his own mother. Pushing him away like that. Calling him a pervert.

But they learned. They all learned. Even his mother. He'd showed her. They couldn't treat him like that. Blow him off, like he was nothing.

Anastasia would learn, too. Or he'd punish her.

Yeah. Punish her.

Pissed him off that she threw the roses away. Shit. The cost of those fucking flowers.

He'd have to make her stop dressing like that, too. Like some street corner slut. Like his mother. God! Did she have to show it all off? Draw all the dogs, like a bitch in heat?

Like that turd sneaking around, throwing eggs. What a loser. Some jilted pissant, trying to get even. He couldn't have that. He'd have to teach the guy a lesson. Give Anastasia a taste of what he could do. If she didn't stop playing stupid games.

Like letting that little pervert hang around. Touching her hair. Her arm. Stroking her back.

Creeped him the hell out. What kind of loser takes an exercise class? Little faggot probably got off seeing women's butts in the air.

He knew that game. He'd seen the little creeps with his mother.

Yeah. Wait until Anastasia found out what it was like with a real man. He wasn't some perv in tights. He'd killed people. Now that was something to get off on.

God! He loved her red hair. Like fire. Redheads were passionate. They liked to fight. He loved it when they fought him. They screamed when he fucked them. He made them scream. Like his mother. She used to scream. He'd made her beg for treating him like that.

The blonds begged. He liked it when they whimpered. He loved their silky hair. The way it caught the light. He loved to touch their hair.

Made him excited, just thinking about it.

Of course, Anastasia would have to pay. For playing games. Humiliating him. Waving him away like he was a nobody. Enough so she'd know not to do it again. Ever.

SIX

"ANASTASIA CAPPELLA?" ASKED A SMALL LATINA WOMAN wearing dark slacks and jacket.

"Stacie," she responded automatically. "I prefer Stacie." But she really wasn't thinking about the words. Her eyes had gone past the woman to the man behind her. Her dark-haired photographer.

"I'm Detective Lauren Cruz," the woman was saying, "and this is Detective Ben Robard."

Stacie barely heard her. She saw the flash of recognition on Ben's face and started to smile. Her lips parted to say something, to acknowledge him, when his brows went down in a frown.

She hesitated and thought better of mentioning their meeting at the South Coast Heritage Park.

Bananas' tags rattled as he came in from the patio and pushed his head under her hand. She curled her fingers in the fur behind his ears.

"Ms Cappella?" the female detective was saying.

Stacie's attention snapped back to Lauren Cruz.

"Yes?"

"Ms Cappella, we're here because there's been a complaint filed against you with the Eden Beach Police Department's Fraud Division."

"What?" Stacie's voice went up a register. "Who filed a complaint against me? For what?" The only thing that came to mind was income tax fraud. She saw her future filled with IRS investigators and lawsuits. She felt sick.

Ben crossed his arms, looked at his partner and leaned back against the sales counter as if he wanted to distance himself from her. From both of them.

"Mrs. Celia Byers says you advertise yourself to be a crystal healer, yet when she asked you for healing, you denied her treatment. Then you tried to extort money from her."

Stacie looked at the detective for at least thirty seconds while the charge registered. She asked the only thing she could. "Who's Celia Byers? What on earth are you talking about?"

"Councilman Byers' wife," said Colin. He closed his eyes and shook his head. "The woman's a menace."

Cruz turned to him. "Why do you say that, Mr. ...?"

"Gates. Colin Gates," he said. "Because she is. She's been to a number of alternative healers in town. When they can't help her—probably because all her *problems*," Colin put sarcastic emphasis on the word, "are in her head—she turns on them, claiming they're frauds."

"You know this because...?"

"A friend in town is an acupuncturist," said Colin bitterly. "He treated the Byers woman for more than a month. It was always something different, and she was never satisfied. He eventually suggested she see a conventional medical practitioner. She became enraged. She eventually refused to pay him for his time. She's suing him now."

Swell, thought Stacie. *It's not the IRS. It's a nut case about to sue me.*

She noticed Ben close his eyes and shake his head almost imperceptibly.

"Be that as it may," said Cruz tightly, turning back to Stacie, "Mrs. Byers came in last week. She said she inquired about your methods and requested...treatment...but she says you refused to treat her in an effort to drive the price up. Mrs. Byers says when she confronted you about it, you became hostile, so she left."

Stacie sighed heavily. "The woman in the perfume cloud. The one with the bad heart."

"I'm sorry?" said Cruz, startled.

Stacie waved her hand. "Yes. Now I know who you're talking about. She didn't introduce herself. I didn't 'become hostile.' She was obnoxious and belligerent. She kept insisting that I treat her. I finally asked her to leave."

Stacie ran a hand into her hair and sighed as she unconsciously pulled the wrap from her ponytail. "Detective," she said, fluffing her hair as it fell free. "I'm not a medical practitioner. I told her that. I don't heal anyone. I can't heal anyone. I'm a bookkeeper. I sell wind chimes, books, meditation tapes," she gestured around her, "with the occasional fountain or pair of earrings. I do it for fun because I inherited the store. It helps me earn a little extra money. I enjoy meeting the people—most of the people," she amended, "who come in."

"So how did Mrs. Byers get the idea you could heal her with crystals?" asked Cruz.

Before Stacie could answer, Colin said, "Mir."

Stacie shot him a look.

He put his hands up in front of him. "Sorry."

"Who's Mir?" asked Cruz.

"Mirabella Nguyen-Collier is the young woman who

69

works for me," said Stacie. "She got it into her head that it was the touchstone I once gave her that healed her acne."

"Why would she think that?" asked Cruz. Her tone made it clear she thought the idea got into Mir's head because Stacie put it there.

"Who knows why anyone believes anything?" said Stacie, an edge to her voice. She was angry now that the terror of federal prison had passed. "Someone buys a touchstone because it gives them something to hold onto during chemo treatment. When their cancer goes away, why do they credit the stone and not the treatment?" Stacie had a customer who had believed just that. "Why do placebos work? Doctors still don't understand that."

She glanced at Ben. His face was closed.

She remembered the odd sense of confusion she'd sensed at the Heritage Park.

Not confusion. Imbalance. Uncertainty. As if his tether to the ground had been cut.

Stacie went to the case where she kept exquisitely formed quartz crystals—smoky, amethyst, colorless—under glass to protect them from damage as well as from too much handling.

"Personally?" she said as she unlocked and opened the case and pulled out the drawer holding the crystals. "I think that, for most people, the crystals, the wind chimes, the music —beautiful things, beautiful sounds—just make them feel better, more connected, calmer." Her hand went unhesitatingly to a smoky quartz the size of her thumb. The specimen was cloudy and dark at the base, but gradually cleared to a lovely gray at the finely pointed termination.

She went back to Ben and held it out to him. Startled, he reached for it, and she laid it in his hand. Stacie saw Colin's puzzled look as she turned back toward Cruz.

"The Tarot, the runes, simply give people a way to acknowledge what they already know. That it's time to change jobs. That their boyfriend is no good for them." From the corner of her eye, she saw Ben watching her, listening to her. She saw his thumb stroking the crystal.

"Just because I sell these things doesn't mean I'm a healer. Nor does it mean I endorse them as a method of healing. In fact, I always tell people—like your Mrs. Byers—to see a health professional if they have health concerns."

"But you let your employee continue to tell people something different," said Cruz doggedly.

"Yes, well." Stacie sighed. "I've tried to tell her the stones don't heal, but she's convinced they've helped her." Stacie spread her hands. "I can't help what she believes. I have asked her not to say things like that to customers. The shop alone creates enough trouble by itself." The last statement came out a little bitterly.

For the first time, Ben spoke. "What do you mean, it creates trouble?"

Shoot, thought Stacie. *Now I've opened a can of worms.*

She flushed. She'd almost forgotten how warm his voice was.

When she was silent a beat too long, Colin spoke up.

"The vandalism for one thing," he said, pulling out his phone.

"Vandalism?" Ben's brows came back together.

"I've reported it several times," said Stacie. Colin was already showing Ben the photo he'd taken a few days before. "I practically have Detective Meissner on speed dial."

"Do you know who's doing it?" Ben asked Stacie, passing the phone to his partner.

"No," she said, "not for sure. But I've got a good idea. Ask them." Stacie jerked her chin toward the front window

71

where they could see the picketers, not shouting, but still circling like piranha.

"The vandalism started when that religious group set up shop in the empty Computers 'n' More store up in El Toro. I'm not the only one in town being hit." She gestured to the front of the store. "Apparently, they've decided to try other methods of intimidation."

"Did you know about this?" Ben asked Cruz, as she gave the phone back to Colin.

His partner nodded. "I've heard Kelly talking about it. It's minor stuff."

Stacie bristled. "It's not minor if you have dog poop smeared all over your windows or graffiti painted on your store front. It's extra work, expense, and lost customers."

"Sorry," said Cruz. "Poor choice of words. But, except for the graffiti, because nothing is damaged or stolen, and no one is hurt, we class it as minor." Before Stacie could say anything else, Cruz went on to Ben. "The patrols are watching for it. But it's been random and they haven't seen anyone."

Stacie felt like she was being ignored. "Actually, they *have* started destroying property. Jacqui, at the Windrift, has had books sliced to pieces. When will these people start breaking windows? Setting fire to buildings? Now they're out there intimidating people. What happens to my customers, my clients, my business? When will they attack people? Attack *me*? Did you see the sign out there that says 'Death to faggots'? But the police barely acknowledge they're a threat. Yet you come out here to investigate a bogus complaint by a crazy woman who says I refuse to do something that I don't claim to do!"

"Ms Cappella, we have to investigate…"

"But you don't!" said Stacie, her voice rising with irritation. "Has anyone talked to those people? A friend of mine attended one of those meetings. She walked out because she was frightened by the ugliness they were preaching. She said the pastor was practically mentioning business owners by name. A woman out there called me a witch this morning!"

She saw Colin wince. *He's right. I shouldn't have said that*, she thought.

"Witch?" asked Ben, a strange look on his face. He refolded his arms across his diaphragm. *Angry.* The thought surprised Stacie. *At me?*

"The crystals. The Tarot," said Stacie with exasperation, gesturing at the cases around them. "Anything people don't understand. Anything they fear." She put both hands in her hoodie pockets and fingered her crystal. Definitely angry. His partner was just all business. *Why is he angry?* she wondered.

Bananas felt it, too. He walked over and surprised Ben by butting him in the hip.

Ben looked down into Bananas' laughing face, and for the first time since walking in, he smiled. He took the side of the dog's face in his hand and fluffed one of his droopy ears. "What are *you* laughing at, you big galoot?" Ben asked him.

A wave of warmth washed through Stacie, unknotting some of the tension in her shoulders. She smiled, too, in spite of herself.

The front door opened, and a slender woman in her sixties dressed in green slacks and cream cardigan over her flowered blouse, stepped in, shopping bag in hand.

Bananas left Ben and trotted over to the newcomer, wagging his tail.

"Good morning, Stacie!" she called as she pulled the door shut behind her and stretched a hand to pet the big dog, her hair falling over her cheek. "I saw all the crazy people out there and thought I'd…" She glanced up and stopped, her

gaze taking in the tense stances of the people in the shop. "…
bring breakfast," she finished. "Stacie? Is everything all
right?"

Colin rolled his eyes at her.

"Eileen, meet Detective Cruz and Detective Robard. A
friend and neighbor, Eileen Kemper. She owns the four-plex
next door."

"You're here about the stalker?" Eileen asked them. "Stacie. You haven't seen him again?"

The energy in the room shifted. Ben dropped his arms and
stepped forward, shoulder to shoulder with his partner. Cruz
shot him a look but Ben kept his eyes on Stacie. He'd stopped
stroking the crystal.

"Stalker?" he asked quietly.

SEVEN

STACIE'S FINGERS, CURLED AROUND THE QUARTZ IN HER pocket, got the pins and needles feeling of a numb hand coming awake at the same moment she realized Ben was suddenly very alert. Very concerned.

His concern scared her almost as much as if Troy had walked in the front door.

She really didn't want to talk about this. She didn't want to look like a fool.

But Troy *did* scare her.

Maybe Colin's right, she thought. *Maybe it* is *time I talked to the police.* Especially if the thought of a stalker caused this level of concern in the police. Or at least in this particular cop.

She didn't realize her hesitation was noticeable until Ben said, "Stacie?"

The jolt of joy at the sound of his voice saying her name was so strong, that the amethyst crystal next to Stacie's heart pulsed in response.

Before she could reply, Colin interrupted. "Some creepy

guy tried to pick her up at the Becker Preserve," he blurted out. "Now he shows up wherever she goes."

"Everywhere?" asked Cruz. She, too, was suddenly alert.

"Not everywhere," said Stacie finally finding her voice. "Places I often go, but have never seen him before." She told them about the bookstore, nursery, and coffee shop.

"When was the last time?" asked Cruz.

"About ten days ago?" Stacie looked at Colin for confirmation. He nodded.

"Not since?"

Stacie hesitated.

Ben raised an eyebrow and cocked his head, questioning without a word.

Eileen had no such control.

"Stacie? You haven't seen him again," she said, walking over to put a hand on her friend's arm.

"No," said Stacie. "Well...no."

"But you think he's around." It was a statement from Ben.

"Yeees...maybe," said Stacie. She waved her hands. "I sound like a nut case," she said. "I'm sorry. It's just that...that thing where you think you see someone from the corner of your eye, but then they're not there. Or you feel like you're being followed." *Or your crystal is buzzing.* "A couple times I thought maybe someone was watching the shop when I was working upstairs."

"What?" said Colin and Eileen at the same time. "You never mentioned that," said Eileen.

Stacie laid her hand over Eileen's. "I didn't want you worrying."

"You could have called me. I would have come over to look," said Colin.

"You live upstairs?" Ben asked Stacie.

"No. My office is up there," said Stacie. "As I said, I'm a

bookkeeper and tax preparer. I do this," she gestured to the space around her, "for fun, part time. My employee..."

"Mirabella," said Cruz.

"Yes. Mir works part-time most of the year, and full time when tax season gets into full swing. Which is about now. This time of year," she explained, and realized she was babbling. "I'm almost always here working upstairs in the office after I close the store and before I open it in the morning." She made an effort to stop talking.

Ben frowned and looked at Stacie, then Colin. "You're working this morning?"

Stacie became aware of her yoga outfit—bare feet, no make-up, black stretch capris, the gray hoodie, and a hot pink spandex tank that, she was sure, left very little to Detective Robard's imagination. She self-consciously pulled the hoodie closer around her.

"Yoga class. Twice a week," said Colin. "Then breakfast. Which we haven't had yet," he added pointedly.

Stacie smiled at his protest.

"The two businesses don't exactly seem..." Ben paused. Stacie could see him search for the right word. "Compatible," he finally said.

She knew what he was hinting. Bookkeeping: intellectual, rational. Crystals and Tarot: mystical and about as irrational as you could get.

Yet there were countless times when her intuition— enhanced by her crystal—warned her to steer clear of a client, or hinted that a client was being less than honest with her.

Like Senator Michaels.

She was not going to try to explain that to the police, however. Two people who were about as intellectual and rational as you could get. She chose to misunderstand him.

"It's almost never a problem," she said, shrugging. "I

usually open in the morning, then Mir comes in. I crunch numbers while she covers the shop. I'm here to answer questions, if she has any—she doesn't know the stones like I do— or if a customer asks to see me."

Mir didn't know the Tarot or runes like Stacie did, either, and customers sometimes wanted to ask her opinion on a reading. She definitely was *not* going to bring that up.

"Tax season does get hairy because the bookkeeping work goes on even when the tax prep picks up. That's why Mir starts covering full time soon." She shrugged again. "Even if I didn't have the shop, I'd be working early and late."

Shut up, she told herself. But something about the intensity of Ben's gaze made her want to keep talking.

"So you're often here on your own late at night," said Ben. Even without the crystal in her palm tingling, Stacie felt his tension underlain by that whisper of deep concern. He was definitely scaring her.

Bananas, sitting next to her again, pushed his wet nose against her hand. Stacie unconsciously slid her hand up to the dog's head, stroking the curly hair.

"Yes, but I keep the outside doors and the door to the office locked," she continued.

"You said you were working upstairs and thought someone was out front watching," Ben prompted. "What made you think that? Did the dog bark?"

"No." She hesitated. Bananas hadn't barked. "He did get up. Usually he just imitates a carpet. When I went to the window..." She paused again. "It was just a feeling. Something about the street when I looked out." True enough. There had been something not right, though she couldn't say what it was. She didn't mention that the cold sense of the crystal slicing through her palm had confirmed Troy was close.

She took a deep breath, gave Eileen and Colin an apologetic look, then turned back to Ben.

"But there's something else." She gave the dog a final pat, moved behind the sales counter and took an envelope out of a drawer.

"The day at the bookstore, I found a rose on my car. I found another one about a week ago, when I left to go home at night. I threw them in the street hoping he'd get the hint." She held the envelope out to Cruz. "But there have also been these." She saw Eileen's blue eyes widen behind her wire-rimmed glasses.

The detective pulled two torn sheets of paper out of the envelope, handling them carefully.

Stacie knew by heart what they said.

"When did you find these?" asked Cruz, handing the notes to Ben.

"The first, the one that says, 'Don't play with me,' that was on the car the day after he approached me at the coffee shop, when I was with Colin."

"What does he mean?" asked Cruz.

"He accused me of lying to him, not telling him I had a boyfriend." She nodded at Colin who raised an eyebrow.

"The other?"

"That was in the outside door, two days after the last rose."

"'If you don't like flowers, I have something I know you'll like better.'" Ben looked up at Cruz. The air almost sizzled between them.

"Look," Stacie said firmly, trying to get a grip on her fear. "He's a creep, as Colin said, and he's given me a bad case of nerves. And it *has* been almost week since the last note. Maybe he's gone away. Given up."

Colin gave her a look that said, *Oh, girlfriend, you are so lying*. But he kept his mouth shut.

"Anyway, Eden Beach has its share of loonies. I'm hoping that if I don't respond, he'll quit and leave me alone," Stacie finished up lamely.

"This is not nothing, Stacie. What did he look like?" asked Ben. Cruz pulled her phone out of her pocket to take notes.

Stacie gave them a rundown. "About your height," she nodded at Ben.

A flash of memory: Ben standing next to her in the sunlight, smiling, his eyes like sapphires.

Distracted, she hesitated. There was a slight downward flicker of Ben's eyebrows.

She shook herself mentally. "Blond-brown hair, longish." She gestured. "About collar length. Medium build. Lean, though. Straight nose. Do they call that Roman? Dark brows. Eyes," she hesitated again. "His eyes are very light blue."

"They're almost white," said Colin. "Like a dead fish." He shuddered and made a face.

"He said his name was Troy," Stacie said finally. "But I don't think that was true. It was like it was made up on the spur of the moment. He was wearing a camo jacket. Jeans, maybe?"

"Was the jacket military?" asked Ben.

"I really don't know," said Stacie. "Everyone wears camo these days. There's even camo underwear in the lingerie department."

Cruz buried a smile.

"You didn't see a car or license plate?" asked Ben.

Stacie shook her head. "No. He always seems to pop out of the ground." *Like a devil*, she thought.

"Have you reported the stalking?" asked Cruz.

Both Colin and Eileen turned their heads toward her.

"And say what?" she said, as much to them as to Cruz. "He hasn't done anything except act creepy and show up at places I've been." *And send my crystal crazy.* "What's to report?"

"Oh, I don't know," said Colin, to the air in front of him. "Maybe the notes?"

Cruz looked at Stacie sternly. "We'll mention this to the detectives who handle this kind of thing, but you need to make a formal complaint, get it on record. Anything you can remember."

"Good thing you've made notes in your vandalism log," said Colin.

Cruz looked at him then back at Stacie. "You were concerned enough that you kept a log but you haven't reported it?"

"I kept telling her it would be too late when they found her body," said Colin lightly.

"Not funny!" snapped Stacie. Cruz turned a penetrating stare on him.

"Sorry," he said sheepishly. "Awful joke. But it's not that bad, is it? I mean, yes, we've been after her to report it, but really, it's not that bad, is it? Just another Eden Beach loony, like Stacie says?"

"Stalkers can be unpredictable," said Ben. "As Detective Cruz said, we'll let the Crimes Against Persons detectives know, but you really have to make a formal complaint." Stacie saw concern in those deep blue eyes, a break in Ben's mask of professionalism.

Colin looked sick. Eileen put her hand back on Stacie's arm.

Stacie remembered every hair on her body standing up when Troy surprised her, the nasty look on his face when he confronted her with Colin, the slicing edges of her crystal. His empty eyes. The black hole he inhabited.

The black hole. No aura. Nothing. Just darkness around him.

All light going in. Nothing coming out.

Stacie felt the room draw away. Cold sweat prickled her skin as bile rose in her throat.

"Stacie? What is it? You've gone white," said Eileen.

"I'll call today," she said shakily.

Cruz nodded.

"Ask for Detective Breckenridge or Danner," said Ben.

"I will." She took a deep breath, and a second. The ringing in her ears faded, and she felt the blood coming back into her face. "But look. What about this fraud thing?"

She saw Eileen look at Colin who mouthed, *Tell you later*.

"I do not heal anyone, Detective," Stacie continued. "I *never* suggest the stones can heal because they don't. I tried to explain that to your Mrs. Byers. She just wouldn't listen."

"I'll talk to her," said Cruz. "Explain that it was a misunderstanding."

Good luck with that, thought Stacie. "Thanks. Sorry you wasted a morning," was all she said.

"One thing," asked Cruz.

Stacie wondered why the detective suddenly was so uncomfortable.

"Why did you say Mrs. Byers had a bad heart? Is that what she asked you to heal?"

Stacie, puzzled by the odd look Ben was giving his partner, said, "No. That was for the alcohol addiction."

"She *told* you that?" Cruz seemed surprised.

Shit! thought Stacie. The woman had never said what she wanted treated.

"I really don't remember, Detective. She must have," Stacie lied smoothly. "Does it matter?"

"No, not really," said Cruz, sliding her phone into her jacket pocket. "But you'd better make it clear to…Mir…that she's not helping your business. If we get similar complaints, we'll have to look into this more deeply."

Stacie saw Ben's eyebrow lift slightly as he glanced at his partner. Detective Cruz was trying to save face. Well, nothing wrong with that.

"Believe me, I'll tell her. Again," said Stacie.

"Since you're here," interrupted Eileen, "can you do anything about those people out there?" She pointed to the sidewalk out front. "They were very unpleasant when I arrived this morning."

They all glanced at the crowd moving back and forth, waving their signs.

"I'm sorry," said Cruz. "There's nothing we can do. It's ugly, but they're within their rights to picket. We'll talk to them about not blocking the walk or coming onto the property. We can warn them against trying to intimidate or threaten you," she looked at Stacie, "or your customers. But beyond that, our hands are pretty much tied."

Stacie rubbed her temples. "Great," she said. "Just what I need right now. Lost customers and clients." She dropped her hands and sighed. "But if you'll speak to them about not intimidating people, I'd appreciate it."

Cruz nodded. As she turned toward the door, Ben said to Stacie, "If you see your stalker again, give one of us or Detective Breckenridge a call. Or Detective Meissner. Or call 911," he said. He handed her his card. "Just let someone know." Then he held the smoky quartz out to her.

"It's yours," said Stacie.

"We can't accept gifts," Ben told her.

"It's not a gift. Or a bribe. Or a thank you," she said. "It's *yours*. Certain stones belong to certain people." She looked back into his blue eyes unflinchingly. "This crystal is *yours*."

Ben hesitated. Stacie felt his uncertainty. *It's calling him*, she thought. *He wants to keep it*.

"It's a *rock*, Robard," Cruz murmured. "No one's going to get worked up about it."

Ben looked back and forth between them, shook his head and slipped the crystal into his jacket pocket. "Thanks. I think," he said. He gave her a small smile. Puzzled.

Stacie's heart did a sidestep, and heart-deep longing seized her. She nodded slightly, and the two detectives left the shop.

The three friends were momentarily silent as the door closed behind them. Bananas snorted as he dropped into his usual place near the patio door.

"She would have thought differently if she'd known how much that 'rock' was worth," said Colin as Stacie went back to the case and pulled out the label that said "Smoky quartz, Bahia Brazil, $175."

"I need tea. Hot and strong," said Stacie. "And coffee cake. And whatever Eileen has in that bag. I'm afraid we'll have to make a fresh pot. Eileen, would you mind locking the door. Today I'm opening late."

"Good," said Eileen. "I want to hear about this."

"I just want to eat," said Colin. "Has no one noticed I'm fainting here?"

EIGHT

"Pray to the merciful God! You have been defiled by a witch." One of the picketers stepped in front of Cruz as she and Ben left The Bell, Book and Crystal.

Witch, thought Ben. *Honestly.*

Cruz stopped. "Sir, clear the walkway," she said.

"I have a right to be here!"

"You have a right to be *there*," said Cruz, pointing at the sidewalk in front of the picket fence. "You have no right to block this walkway."

"I know my rights..."

Cruz pulled her badge out.

"No, you don't. You have the right to *peaceful* assembly and the right to picket as long as you stay on the public sidewalk. But the moment you threaten, intimidate, or harass anyone, *anyone*," she repeated, "going into or out of this business, the moment you come onto this property or block the entrance to this store, you break the law, and the store owner will be within *her* rights to make a complaint and press charges. Do I make myself clear?"

The crowd was silent.

Ben was awed when Cruz went full-on cop. She was like a puffed up bantam rooster, all beak and claws. People rarely argued with her when she was like this. If they did, they almost always regretted it.

Yet no matter how tough *he* talked, people always gave him lip. He didn't know how she did it.

"You might be able to picket out here," Cruz was saying now, "but this is a very narrow sidewalk. If we get complaints from pedestrians that you're blocking their passage, or if you block traffic by standing in the street, you'll be removed. That is my right as a police officer."

She glared at the sullen group for a few more moments. No one protested, and the three people blocking their path shuffled back to the sidewalk. Cruz pocketed her badge, and she and Ben walked through the crowd, which parted like the Red Sea.

When they were about fifty feet down the street, and the crowd remained silent behind them, Cruz's face split into a grin. "There are times I love my job," she said.

Ben grinned back.

"But you," she said and guffawed. "Today, you are the icing on the cake."

Ben stopped grinning. "What?"

She turned around and walked backward in front of him, making a face and waving her hands. "Nothing," she smirked. "Not a thing. But I noticed the witchy woman didn't give *me* a rock."

"Cruz..." he said in a long-suffering tone. He knew better than to say anything else, but tried anyway. "Just leave it will you?"

"Hey, okay," she said, pivoting to walk next to him again. "But you never know. It might clear up your dandruff."

He knew what she wanted him to say. "I don't have dandruff."

"See?" she said, pointing at him, her eyes wide in amazement. "It's already working." She stepped into the street around the back of their car toward the driver's side.

Ben sighed. "Just unlock the door, would you?"

His partner grinned at him over the roof of the car.

"So. What do you think?" she asked, as she got in and rolled down her window to let air into the sun-heated car. She put the key in the ignition but didn't turn the engine over.

"About what?" He rolled his own window down and let the sun beat onto his face. Sweet ocean air rolled through the car. He could faintly hear the waves crashing a couple blocks away. He tried to get a grip on his feelings. Confusion, irritation, disappointment, all twisted inside him.

With more than a dollop of desire. He'd forgotten just how beautiful Stacie was. How whole he'd felt talking to her.

Only to find out she's a fruitcake.

Cruz looked at him incredulously. "Have you entirely spaced the last hour?" She grinned devilishly. "Or did our 'crystal healer' have you bewitched?"

Ben glared at her.

"Are you asking me about the vandalism, your crazy aunt…"

"Husband's aunt…"

"…or the stalking?" he finished.

"Or about why the witchy woman gave you a rock?"

Ben waved a hand as if he'd forgotten the crystal, which he had not. Mesmerizingly beautiful, it was almost burning a hole in his pocket. He was itching to hold it again.

He was not going to reach for it in front of Cruz.

"First, your crazy aunt is crazy." Ben held up one finger. "It sounds like Ms Cappella's friend hit that nail squarely."

He saw Cruz's eyebrow lift.

"Ms Cappella? I noticed it was 'Stacie' when we were in the store."

Ben stopped. He hadn't realized he'd used Stacie's given name.

Crap, he thought. There would be no living with Cruz.

"Your *aunt*," he went on, emphasizing Cruz's connection in a small act of revenge, "is a troublemaker, looking for attention. And no, I'm not going with you to tell her that."

"We're partners…"

Ben shook his head. "Nope. Not on that. That's your baby."

She didn't argue. "I really have to talk to Paul about his relatives," she said. "I should have checked them out before I married him."

Ben held up a second finger and went on. "The vandalism. You said Meissner mentioned it?"

Cruz nodded.

"So she's probably not doing it herself for publicity or anything."

"Publicity?"

"It happens," he says. "A psychic foretells the end of the world, the newspapers make a big thing of it, and her business increases. Making yourself the target of persecution can do the same thing."

"You have a dark mind, Robard," said Cruz, looking at him strangely.

He shrugged. Like he wasn't desperately trying to drown the hope he'd had of seeing Stacie again in the reality that she was an Eden Beach weirdo.

"Just trying to stay objective," he said, and didn't like the look his partner gave him.

He hurried on. "It's pretty obvious that the picketers are

from that group in the computer store. You think the vandalism is being done by them, too?"

Cruz nodded once. "Probably. It makes sense with the group of businesses being targeted. It may only be one or two of them, though. The gang with the signs might not even know about it." She lifted a shoulder. "We've seen it before. Remember the guy shouting hellfire and damnation in front of the bathing suit shop two summers ago?"

Did he ever. Their community officer had had his work cut out for him soothing the merchants who'd wanted the guy arrested. If not shot.

At least Eden Beach's legendary self-appointed "Welcome Man" had only waved and smiled at people. Shaggy and shabby, his only insanity had been his desire to make everyone smile. Postcards with his picture on them still sold by the thousands every summer. There was a statue on his favorite corner.

Ben had to admit, there was some good weird in Eden Beach, in addition to the crazies.

He wasn't sure, right now, which camp Stacie fell into.

"Still," he said, "maybe someone should talk to the folks up in El Toro."

"No proof they're behind it," said Cruz. "Without proof…" She spread her hands. "Not only that, if we went up there, they'd no doubt claim we were trying to restrict their freedom of religion, freedom of speech, yadda yadda… Just like those folks in front of the store back there." She jerked her thumb over her shoulder. "They'll stand on their rights. You know the story, Robard."

He grimaced. He did know it. It was times like this he hated police work. It should be straightforward.

"Not to mention," she added, "it's not our beat."

She was right there, too. Meissner wouldn't be happy if he tried to tell her how to do her job.

He sighed. He couldn't tackle every wrong and make it right. His father reminded him of that constantly.

Probably because his dad, a talented surgeon, had the same problem.

"You know as well as I do, we have to catch them in the act," said Cruz.

"That's going to be tough," he said. "With the way our population's exploding, we barely have enough cops to cover the big stuff."

Cruz nodded. "I agree. Especially since they're hitting a number of places. It'll be a matter of having a patrol in the right place at the right time."

Ben grinned. "Maybe you should talk to your council-man-maybe-soon-to-be-mayor uncle. Get him to raise our budget so we can hire more officers."

Cruz gave him the finger, and he laughed.

His smile soon faded. Their small force meant that the stalker, too, wouldn't get the attention he should. And *that* wasn't funny. Ben barely heard the small voice in his head suggesting he cruise by the shop himself whenever he could.

"You're thinking, Robard. I hate it when you think."

He took a breath, brought himself back to the present and held up a third finger to Cruz. "Frankly, I'm more concerned about this stalking thing, especially in light of the body they just found, and the possibility of a serial killer."

Cruz, who'd been half turned toward him, leaned back against the car door.

"Isn't that a stretch?" She frowned slightly. "Yeah, there's a body that might be connected to some others, but still…"

"She was killed only a month or so ago."

"Yeah, but there's no reason to think the guy's still in the area. Or, even if he is, that he's here in Eden Beach. And that we would just stumble over him."

Rationally, Ben knew she was right, but he wasn't convinced. He didn't like the idea of Stacie being stalked by an unseen nut case when there was—or had been—a killer in, around, or near Eden Beach.

He made some kind of non-committal noise.

"Ben," said Cruz, "the Swallowtail Canyon killing was years ago. The other two Eden Beach victims might not even be connected to that one. The other three deaths are scattered throughout the county. San Diego is a couple hours south. This new one's in Mission Viejo."

"That's only fifteen miles from here."

Cruz frowned. "So okay. Maybe that's not far enough. But still."

Ben lifted a shoulder and made a face that was meant to say, *Okay, you have a point.*

It didn't work.

Cruz grinned.

"You're not buying it," she said. "Is that why you told her to talk to Breckenridge or Danner? Like they don't have their hands full enough?"

Ben raised his hands helplessly. "They're Crimes Against Persons..."

"And they're handling the killings."

"I just thought they should know." *Just in case.*

"Don't tell me you're getting hunches, Robard. You're my 'just the facts, ma'am' partner. Don't turn Hollywood on me here."

"Then you don't think the stalker is a problem."

Cruz stopped smiling. "No," she said. "The stalker is a problem. Stalkers are always a problem. Bad enough when the victim knows who's doing the stalking. Worse when it's a stranger. I didn't like the threatening tone of those notes, either. He's trying to scare her. Or worse."

"I agree."

Cruz went on. "I'll send the notes to Breckenridge's office. When he gets back, I'll have a talk with him. Make sure she files that report."

Ben smiled to himself as she reached for the ignition. Apparently his partner was also having a hunch.

"I'll ask him about having the patrols go by morning and evening, too, when they can," Cruz was saying. "See if we can spot anyone hanging around."

"Probably wise." Ben paused. "You might want to come back and talk to Ms Cappella about her safety. Locking doors. Keeping an eye on her surroundings. Getting a friend to check on her, walk her to her car."

"Oh?" said Cruz, arching an eyebrow. "I think that should be your job."

"Me?" said Ben, surprised. "Why me? It would be less threatening and more convincing coming from another woman."

Cruz turned the keys and the engine came to life. She glanced in the side mirror as she pulled the car out into traffic.

"Oh, I don't know," she said, a smile dancing around her mouth. "I'm not the one she gave the rock to."

Ben huffed. "Lauren…"

"No, really, Ben." She grinned openly now. "From the moment we walked in, she had eyes only for you."

"She probably recognized me. From the other morning."

"Oh, now this sounds promising. Go on."

Ben regretted saying anything.

"I was up in the Heritage Park. Hiking. Taking pictures." Cruz was one of the few people who knew about his photography. "I ran into her there. We talked a few minutes about the trails."

Cruz frowned a bit. "She was alone?"

"She said she often hiked there alone."

"Well, then," Cruz grinned again. "You definitely should go back and talk to her. Maybe you should offer to be her bodyguard." She flashed him a look. "Who knows what parts of her body she'd ask you to guard?"

"Paul ever tell you you're a pain?"

She laughed, a deep throaty sound that made Ben smile.

"I don't know, Robard. This could be just what your love life has needed. Assuming you have any love life at all."

"Do I look like the kind of guy who'd fall for a woman who believes rocks 'belong' to people?"

She sighed. "I don't know who you'd fall for, Ben. You worry me."

But she grinned again.

"Here's the deal, Robard," she said. "I'll take on Celia. You get the witch."

"She's not a witch," he said, sighing. "She's a book-keeper-slash-tax preparer."

"Whatever," said Cruz, flicking a hand off the wheel. She paused. "Though I do wonder...

"What?"

Cruz gave a quick shake of her head. "Nothing. Now, we'd better do what we get paid for. Let's see if we can find that bottom feeder, Todd Huff."

NINE

BEN LOCKED HIS BIKE IN THE SMALL SHED HIS LANDLADY supplied, pulled his pack from the saddle bags and climbed the stairs to the tiny apartment over the equally tiny single-car garage. It was a dream location for Ben. The neighborhood was quiet. He could see a sliver of ocean from the postage stamp-sized deck that overhung the landlady's backyard. Though his old Toyota Camry was parked at the curb a few doors away, he could easily walk or bike to work and usually preferred to.

Ben had changed at the department into jeans, T-shirt and sweatshirt. He went through to the bedroom, pulled his sport jacket and slacks out of the day pack, shook them out and hung them up. He dropped his dress shoes on the closet floor and locked up his gun. In the bathroom, he dropped his shirt into the clothes basket and checked his wetsuit, dry now on the inside. He turned it right side out and rehung it.

Twenty minutes later, he was sitting in one of his two chairs, stockinged feet up on the old footlocker that served as a coffee table, deep into a Robert Crais novel, when Tucker knocked, then let himself in.

He held the pizza box aloft. "Dinner is served!"

"About time. My stomach was beginning to think my throat had been cut."

"You could have bought."

"You lost the toss."

Ben saw half a smile hidden in Tucker's beard as the big man turned to put the box on the kitchen counter/bar that served as a dining table. Ben dropped the novel on the foot-locker and got up to retrieve two Heinekens from the fridge.

Tucker opened the box and pulled up a stool, reaching for the beer. "Table linens?"

Ben snorted, yanked some paper towel off the roll, then sat next to Tucker.

They were silent while they polished off a couple pieces of pizza each.

"Another?" asked Ben as Tucker took the last swallow of beer.

"Sure," said Tucker.

Ben finished his, too. As he went to the fridge for a couple more, Tucker asked, "How's the cop business?"

Ben held up a hand. "Not the day to ask. This has been one weird ass day."

"How weird?"

"Serious weird."

Ben gave him a brief rundown of the fraud charges against Stacie, without saying who filed them.

"Okay, that is weird," said Tucker.

"On top of that, we get there, and there are picketers out front. Yelling about God. All worked up because the woman's a witch."

"They from that nut group up near the freeway? The ones who hate everyone and everything?"

"Quite probably."

"Doesn't it warm your heart," said Tucker, his voice thick with irony, "to know we both risked our necks so they can spew all that crap?"

Ben snorted. "Yeah. I know. But would it have changed your mind about serving?"

"I was drafted, remember. I didn't have a choice. I wasn't too pleased to get back from 'Nam and hear all the shit the hippies were saying about us, either, after all we'd seen and done. Made me wonder why we'd been put through that meat grinder." Tucker shook his head, then grinned. "Pretty ironic. Now I'm a long-haired hippie throwing pots. And not much in favor of sending other men and women overseas to get shot at."

"You mean my perspective will change when I get to be an old guy?"

Tucker punched Ben in the arm. "Respect, bro."

Ben laughed.

"You're right. That sounds like a weird day."

Oh, that's not half of it. We get inside, and I know the woman."

"Really?"

Ben nodded. "Met her up in the Heritage Park. Beautiful woman. Red hair, nice figure." An image of Stacie, her hair on fire in the sunlight, her green eyes dancing, flashed into Ben's mind.

"Oh?" Tucker rotated his hand in a 'give me more' gesture.

Ben gave him a look. "Don't start. I had to hear about it all day from Cruz."

"We love ya, man," grinned Tucker. "Just want to see you settled."

"Heaven protect me from happily married people."

"Hey, beautiful is a good start."

"Weird is a good finish," said Ben.

"I thought just the day was weird. She's weird, too?"

"Shirley MacLaine weird. She believes rocks 'belong' to people."

"What do you mean?"

Ben sighed, remembering. "Cruz is talking to her about the complaint, right? And out of the blue Stacie goes over to a case, gets this rock," Ben reached into his pocket, pulled out the crystal and placed it in Tucker's big paw, "and hands it to me, just like this. When I try to give it back to her later, she says it's mine. That certain rocks belong to certain people, and this one's mine." He gestured to the smoky quartz.

"First of all, my man, this is not a rock," said Tucker, holding it to the light. "It's a crystal. A pure mineral. Rocks are a mishmash of different minerals."

"Oh, no. Not you, too."

"This is a beauty," said Tucker, rolling the stone in his big hand. "She just handed it to you?"

"Yes."

"Did she tell you smoky quartz is good for grounding?" Tucker handed the stone back to Ben.

"Grounding?"

"Yeah, like to center you. Help keep you balanced." Tucker wasn't smiling.

"You believe all this?"

Tucker shrugged. "I don't disbelieve it."

Ben fell forward and dropped his head on the counter. "You sound like my mom."

"Your mom's into all of that?"

Ben sighed and sat up. "Yeah. She really believes all that woo-woo stuff. Her grandma was a *traiteuse*."

"Come again?"

Ben grinned. "Cajun faith healer."

97

"Really?" Tucker's eye brows went up. "Your mom do that, too?"

Ben took another pull on the beer and thought. When he'd been sick as a kid, his mom's touch had always made him feel better.

"You know," he finally said. "I've never been sure. I've always wondered if she did. If she used it in her practice."

"The massage?"

"Umm."

"You never got into it?

Ben shrugged. "She had me doing a bunch of stuff when I was a kid."

"Like what?"

"Like tai chi." Ben moved his hands in half-remembered configurations. Tucker guffawed. Ben dropped his hands and grinned. "Jackie Chan in slow motion."

Ben rolled the crystal in his hand.

"None of that stuff took for you?"

"Nah," said Ben. "It was kind of cool when I was a kid, but..." He lifted a shoulder. He stroked the crystal with his thumb, lost in its depths.

Tucker waited. "But, what?" he finally asked.

Ben looked up, surprised. He'd almost forgotten Tucker was there. He took a deep breath.

"Mom used to say that, if you listen with your heart, you'll find magic all around you," he said matter-of-factly. Then his voice tightened. "All it took was a single tour in Iraq to teach me there's no magic in the world. It's a hard, incomprehensible, unforgiving place."

"Hard and incomprehensible, maybe," said Tucker quietly. "But not unforgiving."

"Yeah, well. Maybe not." Ben stuck the crystal in his pocket and reached for his beer.

"Ben. You aren't responsible for what happened in Iraq."

"Sure feels like it," said Ben. "Have you forgiven yourself for things you did—or didn't do—in 'Nam?"

Tucker lifted his shoulders and bobbed his head equivocally. "Most days. More or less. Throwing pots helps. Maureen helps." He looked at Ben. "I've had longer to come to terms, too."

"Forty years." Ben shook his head. "I don't know if I can manage that."

"We don't have much choice," said Tucker, lifting his bottle and rolling the beer in it, "if you take the nuclear option out of the mix." They'd spent long evenings talking about buddies who had committed suicide. Or had drunk or drugged themselves to death. *Which amounts to much the same thing*, thought Ben.

"I guess not."

"Your job can't help. Dealing every day with the darkness in people."

"No, it doesn't. Especially when it all just keeps recycling. More fraud, more robbery." *More death.* Ben didn't mention the possible serial killer. "Like Todd Huff."

"Huff? Like Ken Huff, the big contractor up in Corona del Mar?"

"Yeah. His son."

"He a contractor, too?"

Ben shook his head. "He's a lowlife, fly-by-night con man. Clean cut, sympathetic. Goes door to door claiming to do contracting. Gives people an ingratiating smile," Ben flashed Tucker a fake smile, "and a hard-luck story. Uses his dad's contracting license for those who ask. He usually brings the materials to the victim's house late in the afternoon, covers it neatly in the drive, asks for reimbursement, promises to start the next morning and never returns. Phone numbers are no good. When people finally check the materials, they're worthless. Roofing shingles melted together with heat. Paint and caulking dried up in the cans and tubes. Scavenged lumber twisted or rotten."

"Can't believe he'd get away with it for long."

Ben shook his head. "Most people are slow to report being conned. They're embarrassed by their gullibility. But Huff's worked Eden Beach too long. This time, he cheated the mother of a hotshot attorney here in town." Ben grinned. "He'll be out on bail in no time, but it was sweet to take him down."

"What happened?"

Ben grinned wider. "He was so sure no one could touch him, he was easy to find. But man, when Cruz cuffed him, he went nuts. Threatened lawsuits, how he'd get even."

"That doesn't worry you?"

Ben made a face, shook his head. "Nah. A lot of people we bust get hot about it. They cool off. Huff'll spend the night in jail, his old man'll bail him out in the morning, and he'll move on."

"Won't his dad lose his bail money?"

"No doubt," said Ben. "He may lose his license, too, if the victim makes enough trouble, but that's his problem. Sooner or later, maybe, he'll stop bailing his son out."

"And junior just moves on to work his con someplace else."

"Yep." Ben shook his head. "That's what frustrates me. We can't stop these guys. We just go round and round with the same cast of characters."

He finished the piece of pizza in his hand and wiped his mouth.

"You thought any more about leaving the police department?" Tucker asked him.

"Sure. Almost every day. But what would I do? And don't say photography."

Tucker grinned and reached for another slice of pizza, now growing cold.

"How about photography?" he said.

"We've talked about this before. It's a hobby, not a living. You want me to zap that?"

Tucker answered by biting into the pizza and shaking his head at the same time. "You don't know it's not a living," he said around the pepperoni. "I never thought I could make a living throwing pots."

"To make a living as a photographer, you have to photograph people," Ben told him. "Weddings. Babies. Bar mitzvahs. Graduations. Blech." Ben shook his head. "I don't do people."

"I didn't make ceramic dragons, either, until Maureen asked me."

Ben grinned. "She really had your number."

"Still does," said Tucker, finishing the pizza. "Maybe you could teach photography. Isn't that what those workshop guys do? They make money."

"True," Ben agreed. He had taken a lot of workshops from an endless number of photographers—learning techniques in framing, developing, printing and manipulating his images. "But that's not for me."

"Why?"

Ben tossed the paper towel into the empty box, flattened it, folded it up, and stuck it into the trash under the sink.

"Coffee?" he pointed at the maker. Tucker nodded, waiting.

Ben sighed to himself as he put water in the machine. Tucker could out wait a stone when he was in this mode.

Measuring coffee, Ben said, "The camera's mine. It keeps

me sane." He flipped the maker on and turned to Tucker. "When I look through the lens, the world gets quiet. It makes sense. It's not something I want to share."

He'd been willing to share it with Stacie that day. He'd still be willing to share it with her. The thought surprised him.

He grabbed the beer bottles, rinsed them and set them to drain. He hated the smell of day-old beer in the apartment.

"That's what I said when I first started throwing pots. Seemed like something a grown man shouldn't be doing."

"Who said you were a grown up?"

Tucker blew him a raspberry.

"Tuck, mugs and bowls are useful," said Ben as the coffee bubbled to a finish. "Photos—especially shots like I take— aren't. People aren't about to buy them." *Especially mine*, he thought.

Tucker looked at him in disbelief as Ben poured coffee into mugs and put them on the counter.

"Bro!" he said. "Have you ever been into that gallery downtown—what's the name? Margot Somerset—when they're having a photo show?"

"Have you?"

"Yeah, I have. I'm married to Maureen, if you remember. She lives for gallery shows. Last one they had was all black and white photos of water. High contrast. Grainy. Close-ups of ripples and foam on sand. The walls were covered with little red dots."

"Yeah. Well. Those are art photos. I'm not an artist."

"So, what you're saying is you take these pictures, but you never look at them."

"What does that mean?" Ben sipped the coffee.

"It means, Robard, that you should take an unbiased look at them. Maybe you should take them to that gallery owner."

"Oh, now you *are* out of your mind."

"No. I'm serious."

"Tucker..."

"Have you shown them to anyone? Besides me," Tucker insisted. "Your workshop guys?"

"No, Tuck. Like I said, these are just for me."

Tucker watched him for a minute. Ben became uncomfortable.

"Have to come out of hiding sometime," Tucker finally said.

"No, I don't."

"Think about it."

Ben paused a moment. "Okay. Thought about it. Dumb idea."

Tucker shook his head and lifted his mug.

"Tucker," Ben insisted, "taking pictures is nice, and all those guys who teach workshops, that's nice, too. But I need more. I need a purpose. I need to be useful. That's why I stay a cop. I want to help people."

Tucker shook his head again. "Gotta help yourself first, Ben. Just because it makes you happy, doesn't mean it's without purpose." Tucker held his hands out to his sides. "Maybe your photos could help someone see beauty where they never thought to look. That could change their lives. That photo exhibition you saw when you were a kid changed yours."

"That was different." Ben sipped coffee.

Tucker watched him.

"Leave the darkness behind, Ben. You've paid your dues. You don't owe it to the world to set it all right."

"Hmm."

After a moment, Tucker asked, "What did you say your redhead's name was?"

"Stacie. Stacie Cappella. And she's not my redhead."

"I'm not so sure about that, man. Not with that look on your face." Tucker grinned and gestured to Ben's hand. The crystal was in it again.

Ben stuck it back in his pocket.

Tucker raised an eyebrow.

"Stop," Ben told him.

"Maybe you should ask her out."

Ben pushed imaginary glasses up his nose with his middle finger. Tucker guffawed.

"Why not?" asked Tucker. "You're obviously attracted to her." He grinned wider. "Or maybe she's sending you signals through your crystal. Quartz is used in radios, you know. Or was, once."

"Tuck, the woman is a fruitcake. I can't see myself seriously dating someone who listens to rocks. Minerals."

Tucker gave him a look, the corner of his mouth disappearing into the beard. "I'm not so sure. You know what they say. Men tend to marry their mothers."

Ben snorted. "*Maureen* like your mom?"

Tucker threw back his head and laughed. "Thank God, no!" he finally said. "My folks were so conservative, if I hadn't been drafted, they would have volunteered me for 'Nam."

He stood, drained his coffee and set the mug on the counter. "You should ask her out."

"Unprofessional, man! I was in there with Cruz. We were working."

Tucker shrugged. "You said the charge was bogus. So, you're not working now."

Ben was shaking his head and waving his hand in negation. "No."

"Go buy your mom a rock." Tucker was grinning at Ben.

Ben stood up. "Go home," he said.

"Chicken."

"Go home." Ben pushed on one of Tucker's shoulders. It was like trying to move a tree.

Tucker laughed. "See you next week?"

"Probably."

As Tucker pulled the door closed behind him, he turned and said again, "Ask her out."

"Go!" said Ben to the closed door.

WHEN TUCKER WAS GONE, Ben washed out Tucker's mug, made another cup of coffee for himself and went out onto his small deck.

The chilly night was clear, a few stars barely visible through the haze of lights thrown up by the town. In the distance, the moon shone on the ocean's surface, lighting a pathway directly to him. The feathery fronds of the tall queen palms next door gently hissed and rattled. A car passed on the quiet street.

Thoughts of Stacie stole back into his mind so softly, he didn't realize he was thinking about her until he was. The scent of warm wool from her jacket when she stood by his shoulder. Another, gentler fragrance from her sunlit hair. The way her eyes lit up when she laughed.

So easy to talk to, he thought. *Interested. Interesting.*

She'd understood exactly what he'd been looking for and directed him to the best places to get the kinds of shots he'd wanted.

She's a fruitcake who thinks crystals talk, he reminded himself irritably.

Just like his mom.

Great. I have a thing for a woman like my mom. I need my head examined.

Whoa.

His mind replayed the previous thought.

I have a thing?

He'd talked to her once. Once. The second time was business.

One conversation on a trail does not a "thing" make, he told himself.

Then why couldn't he stop thinking about her? Even Tuck had noticed she had him distracted. God forbid Cruz noticed. Though she probably had, given the merciless ribbing she'd given him all day.

There was no denying Stacie was beautiful, smiling at him in the morning light, completely at ease by herself on the trail. The copper red hair, the brilliant green eyes, the peaches and cream skin. The freckles, rather than taking away from her beauty, had emphasized it.

Dania was beautiful, too. Look where that got me.

But Ben had never felt such a deep sense of contentment, of happiness, with Dania as he'd felt that single morning with Stacie. Horniness, yeah, sure. He'd been nineteen when he'd married. But such a quiet sense of peace? He was pretty sure that had never been part of their chemistry.

Even at her store, when Stacie had been angry, worried, frightened, Ben had sensed a solid core of sureness in her. A wholeness.

Ben had felt whole once. At least he thought he had. A long time ago.

Why did I lie when she asked me if I sold my photos? he wondered. He never had. He'd only shown his prints once during a high school photo contest. Did he think Stacie would be disappointed in him?

Or was he disappointed in himself, in the way his life had turned?

The way he'd turned his life.

He'd decided to marry Dania. *He'd* decided to join the Army. No one had held a shotgun on him. There had been no draft.

Ben hadn't admitted it to Tucker, but thoughts about getting serious about photography *had* been skittering through his mind for a couple weeks.

Ever since he'd met Stacie.

He'd told Tucker he didn't like shooting people, and he didn't. It always made him feel like some creepy peeping Tom. Yet he wouldn't mind photographing Stacie. The quick, generous smile, set off by dimples. The green eyes, ever so delicately lined at the corners, fringed by long, unusually dark lashes, under dark, auburn eyebrows that were ever so slightly peaked in the center.

Photographing Stacie wouldn't feel like an invasion of privacy, it would feel more…more…

When the right word finally came to him, he wasn't sure he wanted to hear it. Photographing Stacie would be intimate. Personal. It would be the kind of communication he hadn't had with a woman in a long time. Maybe never.

He knew exactly how and where he would photograph her, though. In the Heritage Park, the swelling shapes of the hillsides echoing the shapes of her body. The sunlight flashing in her hair. Her head tipped in that listening posture she had.

Ben shook himself. This was not a good path to follow.

He finished his coffee and went back inside to his novel. He needed to get his mind off her.

A little while later, though, Ben found himself staring at the darkness beyond the windows, novel forgotten in his lap.

The crystal was back in his hand. He looked at how it caught the light. The way the cloudiness in it gave way to transparency. Sometimes he felt like he was falling into the soft gray, so much like the ocean in the early morning when he swam, shading into ever-darker depths.

Maybe it was the resemblance to the morning sea that quieted his mind when he looked at it.

Or maybe it reminded him of Stacie. Her inner stillness.

He sighed. She'd seemed so normal. Until she'd handed him the crystal saying it belonged to him. Like it was imprinted with his DNA.

The weirdest thing, though, it felt like it was. He kept finding it in his hand, but could never remember how it got there.

Like now.

Ben looked back at the darkness and his mind drifted to the stalker following her.

Stalkers bothered most cops. There were far too many of them—former co-workers, former spouses, boyfriends. Strangers. They usually didn't quit. They were into power and control. As long as they had that, they kept coming back.

He rolled the crystal in his hand.

He would ask Meissner to talk to Stacie about the precautions she could take. Regardless of what Cruz said, Ben thought the advice would be accepted more readily if it came from another woman.

But Lauren's right. It's a crazy leap to think this guy might be our possible serial killer.

Breckenridge had been worried, though, when he'd come back from the meeting with the other cops in the county. He'd fended off Cruz's questions, but they'd both seen their colleague's drawn face.

Cruz had said, "You're not getting hunches on me, are you?" But Ben *did* get hunches. Or he had, once.

Like Phillips, there in Iraq. He was a little crazy, but

always played his hunches. He'd told Ben, "You gotta listen to the little voice in your head, man, no matter what the LT says. If he tells you to check something out, and the little voice says 'Watch it!', then you give the LT whatever will get you out of there. Doesn't matter. Your job is to get home."

Ben's little voice right now was telling him that Stacie looked terrific in pink. He could almost feel his hands on her waist, the curve of her hip…

He sighed and shook his head regretfully. Thank goodness Cruz couldn't read his mind. There'd be no working with her.

Too bad Stacie was a kook.

Mom would probably like her though, he thought.

Great. *There* was a recommendation.

Ben got up, tucked the smoky quartz into a pocket, washed his mug out, and set it in the drainer. He'd planned to read a while longer, but instead he went to the file cabinet that held his photos. He pulled open a drawer and took out the shots he'd taken the day he'd met Stacie.

It was almost midnight when he finally left his darkroom —the bathroom—and shut off the lights, leaving the new prints to dry.

The moon had shifted. Moonlight was streaming into his bedroom window. Ben emptied his pockets, setting the crystal along with his keys, coins, and phone on the bureau under the window. He got undressed and climbed into bed.

He glanced toward the window as he settled down. The crystal glowed in the moonlight.

Weird day, he thought.

He was asleep almost immediately. For once his sleep was untroubled by dreams.

TEN

THE BELL, BOOK AND CRYSTAL WAS SO BUSY SATURDAY IT was like mid-summer rather than the first week in March. Stacie had been running since she'd unlocked the door. She blamed it on the warm, sunny weather without a trace of fog. Mir was due in shortly, but if it stayed like this, it would take both of them to manage. Stacie was afraid she wasn't going to get to the work she'd planned to do upstairs.

Fortunately, sales had been very brisk, too. It hadn't been all browsers.

And the damned picketers hadn't shown up. They'd been missing since Thursday afternoon, thank heavens.

Too bad it can't always be like this, thought Stacie.

Stacie's shop wasn't right downtown, but Eden Beach was small enough that she was not out of reach to walkers, especially on a glorious day like this. The sky was crystal clear, the deep blue reflected in the ocean that glittered where the sun struck it. As Stacie had driven down toward the beach from her home in the hills, she had glimpsed the dark purple hump of Catalina Island sitting on the horizon, like Avalon risen from the sea. The view was somewhat spoiled by the brown haze sitting farther out—all the pollution from the inland valleys that had been pushed seaward by the offshore breeze.

Well, she thought, smiling to herself, *even Shangri-La wasn't perfect.*

"Oh, my daughter would *love* those!" gushed the customer at the counter, pointing toward a pair of sterling earrings of dolphins topped by a Celtic knot.

"Would you like to see them?" Stacie was already opening the case and reaching in, smiling. She didn't know if the Celts had known anything about dolphins, but the earrings were one of her best sellers.

While the woman chattered on to her friend, Stacie pulled out a matching necklace, all the while keeping an eye on the rest of the store. There were another two women in the garden, where Bananas lay in the sunshine, trying out the sounds of various wind chimes. A young couple, who appeared to have already selected a book on the Tarot, were consulting a book on Wicca. A mother by the front window was trying to get her young son to reduce the pile of touch-stones he had cupped in two hands.

Stacie understood the boy's dilemma. The natural, undyed stones were hand-polished by a cutter in Costa Mesa. Their silky feel made them irresistible.

Stacie's amused gaze was on the mother and son when a very young girl slipped hesitantly into the shop. Her straw-berry blond hair was pulled back into a tight ponytail, and she wore a cotton cardigan over a sundress that hung loosely on her thin body. She clutched the sweater around her protec-tively as she hovered nervously in the entry, ready to bolt at the slightest provocation.

She'd been in yesterday, too, darting out before Stacie could even say hello.

Frightened, Stacie thought, but of what, she had no idea.

The women with the earrings finished their purchases and headed toward the door, considering lunch. The young girl had to move farther into the shop to let them pass. Just those two steps tipped the balance. Stacie recognized the body language. The girl had come too far into the store to leave without feeling foolish—after all, she was in this far, she couldn't leave without at least looking around—but she was by no means comfortable. Stacie expected she'd make the quickest possible circuit and then leave. She turned her attention to the young couple with the books who were approaching the counter with questions in their eyes.

More customers came in laughing. The sound volume in the store went up even higher when the women from the garden came in carrying chiming and clanging wind ornaments, commenting on how well-mannered Bananas was.

"I'm not sure if he's well-mannered or just lazy," Stacie told them, laughing.

She found boxed versions of the chimes, sold them, then carried the chiming, clanging samples back to the patio and rehung them. She was followed by some of the new customers who proceeded to ring the sample chimes. Stacie caught the flash of a hummingbird investigating the bougainvillea hanging over the fence from the neighbor's yard. *It must be deaf to put up with all the ringing*, she thought.

When she came back in, the mother and son were at the counter. Mom had restricted her son to six touchstones. Stacie could see this had been agonizing for both of them: for him to limit his treasures, for her to lay down twenty-four dollars for rocks.

Stacie sold more wind chimes; the couple took a stack of books; a woman came to pick up a fountain she had on layaway and bought a small ceramic dragon on impulse. Finally, Eileen came in, brown bag in her hand.

Thank you, Stacie mouthed to her friend. Eileen smiled and waved as she passed through to the kitchen. She'd seen the steady stream of customers from her apartment and called Stacie offering to bring lunch.

Bananas, on the patio, heard the rattle of the bag, ambled in and followed Eileen into the kitchen.

As Stacie brought her gaze back to the layaway customer, she was surprised to see the thin blond by the bookshelves going through books on herbs.

Read that one wrong, Stacie thought and frowned. Something still wasn't right. It was then that she noticed the sleeves of the girl's cardigan pushed up to reveal the light bluc-grccn stain on her wrist.

Then, as busy as it had been all morning, the store was suddenly empty except for the thin girl and Eileen out of sight in the kitchen.

Into the silence, a wind chime rang, softly pushed by the sea breeze drifting gently through the store. Stacie could hear the water falling in the fountain for the first time all morning.

"Wow!" Stacie said, smiling at the girl. "That was some rush."

Startled, the girl looked at Stacie guiltily.

Guilty? Stacie wondered. She knew the girl wasn't a shoplifter. She wouldn't have stayed this long.

"I'm sorry I haven't been able to ask you before this, but do you have any questions? Or are you looking for something in particular?"

The girl swallowed. Her eyes were enormous.

Not guilt. Terror.

Stacie kept her face non-committal and open.

The girl took a deep breath and stepped timidly toward

Stacie. She was holding a book on herbs against her chest like a shield. Just above the edge of the book, Stacie saw the glint of a small cross.

"Are you..." she started to say softly. Her voice caught. She cleared her throat and started again. "Are you the witch?"

Stacie's heart sank. *Not this again*, she thought. From the corner of her eye, she saw Eileen framed in the kitchen doorway, frowning. Bananas joined her, intent on investigating the newcomer. Eileen snagged his collar and held him in place.

"I am not a witch," said Stacie gently. She smiled and moved casually from behind the counter. She did not try to get close to the girl. "In fact, I'm pretty sure there's no such thing as witches. I'm Stacie. What's your name?"

"Ginny," the girl replied, almost inaudibly.

"You seem uncomfortable here, Ginny," said Stacie quietly. "Do you have any questions I could answer that might make you less...nervous?"

Ginny looked around wildly.

"All these stones," she said finally. "Are they really magic? Can they... Can they *do* things to you?"

Stacie slowly lifted a hand and laid it against the large smoky quartz crystal on the end of the counter. Her sense of Ginny's fear and guilt sharpened. Stacie wondered for a moment if someone had sent this poor frightened child to try to get "the witch" to say something incriminating.

But just as Stacie knew Ginny was unhappy, confused, and scared, she also knew the girl wasn't deceitful.

"Ginny, they're stones. They can't do anything to anyone. Unless, like any rock, you pick one up and throw it." Stacie smiled and tipped her head to the side. Eileen was motionless in the doorway, her hand on Bananas' collar, listening. If this girl *was* from the computer store church group, Stacie would want a witness to this conversation. "What did you think they could do?"

Ginny looked down, shrugged her narrow shoulders. "Some people just said... They said you could cast spells with them. Or see the future."

That would have been my aunt, Stacie thought, but did not say.

"Was there a reason you wanted to see the future?" Stacie asked gently, ignoring the comment about spell casting.

Surprisingly, tears welled in Ginny's eyes. "No," she said. "I know the future." She choked. "I'm going to burn in hell."

Oh, no, thought Stacie.

Eileen was shaking her head, making small waving motions. *Send her on her way*, she was signaling Stacie.

"I'm sure no one as nice as you could burn in hell," said Stacie kindly. She saw Eileen close her eyes and shake her head.

"But I am," said Ginny wretchedly. "Jer says I am. And he knows." Her throat worked as she tried not to cry.

"Who's Jer?"

"He's my boyfriend."

"Ginny," said Stacie softly, thinking *This really isn't my business*, "How long have you been pregnant?"

Eileen's eyes widened.

The tears came in a rush.

"I told him, maybe we shouldn't, but he said it would be okay. It was God's will for us to be together. But when I got pregnant, he said it was my fault. I did something wrong. That the devil got into me and made this child. If I'd been pure, God wouldn't have let me get pregnant."

Stacie thought that if *she* had a pipeline to God, she'd order a lightning bolt to fry this guy.

"Why would Jer say that?" Stacie asked.

"He *knows*," Ginny insisted again. "God tells him things. And now, I'm going to burn in hell. Jer said so. Unless I get rid of the baby, which is evil."

Stacie didn't know if Ginny meant the baby was evil or that getting rid of it was evil, but Stacie knew what *she* thought.

Before she could say anything, Ginny went on.

"He said you were a witch," she said. "That you had herbs and things that could get rid of the baby. That's what witches do, he said."

For a moment, Stacie was so stunned, she couldn't say anything. Then anger spiked through her in all directions.

Someone had hurt and lied to this girl and was now trying to use Stacie to achieve his own ends: Get rid of the evidence of his crime.

Because crime this was. This girl was not anywhere near old enough to consent.

Stacie's ears rang with the fury raging through her.

"Ginny, how old are you?" Stacie managed to keep her voice calm, the question non-threatening.

"I'm sixteen," the girl replied, a bit defensively, wiping her nose on her sleeve. Stacie reached behind the counter reflexively and offered the girl a box of Kleenex. Ginny pulled out two.

"When will you be sixteen?"

Ginny dropped her head. "Two months."

"How far along are you?"

The head fell lower. "Four months. I think."

Stacie's heart fell to her feet. The girl was so thin, that with the loose dress, nothing showed.

"Have you told your parents?" Stacie doubted it, but she had to ask.

Ginny's head snapped up, mortal terror in her eyes.

"*No!* Oh, please, help me, Jesus, *no!*" Ginny's voice rose with every word. "Don't tell them. Please don't tell them!"

Stacie put her hand out toward Ginny placatingly. "Ginny, I'm not going to do anything. I just want you to have someone to talk to."

"I'm talking to *you!*" said Ginny. "Jer said you could help me get rid of it." Her words hung in the air for a minute, then she started to cry again. "My baby. I don't want to get rid of my baby."

What do I say? thought Stacie. *I'm not equipped for this.*

She glanced at Eileen. Her friend was standing stock still in the door way, her face angry, her eyes brimming with tears.

"Ginny," said Stacie, taking a cautious step forward, touching the girl's arm gently. "I can't help you. Whatever Jer told you is wrong. I don't do that kind of thing. I don't have that knowledge. You need to talk to someone—not your parents," she added as the panicked look returned to Ginny's face, "who can help you."

Ginny dabbed at her nose, swallowed. "Who?" she asked.

"There's a Women's Crisis Center down on Coast Highway," said Stacie. "I can call them. I can take you down there. They can help you. You'll be safe." She wondered fleetingly who had dropped the girl off here. If she was only fifteen, she couldn't drive on her own.

If I ever see that bastard, she thought, *I'll spike him to the ground.*

Ginny was pulling away from her. "No," she said, backing toward the door. "They'll send me to a home. They'll make me have the baby and...and," she sobbed, "give it away. They'll give it to non-believers." Ginny's voice got higher and louder, hysteria taking over. "My baby will go to *hell!* I'll never see Jer again!"

"Ginny..."

The girl spun and ran out the front door, clattering down the front steps. Stacie saw her run down the sidewalk, then across the street in front of a car. The brakes squealed as the driver made a panicked stop. Ginny kept running down the opposite sidewalk.

Stacie quickly went to the window. Ginny turned the corner toward the ocean and was gone.

Stacie lifted both hands to her face as she heard Eileen come up behind her.

Ginny had taken the book with her, but Stacie wasn't concerned about that.

"*Madre santa e tutti gli angeli*," she said, and dropped her hands.

"Sounds Latin," said Eileen, slipping her arm through Stacie's.

Stacie turned toward her. "Close enough," she said. "Italian. Something my father used to say when everything hit the fan."

She turned back to the window, half hoping to see Ginny coming back.

"Eileen, I handled that so badly."

"Actually, I thought you handled it as well as anyone could."

Stacie shook her head. "She needs to be somewhere safe. She's not safe."

Eileen gently pulled her toward the kitchen where Bananas was still standing. The lunch bag had not been opened yet, and he was hopeful.

"There was never going to be anything you could say that would get through to her," said Eileen. "She was too frightened." She sighed. "Too young."

"Do you think she'll come back, maybe?" asked Stacie.

Eileen shook her head. "No. That boyfriend will most

likely take her to some back alley," she said bitterly. "I doubt any legitimate clinic could help her without her parents' consent, she's so young."

Stacie's anger rose again. "He raped her, Eileen. She can't consent at that age. And the lies he told her!" Stacie stopped. "She's so alone."

Stacie had been lucky. She hadn't been alone.

Into the silent communion between them, Mir burst in the front door, resplendent in purple jeans rolled half way up her calves, purple sandals and a yellow oversized shirt under a gray, man's suit jacket. On her shoulder was a palm-sized brooch of her own creation filled with purple and yellow imitation stones and beads. Her dark blond cloud of corkscrews was pulled back and streaked with neon purple that matched the jeans. A broad yellow and purple scarf was tied around her head and knotted over her right shoulder.

"Hi!" she called brightly. "What great weather! It's packed downtown. Lines outside all the restaurants. I bet we'll be really busy this afternoon."

Bananas trotted out of the kitchen, wagging his tail and grinning. Mir bent and hugged him. "Hello, you big old goof."

Mir bounced over to them smiling, her gray eyes ethereal in her medium brown face. "Look what I bought! They were having a sale at that cute little dress shop on Hillside, Forever Young." Out of a white shopping bag covered with neon-orange and turquoise swirls, Mir pulled a bright emerald green sundress and held it up in front of her. The dress was lovely with Mir's coloring, the result of her complicated Vietnamese, Swedish and African heritage.

"And," she went on, bending over her bag like a magician, "I got a bag and shoes to go with it!" The shoes and bag were shocking pink.

Stacie's energy rose and her mood lightened.

"What's the occasion?" she asked, smiling.

"Ace is taking me out to dinner at the Hungry Pelican down in Cabrillo Point. We're celebrating! I cracked $300 bucks this month making jewelry!"

Stacie held out her arms. "Congratulations!" Mir walked unhesitatingly into the embrace. If Stacie held her a bit longer than usual, Mir didn't notice.

"From me, too," said Eileen, hugging Mir in her turn.

Mir poked everything back into her bag. "Has it been this quiet all morning?" She went around the counter to tuck her package and her purse into the cupboard under the register. She didn't see the look Stacie and Eileen exchanged.

"No," Stacie managed. "I had a rush this morning."

"Well, I'm here now," said Mir, pulling out the spray bottle of window cleaner and a cloth. "You go enjoy your lunch."

"Good idea," Eileen said quietly to Stacie. "Why don't we eat in the garden?"

Stacie took a deep breath. "Shout if you need me."

Mir gave her a thumbs-up. "I've got it under control." Then she began to spray and clean the counter.

Stacie looked at her fondly for a moment. Tears rising to her eyes, she turned and followed Eileen into the kitchen.

ELEVEN

"You know, if you'd tried, you could have found a harder piece of ground to plant this thing in," said Ben, jamming his foot against the shovel.

His dad grinned. "I did try. The whole yard is harder. I thought you'd appreciate me making it easy on you."

Alain Robard was the image of what Ben would look like in twenty-five years. Dark hair going gray at the temples, brilliant blue eyes surrounded by laugh lines, strong articulate hands, now hidden in leather gloves. He was still fit, providing an example to the patients he urged toward a healthy lifestyle.

He drove a shovel in at the opposite side of the hole from his son.

"You could have picked a tree with a smaller root ball."

Alain shook his head. "Take that up with your mother."

"Take what up with his mother?" As if on cue, Emeline Robard stepped onto the deck, setting a laden tray on the table. Petite, with short, curling hair still dark, Ben's mother had a lithe body with surprisingly muscular forearms and hands.

His dad shot him a warning look and a grin that said, *Ask at your peril.*

"When we're going to eat," said Ben, dropping the shovel and peeling off his gloves. He shoved up the sleeves of his gray sweatshirt, revealing arms lightly covered with soft dark hair.

"Smart man," murmured Alain. "Take after your father." Alain drove his shovel into the pile of dirt they'd accumulated and joined his family on the deck.

"You were probably complaining about the size of the root ball," said Emeline. "You're like your father." She finished transferring plates to the table and went back into the house.

"Just how good *is* her hearing?" asked Ben, as he dropped into a chair. He stretched out his legs in their worn and faded jeans.

Alain held up his hand. "It's my professional opinion that she's telepathic."

"Mom! You need help?" Ben called over his shoulder into the house.

"No," she said, balancing the tray on one hand and sliding the screen door open. "I'm here."

Ben got up and closed the door behind her as she crossed the deck and put glasses and a pitcher on the table.

"Sit. Eat," she said, waving her hand to the sandwiches as she sat down. "Bon appétit."

As Emeline picked up a sandwich, she turned to her husband. "I cannot read minds." Alain raised an eyebrow at his son, and Ben almost choked as he started to laugh. "I've just been married to you for so many years that it seems like it."

"My mother warned me not to marry a woman whose grandmother was a *traiteuse*," said Alain, smiling.

She waved her hand. "Yes, yes. You've said that many times before."

"I should have had you with me this week," said Ben, adding fruit salad to his plate and pouring iced tea for them all. He was regretting his sweatshirt and bent forward to pull it off.

"Why is that?" his mother asked the moment his head was enveloped, and his arms were caught in the heavy cotton. Her timing was impeccable.

"I had a call out at a shop over on Glen Eden," he said, popping his head out, tugging his arms out of the sleeves and pulling down the blue T-shirt he wore underneath. "Some place that sells wind chimes and rocks. Crystals," he corrected himself, dropping the sweatshirt on the extra chair. He snagged his tea and leaned back.

Much better.

"The Bell, Book and Crystal," said his mother promptly. "Used to be the Crystal Tea Room."

Startled, Ben paused mid-swallow, then gulped his tea down. "You know it?" he asked. *Of course, she does*, he thought.

"Yes. Amelia was a great friend of mine."

"Amelia?" Ben asked

"Yes. Amelia Travers." His mother gave the last name a French pronunciation. "Stasha's aunt. Great aunt, really. She ran the tea room. She raised Stasha."

Ben felt a tiny thrill of pleasure at the name. Stasha. It was lovely.

"She used to help wait tables after school." His mother smiled. "She had lovely manners. Took it all very seriously. I've only seen her a couple times since her aunt died." His mother frowned. "Why did she need the police? Is she all right?"

Ben shook his head. "She didn't call us. We had a woman come in who claimed Ms Cappella advertised herself as a healer, but when she asked to be healed, Ms Cappella refused. Woman claimed she was trying to bump the price up."

"That's nonsense," said Emeline firmly. "Stasha doesn't heal and would never say she does. She doesn't even do readings, though Amelia said she had the gift."

"Readings?" asked Ben, but his mom didn't hear him.

"Amelia. Now *she*," Emeline raised her finger to Ben, "she had an incredible gift."

"She was a healer?" Maybe that's where the Byers woman got the idea.

"No," said Emeline. "Amelia was not a healer. And did not claim to be. She was a seer." There was awe in his mother's voice.

"A seer?"

"She could look right into you. Knew you were ill, even before you did. She could even see the future sometimes. In fact, maybe more often than she let on."

"You went to her?"

"Yes," said Emeline.

"About what?" Ben was curious.

"When you went to Iraq," she said matter-of-factly. "I wanted to know if you would be safe."

"What did she say?"

"She said you would come home safe. But not unchanged."

"Oh, for heaven's sake, Mom. *I* told you I'd be okay. You don't call me a seer. She just told you what you wanted to hear." *And got lucky*, he thought.

"No, she didn't," Emeline told him seriously. "I heard other mothers ask the same thing. She told them she could not see the future and sent them away. Later, after you were home, I asked her why she didn't tell me the same. She said she knew she could trust me to understand. She knew about Grandmère."

Ben leaned back and shook his head. "I still say it was a safe guess. No one goes to war and returns unchanged."

"She told me Dania would betray you."

"Hell," said Ben, "I should have been able to see that." He waved a hand at Alain. "Even Dad told me it wasn't a good idea to marry her before I left."

"You're right," said Emeline. "You should have seen. But you were blinded by sex. You let your..." She waved a hand at his groin, "...lead you."

"Not having this conversation," said Ben.

"You never learn, do you?" grinned his father, arching an eyebrow. "You can't win."

His mother lifted her head and gave them both a superior smile. Ben laughed.

As he was biting into his sandwich, Emeline asked, "So how was Stasha?"

Considering his thoughts about Stacie over the last few days, he was glad his mouth was full. He wasn't sure how to answer that question.

"What do you mean?" he equivocated, after taking a long time to chew.

His mother shrugged. "Last time I saw her, I thought she was a strikingly beautiful woman."

Talk about Amelia looking right through a person, he thought. When he'd been a kid, Ben had always been sure his mom knew exactly what was going on in his head. Maybe his father was right. Maybe she *was* telepathic.

He made a noncommittal noise. "We were there on business."

"Of course you were." There was a knowing look in her eyes that made Ben uncomfortable.

Changing the subject, Emeline went on. "Amelia said Stasha had a strong gift, too, but she was afraid of it. Wouldn't use it." Emeline's gray eyes watched him. "At least, not overtly."

Definitely telepathic.

Ben hesitated. Impulsively, he reached into his pocket. "She gave me this."

Emeline took the stone. She looked at it for a while, turning it, looking into it. "Did she say anything when she gave it to you?" she asked him, her eyes pinning him again.

Ben waved his hands, trying to brush the question away.

"What?" Emeline insisted.

Ben gave in.

"She said it was mine. That certain stones belonged to certain people, and this one was mine."

"Ah. I see." Emeline sat back and took a deep breath. "Amelia was right."

The rational part of Ben's mind told him this was all metaphysical crap, and that he should just get back to planting that tree. But another part was deeply curious about this stone.

The rational part of his mind lost the argument.

"What do you mean?" he asked.

Emeline answered with a question. "Did she ask you anything? Did she know anything about your background?"

"She knows I take pictures. I ran into her up in the South Coast Heritage Park a couple weeks ago."

"But not about your time in the Army."

Ben frowned at her. "Of course not. We were there officially."

She nodded. "I ask because smoky quartz is for grounding."

Ben waved a hand irritably. "That's what Tucker said. But what does that *mean*?"

"Just what it sounds like." Emeline smiled at him. "It puts the ground back under your feet. Roots you. Helps you find a path when you feel lost. It clears your mind of darkness and negativity. Calms anxiety and anger so that you can find your way. It can help you realize your dreams. For some people," and she looked deep into his eyes, "it dispels nightmares."

Ben had an uncomfortable twitching between his shoulder blades. The stone did calm him. He'd already noticed that. How had Stacie known it was "his?"

Crap. Am I believing this?

"Amelia told me you would come back confused. Angry. Guilty. Lost." Emeline handed the quartz back to him. "Seems like Stasha felt the same thing."

Ben sighed. "Mom, you know I don't believe all that."

"Don't you?" she asked him. "You used to trust your intuition. That's all, really, that seers do." She shrugged. "Well, almost all. Except when they see the future. That's something else."

"So what's the story there?" Ben knew he shouldn't ask, but he couldn't help it. He was curious about this woman.

"Story?"

Ben nodded. "You said her great aunt raised her. Why?"

"Ah. That story." Emeline sighed. "Stasha's father, Joe, died when she was very small. Nice man. I met him several times at the tea room. He and Stasha adored each other. Her mother," she made a derogatory sound, "was almost worse than no mother. After she remarried," here she gave a small shrug, "Stasha ended up living with Amelia. Pamela and the new husband moved away," she waved a vague hand, "up north some place."

"Her mother didn't take her?"

"I got the sense that Amelia wouldn't let her. Joe was Amelia's nephew. They were very close. Pamela was always jealous of that. Worse, she was jealous of her own daughter. She and Amelia never liked each other."

Ben looked down at the crystal in his hand, the way it caught the light, its smoky transparency. In between the flashes, he saw Stacie's face.

"Maybe you should talk to Stasha," said Emeline into the silence. "Maybe she can guide you."

"I don't need guiding." Irritably, Ben leaned back, slipped the stone back into his pocket. He leaned forward for another sandwich. He groaned and changed the subject. "I'm going to feel this tomorrow, aren't I?" he asked Alain.

"I guarantee it," Alain laughed.

The phone rang in the house. "I'll go," said Emeline. She glanced at Alain. "I hope it's not for you."

Alain sighed. "I do, too."

Emeline rested a hand on Ben's shoulder briefly as she rose, and the phone rang again. "Let me massage you before you go," she said. "It'll help those muscles."

She went into the house. A moment later, Ben heard her speaking Cajun.

Family from Louisiana. Probably her sister.

Alain was pouring himself another glass of iced tea. He held the pitcher up questioningly. Ben nodded, and his father refilled his glass.

"Dad," Ben asked hesitantly after a moment. "What do you think of all this? Seers and faith healers. Magic crystals."

Alain raised his eyebrows, settled back in his chair and

looked across the yard. "I've seen your mom do some things," he said finally. "And her grandmother."

Ben knew their story. They'd met in Louisiana when Alain was finishing his residency. Emeline was working with a researcher at the hospital studying the effect massage could have on healing by relieving pain and fear.

He started to say he knew all this when Alain looked back at him. "And so have you."

"*Me*?" Ben said surprised.

Alain waved a hand toward the house. "You just said it yourself. Emmie always knows what's going on in your head."

"We were joking!"

"Were we?"

Ben paused. *Good question.* When he'd been a kid, his mom always knew what he was going to do before he did it. He'd always assumed it was a mom thing.

"But you're a surgeon. Surely you don't believe in...voodoo?"

"I've seen things in surgery, you'd have to ask yourself what caused it."

"Like what?"

Alain was silent a long time. Ben waited, listening to the Cajun flowing inside the house. He could still understand bits and pieces. He'd spoken it with his mom, aunt and grandmother when very young, but once he'd started school, he'd quit using it. He'd forgotten most of it.

"Something I learned from another surgeon, a long time ago," his dad finally said. "He didn't allow any negative talk in the OR, about the patient or the potential outcome of the surgery. Insisted the patient was listening. He had a nurse once who made a snide remark about a patient. He threw her out of the OR and apologized to the patient—who was still anesthetized."

Ben cocked an eyebrow. Alain shrugged slightly.

"Not long after I finished my residency, I was assisting him. The patient started bleeding too heavily. He calmly said, 'Margie, would you give me a hand? Can you slow the blood flow here a bit?'" Alain shook his head. "Ben, it slowed. Then he thanked her. Said 'Thanks, Margie. That's just right.' And patted her on the shoulder."

"A fluke," said Ben.

"No. I've done it myself many times. It can work."

"Not always?"

"I wish it did. But no. Every person is different."

"But magic crystals?"

Alain smiled slightly. "Could be anything someone believes in." He sat up straight, stretched, then leaned back in the chair again. "I stood in once for a surgeon. When I went in to talk to the patient before surgery, she was almost hysterical, convinced she would die. Her doctor wouldn't let her take her medal of the Virgin Mary into the OR with her. Blessed by an abbot at some monastery. It was very special to her. She was convinced that without it she wouldn't make it."

He tsked. "I've seen that look. Too many times. If someone is convinced they're going to die, my job is so much harder.

"I told her I'd be happy to let her have her medal. She started crying with relief. I told her daughter how to clean it, then we taped it to the patient's thigh while she was still awake. I told the nurses to put it in her hand as soon as she got to recovery." Alain smiled. "She recovered beautifully."

"But she would have recovered anyway, right?" asked Ben.

"Probably," smiled Alain. "But why take a chance?"

Ben remembered Stacie saying someone with cancer believed it was the touchstone and not the chemo that cured him. That her shop assistant believed a stone cured her acne, even though Stacie had told her it hadn't.

That she couldn't help what people believed.

What does she *believe?* Ben wondered. *Besides the fact that certain stones belong to certain people. Does she believe she has a gift?* She hadn't made a big thing about giving him the quartz. Just handed it to him. No questions. No woo-woo.

The men sat together quietly for a while, but Ben's mind was going feverishly, one thought leading to another.

"Dad."

Alain looked at him.

"Have you lost people? During surgery?"

Alain heaved a great sigh of regret and nodded. "Not many, but yeah. Every surgeon does. Sometimes it's nothing you can control. But one time…" He shook his head. "I've never been sure." He looked across the yard. "He was a teenage boy. About your age at the time, which made it all the harder. He shouldn't have died. I still don't know why he did."

"Do you blame yourself?" Ben asked quietly.

His dad turned back to Ben. "Not as much as I used to." Ben looked into eyes as blue as his own. "But I haven't forgiven myself yet, either."

Maybe he knows more about Iraq than I give him credit for, thought Ben.

"Do you ever consider giving it up?"

Alain gave a rueful laugh. "After every difficult surgery. But when the patient recovers, I know it's worth it."

Ben was quiet for a few minutes, thinking about what Alain had said. Trying to fit it into his perception of his father.

"So how about you?" his father asked quietly. "Have you forgiven yourself?"

Startled, Ben gave the automatic answer. "I'm okay."

"Are you?" Alain probed. "How are the nightmares?"

Ben shrugged and made a face. "Still there. Depends on what happens at work. Depends on what's on the news. Depends on nothing at all," he said. "I can never tell what will set them off. Sometimes talking to Tucker does it. Sometimes that keeps them at bay. I don't know." He shrugged again.

"You might try yoga again," called Emeline from the house. Ben hadn't heard her hang up.

"Do you hear through walls?" he called back.

"I'm a mother," she said, opening the door and coming onto the deck with a plate of brownies. "I hear with my heart. You used to like yoga."

"That's because I thought it would turn me into Yoda."

Emeline smiled. "You're too tall. And," she pointed to him, "your ears are too small." She passed the plate to Alain, who plucked a couple brownies off. Emeline pushed the plate toward Ben.

"Maybe you should try yoga to develop your flexibility," she continued. "You won't get so sore digging."

"I don't plan to make a habit of this," Ben laughed, biting into a brownie.

"It would help center you, too," said Emeline. "Maybe help you sleep better."

An image of Stacie in her stretch leggings and pink tank flashed into his mind. "People will think I'm there for the women," he said.

Alain laughed again. "That's not a bad side benefit."

"You're still swimming?" asked Emeline.

"Yeah," Ben told her.

His mother smiled. "Water yoga, see?" she said.

Ben laughed. His dad was right. With Emeline, you couldn't win.

"The swimming helps?" Alain asked.

"Yeah. And the camera. Got some great shots at the Heritage Park. They're in the car. Want to see them?"

"Yes," said Alain, rising and reaching for his gloves on the table. "As soon as that damn tree is in the ground."

"Now, Dad," said Ben, getting up, "No negative talk around the patient."

"Get out." His father grinned.

They wrestled the tree into the hole, backfilled it and watered it in, which took another hour or so. Then Emeline came back out and said that, since they had extra hands, they should get the border planted, too. When they'd finished that, Ben stayed for dinner. Afterward, he brought his photos in from the car.

"You're getting stronger," said Alain, after they'd gone through his folder a couple times. "Those workshops are really paying off."

Ben hesitated. "Tucker's pushing me to make it a career."

"What about you?" Alain asked.

"I don't know. I feel like I need some kind of... purpose...in my work," said Ben. "Taking pictures because I like to doesn't seem like I'm doing much."

"Haven't you done your share? First the Army, now the police?"

"I don't know," said Ben again. "Even if I wanted to, I can't quit just now."

"Why not?"

Emeline came from the kitchen and put coffee on the table in front of them. "Yes," she echoed her husband, as she sat next to him. "Why not?"

Ben hesitated. "We may have a serial killer in the area."

"*Mon dieu*." His mother clapped a hand to her heart.

Ben reached out and took her other hand. "Mom. That's not for publication. Not here. Not in Louisiana."

She nodded. "I understand."

Ben told them what little they had and what they suspected. He found himself telling them about Stacie and the stalker.

"You think they're the same," said Emeline, though Ben had said no such thing.

Ben paused. "Cruz says it's a little far-fetched."

"But what do *you* think?" Emeline asked.

"She's probably right," Ben said slowly. "But..." He hesitated. "But I don't like the coincidence."

His mother rose. "You're right. You can't quit. Even if they are not the same, you have to stop that awful man from following Stasha."

"Mom," said Ben looking up at her, "there's a whole police department..."

"Yes, but I don't know them. I know you. You'll take care of her."

Ben looked across at Alain. His father spread his hands and gave him a wry look.

"Yeah, yeah. I know. I can't win."

Alain shook his head.

"Now, you," said Emeline, pointing at Ben then jerking her thumb toward the hall. "Massage."

BEN FINALLY LEFT HIS FOLKS' home about 10:30. He shivered in the cool air after the warmth of the massage room. He pulled his sweatshirt on before climbing into the Camry. The car smelled a little strongly of salt, sweat and mildew. Time to spend a weekend cleaning it out.

As he drove north from Sycamore Canyon along the Pacific Coast Highway, Ben was warm and relaxed, glad his mom had strong-armed him into the massage. Maybe she'd inherited more than a little of the *traiteuse* from her grandmother.

He smiled.

He reached the junction of Tamarind with PCH and, with only the slightest hesitation, swung right, then left onto Glen Eden. It wouldn't hurt to roll by Stacie's shop, just to be sure all was quiet. It was on his way, he argued to himself.

The shop was dark. No light showed upstairs. *Not working late*, he thought, *or already gone home*. He pulled to the curb in front of the building next to the store, turned off the car engine and rolled down the window.

It was after eleven and the neighborhood was still. A car heading up the hill behind him on Tamarind. The distant sound of waves breaking at high tide two blocks away. A dog walker several blocks down stepped into the circle of light cast by a street lamp, then disappeared again.

Nothing.

A normal, quiet neighborhood, late in the evening in Eden Beach.

Ben felt foolish sitting there. *Neighbors will probably report me*, he thought, smiling to himself. He reached for the ignition as he glanced around the neighborhood one more time.

Then...something.

Ben hesitated, hand on the ignition key. The thought of Phillips in Iraq flitted through his mind so quickly, he was almost unaware of it.

Slowly, he got out of his battered Camry, closed the door softly and looked around again.

This stretch of Glen Eden had once held homes. A number of them had been converted to small businesses, like Stacie's. Besides The Bell, Book and Crystal, a cluster of old homes at the corner of Tamarind held a truffle maker, a bakery, a quilt shop, a sandwich shop and an Italian restaurant. Some of the larger houses, like the one next to Stacie's store, had been converted to apartments. A few of those were still showing lights.

Most of the original homes, though, had been replaced by nondescript, small office buildings filled with financial consultants, real estate offices, attorneys, a dentist, a chiropractor. There was a dance studio upstairs across the street. A few of the businesses had night lights glowing deep inside them, but most were dark.

A few cars were parked on the street: an older truck that had seen better days in front of the restaurant, a late-model Honda Civic in front of the apartment building. A couple Toyotas, a Mercedes, and a motorcycle were scattered farther along. He could see the tail end of a car around the corner at the end of the block. The public parking lot across the street was dark, the only light came from an upstairs apartment on the far side. The few scattered cars in the lot probably belonged to people who lived nearby. A line of thick oleanders stood in pools of dark shadow at the edge of the lot, next to an office building.

Ben was feeling a bit silly again, but then he frowned, looking at the dark offices across the street. Near the corner he noticed a "For Lease" sign in an upper window. Blinds were drawn.

It would be an ideal place for someone to watch the shop.

In fact, there were too many places for someone to hide,

he thought, eyeing the shrubbery and empty cars again. The hair on his neck rose. Too isolated for a woman who was being stalked and who often worked late.

Right now, though, it was quiet.

Ben turned to get back into the car. He'd check the patrol reports on Monday, he promised himself. And make sure Meissner came by to talk to Stacie.

Casting one more look up and down the street, Ben started the car, pulled out and headed home. He didn't look back.

He'd just reached the corner when someone slid out of the shadows next to Stacie's shop and ran to the truck. The ignition turned over and the engine caught. Lights off, it made a U-turn to follow Ben.

TWELVE

STACIE PUNCHED THE "CLOSE" BUTTON ON THE GARAGE DOOR and walked to the gate at the top of her stairs where Bananas waited patiently. She fondled his ears and watched the sun setting on the ocean in the distance. Even from this height, Stacie could hear the rush of traffic on Pacific Coast Highway at the bottom of the hills.

Below her, to the right, the town of Eden Beach lay like scattered toy blocks around the cove. Behind it, the hills rose steeply, cut by canyons, carpeted in chaparral, and punctuated everywhere with hidden houses. When driving the twisting lanes through the hillside neighborhoods, it was easy to believe there were no homes there, just garages. Most homes, like Stacie's, were accessed by steep steps leading down—or up—from the street-side car ports and garages.

As she gazed out toward the purple hump of Catalina, Eileen pulled past her to the end of the street, turned in the cul-de-sac, and came back to park in the tiny pull out close to Stacie's fence. Unsettled after the meeting with Ginny earlier, Stacie had asked Eileen to join her for dinner.

In her mid-sixties, Eileen had remained slender, despite

having had three kids. Her straight hair, kept tinted blond, curled just behind and below her ears, showed off large, gold hoop earrings that matched the gold rims of her glasses. She was dressed against the chilly night, with a collared shirt showing above the edge of a bulky cotton sweater worn over chinos and light hiking boots.

"This truly is a magnificent spot," she said, as she joined Stacie.

"Yes. Not a day passes that I don't get an offer from a realtor." Stacie plucked a flyer out of her gate. "Like this one."

Stacie opened the gate, and Bananas loped down the stairs. Stacie went down a few steps, stood aside for Eileen to pass her, then reached up to latch the gate behind them.

The two women picked their way down the long staircase along the terraced slope, planted over the last century by four generations of Stacie's family, though most of it had been done by Amelia and Stacie. California redbud, shrub manzanitas, and ceanothus were filled now with bees finishing their evening nectar runs. Near the patio, wildflowers sprouted among Mediterranean shrubs and ground cover, such as lavender, rosemary, and thymes. Lupine provided nectar for bees and hummingbirds and plenty of color for Stacie. Star jasmine filled the air with fragrance. California poppies exploded from the slopes and sprang exuberantly from the cracks between the flagstones. Stacie never had the heart to pull them out until they'd finished blooming. By then, they'd set more seed for the next year.

The hum of bees, the thrum of a hummingbird as it shot by, the trickle of water washing over a large smoky quartz crystal in the fountain in the middle of the patio—all of it calmed Stacie's heart as she descended. This was her sanctuary. The place she always felt safe. Protected. There were a few houses on the hills high above her that overlooked her patio, but Stacie always felt she was invisible to them here in her garden.

Eileen inhaled the fragrances deeply. "You've made this so beautiful. I don't know how you bear to leave it each day. I'd become a hermit."

"There *are* days," Stacie said, then sighed. "But since the last tax bills came in, I've been considering renting it. Or selling it."

Eileen stopped dead. "Oh, Stacie. You couldn't. This is your home. Your family's home. This place has defied fire and earthquakes. Certainly it can't fall to taxes."

Stacie looked over the garden. "I don't know what other choice I'll have. The tax bill for the shop alone went up more than $2500 over last year." Her eyes rested on Eileen. "You know that. I'm sure you got an increase, too."

"I did. But the tenants offset that. I have to remember that you don't have that."

Eileen and her husband had owned the large house next to The Crystal Tea Room. After their kids had grown, they had wisely decided to convert the huge old home into four apartments. They lived in one and rented the other three. Several years after the conversion, her husband had died. Now Eileen had a place that was small enough for her to handle alone, and an income to supplement her Social Security.

She shook her head. "It's all the people tearing out the small houses, building the mini-mansions with thousands of square feet. It's driving the tax base up."

Stacie nodded. "At least I'm lucky both the shop and the house are paid off. But the taxes. Well." She sighed. "Sooner or later I'm going to have to choose which one to sell. I could get a fortune for either." She rubbed her forehead.

"There's no other solution?"

"Not that I can see," Stacie told her. "I could live on what the shop brings in, move into the apartment above it and rent the house. I could get enough that way to pay the taxes on the house, but I'd still need to crunch numbers to pay the taxes on the shop property. It would not be impossible, but the shop apartment is just two bedrooms. It's pretty small for me, the business, and Godzilla, the dog."

Eileen chuckled. "You're right. I can't see all that squeezed into that little space. I can't imagine anyone living here but you, though."

"No. Neither can I." Selling or renting, either thought sickened her. "But even now, I need a significant part of the bookkeeping and tax work just to pay the taxes on both places and put money aside for repairs. Even if I hired someone in the shop full time, I couldn't do all the number work I'll eventually need to do to keep up."

"Couldn't you hire help with the bookkeeping?"

"I've thought about it. It's an option. But that entails wages and insurance. I should already raise my rates. And the prices in the shop. Another employee would mean higher fees all around." Stacie sighed again and took a long look around the garden. She thought about the lost CPA. *It would have helped,* she thought.

"What about renting the apartment above the shop and working at home? You could rent the apartment under the garage, too." Eileen gestured to the door tucked in the corner of the garden.

"I did look into converting the shop apartment. It's out. I'd need a separate entrance and would have to remodel the space upstairs. Would require way too much debt. Here," she pointed up at the street, "there's no place to park but that one little spot in front of the fence. The neighbors would rise against me if a renter parked there all the time. Parking is jealously guarded here."

"I see the problem."

"Anyway. This is depressing. Let's go get that dinner I promised you."

Eileen noticed two large pieces of rose quartz flanking the French doors leading into the house. "Are those new?" she asked.

"It's an addiction." Stacie laughed. "Got them at a gem show just before Christmas."

Over the years, Stacie had collected more than two dozen stone spheres and pillars, situating them in a rough circle around the patio: carnelian, poppy jasper, bloodstone, blue lace agate, moss agate, rose quartz, among others. Though they varied in size, most of the pillars were about twelve inches tall. The spheres were about six inches in diameter. She had spent a lot of time idly—and not so idly—arranging and rearranging the stones. The day she put the last pillar into place—a rutilated quartz—her stress level dropped. It was like a cone of silence had fallen over her. Outside noise, in terms of worry or thoughts of clients and audits, all disappeared. Perfect peace.

Stacie unlocked the door, leaving it open. Bananas had galloped down the slope behind the house to the ragged lawn that served as his dog run. She dropped her keys in the agate bowl next to the phone on the table in the small alcove by the door, stowing her messenger bag under it in the same movement.

"I love this house," said Eileen.

Stacie looked around the compact space with love and pride. "Yes," she said.

Eileen shook her head. "I can't believe Pamela would have sold it to developers."

"That makes two of us. I bless my grandmother every day for thwarting her," said Stacie.

When Stacie's grandmother, Mary, had entered her final illness, Pamela had expected her husband, Joe, to inherit the property. Smelling a great deal of money, as Eden Beach was booming, Pamela had started plotting with a local realtor named Carla Towne. She planned to browbeat Joe into selling the house when Mary was gone.

But Mary got wind of it, changed her will and left the house to her sister, Amelia. Joe had just shrugged, saying it was his mom's house to do with as she wanted and they already had a house anyway. But Pamela had been incensed. Towne had spouted empty threats about agreements and contracts, but there was nothing she could do. Pamela didn't own the property.

"I'm going to change, Eileen. If you want to put on some water…"

"I thought we could both use some wine." Eileen pulled a bottle of pinot noir out of the bag in her hand and gave Stacie a questioning look.

"Oh, ever so much better! Bless you!" said Stacie, putting her hands together in a prayer position and bowing slightly toward Eileen, who laughed. "You know where the glasses are," she called, going through the arch into the tiny hall and her bedroom beyond it.

She came back to the living room in comfortable, worn jeans topped by a long-sleeved, deep blue tunic, and a long wool vest of deep violet. To further ward off the chill of the early spring evening, she had pulled on bulky socks and slipped into felt clogs. The amethyst crystal, only worn outside her clothes when she was at home, glowed richly in the late-evening light coming through the sliding glass doors.

They overlooked a small deck, the roof of a neighboring house below, and the hillside falling to the ocean.

Eileen came in, set their glasses on the coffee table and settled against the bright tapestry pillows on the curved brown sofa facing the fireplace. Stacie's pendant swung free as she bent forward to pick up her wine.

"I always forget what an incredible color that amethyst is," said Eileen.

Stacie sat in one of the wing chairs flanking the couch and lifted the pendant to look at it. "It is. As many gem shows as I go to, I've never seen anything like it." She set it back against her heart. "It's truly unique. I can't imagine what the tsar would have done if my ancestor had been caught smuggling it out of the mine. Especially if anyone had known it was 'magic.'" Stacie widened her eyes and lifted her brows in mock awe at the last word.

According to family legend, a many-times-great grandfather had seen a vision of a woman when he touched the amethyst. Convinced he would marry her, he risked stealing the crystal. Several days later, at the market place, he'd seen that lovely woman, and they had married.

"Ah. So, you *do* believe the story."

Stacie laughed. "I did when I was a child. Every time I met a boy I liked at school, I'd race home to Aunt Me and ask to hold the amethyst. Sadly, it never gave me even the slightest buzz," she said in mock despair.

"So, no true love for you there, then."

"Nope. Not a whisper."

"You never know," said Eileen conspiratorially, "maybe you've just never found the one."

Stacie laughed again, a bit sadly, and sipped her wine. "Aunt Me believed the magic didn't work anymore. Not since it broke."

"Maybe you should try it on that good-looking detective." Eileen smiled at her mischievously.

Stacie rolled her eyes as she picked up the pendant again and held it, warm from her body. She was surprised by the strength of her disappointment. She wouldn't have minded the amethyst crystal responding to Detective Robard, she thought, staring into the red-purple depths of the crystal.

The room darkened...

...faded. She smelled wood smoke. The tick of the mantel clock was loud in the silent room. Light from the dying fire reflected in the glass in front of the slowly moving hands. The rocking chair creaked as she stood up, crossed to the door. Silent snow touched her face feather-soft as she stepped out to search the darkness. Worry. Throat-binding fear. For him. For their daughter asleep under the stairs. For the child he didn't know she carried. She'd begged him not to go. She'd seen betrayal in the scrying crystal. But he'd smiled and gone. Now he was hours late.

The amethyst in her hand was cold as ice. Cold as death.

A muffled crack. Sudden, slicing pain. Blood.

Stacie gasped.

The room righted itself, but everything was outlined in a halo of light.

"What is it?" asked Eileen.

What was *that?* Stacie's mind echoed in rhythm to the racketing of her pounding heart. Even as the thought formed, though, Stacie knew.

A memory. And one not hers.

"Stacie?"

"Nothing," she said belatedly. The amethyst in her hand was warm, but Stacie was chilled.

"Shall we have a fire?" she asked. She dropped the pendant and got up, pretending not to see Eileen's concerned look. "It gets chilly in here as the sun goes down." She flipped a switch on the wall. With a hiss and whoosh, the gas caught. "One of the best things Amelia did," she said.

"Putting the gas in?" It was said lightly, but Eileen was watching her shrewdly.

"Yes. I love a fire at night, but no one's going to bring wood down those stairs."

The fire was going out, dying even as he died. No tears. Not yet. They'd come for her, the soldiers. For her and her daughters. They must go. Now.

Stacie shook her head, trying to clear her head of the persistent vision, of the *knowing*.

"It was easier in your great grandfather's day."

Stacie nodded absently, dropped back into the chair, picked up her wine.

What were they talking about?

Wood. Fires.

"Yes. Lots of trees close by. Just cut them and skid them home."

He had just cut fresh wood, so the neighbors would not suspect anything. They'd steal it as soon as they knew she had gone. But they would not take his tools. The worn leather strap cut into the wound on her hand as she hefted the heavy bag into the cart.

"Can't do that anymore. Not without a lawsuit." Eileen smiled, but she was still watching Stacie carefully. She frowned. "Stacie? Are you all right?"

"Umm," agreed Stacie, only half hearing. "Too many things on my mind." *How can I have a memory that isn't mine?* she wondered.

Eileen had been Amelia's friend for decades. Stacie knew she wasn't fooled.

Stacie rose abruptly. It was difficult to breathe. "Just let me get that casserole in."

Eileen watched her as she crossed the room.

In the kitchen, Stacie leaned on the counter, gulped air and tried to collect herself.

Am I losing my mind?

She knew the story, of course. Her great, great grandfather, Tomasz, a leader of partisans, betrayed by a friend, killed by Imperialist soldiers. The amethyst, the bond between him and Anastasia, supposedly breaking at the moment of his death. Anastasia's flight from Bohemia into Russia in early winter, walking behind a pushcart loaded with her most treasured possessions, and her daughters—Magda, just nine, at her side, and the future Ludmilla, just two months in the womb.

She *knew* the story. But she'd never *remembered* it.

Never felt the cold penetrating her boots as they crunched the frost.

Never smelled the snow melting on the goats' hair.

Never felt the gut-twisting fear or the blood-thick grief knotting her heart.

Stacie looked down at her left palm, still tingling.

Never felt the pain as the broken edge of the amethyst crystal sliced across her palm's lifeline.

What was that? Stacie asked herself again.

Was that what Amelia had felt when she was seeing?

Stacie went cold at the thought. She'd go crazy not knowing the real world from some sort of dream state.

Bananas strolled in, nails clicking on the wood floor, crunched some kibble then dropped onto his bed in the dining room corner, big head on his paws. He rolled big brown eyes at her and thumped his tail, twice.

The familiar sight and sounds of the enormous black dog

steadied her, rooted her again in the present. She took a deep breath.

Whatever this was, she'd sort it out later.

The living room floor creaked as Eileen got up to close the French doors to the patio.

Remembering why she was in the kitchen, Stacie popped the chicken and barley casserole into the oven. She set the timer, took another calming breath and went back to her friend.

Eileen was sipping her wine near the fountain that stood by the sliding doors leading onto the deck. Bubbling water ran over a large, perfectly transparent quartz crystal. About eight inches tall and three inches wide at the base, the crystal tapered slightly toward the sharply terminating end. Captured inside, appearing to float, was another clear quartz crystal at an angle to the host crystal. And inside *that* crystal was a fluid-filled inclusion, almost an inch long, containing a large gas bubble. Like the bubble in a spirit level, the bubble moved when the crystal was tipped back and forth.

Anastasia's scrying crystal. Later, Amelia's.

Eileen, her face sad, reached out and touched the point of the crystal.

"Looking into the future?"

Eileen gave her a small smile. "I miss her."

Tears pricked Stacie's eyes. "Me, too."

"I've never known anyone with as big a heart." Eileen looked at Stacie. "Except you."

"Thank you, but I'm not sure that's true."

"Never tempted to try?" Eileen asked her, tipping her head to the crystal.

"Never. That was Amelia's gift."

And Anastasia's, she thought.

But if it was their *gift, what just happened to me?*

It didn't bear thinking about.

"Amelia thought you had it. That it might be stronger than hers."

Stacie reached out to stroke one of the terminating faces of the quartz crystal lightly. Her touch did not linger. Aunt Me had held this crystal when she did readings. She'd wanted to teach Stacie, but Stacie hadn't wanted to enter that frightening realm. Even touching the stone lightly could give her strange sensations.

It gave her one now. A buzz in the tip of her finger. A shadow on her mind, a raven wing passing in front of the sun. Darkness. Death.

Stacie lifted her hand, disoriented.

More death.

Enough, she said to herself firmly. *I won't.*

Stacie dipped her fingers into the flowing water of the fountain to wash the sensation away, then wiped her hand on her jeans.

"No," she told Eileen. "I like my privacy. I saw what happened when Aunt Me did readings. The demands. The scenes. The threats. I have enough trouble just running the shop. Look at that crazy Mrs. Byers, the egg throwing, and now those horrible protesters." She shook her head. She smiled to lighten the moment. "If I have any latent ability, I'd rather keep it a secret. Let my clients think I'm clairvoyant. It'll keep them honest."

"You already do readings, in a way, you know," said Eileen. "I saw you do it today, with Ginny. You knew she was pregnant."

"A lucky guess."

Eileen's eyes said she didn't believe her.

"Colin said you gave that detective a crystal. That surprised me. What was that about?"

What, indeed? wondered Stacie.

"He needed it," she finally said. "He just…" Stacie was reluctant to say much about the emptiness circling Ben Robard. The sense of loneliness and self-doubt that she'd wanted to ease. He deserved his privacy, too. "He just needed it." She gave a small shrug.

"You're right," said Eileen. "I shouldn't have asked."

Stacie touched the older woman's arm. "Come on," she said. "Let's watch the last of the sunset."

They pulled the old rocker from the corner, and Stacie dragged the wing chair over. Eileen kicked off her shoes and curled up in the wing chair, pulling a bright yellow, orange and brown crocheted blanket over her lap and feet. Stacie snagged her wine from the coffee table and sat in the worn rocker. When it creaked, Stacie had a moment of vertigo as the vision she'd just had flashed in her mind.

No, she told herself. *Just, no.*

She breathed deeply, willing the feeling to go.

The friends sat in silence, watching the fog rising in the distance. One by one, the lights on the oil rigs, far out in the channel, winked out in the mist. The sun slipped slowly into the purplish-gray haze. A car passed on the road above the house. Water trickled in the fountain.

"What will become of her, Eileen?" Stacie said after a while.

"I don't want to think."

"She was so frightened. I didn't even get her last name."

Eileen reached out and laid a hand on Stacie's. "You did what you could."

"That's what the counselor at the Women's Crisis Center told me." Stacie had called them to find out what she could do better if, by any chance, Ginny came back. "But I still feel guilty." She sighed. "I just wish I knew she was safe."

Eileen made a doubtful sound. "I'm afraid she isn't, if she's with that boyfriend." She slowly shook her head and leaned back in her chair. "Such a dreadful decision to make. And so young. So alone. To keep a child. To...lose...a child. Or give it up." There was a long pause, and Eileen turned toward the window.

Surprised by the tears in her voice, Stacie asked her quietly, "Did that happen to you?"

Eileen seemed not to hear her. "It changes your life. Changes who you are. You'll always question your decision. Wonder, 'What if?' Wonder what kind of person you are."

She turned back to Stacie, blue eyes pained. "Not me. My younger sister. Same old story. Wrong boyfriend left her pregnant. Angry parents demanded she give the baby up." She shrugged slightly. "So she did. Finally."

"How old was she?" asked Stacie.

"Not much older than Ginny."

"There wasn't much choice, was there, if your parents were adamant? An abortion wasn't legal then, was it?"

"It was, just barely, though it wasn't easy to find a doctor who would do it. But my parents were set against it.

"And she did have another option. I was newly married and offered to take the baby so she could stay part of her life." Eileen shook her head slightly and looked out the window. "She was furious. Said if I wanted a daughter, I should have my own." She looked back at Stacie. "The grief finally killed her. She took her own life a few years later."

Stacie closed her eyes. "I'm so sorry, Eileen."

"Long time ago. Maybe worked out for the best, for the little girl anyway, as that husband was not a keeper. At all. But it felt like yesterday when I listened to Ginny this afternoon."

Stacie was silent as she finished her wine. The sky

outside had gone dark violet and the lights in the town at the edge of the sea glimmered, not yet blotted by the distant fog.

"I often wonder what would have happened to me without Aunt Me," she said finally.

"Pamela?"

"Umm."

"You were lucky."

Stacie nodded and wrapped a hand around the amethyst crystal on its chain.

"You know, my dad always said he didn't believe in intuition, but he always trusted Amelia's. Except when he wanted to marry Pamela. Aunt Me tried to warn him, but he didn't listen." *Big mistake there*, thought Stacie, bitterly.

"Where our hearts are involved, none of us do," said Eileen, finishing off her wine.

Later, Amelia had tried to warn Pamela about that filthy creep, Chuck, who she married after Joe died. But Pamela despised Amelia, thought she was a fraud. She hadn't listened.

Chuck.

Stacie never said his name aloud and could almost not bear to have it in her mind.

What would have happened to me without Aunt Me? she thought again.

Who will protect Ginny?

"Maybe I should have called the police," said Stacie.

"I doubt there's much they could do. She's one, lost, pregnant teenager among probably hundreds, just in Orange County. And she didn't tell you much beyond her first name. And his," said Eileen.

Stacie sighed. "What a mess."

"Perhaps you could call that detective," said Eileen after a moment. Stacie heard the teasing in her voice. "Ask his advice."

Stacie blushed, and the amethyst warmed in her hand. *The wine*, she thought.

"You're smiling." Eileen grinned back at her. "I don't blame you. If I were younger, I'd smile, too, thinking about that detective."

The oven timer went off.

"Saved by the bell!" Stacie laughed and got up.

Eileen followed her into the kitchen. Stacie pulled the casserole out to cool. Together they set the table. Eileen pulled the salad out of the fridge, Stacie zapped some green beans, and they were ready to eat.

"More wine?" Eileen indicated the bottle on the counter.

Stacie waved a hand. "Not tonight. I have to work."

Eileen frowned as she sat down. "Stacie. You shouldn't go back down to your office. Not with that...man...following you. And what about the protesters? What if they become more...aggressive?"

"I'm not going down," Stacie told her, gesturing to the living room. "I brought files home. I've got to get started on the worksheets for a couple clients—here, where it's quiet—before I begin their returns. When we're as busy as we were today at the shop, and I need to help Mir, it's too hard for me to run up and down the stairs and keep my concentration, too."

"That time of year."

"Yes. Every year, I think I'm out of my mind to do this, but I need the tax prep fees. I've been putting money aside to renovate the bathroom. Though after those tax bills..." her voice trailed off.

They talked some more about things Stacie wanted to do in the garden, the new grandchild Eileen was expecting, and they speculated about Colin and Matt. After dinner and dishes, they got back to talking about Ginny. Neither of them could come up with any answers.

About 7:30, Eileen got up. "I'd better let you get to your work," she said. "I know it's hard, but try not to worry about Ginny. Maybe she'll come back. Maybe she'll change her mind and find her way to the Women's Crisis Center on her own."

"I hope so," said Stacie. As they walked across the patio, the security lights on the garage popped on. Haloed in fog, they illuminated the long climb to Eileen's car. Stacie hugged her friend, waited until she let herself out the gate, waved, then went back in, locking the door.

As she turned, her glance fell on Amelia's scrying crystal. She went over and looked into it, the bubble within a crystal, within a crystal, the water shining as it slid over the surface. Stacie ran two fingers across the palm of her left hand where she imagined—could swear—she still felt the slicing pain.

But she didn't touch the scrying crystal again.

She got her messenger bag, pulled the files out and took them into the dining room where Bananas whined softly in his sleep. She made tea, flipped open her laptop and settled down to work.

IT WAS ALMOST midnight when she closed the second file, backed up her work onto a jump drive, got up and turned off the lights. Bananas' feet twitched as he dreamed on his bed.

She was tired, but she'd gotten a lot of work done. She could take tomorrow off. There would be few Sundays from now until April 15th that would be free. The weather had been so lovely, maybe she'd work in the garden, she thought as she walked into the living room.

The phone rang.

Surprised, Stacie hesitated. Only a few long-time family friends knew the land-line number. Everyone else called on her cell. Probably a wrong number. But there was no voice mail on this line. If she didn't answer, it might ring a long time, or the person might call back even later.

It might be one of those old friends. The thought worried her.

She went to the alcove and picked up the receiver.

"Hello?"

"I told you not to play with me, Anastasia. Get rid of your boyfriends, or I will."

THIRTEEN

STACIE SLAMMED THE PHONE DOWN, DROPPED TO THE FLOOR and tore the jack out of the wall under the table. Her heart slamming against her ribs forced her breath out in gasps. Her legs were so shaky, she couldn't stand up.

How had he found her? Her home number was unlisted, and it was still billed to Amelia.

The hair on her arms stood up. *How much trouble had he gone through to find her?* she wondered. *And* why*?*

Feeling suddenly exposed in front of the undraped French doors facing the patio, she scrambled to her feet, yanking the curtains closed and kicking the floor bolt into place. She swiftly crossed the living room, double-checked the locks on the sliding door to the deck, then jerked the drapes into place. She did the same in the dining room and kitchen, then ran to the bedrooms. All was secure.

She snatched up her jacket from where she'd tossed it on the bed and pulled her quartz crystal from the pocket. It magnified her fear and it was buzzing, but there was no sensation of slicing razors that indicated Troy was nearby.

He wasn't close.

At least not right now.

But he knew her number. He must know where she lived.

He'd called her Anastasia.

Like Chuck had.

What else does he know? Why won't he go away?

Shaking, Stacie walked back into the living room clutching the crystal.

She was so cold. She couldn't think.

Breathe, she told herself. *Breathe*. But there was a vice around her ribs.

She had to calm down. She had to get warm.

Going into the kitchen, she flipped on the lights. The kettle chattered against the faucet as she filled it. While the water heated, she tried to clear her mind.

Call Detective Robard.

It was her first clear thought. She had his card. He'd said to call. Any time.

Stacie dumped everything from her messenger bag onto the dining table and scrabbled through it.

No card.

Shit. It was at the shop. She'd put it next to the register.

Call the police station. Ask them to call him.

It was after midnight. They'd never do it.

911? And say what? What would they do?

She'd have to call tomorrow, maybe ask for the other detective, the one Ben Robard said took care of Crimes Against Persons.

On a Sunday?

Besides. She couldn't remember his name.

She couldn't remember Ben's partner's name, the woman.

She could only remember Ben Robard. The steadiness

she'd sensed that morning in the South Coast Heritage Park. His concern when he'd learned about Troy.

He made her feel safe.

She needed to feel safe.

The kettle whistled. Stacie poured hot water over the chamomile flowers. As the fragrance rose, she clutched the mug, almost too hot to hold. She took a shallow breath, felt her ribs relax. Took another.

Chamomile tea. Her Aunt Amelia's sovereign remedy for any upset.

Aunt Me had made her chamomile that night, almost twenty years before. The last time Stacie had needed to feel safe.

Stacie's father had died without life insurance, choosing to put any extra money into his business—or to pay Pamela's credit card bills. Without his income, Pamela's debts had cost them their home on the bluffs downtown. She and Stacie had moved in with Amelia, taking over the tiny garden apartment under the garage. Pamela had fumed. She still thought the house should have been hers and that Amelia should either move into the small apartment herself or relinquish the house entirely and move back down to the bungalow on Glen Eden where she'd lived before Stacie's grandmother had died.

Amelia had flatly refused. She wasn't going to give Pamela a second chance to sell the house. The only reason she allowed Pamela to live in the apartment was because of Stacie.

Not quite two years later, Pamela married Chuck, a well-to-do attorney. Pamela and Stacie moved into his house up on Sky Vista where Pamela could look down on everyone else, literally as well as figuratively.

Stacie had hated him from the first day she met him.

Always petting her hair, trying to hug her, kiss her. "Anastasia," he would croon. "My special girl. My little Russian treat."

Pamela had never wanted children. She'd resented the bond between Stacie and Joe. Now, she was jealous of the attention Chuck paid to Stacie. She started making barbed comments to her daughter even more frequently than ever before. Stacie spent as much time at her girlfriends' homes as she could. After school, she biked to Aunt Me's tea room. When she had to return to the house on Sky Vista—it was never her home—she'd eat dinner fast, then close herself up in her room.

Six months after they'd moved in, Stacie woke from a nightmare, her heart pounding.

A girl. Darkness. The bed sagging. A hand over her mouth. A voice. "Our secret. Your fault." Pain. Blood. Revulsion.

Hatred. Bone-deep and searing.

Self-loathing. Guilt.

The house around Stacie was dark and silent, the only illumination the moonlight coming in the window.

As her heart quieted, Stacie wondered, *Who was that girl?*

Was it even a dream? It felt...different.

Stacie was puzzling over the strange vision, when she heard it. A footstep on the carpet. A shadow moved. The door closed.

She gasped in fear.

"Shh, Anastasia," Chuck breathed. "Shh, my special girl."

Stacie, panicked, sat up quickly. She curled into a small ball against the headboard and pulled the blankets up against her.

Not a dream. A premonition.

Stacie knew what a premonition was. Her aunt had told her.

Scream! The thought ricocheted around her mind. *Scream*!

She tried. Her throat wouldn't open. The fear sitting on her chest stopped her breath.

The single bed sagged as Chuck sat on the edge near her. Stacie made herself even smaller.

He reached out a hand and stroked her face. Stacie flinched.

"It's all right, my special girl. So soft. Your skin is so soft." He raised a hand to her hair. "So beautiful. So soft." His hand slipped down to where Stacie's fists gripped the blankets under her chin. He pried one of her hands loose.

"Go away," Stacie managed to choke out. "Go away. Leave me alone."

"Shh, Anastasia, my pretty Anastasia," he crooned as he slowly pulled her stiff arm toward him, toward his lap. "This will be fun, my little gift. You must trust your daddy."

Stacie was resisting with all her strength when he pressed her hand against something firm but soft in his lap."

Stacie gasped.

"See? You like…"

Stacie's ear-splitting scream shattered the night.

Chuck leaped away, dropping her hand. Stacie screamed again, louder. Her window was open. The neighbors would hear. They would call the police.

It never occurred to her to call for her mother.

"Shut up," snarled Chuck. "Shut up!"

Stacie kept screaming. It was what they'd told her to do at school.

Stacie heard her mother stumbling down the hall.

"What the hell?" Pamela slammed open the door. It hit Chuck in the back. He yelped.

"What...?" Pamela flipped on the overhead light, blinding all of them.

Stacie stopped screaming.

"He was touching me!" she cried to her mother. "He got in my bed. He was touching me!"

"What?" Pamela said again, looking from Stacie to Chuck.

Chuck waved his hands and smiled. "It's not what you think. I heard her moaning in her sleep. She was having a nightmare. I wanted to wake her so she wouldn't be scared."

"That's a lie! You're lying!" Stacie shouted. "He was trying to make me touch him!"

"Stacie! Stop it!" said Pamela. "What a horrible thing to say. Chuck would never do anything like that. You've been listening to too many stories."

"It's not a story. Ask him. Ask him what he did to Clarey."

"What?"

"Clarey! He did it to her, too!" Stacie pointed at Chuck. "You hurt her, too. You hurt your own daughter. You lied! You're a bad, wicked liar! I hate you, just like she hates you!"

"*Stop it*!" Pamela shouted.

Stacie stopped, panting.

"It was a *dream*, a bad dream! Chuck doesn't have a daughter."

"Not anymore," Stacie interrupted. "Her mother took her away."

Chuck's face went blank, his eyelids drooped. His eyes glittered in the narrow slits.

The slap came out of nowhere.

"I said stop it!"

Stacie, too shocked to cry, simply glared. Pamela dropped her hand.

In the silence, Pamela turned to Chuck. "Honestly. These school counselors. I know they mean well, but telling stories to imaginative girls. Well. This is where it leads."

Chuck nodded. "I completely understand." He turned to Stacie and gave her a bland look that scared her so badly, she was afraid she'd wet the bed.

"Stacie, go back to sleep. You have school tomorrow. And don't try this again," Pamela told her irritably.

Pamela stepped back, and Chuck, with one more glance at Stacie, left the room. Her mother flipped off the light and closed the door leaving Stacie, shaking and terrified, in the darkness. She put a hand to her stinging cheek.

He would be back. If not tonight, another night. Stacie knew it down to her bones. She had to run away. But where could she go? It was the middle of the night. Her friends' parents would be angry if she went to them. They would call Pamela. Her school counselor might listen, but not until tomorrow. And then, what could she do? They might put Stacie in foster care. And she'd heard stories. All the kids had.

Then she knew. It was so obvious.

Quietly, she slipped out of bed and padded across the deep carpeting. She pulled a sweatshirt and jeans on over her pajamas, afraid to get undressed in case Chuck burst back in.

She put on her runners and stood quietly by the bedroom door. If he came back in, she would duck out and run.

Gradually the voices down the hall got quiet. The house became silent. Stacie forced herself to wait until the clock downstairs chimed. It was 2:00 a.m.

Soundlessly, she crept out of her room and down the stairs. She tiptoed across the hall and living room, through the kitchen, the laundry room, carefully unlocked the door and slipped into the side yard.

She unlocked her bike and rolled it to the gate. Holding the bike with one hand, she unlatched the gate and pushed it open.

She'd forgotten the horrible screech.

Stacie shoved it hard, out of her way, wrestled the bike through. With a leap, she was on the saddle and moving. She raced down the driveway, gaining speed as she rode into the street, turning wildly onto Scenic. Down a long block, swinging wide onto Tamarind.

Pumping hard, she flew down the middle of the dark street. She never thought about falling. Walls, hedges, fences flashed past her as she darted from one puddle of light to the next, each patch of streetlight glare making the night in between darker. No cars came, but Stacie was sure they'd be after her in no time. She kept pumping, leaning into the curves.

She was moving so fast, she almost missed the turn onto Canyon View. She slammed on her brakes, skidded, fish-tailing wildly. As she started up the long hill, the adrenalin rush began to fade. Her legs wobbled.

Part way up the hill, gasping for breath, her blood pounding in her ears, she had to get off and push. A stitch stabbed her side, but panic drove her on. She couldn't stop. They would find her. They would stop her.

She would scream. She would scream until the police came.

No one came.

Finally, Stacie got to Aunt Me's house on Fern Dell, a little cul-de-sac off Canyon View. With a shaking hand, she opened the side door to the garage to hide her bike. Legs threatening to buckle, she stumbled down the stairs to the front door.

When Amelia opened it to Stacie's frantic pounding and shouting, Stacie fell sobbing into her aunt's arms. It took more than half an hour for Stacie to calm down enough to tell Amelia what had happened. Her aunt held her close and let her cry. But beneath the softness, Stacie felt steel. Amelia had seen the hand print, still livid, on Stacie's face.

"You're safe here, Stasha. You'll stay with me."

"But she'll make me go back!" Stacie cried out. "What will I do?"

"You won't go back," Amelia told her calmly. "I'll see to that."

Stacie looked at Amelia with the first hope she'd felt since she'd woken in the dark. "Really?"

"Really."

A sense of calm descended on Stacie. She nodded. "Okay. I won't be any trouble. I promise."

Amelia smiled. "You've never been any trouble, Stasha," she said, giving her a hug. "Now. You need some nice hot tea, with lots of sugar. Maybe some toast with sugar and cinnamon?"

Stacie never did go back to the house on Sky Vista. Later that morning, Amelia woke her, told Stacie she was going out, that Stacie was to stay in the house and was not to answer the door for any reason, to anyone.

"But school?"

"No school today," Amelia told her. "You can get breakfast later? I may be gone a few hours."

Stacie's panic rose, but Amelia calmed her. "You're safe here, Stasha. I'll be back. Everything is locked. No one can get in. Just don't answer the door. Pretend there's no one home if anyone comes. No matter how loudly or how often they knock. Do not answer." She smiled. "Pretend you're invisible. Can you do that?"

"What if they break a window?"

"No one will break a window. You will be perfectly safe as long as you're quieter than a mouse and you don't answer the door. *For anyone*. Not even if they say they're police. Promise?"

Stacie nodded. "I promise."

"Good. Now, I have to go. Close the drapes after I lock the door."

With a kiss to Stacie's forehead, Amelia was gone, waiting only to see that Stacie pulled the drapes. Only then did Stacie realize that all the drapes in the house were closed.

That was when Stacie discovered the way light fell through the skylight in the tiny hall between the bedrooms. It set the rag rug there glowing. She closed the bathroom and bedroom doors, then dragged the big wing chair across the arch between the hall and the living room. At the last moment, she got the big scrying crystal from the fountain and took it into the hall with her. With the protective chair in place, it became her magic cave. She watched the light play through the crystal, throwing rainbows, painting the walls with color. It was the safest place in the world.

She slept a bit on the rug, the crocheted blanket over her. She crawled out once, made toast with peanut butter and jam and brought it and a glass of chocolate milk into the cave with her. At one point, she heard angry voices. Someone clattered down the steps from the street onto the patio. For a bad few moments, as Pamela pounded on the door, shouting, Stacie panicked. But she did what Aunt Me had told her. She sat quietly in the soft light, clung to the crystal and pretended she was invisible. Eventually, Pamela had left.

Amelia finally came home about mid-afternoon. Stacie

was curled in the wing chair reading a book she'd found about a wizard and little people who lived in holes with round doors. She was pretending she was a hobbit when the key rattled in the door.

"Stasha? Honey, it's me. Are you hungry?"

Stacie pushed the chair aside as the smell of pizza floated into the cave.

As they ate, Amelia told her she would not be going back to live with Pamela and Chuck. She'd live with Amelia. Only many years later did Stacie learn how Amelia had threatened Chuck, who had political aspirations, with exposure as a pedophile.

Stacie had seen her mother only once after that, at the hearing where she gave all custody of Stacie to Amelia. When the judge had asked Pamela if she was sure, Pamela had told him, "The witch can have her. She's been nothing but trouble to me."

Soon after, Pamela and Chuck sold the house in Eden Beach and moved to LA. Stacie had no idea what had happened to them. She didn't care. She had stopped caring about her mother that dark night when she'd slapped Stacie for telling stories.

It had been many years before Stacie wondered how she'd known about Clarey.

Now she stood in the house that had been Amelia's remembering that ten-year-old's terror. The awful isolation of being alone.

This time there was no Aunt Me. She truly was on her own.

Stacie set her tea down on the counter and held her crystal between her hands. She calmed herself as much as she could, then sent her intuition outward. In the distance, she heard a few cars. A mockingbird sang a night-time song of love in a dark canyon far away.

The crystal remained calm except for the faint buzzing that confirmed what she knew. Troy was still a threat, but he wasn't anywhere close.

Knowing that cleared her mind. Her breath, her heart, and her mind settled.

She thought.

Troy's call was meant to rattle her, she realized. If she was frightened, she might not think clearly, might make mistakes, become his victim.

His victim.

She'd known all along that he was dangerous. But this was more than stalking. This was... It was... Whatever it was, it was far too scary to think about right now.

How would she convince the police he was a threat?

Detective Robard will believe me, she thought.

Intuition or hope? she wondered.

It didn't matter right now. He wasn't here. She had to depend on herself.

So think, she told herself.

Avoid being alone, she thought, rolling the crystal between her palms.

That would be difficult. This was tax season. She spent many late nights in the office, working on returns.

She was alone right now.

But she was locked up tight. She had to be content that she was secure, at least for the night. She'd sleep with her phone. Monday she'd call a security company for both the store and the house.

There goes my bathroom renovation.

A rational thought. She was calming down.

Don't be predictable, was her next thought.

Running a store, that, too would be difficult, but she could change other patterns.

Tomorrow—today—was Sunday. Her friend Gayle, in Pasadena, had been asking Stacie to spend a weekend so they could go to the Huntington Library. Stacie would call her later this morning and see if she was free today.

She had a tour at the botanical garden on Monday. It was too late to switch with someone, but she could let security know about Troy. Maybe one of them could walk along with her group. She'd let the staff and other docents know, too.

Stacie winced. She felt like Chicken Little, crying the sky was falling. She'd always hated the story about the idiot bird who couldn't tell a falling acorn from the end of the world.

I'd rather look a fool than end up dead.

She froze. The crystal cut into her hand, she was squeezing it so tightly.

End up dead.

Was that what she feared from Troy?

Was the sky falling?

For a moment, two, she didn't move.

Then ten-year-old Stasha, who'd screamed away one predator, stood up in her heart, and Stacie became angry.

How dare he? she thought as anger and resentment flickered.

She would not be driven from her home. She would not be driven from her shop. She would not allow him to hunt her and terrorize her.

She would, however, be smart. She'd stay safe this weekend, and Tuesday, when she got to the shop, she'd call Detective Robard.

She tucked her crystal into her jeans and took a deep breath.

What about tonight?

Tonight, she would try to sleep.

"Bananas." The dog woke and rolled onto his stomach. "Come." The dog lurched to his feet, wagging his tail.

"You're sleeping with me tonight." She reached for the knife stand on the counter and pulled out the largest knife she owned.

"Come," she told the dog again and went toward the bedroom, leaving all the lights burning.

FOURTEEN

B<small>EN WAS AT THE SIDE TABLE, HELPING HIMSELF TO COFFEE</small> when a hearty slap on the shoulder announced Tucker.

"Ben! How goes it at the cop shop?" Tucker boomed.

"Still fighting for truth, justice and the American way," Ben told him reaching out to grip Tucker's hand.

Tucker looked significantly at the plate in Ben's hand. "Thought you were swearing off the goodies."

"Trying," said Ben, "But Maureen's cookies should be listed as a Class A narcotic. Impossible to kick the habit." He shook his head as Tucker laughed. "Besides. Been a shitty weekend."

"Last time I saw you, life was weird."

"This isn't weird. Some asshole keyed my car."

"Seriously?" Tucker's eyebrows shot to his hairline. "Not a parking lot thing?"

"No, this wasn't a shopping cart. It was done sometime Saturday night while I was parked at the curb in my neighborhood. It was gouged pretty good, too, in some places. More like a screwdriver than a key."

"What kind of a moron would do that to a cop's car?"

"Oh, I'm pretty sure I know who did it," Ben told him, irritation in his voice. "A somebody who was pretty wound up. The trouble is, I can't prove it."

"Who'd you piss off?"

"That's what really gets me," said Ben half in jest. "Remember Huff, the con man I told you about? When we busted him, it was Cruz who cuffed him. Cruz he was swearing to get even with." Tucker started to laugh. "So how the hell did I get sucked into this? And how did he find me?" Ben snapped off a bite of cookie, chewed and swallowed. "Must have had to work pretty damned hard to do it. Maybe he should work that hard at a legitimate job," he said, brushing crumbs away from his mouth.

"Probably didn't have to work that hard. A lot on the Internet," said Tucker.

Ben snorted. "Internet. Makes so many problems for us, you wouldn't believe." He bit off another chunk of cookie.

"Look on the bright side. A few gouges in the paint probably improves the look of your POS." The corners of Tucker's eyes were crinkling as he tried not to laugh.

"Just because it's not a black, chrome-covered SUV doesn't mean it's a POS," Ben told him. Then Tucker did laugh.

Ben shook his head. "Vandals," he said. "As bad as Internet trolls and hackers. Hide in the dark, lash out, then crawl back into their holes. Bunch of cowards." Ben looked around the room, then back at Tucker. "That's why I hate terrorists. I don't give a damn what their cause is. They're just cowards armed with guns or bombs instead of spray paint and screwdrivers. Glorified murderers killing people at random." *Children. People shopping, going to concerts. People planning weddings,* Ben thought. He had no sympathy for the killers who died during the course of their killing sprees. *Good riddance*, he thought. *If only they'd killed themselves first.*

Tucker gripped Ben's shoulder. "Yeah. I know."

"Hey, Ben. Tucker." A guy about Ben's age was heading toward the refreshment table.

"Hey, Justin," Ben replied. Justin was an Iraq vet, too. They'd talked often when Ben first got back. "Stay away from the cookies. They'll ruin you for Mrs. Fields'."

"Too late," said Justin. "I'm already parked at the curb in front of Tuck's house every day. I've got a standing order with Maureen." He grinned and slapped his stomach. "Can't you tell?" He walked on.

Ben and Tucker headed to a table in a corner. Ben spotted Christa, a Navy helicopter pilot, and raised a hand. She waved back.

"You know," said Ben, as they scraped chairs back and dropped into them, "I've always thought vandalism was just a nuisance thing. Nobody is hurt." He remembered Cruz saying the same thing to Stacie at her shop. "But now I get it. I understand why people are pissed off when it happens."

"Makes you want to punch someone, but there's no one to punch."

Ben nodded and reached for his coffee. "Pretty much."

They sat for a while and watched the room.

For Ben, as for the other vets, such as Justin and Christa, the twice-weekly meetings gave them a place to talk to others who had shared the same experiences or had the same difficulties re-entering civilian life after the military. It allowed them to continue the kind of camaraderie they'd had in the service.

"Small turnout tonight," Ben leaning back.

"Some sort of game on TV tonight," said Tucker. "Game of Thrones or something?" Ben laughed. "You know me," Tucker went on. "If it's not football, I'm not interested."

"Yeah. I heard Maureen was lining up her boy toy already." Tucker's wife always joked that she planned her gigolo getaways to coincide with football season because Tucker never noticed she was gone. "What is it this year?"

Tucker hid a grin behind his beard. "A series of ceramic workshops somewhere back east. Works for me. I mainline football. She does the hard training. Then she teaches me what she's learned afterward." He took a big swallow of coffee. "Wins all around."

"I can't decide if you're born lazy or studied for it," said Ben.

"Born this way," said Tucker. "Too much work to study for it."

Ben guffawed.

Tucker, despite claiming to be lazy, had worked very hard to expand the vet gatherings, bringing in speakers, seeing that services for vets were available in Eden Beach. He'd worked with Alain Robard to sweet talk the hospital into providing many of those services, and into giving them the space to meet. Besides Maureen's cookies, there were always sandwiches, fruit and hot soup Tucker had strong-armed from local restaurants. For a few of the vets, it was the only place to get a good meal. There were always brochures out about drug abuse and alcoholism, counseling for PTSD and suicide prevention. Counseling offices were just down the hall, and counselors made a point of coming in, becoming familiar faces to the vets, building trust for those who were ready to reach out for help. Maureen, or another local artist, came in every week offering classes for vets and their families.

Tonight, there was no program. Ben had just come down the coast to visit with Tucker and other friends. After an hour or so, he was finishing his third cup of coffee and rising to leave, when a man walked in, someone he hadn't seen before.

The newcomer paused in the door and looked around.

"New guy," said Tucker, standing up next to Ben. "Guess I should say hi, break the ice."

Ben automatically filed away the new vet's details. Good-looking. About Ben's height. Straight, medium-brown hair cut short. He was well built but not overly muscled, from what Ben could see under the camo jacket and jeans. There was an arrogance to his walk, though, a slight smirk to his mouth, like he thought he was smarter than anyone else. It put Ben's hackles up. It was a look Ben saw too often on the con men they investigated. Smug. Sneaky. Contemptuous of the people they cheated.

Ben disliked him immediately, though he tried not to show it. The name on the jacket read: Fowler. As he got closer, Ben noted his pale blue eyes behind wire-rimmed glasses.

Tucker held out a hand. "Tucker Hayes. Welcome."

"Carson Fowler."

"Glad you could make it. How'd you hear about us?"

"Buddy of mine mentioned it. Thought I'd drop in."

"Well, you're welcome." Tucker smiled at him, but Ben noticed that Fowler kept looking at *him*.

Fowler put out his hand. "You are?"

It was more demand than request. Ben's hackles rose higher.

Tucker was making the introduction. "Ben Robard. Good friend of mine. Iraq."

"Pleasure," said Fowler as Ben, reluctantly, shook hands. "I was in Iraq, too."

He's lying, thought Ben, and wondered how he knew that.

"Anything in particular bring you in?" Tucker asked Fowler.

"Understand you've got some kind of job referral service. Been having trouble finding work."

"We do," Tucker told him, gesturing across the room. "Hal Marsdale. VA."

"What's your line?" Fowler asked Ben, ignoring Tucker. Again, Ben felt it was a demand.

He was pleased to see Fowler recoil when he said, "Police officer."

"Being modest," said Tucker. "He's a detective with Eden Beach. Been there for years. MP before that."

Ben hadn't taken his eyes from Fowler. *Something's off there*, he thought. It was something working behind Fowler's eyes. Cruz would have said he was getting hunches.

In this instance, though, he was sure she'd agree with him. Fowler was some kind of lowlife. Ben felt it in his gut. He'd seen guys like this in Iraq. Not many, thankfully. Guys who'd come spoiling for a fight. Waiting to exert power. Waiting to kill.

Cowards and bullies, hiding behind the uniform.

He didn't like them then. He didn't like this one now.

"What kind of work you looking for?" Tucker was asking.

"I'm good with numbers," said Fowler, almost defiantly. "Kind of hoping to find work with an accountant. Work my way up." He looked directly at Ben.

"VA rep can probably give you information on that," said Ben, nodding toward Marsdale who was talking to another vet.

There was an undeniable flash of anger on Fowler's face. He'd heard the dismissal in Ben's voice.

"Thanks," said Fowler, sarcasm in his tone. "I'll check it

out." He spun and walked off without another word to Tucker.

"Well, that was a pissing contest and no mistake," said Tucker. "What was that all about?"

Ben gave a small shrug, as he watched Fowler stalk across the room. He saw the VA rep take a step back before shaking hands.

"Something's not right there," Ben told Tucker.

"Yeah, he is a bit rough," said Tucker. "But since he was in Iraq, maybe you could help him soften some of those edges."

Ben paused. "No, Tucker. Not that one." He shook his head, just as Fowler glanced over at them.

"Okay then," said Tucker.

Ben reached out for his friend's hand. "I'm calling it a night," he said. "See you next week, if not before?"

"Yep," said Tucker as his hand enveloped Ben's. "I'm always here."

As Ben turned to leave, he saw Fowler throw another look his way.

Nope, Tucker, he thought again, *definitely not that one*.

TROY

A fucking cop! She blows me off but lets that prick of a cop sniff around? That's bullshit!

What kind of a faggot name is Robard, anyway? Look at him. What a pussy. Not even man enough to drive. Just hands that Spic bitch the car keys.

What do you expect? He's probably a Spic, too. Pussy whipped.

Where does he get off, blowing me off like that? Telling me to talk to the VA guy. Like I'd take any half-assed job the VA has to offer? Like I'd be stupid enough to go into the Army. All that bullshit about IDs and records. Some ball-buster telling you what to do all the time. Fuck that.

Bet he never thought someone would cut up his car like that.

But a cop. Never done a cop before. Yeah. That could be a rush.

Yeah, but cops get pissed when you off one of theirs. Bunch of little whores, they don't look too hard. But hit a cop, you get problems.

Stay calm. Stay cool. You get upset, things happen,

remember? They make you do things you don't want to do. They fuck up the plan.

Like that stupid blond bitch. Called me little man. Scratched me.

She got hers, though. I made her pay. She tried to screw it all up. But I stuck to the plan. Had that fire road scoped out way ahead, stupid bitch. No one's ever gonna find her, because I'm smart. Careful. No one's gonna call me stupid again. Not like that pumped up faggot screwing my old lady. Surprised him, didn't I? Knife almost took his fucking leg off. Now who's stupid?

Fucking Angelina.

Now this bitch.

You're pissing me off, Anastasia. Hanging up on me. Blowing me off. Cheating with your pussy men. You need a lesson. Oh, yeah. And I'm just the man to teach you. You'll never misbehave again. Ever.

Things happen when I get angry, Anastasia. If you bitches wouldn't piss me off, things wouldn't happen. But you never get it.

And where the fuck is she?

Wouldn't have lost her if I could set up near that house. But, oh, no. Fucking asshole had to come out and act like a big bad-ass. Fuck. Like he owns the street. Standing there staring, gun at his side. Like he's so scary. I'll fix him. Later.

Even so. I almost had her. I was right on her tail. Then that asshole cut me off.

She's probably fucking some loser, like that rent-a-cop at that place she's always going to. Now there's a limp dick. But it'd be like her. Throwing all her pussy friends in my face. Like that faggot cop.

Almost caught that one the other night, too. If that faggot cop hadn't distracted me, I would have caught him. If this piece of shit truck would turn tighter. Could have gotten rid of one of her pals, anyway. Then she'd know she shouldn't fuck with me. What a loser.

I'll have to teach him a lesson.

Oh, Anastasia, baby. You're going to be so surprised to find out what it's like to be with a real man.

Redheads. Hot and horny in bed, but always fucking with your head.

Just like Angelina. Another red-haired bitch. Screwing every guy that comes near her. You could just tell. Even the perv. Can't tell me they're not fucking. He's over at her place enough.

Angelina. We should have been together forever.

She called me a pervert.

Don't think about that. Can't think about that. Can't lose focus.

Are you getting excited, Anastasia, about what's going to happen? I left you a message. Oh, baby. Just wait.

Shit! Fucking red-haired bitch! Where are you? I'm tired of waiting. Got the fire up. Ready for action. Need the action! Should've been in that bitch's pants days ago. Tired of fucking waiting!

Be cool. Be cool. Stick to the plan. Like the last one. Last one is nice and safe. Cops'll never find her. No one'll find her. She's gone, gone.

Maybe a little appetizer. Something small. Quick. Yeah. Feed the fire. Calm me down. Don't want to make a mistake. Not with Anastasia. Gotta be cool. Been waiting too long. Want to enjoy it.

Can't stay on this street any more. That bitch dyke at the restaurant keeps watching me. And that goddamn wino in the bushes last night.

Gotta find some place. Some place private. Maybe an empty house. Where we can take our time.

I'll show her. No one plays games with me.

Then after. After, yeah, I'll take that sucker down. Mr. Scary.

I'll fix that cop, too.

FIFTEEN

IT WAS TUESDAY BEFORE BEN GOT AROUND TO CHECKING patrol reports. He found the reports of vandalism on Stacie's shop and a prowler report from two weeks before.

Another one Saturday, he noted. *Probably me.*

Ben hoped the person who'd called it in hadn't gotten his license. That would be embarrassing. He cringed to think what Cruz would say.

He found Kelly Meissner kicked back at her desk, one ankle-booted foot on a pulled out drawer. Tall, blond, older than Ben, younger than Cruz, Meissner had formerly worked LAPD. She'd joined the Eden Beach department the year after Ben.

He told her about the fraud complaint at the crystal shop and asked about the vandalism.

"The crystal shop owner said it started when that fanatical church moved in up near the freeway," he added.

"Yeah, it did. The Holy Star Evangelical Church. They moved in about six, eight weeks ago. The vandalism started not long after that."

"They've given up on anonymity," said Ben. "When we

got there the other day, there were a bunch of protesters in front, waving signs. Yelling stuff."

Meissner sighed and ran a hand through her cropped hair. "Yeah. I heard. Not about the crystal shop. They were outside the bookstore over the weekend." She grinned. "The store owner didn't take it lying down. Came out with a hose to 'wash the sidewalk' while they were there. Gather they were using all kinds of Biblical language against her."

"Yeah, Ms Cappella said there were others getting hit."

Meissner nodded. "The acupuncturist on Mockingbird and the crystal shop are getting the worst of it. They're both on streets where there's little traffic late at night. The bookstore on Canyon and the psychic on the highway have gotten some grief, but they're more visible. We're more likely to bust them there."

"I kind of get why they're targeting the crystals place and the psychic, but why the acupuncturist and the bookstore?"

"Matt Harrelson's a pretty outspoken gay rights activist," Kelly told him. "And Jacqui Runion runs a banned books campaign. Features controversial books and authors prominently every month. The one over the weekend was a reading by a transgender author."

"Ah," said Ben, and hesitated. "I don't suppose it would do any good to have a word with whoever the minister is up there?"

Meissner shook her head. "Right after all this started, I tried that. Went up there. Listened. Pretty inflammatory stuff. Talked to the preacher. The Reverend Obadiah Hammond. Tall guy, gray hair. Trying to look like Billy Graham, remember him?"

Ben nodded.

"No finger pointing, just told him the trouble. I said maybe some folks were taking his sermons the wrong way.

He got his back up about religious freedom and freedom of speech. Said he'd sue the police department."

"And?"

"I talked to our lawyers. It's pretty shaky ground. All we can do is send the patrols by all the locations more often. Which we're doing. The crystal store owner has been particularly good about reporting and documenting the incidents. But I keep telling her that until we catch them…" She held her hands out helplessly.

"Nada," Ben finished for her.

"'Fraid so."

"When we were there the other morning, some of the signs said 'Death to Faggots.' Sounds pretty threatening." Though Colin had been more angry than intimidated, thought Ben.

"Were you here when we had that case up in LA?" asked Kelly. "Some loony going around the businesses in a strip mall, yelling obscenities, saying God had instructed him to cleanse the Earth?"

Ben shook his head.

"Merchants were freaked out. They called LAPD repeatedly to complain. But we were in the same position. It was just words. Our hands were tied until he actually did something." She sighed. "So he did. He came back with a gun and put five bullets into a teenaged girl working there. Killed her. Then we could lock him up."

"Shit."

"Yeah. I know."

Ben crossed his arms and leaned on the cubicle wall. "Is that what we're looking at here?" he asked her. "Could it escalate to that? I mean, with them actively protesting now?"

She made a skeptical face. "Doesn't feel like it," said Meissner. "Right now, it *is* just words. Harassment, with the picketing. Minor vandalism. Frankly, I think they're trying to provoke a confrontation with police or the press to get publicity to build their church membership or raise money."

Ben felt queasy. He'd floated the same idea to Cruz about Stacie.

"I guess we have to wait then."

"Unfortunately, yes. Unless we can catch them."

Ben changed the subject.

"Did you know that, on top of all this, Ms Cappella's being stalked?"

"Yeah," said Meissner. "Cruz told me. And Ms Cappella called this morning."

A relief he didn't examine too closely washed through him. Stacie had taken their advice and reported the stalker.

Then Meissner went on. "Apparently the guy called over the weekend." Ben tensed. "Freaked her out. Understandably. He called on an unlisted landline still billed to her aunt. Had her hiding out with friends all weekend."

"She just called *today*?" Ben was incredulous. "Why the hell did she wait?"

"Said she wanted to talk to me directly. But that's not all. When she got into her store this morning, she discovered it had been vandalized again. We had a report after midnight Saturday from a neighbor who saw someone climb over the fence from the store's yard, then cut along the side of her apartment building to the street."

Not me, thought Ben, then frowned.

"Has there ever been vandalism in the back before?"

"Nope. Always the street side. And this is different. Take a look."

Meissner dropped her foot to the floor, leaned forward, opened her e-mail program and brought up a picture. "Her friend sent this to me."

It was the garden in the back of The Bell, Book and Crystal. A bunch of female statues were lying down. Rocks had been set on top of them. It made Ben's skin crawl.

"I told her to leave them. We'd get someone out to document it. Later this morning, I hope.

"But there was a note on the back door, too." Meissner scrolled down the e-mail to a photo of handwriting on a torn piece of paper. "'You think you're clever. But I'm watching you,'" she read.

"Stalker." It wasn't a question.

She nodded. "That would be my guess. I'm going out later to talk to her about it, but I have to finish this first." She gestured to a report on her computer screen.

"What's that?" asked Ben.

"More squatters." The financial crash in 2008 had bankrupted a lot of people in Eden Beach and left lots of homes sitting empty. Now that the economy was picking up, realtors wanted to show the houses, but kept finding squatters in them.

"Much damage?"

"When it's just people looking for a place to sleep, not usually. Some have kids. But this," she made a face, "Yeah. Looks like meth heads. They trashed the place. It's going to take a lot of clean up to make it saleable. If it even can be."

"If you're going to be tied up," Ben said, offhandedly. "We were just about to head out. We have to go right by the crystal shop." *Cruz'll be surprised to hear that*, he thought. "We can stop and talk to Ms Cappella for you."

"Thanks, Ben. That would be great," said Meissner, smiling gratefully. "She was pretty upset. And this is going to take a while." She waved again at the screen.

"No problem," said Ben.

"Do you have a camera in the car?"

"We do. We'll let you know what we find out." He turned and went to get Cruz.

She looked up as he got to her desk and grinned. "I'm guessing that look on your face means you found out how much it's going to cost to repaint the Camry."

"Just be glad it wasn't your new Prius," said Ben, "You're the one who busted Huff." He grabbed the car keys from her desk. "Come on." He made a U-turn and left her cubicle.

"Hey!" she called after him. "What? Where are you going?"

"The crystal shop."

"I beg your pardon?"

Ben raised his right hand, rattled the keys and kept walking.

"Oh, no, you don't," she said grabbing her jacket and trotting after him. She didn't see Ben smile to himself.

"HE CALLED on an unlisted landline still in her aunt's name?" asked Cruz in disbelief. "He's digging pretty deep to find that."

"Yeah," said Ben, who had won the tug of war and was behind the wheel.

He felt Cruz's eyes on him. "And you think the damage in the garden is part of it. Not the vandals."

"Yes, I do."

"Is that a hunch?" He could feel Cruz smile.

"You didn't see the pictures. Kelly thinks it's him, too."

"Shit," said Cruz, her voice serious.

"Yep."

"So. You want to tell me why, exactly, we're doing this rather than leaving it to Meissner? Or Breckenridge?"

Why, indeed? Ben thought.

"We do have our own workload to handle, you know," she added.

"Meissner can't get out there right now." Ben hoped he didn't sound defensive. "She's tied up with the squatters. If this guy's escalating, the sooner we get on to him, the better. So I told her we'd stop by."

Cruz didn't say anything, but he knew she was smiling.

"And," she said, "you want to see her again."

"Cruz," he said warningly.

She laughed. "You are so transparent. I don't know why I thought you were hard to read."

Ben cut his eyes to her but didn't respond. He was trying not to admit to himself that his reason for returning wasn't entirely professional.

"It's okay," said Cruz, still grinning. "My hunch says she'll be glad to see you, too."

Ben clenched his teeth. If he argued, it would only get worse.

They were quiet for a few blocks as Ben navigated the one-way streets through fog so thick the streetlights had not yet gone off. He hit the wipers periodically as the droplets condensed on the windshield.

"Lauren," he finally said. She turned toward him. "Is it worth it? What we do?"

His partner was quiet. He knew she was frowning. "What brought this on?"

"Just sometimes… It's like Huff. He gets out, maybe jumps bail. Father loses the money. Then what? He goes somewhere else. We never make a dent—robbery, burglary. The vandals. Even the killer Danner and Breckenridge are after." Ben raised a hand from the wheel, then dropped it back. "How many has he killed? How many more before he's caught?"

Cruz studied him. "It's nothing new," she said. "What's really biting you?"

Ben sighed. "It's just that sometimes… It seems like there should be more."

"You mean the pension isn't pay off enough?"

He glanced at her, saw a small grin.

"Okay, yeah. I know what you mean. And yeah, sometimes I wonder, too," she said. She was quiet for a moment or two. "But somebody has to try, Ben," she finally added. "And sometimes… Sometimes we win."

"I guess," he said. He turned onto Glen Eden.

And pulled abruptly to the curb.

"What the hell is all this?" said Cruz.

SIXTEEN

"Is she coming?" asked Colin.

"Not right now," said Stacie, her voice tight.

"Why not?" asked Mir, her voice shaking only a little.

"She has to finish something she's in the middle of. She said she'd come as soon as she could." Stacie's fingers were curled in Bananas' fur.

"We can't just leave the garden like it is," said Mir. "What will customers say?"

"I don't think we have any choice," Stacie told her.

"I'm going to take more photos," said Colin.

Stacie nodded. "Just don't move anything."

"I'll put the tea on," said Mir.

"I'm not hungry," said Stacie, as Colin opened the sliding door.

"Well, I am," he threw over his shoulder.

"You always are," Mir called back to him. She turned to Stacie. "Come on. We'd better try those cookies before Colin eats them all."

"I heard that." Colin's voice floated in from outside.

A few minutes later, Colin joined them in the kitchen.

"You know, that is seriously perverted shit back there," he said. "How did he even get in? He had to climb over the fence. Even I'd have a hard time doing that."

Stacie smiled wanly. "My friend Spidey."

"I'm serious, Stace. I'm good with board fences."

"Misspent youth?"

"Nothing misspent about it," Colin told her. "I enjoyed every minute."

She knew Colin was trying to distract her. He was as angry—and as upset—as she was. As they all were. She glanced at Mir.

"Are you okay?" she asked the younger woman.

"I just want him caught. And jailed. Forever," said Mir.

"Hear, hear," muttered Colin as they all sat down.

They were critiquing a range of Greek cookies when noise started coming from the front of the store.

"Oh, no," moaned Stacie. "I thought maybe they'd gone for good." She jumped as there was a loud *crack* against the front window.

"What the fuck?" said Colin. There were more hollow thuds as missiles hit the siding.

Stacie looked at Colin. "They're throwing eggs. Mir, call 911. Tell them we're being vandalized right now. We need the police. Colin, grab your phone. I want a record of this."

"My pleasure," he said grimly.

Stacie was halfway to the front door, Bananas at her side, when the scene outside stopped her in her tracks. Another egg cracked into the window, spilling its yolk and bits of shell down the glass.

"*Madre santa e tutti gli angeli*," she whispered.

Today, there had to be at least two dozen people gathered in front of her store, chanting "Burn, witch, burn!" More were getting out of a car at the curb.

In rhythm with the chant, a balding, middle-aged man pumped a sign up and down that read, "Be not defiled by witches!" A dark-haired young woman held a sign in one hand that said, "They shall stone them with stones." Her other hand held the wrist of her daughter. The girl couldn't have been more than four, but she was chanting along with her mother. Stacie saw another mother offer her first-grade-sized son a carton of eggs. He took two and hurled them at the storefront.

"They have children with them!" she said to Colin in disbelief.

But it was their faces, twisted with hate, that staggered Stacie.

Across the street, veiled by the fog, several people were gathered in a knot, watching. A car slowed as it passed, the driver gawking out the window.

"Holy crap!" muttered Colin.

A tall gray-haired man in an expensive suit separated himself from the crowd, and strutted up the walk toward the store. Several people followed him.

"Is the door locked?" asked Colin urgently.

"Yes," said Stacie.

The man did not try the door, but stood on the stoop and turned to the crowd.

"Brothers and sisters! We are here today in the name of the Righteous!" he shouted. Stacie and Colin could hear him clearly in the store. "We bring a warning. The followers of Satan are here, in this town. And right here," he flung his arm toward Stacie's store, "right here, one of his brazen hand-maidens claims to see the future! Blasphemy! Only the one true God knows the future. And he vouchsafes it to no man!"

"Glory to God!" shouted a blond man in the crowd.

"This witch," the man continued, with growing contempt

in his voice, "claims to heal with the laying on of 'magic' stones and crystals. Evil lies! A trap for the unrighteous!"

"Amen!" shouted someone in the crowd.

"That grace is not given to some red-haired bride of Satan! Only the merciful Jesus can heal with his mighty hands! The word of God, recorded in His Holy Bible, tells us this! And we do not doubt!"

"Amen, Reverend, amen!"

"Yet she does not stop at that! There is no evil this witch will not stoop to. Like all her kind, she can murder unborn babies in the womb with her poisonous herbs and dark sacrifices!"

"Burn, witch, burn!" screamed the crowd.

"That lying bastard," muttered Stacie.

"She consorts with all manner of debauched and depraved demons masquerading as humans. But we know them! They pervert God's law with their talk of unholy *love*," scorn dripped from his words, "between two men or two women!

"God has ordained that we stop them! We must drive these blasphemers, these fornicators and children of Satan into the sea! In the Holy Name of God!" the gray-haired man shouted, throwing his head back and punching both fists into the air.

"Amen!"

"Drive them out!"

"*Glory* to God!"

Stacie heard Mir talking to the 911 dispatcher. "About twenty of them. Maybe more," she said, her voice shaking. "They're throwing things and screaming at us." She paused. "Yes, of course, I'm frightened! You should see these people!"

Stacie's fear morphed into anger, like lava exploding into

the volcano's throat. Her face hardened as she headed toward the door.

"Stacie, I don't think that's a good idea..." Colin was saying, but Stacie didn't hear him.

"Shit," muttered Colin and went after her.

Stacie threw open the door and went out on the stoop. Bananas, like a black torpedo, shot out behind her. He barked once before she caught his collar to keep him from charging the crowd.

The gray-haired man spun to face her. He produced a nasty smile.

"Get off my property. Now," Stacie told him, her quiet voice vibrating with fury. "You're trespassing."

"Behold the witch!" The gray-haired man flung his arm toward her. "Behold her familiar! Beelzebub incarnate!"

Bananas was rigid under Stacie's hand, his tail perfectly straight behind him. Stacie felt him rumbling low in his chest.

"Get off my property," she said again more loudly, taking a step closer to the leader. "You are trespassing."

The man heard the low-throated growl and glanced at Bananas whose lip twitched, showing a strong set of teeth. He took one step down.

Stacie saw someone rise from a crouch next to the fence, spray paint can in his hand. "What the hell are you doing?" she shouted at him. "Destruction of property is a crime!"

An egg whistled by her. It hit something next to her. "Death to faggots!" a woman screamed.

"Yeah, yeah. Fuck you, too," Colin muttered. Stacie glanced sideways. Egg yolk rolled down his sleeve. "Got you, bitch," she heard him murmur as he slowly panned the group with his phone, recording video. "Film at eleven."

"And that is assault!" Stacie was shaking, but was surprised to discover her mind was crystal clear.

"Excuse me! Clear the walk, please," she heard a familiar voice. Eileen was trying to force her way through the crowd.

"You have no right to block my business," Stacie shouted at the crowd. "Now all of you, get off my property!"

"Or you'll what?" taunted a man. Another egg hit the siding behind Stacie just as she saw a woman shoulder-butt Eileen and scream into her face, "Those who associate with witches will burn!"

The world faded to dark, then became brilliantly clear. Everyone in the crowd was haloed in light. Anger drained from Stacie and peace settled on her.

She pointed at the man who had shouted. "Or I will tell you the day, hour and manner of your death," Stacie called to him, her voice calm and clear.

"Oh, no," Colin muttered next to her, but she hardly heard him.

Stacie turned to the woman with the little girl as the crowd started to fall silent. "I know that the true parents of the child you have stolen search for her even now." The woman faltered in her chanting, and her face went white.

"Witch! Bride of darkness!" the gray-haired man yelled in her face, as the heavy engine of a police cruiser stopped across the street. "God says thou shalt not suffer a witch to live! God will burn you!"

Stacie turned to him, her eyes dilated so wide there was just a rim of green around her pupils. He took a step back, down another step.

"I will say to these people that you cheat them. You spend their money in the casinos and brothels of Las Vegas, where you have built your mansion," she said, her clear, calm voice carrying to the back of the now-silent crowd. "I will say to them that you are wanted for fraud in Austin. And Lincoln. That your families there are left destitute."

The leader's eyes narrowed, but there was fear as well as anger in his face.

"Okay, folks someone want to tell me what's going on here?" A tall, dark-skinned police officer stepped onto the curb.

Some of the people in the crowd started to edge away. "Nope, nobody leave, please. We need statements from all of you," called his wiry blond partner.

Eileen pushed through the crowd toward Stacie.

"A woman that hath a familiar spirit shall surely be put to death. Their blood shall be upon them!" hissed the gray-haired man, as one of his followers pulled him away from Stacie.

"Excuse me, Reverend. Care to repeat that?" Stacie heard Ben Robard's voice.

"Stacie?" Colin murmured in her ear. "Stace?" His hand was warm on her cold skin. "Best you come inside now."

"Yes, I think so, too." Eileen was at her other side. "I've got Godzilla. Go with Colin, now."

The world's brightness started to fade. Stacie blinked. Suddenly, she had the worst headache of her life. She began shaking.

"You cannot stop us exercising our right to free speech and peaceful assembly!" Stacie heard someone shouting.

"Not so peaceful," she heard a voice... Detective Cruz?... saying. "Vandalism. Destruction of property. Assault. Threats of bodily harm. Not to mention trespassing."

Stacie let her friends lead her back inside while the police moved through the crowd, and the members of the Holy Star Evangelical Church tried to slide anonymously away.

"Excuse me, sir. Stay right there..."

The sounds muted as Colin closed the door behind them.

"Come sit down," said Eileen.

"In a minute," said Stacie. She went to the large smoky crystal at the end of the sales counter, laid both hands on it and rested her forehead against the smooth stone. She closed her eyes and tried to focus only on the cool surface of the quartz.

"I'll get her some tea," she heard Mir say.

Breathe. In. Out. Stacie thought. *In. Out.*

"Did you hear what they were saying? What a bunch of bottom feeders. But I got it all on video. Close-ups of all their faces, too." Colin was saying gleefully. "I can't wait to post it online."

"I don't know where people find that kind of hate," Eileen told him. "And to bring children..."

"I'm so glad the police came," Mir said. "Maybe they'll stop harassing us now."

"They're the kind of people who have attorneys on speed dial," Colin snorted. "I'm sure they'll claim religious freedom. They totally ruined this jacket. And it's new."

In. Out, thought Stacie. *Breathe.*

Slowly, the shaking subsided, the crystal taking in the darkness.

She straightened.

"Here." Mir pushed a mug of hot tea into her hand.

"Thank you," she murmured.

"Sit," said Eileen, taking her arm. It wasn't a request.

Stacie sat. Bananas dropped his heavy head on her lap. She laid her hand between his ears, closed her eyes and sipped her tea. The headache began to fade.

"How do you feel?" Eileen asked her quietly.

"Like I've been hit by a truck." Stacie opened her eyes to see her friend kneeling next to her.

"Ah. Back with us. You should have seen your eyes,"

Eileen said, with a faint smile. "I've seen Amelia look the same way, many times."

"I said things..."

"You certainly did."

"Man, their faces!" Colin grinned.

"What? What did she say?" asked Mir.

Eileen raised a hand to stop her and looked daggers at Colin, who closed his mouth.

"*Madre santa e tutti gli angeli.*" Stacie closed her eyes again.

"You'd better figure out what you want to say to the police," said Colin.

"Police?" Her eyes snapped open. "Oh. The police. Shit."

"Lie, is my advice."

"Colin! She can't lie to the police," Eileen told him.

"Why not? Tell them it was all a show. Just as long as none of them saw her eyes."

"Decide fast," said Mir. "They're coming in."

BEN OPENED the door of The Bell, Book and Crystal, letting in both his partner and the welcome scent of the sea. They both stopped and looked at the three friends. Though they were silent, Ben was sure they'd been talking just a moment before.

Stacie was in a chair by the window, clinging to a mug of what looked like tea. The dog stayed next to her, not getting up to greet the detectives, although his tail moved briefly against the floor. Colin, wearing a lime green tank, yellow yoga pants and holding a teal green warm-up jacket, was standing nearby looking far too innocent, thought Ben. The neighbor was crouched next to Stacie, hand on her arm. Near the counter

197

there was a young, multi-racial woman he thought must be Mirabella. Compared to Colin, she was almost conservatively dressed in black stretch capris and a bright purple T-shirt that read, "Well-behaved women seldom make history."

Tuesday. Yoga morning, Ben remembered.

Ben hoped Cruz hadn't heard his intake of breath. It had only been a few days, but it hit him again how beautiful Stacie was. Her auburn hair was up in a ponytail, and she was barefoot. The emerald-green hooded sweatshirt that she was clutching to her as if she were cold, intensified the green of her eyes. Her face was drawn and her freckles stood out starkly against pale skin.

"The patrols are taking people's names," said Ben, tipping his head toward the front of the store. "They'll be in to get statements from all of you as well."

He looked at Stacie. "Are you all right?"

She nodded.

"It wasn't a good idea to confront them like that," he said.

"Someone told her that," murmured Colin.

"It could have turned ugly," Ben went on, ignoring Colin. "You should have waited for the patrols."

Stacie sighed and rubbed her forehead. "You're probably right," she said. "I guess I'd just had enough." She looked up at Ben. "Detective, there were children out there. Little children. Being taught to hate."

"I understand. But 'cursing' them, or threatening to expose them, or whatever you were doing out there, probably didn't make things better."

"No. Maybe not." Stacie massaged her forehead.

Mir saw the gesture. "I'll get you a painkiller."

"I'm not sure it will help, but thanks," Stacie told her.

"The officers outside will take care of those people," Ben continued. "But they're not why Detective Cruz and I are here. Detective Meissner asked us to come by because she couldn't get out here as quickly as she wanted." Cruz, to her credit, did not roll her eyes.

"She said you'd had more vandalism," Ben continued. "And a call over the weekend."

"This isn't the vandals," said Stacie. "It's Troy."

"How do you know?" asked Cruz.

"Come look at this."

Stacie set her tea down and stood. Eileen stopped her.

"Are you sure you're okay?" she asked.

"Yes," said Stacie firmly. "I want to get this taken care of so we can clean up the garden."

Stacie opened the sliding door, and Ben and Cruz stepped past her onto the bricked patio. Stacie slipped into sandals lying by the door and followed them.

"Bananas. Stay." The big dog halted, went to his usual place and sighed as he dropped down.

Stacie stepped outside into the mist. Colin was right behind her. Eileen and Mir stayed in the store.

It was even creepier than it looked in the pictures, Ben thought.

The female statues had been laid in a straight line. What Ben hadn't seen in the photo was that they were all *face down*. Set carefully on the head of each one was a rock. Ben could see the gaps along the garden where the rocks had been removed.

"Guy's a control freak," said Cruz.

"Guy's a serious mud-sucker," muttered Colin and linked his arm with Stacie's.

Cruz took out the camera and started taking pictures. "What are those?" she pointed to statues that, just beyond the heads of the female statues, were half buried with only their bases showing.

"They're all Buddhas. Or Jizos."

Cruz paused. "Jizo?"

"Japanese bodhisattva." Stacie didn't explain further. Fear radiated from her. Or was it...anger?

Ben began to understand why she'd confronted the protesters. She'd had to scream at someone after this.

"Has this happened before?"

"No," said Stacie. "No one's ever done this before." She gestured without taking her hand from her pocket. "This was carefully thought out. It's a message. A threat."

"Message?" asked Cruz. "Threat?"

Stacie nodded tightly. "Like you said. Letting me know he's in control. That he can get at me whenever he wants. That women should be face down in the dirt. Is it me or do those," she took her hand out of her pocket and pointed at the buried statues, "look like tombstones?"

Ben felt a chill that had nothing to do with the fog. That's exactly what this looked like. Cruz's face was shuttered, angry. She agreed with Stacie.

He glanced at Stacie, huddled in her sweatshirt.

"Do you have what you need?" he asked his partner. She nodded. "Then let's go inside."

Cruz turned to Stacie as she shut the door behind them. "There was a note, too?"

Stacie nodded.

"I'll get it." Colin went into the kitchen and came back with the note in a plastic bag. "I only touched the corner," he said, handing it to Cruz.

"Detective Meissner said Troy called the other night." Ben turned to Stacie.

"Yes," she said shortly.

"What did he say?" asked Ben quietly.

"Told me to get rid of my boyfriends or he would. Called me Anastasia."

"Boyfriends?" Ben's heart plunged.

"He meant Colin. That's what he said when he approached me at Del Mundo."

"Was that the first time he'd used your name?" asked Cruz.

A slight head shake. "No. He always uses it. Makes a point of using it."

"That bothers you?"

"No one calls me Anastasia." It was clear she didn't intend to explain.

"Did he threaten you?"

"I didn't give him time. I hung up and pulled the jack out of the wall." Stacie pulled her hoodie closer around her neck and crossed her arms, rubbing her upper arms as if she were cold.

"His voice." She hugged herself even tighter. "It was low. Insinuating." She swallowed. "Intimate. But violent. Made me sick to my stomach."

Ben thought she was getting sick again, just talking about it. A surge of anger knocked the breath out of him.

"You didn't call the police at that time," Cruz said.

"No," said Stacie.

"Why?"

Stacie hesitated. "It was late. I was tired. Scared. I didn't want to have to explain everything to an officer. I wanted to talk to someone who already had the background. You two. Or Detective Meissner. I needed someone to listen to me. To believe me. To understand it wasn't a prank call. That it was a..."

"A threat?" asked Cruz.

Stacie nodded.

"I told her she should have come to stay with me," said Colin.

Stacie gave a small shake of her head.

"You didn't think that was a good idea?" Cruz asked her.

When she hesitated a bit too long, Cruz encouraged her. "Ms Cappella?"

"I had the feeling," said Stacie almost reluctantly, "that he wanted to frighten me. Throw me off balance. So I'd make mistakes. I felt…" She paused. "I did think briefly about calling Colin. But..." Her hand was back in her pocket again, fist balled. Ben saw her come to a decision.

"I think he wanted me to run. Like a rabbit. He was trying to force me out into the open." She paused again. "He wanted me to leave the safety of my house in the middle of the night. Alone. I thought I was safer where I was."

The hair on Ben's neck rose. *She's right*, he thought. *She's right*.

He wanted this guy. Oh, how he wanted this guy.

Stacie looked away from Cruz to Ben. "I know that sounds like a lot to get from a few words, but I'm sure of it. He meant to scare me. He wants me so scared I can't think.

"And I wanted… If he was watching the house from somewhere, I didn't want to give him the satisfaction of seeing police cars roll up outside," she finished. Now Ben was sure of the anger in her voice.

"You could have called me. I would have come," said Colin. Ben knew he'd said this before.

Stacie shook her head, looking at her friend. "No. I didn't want him turning on you, too." She turned back to Cruz and Ben. "I'm afraid for my friends. If he's watching, if he knows where they live. Where they work. I'm afraid… I'm afraid for them." She nodded toward Colin. "Especially Colin."

"Let him fucking try," said Colin.

Ben was surprised by the vehemence in the slight man's voice, all joking and cynicism gone.

Cruz nodded. "You're not wrong. He'll try to separate you from help and support. From friends and family. By threatening them, getting them to pull back. But staying locked up all weekend also gives him control."

Stacie nodded. "I know. So I didn't."

Cruz raised her eyebrows.

"I spent Sunday with a friend in Pasadena. Yesterday, I had a tour at the garden."

"Garden?" asked Cruz.

"The Becker Botanical Preserve. I'm a docent there. I couldn't cancel. Since he knows I volunteer there—that's the first place I saw him—I called ahead. I asked the security guard to meet me at the gate. He stayed with me on the tour and walked me to my car after. I let the staff know what Troy looked like and what was happening."

"Did you see him?" asked Ben.

She shook her head. "No. Thank goodness."

She nodded at Colin. "Then Colin came here with me, to the office, so I could get some work, and Bananas and I spent the day in his apartment." Stacie gestured to her messenger bag on the floor near the counter. "I'd taken my laptop and files home with me to catch up on some work. I spent last night on his couch."

Cruz nodded in approval. "You did well. Not being alone. Changing your habits."

"Thanks," said Stacie. "My friend in Pasadena and I searched the Internet on ways to protect yourself from a stalker. But I can't keep this up. I have accounting clients," she glanced at the clock, "including one today at 11:30."

Mir followed her glance, then looked back at Stacie. Stacie nodded. "Go open," she said. "Business as usual. I can't let him know I'm afraid." She nodded toward the front of the store and the thinning crowd. "Or them."

Ben thought Mir looked at Stacie with something like awe before she picked the keys off the counter and went to unlock the door.

"But some of my clients can only come after work, at six or seven o'clock. Or even later," Stacie continued.

"Could you meet with them at their homes?" asked Ben.

Stacie wrinkled her nose. "I could, but I'd have to explain. And I'd really rather they didn't know I was being followed. I don't want to bring this into their lives."

"The Becker Preserve?" he asked.

She shook her head. "I don't have any more tours—the garden staff knows I can't do them until after April 15th. But, Detective, I have to be here to cover Mir. I can't leave her alone, not with Troy snooping around."

"Do you have an alarm system here or at home?" Ben asked.

"No. I called a couple alarm companies yesterday, but they can't get out for a week or more. Detective Meissner recommended a few companies she's worked with. I'll call them later. I want to have more motion-sensitive lights and an alarm put in, here and at home." She gave him an ironic smile. "Will probably drive me nuts. The coyotes and opossums come through my yard all the time, not to mention rabbits and the neighbor's monster cat. They're always setting off the light near my front stairs."

"Until that system's installed?"

"I'm staying with a friend in Costa Mesa. We were at school together."

"Have a silent alarm installed, too," suggested Cruz, "both here and at home."

Stacie nodded. "I will. Thanks. That will make me feel better about having Mir down here while I'm upstairs."

"Me, too," said Mir, frankly.

Stacie frowned a bit. "Mir, maybe you should wait this out at home."

Mir shook her head. "Not a chance," she said. "With a silent alarm, my pepper spray, and Colin on speed dial. I'm ready for the sucker."

Stacie produced a short, surprised laugh that sounded a bit too close to a sob. Stacie put out a hand and squeezed Mir's arm. "Thanks. I needed that," she said.

Mir smiled, but Ben could tell she was scared, too.

"As long as someone is here, or people are coming in," he said, "I doubt he'll approach you. He won't want to be seen by others. Stalkers want it to look like you're crazy. Imagining things."

Eileen spoke up for the first time. "Yes. Make you look hysterical." She looked at Stacie. "Too often, everyone is willing to believe it."

Cruz and Ben looked at her in surprise.

"You sound like the voice of experience," said Cruz.

Eileen nodded. "First husband. Don't ask."

Stacie looked at Ben. "Do you believe me?" she asked.

"Yes," he said.

She closed her eyes and let out a long-held breath. Ben could see some of the fear drain away.

"Stacie," said Eileen hesitantly, "with all that's going on, maybe you and Mir could use another person over here? I'd be happy to come over, sit with Mir, clean cases or something."

Ben saw the look of relief on Stacie's face.

"Thank you," she told Eileen. "I'll feel better about Mir being downstairs if someone's with her."

"Good," said Eileen. "I'll run home and get some knitting." Then she smiled at Colin. "But first, I know someone who's always hungry. Which is why I came over this morning in the first place." She picked up a bag from where she'd set it next to the chairs.

"*Bless you!*" said Colin, feigning a faint. He took the bag from Eileen.

"Let's see if we can get that egg washed out of your jacket, too."

"Food and laundry, too. You are a saint, Eileen." Eileen held her arm out toward Mir, and the three of them headed toward the kitchen.

"You have good friends," said Cruz.

"I do," Stacie replied. "I don't know what I'd do without them."

"You'll be most vulnerable at home," said Ben.

"I know."

"Do you have any neighbors you're close to?"

"Yes. I called them last night. Some I've known since I was a kid. I asked them to call the police if they saw anyone hanging around who shouldn't be there.

"But," she went on, "I live up on Fern Dell, off Canyon View."

"Ah," said Cruz.

"You know it?" Ben asked his partner.

She nodded. "It's a sweet, but secluded little cul-de-sac."

"We see very little of what happens at each other's houses." Stacie shrugged. "Best I can hope for is people walking their dogs spotting someone. So I'll be counting on the security system, my neighbors and," she nodded toward Bananas, ambling toward the kitchen looking for a handout, "Mr. Friendly."

"Speaking of walking," said Ben. "You've done such a

good job of covering your bases, you probably know you shouldn't walk in the Heritage Park alone."

"I know," Stacie sighed. "Really pisses me off. Besides yoga, it's my stress reliever this time of year." She raised clenched fists. "God, I hate this bastard!" she cried.

Colin popped back out of the kitchen, cookies in his hand.

"I can bring you a bat," he said, walking up to her. "To keep by your bed?"

"A bat?" asked Ben.

Stacie gave a faint laugh. "Colin plays for the Blue Jays. No, once the security system is in, I'll be fine. Besides, I have Bananas. And a very large kitchen knife. Until then, I'll be safe with my friends in Costa Mesa."

"Let me know if you change your mind." Colin hugged Stacie. "I'll take you to your car tonight. I'm just across the parking lot. Call me whenever you're feeling uneasy." He put his arm around Mir, who'd come out to stand next to him. "You, too, girlfriend."

Eileen had sent Bananas to the patio with a treat. "I can be an extra set of eyes most days," she said, joining them. "Unlike Colin, you won't have to feed me."

"Again, sullying my reputation," said Colin around a bite of cookie.

Cruz almost smiled at the exchange, then became serious.

"We'll do all we can to stop him," she said. "But I have to be honest. Stalkers are difficult."

"I know," said Stacie. "That's what the websites said."

"Have you called Detective Breckenridge?"

Stacie nodded. "I left a message for him this morning, right after I called Detective Meissner."

Ben reached in his jacket, pulled out a card, stepped to the counter and began to write. "I'm giving you my cell number." He pointed his pen at his partner. "And Detective Cruz's."

Cruz gave him a strange look. Ben looked at Stacie with a small smile. "You said you had Detective Meissner on speed dial already."

Stacie looked embarrassed. "Sorry. I was pissed that day."

"We could tell," Ben said wryly. He handed her the card. As she took it, her fingers touched Ben's, almost embarrassing him with a rush of desire.

Stacie folded it into her hand and put both hands back in her pockets. "Program them into your phone," said Ben. "Call any time." He gave a fast glance at Cruz, then looked back to Stacie. "Any time. Right after you call 911."

Ben saw Colin look at him oddly, then flash a glance at Stacie. Suddenly his eyes widened and he looked back at Ben. He stuffed another cookie in his mouth, hiding his smile. But not before Cruz had noticed, Ben thought.

"You okay if I go?" Colin asked Stacie, swallowing his cookie.

She gestured at the detectives. "I'll be fine."

"Be sure to give the officers outside your contact information," Ben told him. "They'll need your statement about this morning."

"All I can say is that those people," he gestured to the street where the two officers were finishing with the last of the crowd, "are lucky that egg washed out." He held up his warm-up jacket, now damp.

"I'll go with you," said Eileen. "I'll be back shortly."

Colin hugged Stacie. "Stay safe," he said. "Let me know if you change your mind about the bat." He headed out the door.

"I'm serious about the call," said Ben, as the door closed behind Colin. "And Stacie," he said, looking into those green eyes. "Don't take chances. Don't ever assume he's gone.

Sometimes stalkers appear to disappear." He hesitated. "He could be very dangerous."

She looked at him for a moment. "There's something you're not telling me," she finally said. "Isn't there?"

Ben felt Cruz's glare on him.

"It's just that women on their own can be vulnerable, and stalkers are unpredictable." He nodded to the backyard. "This may be nothing more than an effort to control you through fear." He looked back at Stacie. "It might be more."

"Yes. I know," said Stacie quietly.

No, thought Ben. *You don't.* But then he remembered what Emeline had told him about Stacie's gift. Briefly, he wondered if she knew more than he gave her credit for. Then cursed himself for being an idiot.

"We'll do everything we can," said Cruz again.

"Thanks," said Stacie. She looked at Ben. "Thanks for believing me."

She smiled softly, and Ben's heart rate went up.

He gave her a nod. But as Cruz headed for the door, Ben turned back to Stacie. An impulse drove him to ask: "Stacie. If you were to give Troy a mineral, what would it be?"

Cruz glanced at him like he'd lost his mind.

"Lead," said Stacie without hesitation. "It's heavy. Dark. Dead. Like he is."

Ben nodded. "Be careful."

THEY WEREN'T six feet down the sidewalk when Cruz spoke. "What was *that* all about?"

"I don't like this, Lauren," he said.

"Well, neither do I! But you're not a one-man frigging police department. There are a hundred and fifty of us. Are we all useless but you?"

She stopped as they reached the car. "Keys," she said. He handed them to her.

"This guy is not a garden-variety stalker," he said mildly. He'd seen Cruz's reaction to Stacie's story. She wanted this guy as badly as Ben did.

Cruz walked around the car and unlocked it. Then she looked at Ben over the roof. She wasn't smiling.

"And what was all the mumbo jumbo about what rock she'd give him?"

"I was just curious."

"About what?"

He hesitated. "About her...intuition."

Cruz gave him a look of pure disbelief.

"You're not giving this up, are you?" she said. "You really think he could be a killer, or even *the* killer?"

Ben returned her look, then turned to gaze at the empty offices in the building across the street. He remembered his sense on Saturday night that there were too many places to hide.

Good thing Cruz didn't know about that.

Did he think this stalker could be the serial killer? Really?

Ben looked back at Cruz, serious. "Call it a hunch," he said.

Her face split into a grin.

"I'd call it love," she said and yanked the car door open.

SEVENTEEN

STACIE WAS FEELING THE STRAIN OF THE LAST FEW DAYS. HER friends in Costa Mesa were welcoming, and they loved Bananas. They'd given her a key to the house so she was free to leave early and return late. But she resented the time she lost every day making the drive, and she really hated the traffic. By time she got to the shop, her nerves were already tight. Every day that passed, she got angrier at Troy for forcing this on her.

And, of course, now he was silent and invisible, making her feel ridiculous.

But she knew he was still there.

Of the three alarm companies Detective Meissner had recommended, one had been able to send someone out almost immediately. The technician had wired a silent alarm, outside alarm, lights, cameras, and a keypad. Stacie had spent the last few days running up and down the stairs, answering questions from the tech, while trying to focus on her work with her tax clients who were curious about the new security. Stacie told them it was due to the vandalism.

The tech had finally finished training Mir and her on the system and was about to leave.

"What time do you want me up at the house tomorrow?" he asked.

"The earliest you can be there," she told him. "I want to get back into my own home."

"Eight?"

"Fine," she told him. "I'll meet you there."

Stacie blew out a breath when the door closed behind him.

"Would you like some tea?" asked Eileen from the corner where she sat quietly knitting, a calm center in the hurricane of activity.

Stacie glanced at the clock. Her last client was due in an hour, just before the store closed. Few people wanted to talk taxes on a Friday night when they were planning a weekend. Stacie was glad of that, too. She needed the time to catch up this evening.

"I'll make it," she said. "We could all use a break. It's been a bit hectic."

"Yes, but I'm sure you'll feel better, now the alarm is in," said Eileen.

"I do," said Stacie. "I'm especially glad for the silent, for Mir." She nodded to the younger woman at the counter.

"What?" Mir shrugged and held her hands up. "Killer Dog over there isn't enough to scare him off?" She jerked her chin at Bananas, sprawled on his side in the sun, feet twitching as he dreamed.

"Speaking of the hound," she added, "If you're going to be downstairs for a bit, I'll take him down the block for a quick potty break in the park."

Mir picked the leash off the hook behind the counter. At

the sound, Bananas' eyes snapped open. He scrambled clumsily to his feet and bounced over to Mir, tail in motion.

The three women laughed. "I think the sound of his leash would bring him back from the dead," said Stacie. She glanced out the front window as Mir clipped the dog's leash in place. "I wish you didn't have to run the gauntlet outside."

"It's okay," said Mir. "They've been subdued since the police took names, and you and Colin and Jacqui pressed charges against them."

"At least they've stopped bringing the children with them," added Eileen, not looking up from her knitting.

Stacie sighed. "I guess we can put up with sign waving and nasty looks. At least until they've moved on."

"Have you lost any customers because of them?" asked Eileen.

"I had a couple people call and ask if it was safe to walk by them," said Mir. "Most of our customers think they're ridiculous." She started toward the door. Seeing Stacie open her mouth, she held up a hand. "I'll keep my eyes open." She grinned. "Come on, hound, let's walk."

"Are your bookkeeping clients okay with the picketers, too?" asked Eileen.

"Some are. But most are uncomfortable with it. Especially since they've started copying Colin, filming people who come in. People carrying tax and business documents are not happy that they might be posted online somewhere. I've had to meet some of them at coffee shops or at work." She shook her head. "My schedule is already a mess. Trying to keep my clients satisfied is becoming a real hassle." She shrugged. "But what else can I do? At least they don't know about Troy." Stacie shuddered. "Let me get that tea."

A few minutes later, she came back with two mugs on a

tray, set it on the table and sighed as she sank into the chair next to Eileen. She looked around the shop.

"I should be cleaning cases," she said. "The alarm guy left fingerprints everywhere." But she made no move to get up.

She watched Eileen knit for a while, the movements soothing. "Eileen," she said finally. "I want you to know how grateful I am to you for coming over the last few days. Keeping Mir company." She rolled her shoulders. "Frankly, you make *me* feel better, too." Stacie hesitated.

"But you're worried about me. Afraid I'll become a target for this crazy."

"I am. You're here every day. You live next door. Alone. He could turn on you."

Eileen shook her head. "Don't worry about it. People see me, they think I'm a nobody," she'd said. "Even if he's watching, I'd be surprised if he notices me."

"I'm not so sure, Eileen. It's selfish endangering you and Mir."

"Detective Meissner thinks he's focused on you. Not that that's a comfort."

Stacie made a sound that was supposed to be a laugh, but there was no mirth in it. "No. It isn't. But I don't think this guy is so...textbook. I'm not sure anyone knows what he'll do."

"I'll be fine. Besides. I owe it to Amelia. I'd have been lost without her after my husband died. Consider it payback."

"A lot of people are lost without her." *Starting with me*, thought Stacie. She picked up her mug to blow on her tea.

"I'm more worried about Colin," said Eileen. She reached the end of her row, set the work down, and reached for her tea. "Especially after the threats. It's a bit suspicious that someone smashed the pots on his stairs the other night while he was at practice."

"I'm worried, too. I don't know if that was Troy or one of these people." Stacie waved her hand toward the front of the store. "But regardless, I can't get him to take it seriously."

In fact, Colin was fired up. He'd gone to all the merchants and offices nearby asking them to report anything or anyone unusual. He was even talking about organizing a gay pride counter-demonstration at the church. Stacie didn't know if he meant it or not.

"I guess he's dealt with enough bullies in his life that, to him, these threats are just one more," Eileen told her.

"Umm. Maybe you're right."

They sipped tea quietly and listened to the hummingbirds squabble in the garden outside. A chime rang softly.

"He's quite good looking, isn't he?" said Eileen, taking up her knitting again.

"Colin? said Stacie, surprised. "Yes, he is kind of cute."

"Your detective," said Eileen, eyes on her needles.

Stacie stared at her open-mouthed.

Eileen glanced up and caught the look. "I've known you a long time." She smiled. "I've seen how you look at him. That look is on your face right now."

"Oh, Lordy. I hope no one else has noticed."

"I'm pretty sure Colin did. And that sharp-eyed partner of his."

A blush rose into Stacie's face.

"How did he know you walk at the Heritage Park?"

"I ran into him on the trail one morning. Oh, Eileen!" said Stacie, surprised at the intensity in her voice. "He was so easy to talk to. Smart. Funny. I thought he was a photographer. I had no idea he was a cop."

"He didn't tell you?"

"We never got that far. It was just idle conversation. I never even got his name. Until they walked into the shop that day, about the Byers woman. And now. Well, now things are a bit complicated."

"Umm. There are probably rules about officers dating crime victims."

"I'm sure there are. But sometimes I wish we could go back to that trail and start over," said Stacie sadly. "It's pretty ridiculous, really. We only talked about ten minutes, but I felt like I'd known him forever."

"Sometimes love happens like that."

Stacie laughed with bitterness. "I doubt it's love. I'm sure he thinks I'm crazy. The crazy crystal healer." She rolled her eyes.

"Maybe not."

Maybe Eileen was right, thought Stacie. Ben's casual question, about what mineral she'd give Troy, had caught Stacie off guard, and she'd answered without thinking. Her answer had shocked her.

Lead. Dead. Lifeless. Soulless.

What do they know that they're not saying? Stacie wondered. Whatever it was, she was sure it would scare her more than she already was.

Stacie tilted her head and inhaled the fragrance of bergamot in the Earl Grey tea. She changed the subject.

"What are you making?" She gestured at the pink and white knitted fabric spooling out from Eileen's swiftly moving hands.

"A little afghan."

"A new grandchild?" asked Stacie. Eileen had a son in Texas with two small boys.

Eileen smiled. "Yes."

"Let me guess. A girl this time?"

"The pink a giveaway?" They both laughed.

"Stacie." Eileen set her work down and reached for her tea again. "I know you want to stop driving to Costa Mesa. But I wonder if it's wise to be alone at night? Your house is beautiful, but you're so isolated.

"I'm sorry," she added quickly. "I shouldn't have said that. You're probably nervous enough as it is."

Stacie nodded and gripped the mug tightly. "I am. But the security system will make me feel better." She smiled. "And Fred Langley has offered to shoot anyone he sees prowling around."

"Ah, Fred. No matter what he did, he couldn't convince Amelia he was 'the one' for her."

"No," said Stacie. "But he's always been a good neighbor. To her and to me."

They glanced up as Mir and Bananas came back in. Unclipped from the leash, the dog made a beeline for the kitchen.

"Oh, for heaven's sake," said Stacie, as Mir and Eileen laughed. "That dog is so much like Colin, I think they're related."

"I'll get him a treat," said Mir. "Bananas. You want a carrot?" The dog wagged at her from the kitchen door.

Stacie's phone rang and she pulled it from her skirt pocket. She smiled at the caller ID and opened the connection. "Hey, Frances. How are you? How's the new grandmother-to-be?" She looked at Eileen and mouthed, "Another one."

"At my wit's end, Stacie," said her friend and fellow docent at the Becker Preserve. "I have a tour scheduled for next week, but I just got a call from Monica. She's gone into labor early. Steve and I are heading up there tonight. I don't know when I'll be back. I know it's the absolute worst time to ask you, but I haven't been able to find anyone else. I'm hoping you can cover for me."

Stacie's heart sank. *One more thing*, she thought. But Frances had covered Stacie's tours numerous times when business got out of hand. She'd never asked for help before. Besides, this was her first grandchild, and Monica was having a very difficult pregnancy. "When are you scheduled? Is it just a straight up tour?"

"A week from Sunday, and no, it's the poison garden."

The poison garden was unique. There were only a few in the world. The Becker's version was Frances' brain child and baby rolled into one. She had lobbied the Becker to establish it, funded the enclosure that would keep people from abusing it, researched the plants, and helped install many of them herself.

Stacie sighed to herself, but thought, *This could be fun*. She'd never given the poison tour before.

"Can you drop some notes by the shop?" she asked. Frances' notes were encyclopedic. "I can't do that one without some prep."

"I've made you a set of note cards, one for each plant, with a map showing where they're located and a photo."

"Wow! I can't ask for better than that."

"Again, I hate to ask, but can you pick them up at the garden? We're heading out in a half hour, and the Becker's on our way to John Wayne. Easier for me to drop them there."

"Sure," said Stacie. "I can cover you."

"Thank you!" The relief in Frances' voice was clear.

"You have a safe trip. Do you know if it's a boy or girl?" She glanced at the blanket on Eileen's lap.

"Don't know yet. They want to be surprised. I'll text you. And thanks again, Stacie!"

"You're more than welcome." She slipped the phone into

her pocket as Mir opened the sliding door to let Bananas out and some fresh air in. Mir picked up the window cleaner and began working on the cases.

"You know that garden backwards, forwards, and blind-folded," Eileen teased Stacie. "How much prep can you need?"

"The poison garden," said Stacie, taking a sip of her tea. It had gotten cold.

"Oh, that's fascinating!" said Eileen. "I did that tour a few years ago. It brings out the Lucretia Borgia in a person."

Mir laughed. "Eileen, there is no one in this world less like Lucretia Borgia than you," she said.

"Oh, I have my moments," Eileen replied, smiling.

The front door opened, and they all looked up. Mir turned, but Stacie rose swiftly and put a hand on her arm to stop her.

"Ginny," said Stacie, moving toward the girl, "I'm glad you came back." Then she saw Ginny's ashen face. The bruises on her throat.

"Come," she said going to the girl's side. "Come sit down."

Eileen, hearing the tone in Stacie's voice, set her knitting down and got up quickly. "I'll make more tea."

Stacie glanced at the clock as she guided Ginny into a chair. It was thirty-five minutes until closing. Her client would be here in about twenty minutes.

"Mir, lock the door, please. We're closing early tonight. An emergency." Stacie glanced at Ginny, then back to Mir. "Let *only* my five o'clock appointment in. No one else. No one at all."

Mir nodded grimly and moved quickly toward the door.

Stacie helped Ginny sit, then took her hand. The girl's icy fingers curled reflexively around Stacie's warm ones.

She looked at Stacie, her blue eyes huge. "I didn't know where to go," she said. "I didn't know where to go."

Stacie knelt by Ginny's side. "You're safe here. We've locked the door. No one can harm you."

"You were kind. No one's been kind," Ginny told her.

Eileen came in with the mug of tea and quietly set it on the table next to the girl. She took her seat and simply started knitting again. Stacie was grateful for her calm.

"Mir," she said over her shoulder, "would you wash one of the rutilated quartz touchstones and bring it to me?"

Mir detoured to the bins by the front window and started looking the stones over carefully.

"Can you tell me what happened?" Stacie asked Ginny quietly.

"He tried to kill me," whispered Ginny, staring with disbelief into Stacie's eyes. "I told him I didn't want to get rid...that I wanted to keep my baby. I told him I'd be a good wife and mother. He got so angry! I've never seen him so angry. He called me a liar. He said the baby wasn't his. He said I was such a...a...whore," Ginny could hardly say the word, "that I didn't know who the father was. It isn't true! It isn't!" She clutched Stacie's hand desperately.

"I know it's not Ginny," said Stacie gently. "I know you're not lying. I believe you."

Mir came up quietly and held out the rutilated quartz. She'd chosen a beauty. Stacie took it and, without saying word, slipped it into Ginny's palm. The girl clutched it convulsively.

"I told him I'd go to Reverend Hammond," she continued.

"Reverend Hammond?" asked Stacie.

"The preacher at the Holy Star Evangelical Church."

Of course, thought Stacie. *The gray-haired man among the picketers. The one who threatened her.*

"Then he…he grabbed my throat." Ginny put her free hand protectively against her neck. "And he…he tried to…to…to kill me." The last words came out as a whisper.

From the corner of her eye, Stacie saw Eileen stop knitting.

"How did you get away?" asked Stacie calmly, though her mind was churning. Was this maniac coming to her store?

Ginny swallowed and winced as if her throat hurt.

Eileen quickly reached over, picked up the mug of tea, and offered it to her. "Here, love, it will help."

Ginny turned and saw Eileen for the first time. Eileen gave her a small smile. The girl reached for the mug, then paused. "What is it?" she asked.

Still afraid I'm a witch, thought Stacie sadly. *Probably thinks Eileen is one, too.*

Eileen gave Ginny her best grandmother smile. "Just chamomile, love. It won't hurt you. Women give it to babies when they're teething."

Reassured, Ginny took the mug in her free hand and drank the tea. She took a deep breath.

"How did you get away?" Stacie asked again, more quietly.

"Someone came," said the girl. "They knocked. He pushed me into the bedroom. I fell. He told me he'd kill me if I made a sound."

Ginny looked at Stacie, her face pale as death.

"He meant it," she whispered. "He wanted to kill my baby." Ginny took another sip of the hot tea. A shudder ran through her.

Shock's passing, thought Stacie. She remembered that night long ago. Being terrified. Then being safe.

"Someone came in. They were talking. Jer started to laugh. I was so afraid. I had to save my baby. The window

221

screen was loose. I climbed out. And I ran. I kept hiding all the way here. I was afraid he'd find me."

She looked at Stacie apologetically. "I didn't know where else to go," she said again. "You were kind to me."

Holy Mother, thought Stacie. *Now what?*

"We'll have to call the police," Eileen said. "He tried…"

"No!" Ginny cried. "I can't! They'll make me testify. Everyone will know. He'll find me. They'll curse me!" Hysteria was a moment away.

"Ginny. Ginny," said Stacie firmly, clutching the girl's hand in her own. She reached up with her free hand, took the mug and set it down, then took Ginny's other hand. "No one will make you do what you don't want to. Ginny," she said again urgently, trying to get the girl's attention. "We want to help you."

"Not the police," said Ginny terrified. "Not the police." She took a short, shivery breath. "That other place. That other place you told me about. The women's place."

The crisis center. *Yes*, thought Stacie. *They'll know how to handle this. Because I certainly don't.*

"Mir," she said, without taking her eyes off Ginny, "Would you call, please? Ask for Danielle if she's there. The number is on the counter, next to the register."

"They won't take my baby away?"

"They'll keep you safe," said Stacie. "I'm sure they'll talk to you, yes, to be sure you're doing what's best for you and the baby." Ginny's grip threatened to break Stacie's fingers. "But I'm sure they won't make you do anything against your will.

"You need someone to help you, Ginny. They know how to keep you safe. I don't know how."

Ginny looked at Stacie for a long time, then gave a small nod.

Hallelujah, thought Stacie. She heard Mir talking to Danielle.

"She wants to talk to you," Mir told her.

Ginny slowly released her hands. Stacie stood and took the phone. She talked to Danielle for a few minutes, giving her a brief synopsis of the situation.

"We're only a few blocks away," said Danielle. "I'll come get her myself. Less than ten minutes." She hung up.

Stacie turned and was surprised to see Mir holding Ginny's hand. They were talking baby names. Eileen was back to knitting, throwing an occasional glance at Ginny. Stacie had a hunch there was a baby blanket in Ginny's future.

Stacie went to the window to watch for Danielle. She glanced at the clock. Her client was just about due.

The ten minutes was only six. Danielle came in, introduced herself, assured Ginny she'd take good care of them both, and whisked her out the door. Stacie barely had time to say thank you.

They were just getting into Danielle's car when Stacie's client, Marjorie, parked a couple doors down.

"Mir," she said, turning. "I'm sure you probably know this, but you shouldn't mention Ginny or the crisis center to anyone. Not friends, not family. Not even Ace. Definitely not customers. It could put them all in danger."

Mir nodded. "He's a real bastard, isn't he?"

"Yes," said Stacie.

"Will they call the police?"

"I'm sure they'll do whatever is best and whatever the law requires," said Stacie. She sighed. "I just don't know how to reconcile those things. They'll know."

"Why did she come to you?" Mir asked. "She said you were kind."

"Her boyfriend told her I could give her herbs to make her abort."

Mir looked appalled. "This is my fault, isn't it? Telling people that herbs and gems can heal."

"No, Mir," Stacie told her firmly. "It is not your fault. If it's anyone's fault, it's that preacher's." Her voice was bitter.

Marjorie was coming up the walk.

"Now, we need to stop talking about it." She reached out and hugged Mir. "It is not your fault," she said again, fiercely.

Stacie took a deep breath as Marjorie appeared at the door. "Right on time," she said, and smiled. "It's good to see you. It's been a hectic day. Why don't I make us both some tea?

"Lovely," said Marjorie.

"I'll bring it up," said Mir and went to the kitchen.

As Marjorie started up the steps to the bookkeeping office, Stacie cast a worried glance toward the kitchen.

"I'll see she's okay," said Eileen.

"Thank you," said Stacie, and followed her client upstairs.

EIGHTEEN

BEN HEFTED THE CAMERA BAG ONTO HIS SHOULDER. WITH A disgusted look at the Camry's vandalized hood, he headed to the entrance gate of the Lillian Becker Botanical Preserve.

I'm not the only one who thought this would be a good day to be out, he thought, looking at the half-full parking lot. It was a perfect sunny Sunday. His Black Watch plaid flannel shirt was just warm enough for the hint of coolness in the air. He took a deep breath of the sharp, dusty fragrance of the eucalyptus trees warming in the sun, and relaxed.

He was pushing his entry ticket into his pocket, when he saw Stacie Cappella come out of the interpretive center tucking a file folder into her messenger bag. Her auburn hair glowed in the sun as she stepped out of the doorway. A wide belt showed off the slimness of her waist between a white tank and snug blue jeans. The sleeves of her blue-and-black-checked flannel shirt were rolled up to mid-forearm.

Ben's heart kicked to see her. His mood, already good, lifted even more. A grin began to spread across his face.

A tall, blond man stepped into the sunlight behind her.

The grin stopped.

"Stacie?" he called, tension in his voice.

She looked up, startled. A smile lit her face. Something eased deep inside Ben.

He saw the khaki uniform as the young man stepped forward nervously.

"Sir," he said, "I'll have to ask you to stand back."

Ben halted.

Stacie reached out and touched the young man's arm. "It's okay, Steve. This is Detective Robard, Eden Beach Police."

"Oh, sorry." The young man flushed.

"No need to apologize," Stacie told him. "I'm grateful you're here. Detective Robard," she turned to Ben, "this is Steve Toleffson. He's one of the security staff. He's been kind enough to join my tours and to walk me in and out of the gate."

The two men shook. "I'm glad you're taking precautions," Ben told her.

"I wish I didn't have to," said Stacie ruefully. "On a day like today, I'd love to spend a few hours walking out here. But…" She shrugged and put her hands out. "What can I do? I can't monopolize Steve's time. He has work to do."

Ben found himself speaking before he thought much about it. "Well, I just got here. If you'd like to join me," he nodded at the security guard, "I'd be happy to take Steve's place."

What am I doing? he thought. He liked to spend this time alone.

As soon as he saw her smile, Ben knew he'd made the right choice.

"I'd love to," she said, "but I don't want to be in your way."

"You won't be," Ben told her truthfully.

"Then I accept. And Steve," she turned to the young man, "can get back to doing his job. Thank you," she added.

"Sure," he said. "Nice to meet you," he said to Ben and walked away.

Stacie lifted the strap of her messenger bag and pulled it over her head to cross her body, freeing her hands. Ben tried not to see how the strap lying between her breasts accentuated her curves.

She looked at Ben, and there was an awkward moment. "So," she finally said, nodding at the camera bag. "More pictures."

Ben grinned a bit sheepishly. "Yeah. Kind of an obsession. Cruz says I should have a sign over my desk that says, 'Will work for film.'"

Stacie laughed that delightful full-throated laugh, tossing her head back in the sunlight. Ben couldn't help but laugh with her.

"I know how you feel. My addiction is plants. My garden at home hardly has room for one more root." They began to move down the path past the koi pond.

"How did the pictures you took the other day come out?" she asked him. "The ones up at the Heritage Park."

"Good. The suggestions you gave me were excellent. It was a great time of day to be up there."

"I know," she said wistfully. "I miss going up in the mornings."

They had fallen into step unconsciously as they moved slowly up the sun-dappled path, the scent of warm eucalyptus and chaparral around them. Ben smelled the light fragrance he'd detected the first day he'd met her.

Steady, he thought to himself.

Stacie paused at an intersection of two paths. "Tame or wild?" she asked. She pointed to her left. "The teaching

227

gardens are down there. Herbs. Medicinal. Plants by biome. It's where I spend most of my time, doing tours."

Ben looked at the crowds, dismayed.

Stacie laughed. "That face says 'maybe not.'"

"Sorry." Ben made another face.

"No need. When I'm here on my own, especially when it's this busy, I don't spend my time here." She pointed in the other direction. "Wild it is."

They turned and began to climb slowly, then more rapidly uphill.

"There are almost sixty acres here," she told him. "More than forty are wild. Mrs. Becker wanted visitors to experience what California was like before we started taming it. Her house is up there." She pointed up a gated, stone-flagged path that went to the left. "It's just used for training now, but it has a wonderful view of the coast. On clear days."

Stacie took a deep breath of the chaparral-fragrant air. "I miss coming out here, hiking the hills. But it's too big a place, with too many secluded places, for me to risk being alone." She shuddered. "Not since that creep started following me." She gave an odd shrug, like something was tickling between her shoulder blades.

Something about it made Ben say, "You've seen him."

"No." She looked away.

Ben waited

"No," she said again, reluctantly. "But I know he's there." They had gone another fifteen feet when she added quietly, "I wish I could tell you why."

He remembered Phillips in Iraq.

"A little voice?"

She lifted her eyebrows slightly. "Something like that."

She waved her hand, as if brushing Troy away.

"Anyway, Detective Robard. I really don't like talking

about him. He's already taken over too much of my life. I don't want to give him this day, too."

"I agree." He smiled at her. "Why don't you call me Ben?"

She smiled in response, and he just barely refrained from reaching for her hand.

"So, Ben, are you looking for anything in particular?"

He let her change the subject. He, too, wanted to enjoy the day. It had been a long time since he'd just wanted to walk in the sunlight with someone.

"Not really," he said. "Just getting familiar with the place. I haven't been out here for a long while. In fact, until you reminded me, I'd forgotten it."

He paused as a family passed. "This way!" yelled one of the kids, running by and waving a map. His sister was close behind him.

Ben watched them with a puzzled expression. "I can honestly say I was never that excited about gardens when I was that age."

Stacie laughed. "They're looking for the carrion plants."

"The what?"

"We have a variety of plants that smell like dead meat when they flower."

Ben grimaced. "They like that?"

She laughed again. "They're kids. They're all about the 'Ewww!' Those and the predator plants, like Venus flytraps, are the most popular spots on my tour when I'm shepherding school kids."

"I guess you're right." Ben grinned as the family went out of sight around a corner. "When we did field trips to the zoo, we were always hoping the elephant would take a dump."

"Or pee!" said Stacie, and threw back her head and laughed. Ben joined her.

A little farther on, a well-groomed dirt and gravel trail led uphill to the left. "This way," said Stacie, pointing. Not ten feet up the trail, the sound of garden visitors fell away behind them.

"Much better," said Ben. "Sometimes I get too much of people in my job."

"I can imagine."

"Didn't you say you liked California plants?" Ben asked her as they started to climb.

"I did. I do!" She smiled. "That's one of the reasons I like to come up here. But California makes it difficult to be a purist. It's so easy to grow things here. We can't get *every-thing* here, in Eden Beach, because of the coastal weather— the fog, the cool temps at night. Some plants just aren't happy. But we get a lot."

"Do you bring tours up here, too?"

"Rarely. Not unless we have a special request. Mostly docents stick to the teaching gardens where the plants are concentrated and well labeled and the paths are paved. And kids are easier to corral. There are rattlers up here, too, this time of year. Too risky for a group on the trail."

"You've seen them?"

"Oh, I've seen them. Not often, but enough to remind me to stay alert." She gasped and rested her hand on his arm. "Like that one there!" she stage-whispered.

Startled, Ben looked, then turned back to see her dancing eyes. "It's a stick," he said.

"I know," she said. "But I made you look."

He sighed dramatically. "I'll get even."

"You can try," she said, laughter in her voice. She started moving uphill again. "You said you liked strong patterns? High contrast?"

"I did. I do."

Stacie smiled, hearing her words come back to her.

"I'll show you a stand of manzanita. The bark is peeling and there should be some great contrast for you. The light should be good. That area of the canyon faces southeast."

"Sounds great."

"This way." She pointed toward a steep trail that branched to the right. "Let me know if you see something particularly photogenic."

Ben paused for a moment as Stacie pulled ahead of him. *Photogenic*, he thought, watching her strong legs in the worn jeans sway her lovely behind up the trail.

He took a moment to slip his flannel shirt off and tie it to his waist.

They climbed slowly, the sun warm where it fell through the trees. Stacie moved smoothly, comfortably, at home in this place and at home in herself. Her gestures were open and free. She was a good teacher, enthusiastic about her subject and knowledgeable. She pointed out some of her favorite plants, telling him what they had been used for in the past. She noted other plants that she thought he might like to visit another time in the year when they flowered or set seed.

Ben only half listened. In fact, he almost forgot the camera on his shoulder. He relaxed into the sound of her voice, the crunch of the leaves and gravel underfoot, the rhythm of their boots on the trail.

Stacie paused as they came out of the trees. She pointed to a stand of live oaks a couple hundred feet away. "The manzanitas are just beyond those trees."

As they moved out onto the open hillside, she reached into her bag, pulled out a faded and worn Cubs' baseball cap, and put in on.

She saw Ben look at her. "Redhead." She pointed to herself. "Sunburn. Freckles."

"Cubs?"

"Yeah," she said. "My dad's favorite team. The hat was his. He was a big supporter of underdogs. He always hoped they'd win the Series someday. He'd have been sorry to miss their big moment."

"He's gone? Your dad?"

"Umm. When I was about eight."

"That must have been hard."

"It was."

"You remember him much?"

"Umm. Some." She smiled to herself. "He was a lot of fun for a kid. Like I unrolled my socks one day and there was a note that said, 'Don't tread on me'." She looked at Ben. "I remember that one every time I'm up here in the summer. Keeps me alert for the snakes."

"Or the sticks."

Stacie grinned.

"What did he do?"

"He was an architect. I used to sit and draw at the table next to him." She glanced at Ben. "Before digital. I still have some of his blueprints. And all of the cartoons."

"Cartoons?"

They walked quietly for a few steps before she went on.

"He drew cartoons with me as a superhero, leaping over trees, winning dance contests, and whipping bullies all at the same time." Her smile was sad. "He'd tuck them into my lunch box." She looked at Ben. "I was the dorky girl who carried a lunch box."

"I can't imagine anyone thinking you dorky."

"Redhead," she said again. "We tend to take a beating in school with the name calling. The hair color. The freckles. The pale skin. And if you're different in other ways…"

Ben waited for her to finish. When she didn't, he asked, "How were you different?"

"How wasn't I?" She laughed ruefully. "I didn't have parents. I was adopted by my great aunt. And *she* had a tea shop where she…gave advice based on what she saw in her crystal. Kids called her a gypsy. A witch. Gave me this all the time." Stacie rotated her finger by her temple. "I was a certified weirdo."

"Hard," said Ben, embarrassed that he'd had similar thoughts.

She shrugged. "I survived. We head uphill here." She pointed to a narrow path that led toward a small canyon.

"Why did your aunt adopt you?" Ben asked as he dodged under a low-hanging branch. Although Emeline had told him a little of Stacie's background, he was curious. "Did you lose your mom at the same time as your dad?"

"Not long after, thank heavens." Ben was surprised by the harshness in her voice, and his face must have shown it. She went on. "My mother was not much of one. She never really wanted me. And her second husband was no one a ten-year-old girl should ever be around."

"Not kid friendly?"

"Pedophile."

Ben inhaled sharply. "Shit."

"Yeah. A charmer. My Aunt Me saved me. Protected me. Gave me my home. Put me through school. Gave me all the love in the world. I owe her everything."

This was a different side to the fortune-telling kook, he thought, and remembered his mother's respect for Amelia.

They walked a bit farther up the side canyon, then Stacie stopped and pointed. "There," she said.

She was right. The manzanita was crying out to be photographed.

233

Ben thought he said thank you, but he was already moving forward toward the group of trees. They were old, the ground around them littered with fallen branches and curls of bark.

He didn't see Stacie smile, pulling off the ball cap as she sat down on a boulder in a patch of shade to watch him.

He pulled a digital camera out of his bag and began to move around the grouping.

"I thought you were a film guy," Stacie teased him.

He nodded. "I am. But digital is like my rough draft. I can look at the composition, the light, know if I screwed up or not before I take the final shot." He glanced over. "Saves a ton on film and wasted time."

"Then you're not a total dinosaur."

He laughed and shook his head, surprised to be enjoying the banter when he usually worked in silence. "Let's just say I'm evolving."

"So why don't you just stop with the dig photo?"

Why, indeed? It was what everyone asked.

"I like working with the film," he finally said as he moved around the manzanita. "Manipulating it."

"But can't you do that in the computer?"

He gave a small shrug. Framed a shot. Adjusted his settings. Took the shot. Looked at it. Then looked at Stacie who was still waiting.

"For me, there's a...a quality of attention that I get working in the darkroom. A kind of quiet. Co-ordination between my eyes, my hands, my head. I don't get that with the computer."

She produced a slight smile. "A 'meditation,' as we of the lunatic fringe would say."

It was what his mother would say, too.

"Yes," he told her. "I've never thought of it that way, but yes."

She smiled fully now. "I'll let you work."

He did, turning his attention back to the camera, shooting dozens of photos on the digital, checking them, discarding them. Finally, he went to his bag and pulled out the SLR and tripod. Using the images and angles he liked in the digital, he set up, adjusted, and finally took his shots.

He moved quickly, working intensely to capture the light.

When he finally finished, he turned and saw Stacie watching him. He stared at her wordlessly for a moment.

He'd forgotten she was there.

"Crap," he said, embarrassed. "I'm supposed to be looking after you."

She laughed. "Believe me. If that creep had shown up, they would have heard me in Tijuana."

Ben snatched up the bag from where it waited on the ground and went to sit next to Stacie on a neighboring boulder. Again, he smelled her light fragrance.

"Anything worthwhile?"

Ben surprised himself. He leaned over his bag, pulled out the digital camera, flipped open the screen, and handed it to her. "It would be pretty rude not to share these since you're the one who brought me here. They won't be exactly as you see them here." He gestured to the images she was bringing up. "It's amazing how the light changes so quickly."

"Ben," she said after she'd screened several of them, "these are really good."

"Thank you," he said, putting his hand on his heart and bowing slightly.

"No, seriously. You could do this professionally."

"You sound like a friend of mine."

"I have a neighbor. Margot Somerset. She runs a gallery downtown. You should show these to her."

"It's just a hobby."

"That doesn't mean you couldn't sell them."

Ben made a face. "I'm just a cop who takes pictures."

Stacie looked at him, green eyes serious. Her pupils grew large.

Time slowed. Ben could almost see the sunlight creeping across the path. A mockingbird sang out, a long complicated song.

"You are a great deal more than that," said Stacie quietly.

Ben felt exposed, as if every corner of his soul had been laid open. He felt each beat of his heart pushing blood through his body. The air around them shimmered.

Stacie looked at him a moment longer, then turned back to the tiny screen, breaking the spell.

"I really like this one." Stacie had thumbed back to one image in particular.

"It'll be even better in film," Ben managed to say as the world snapped back into place.

"I look forward to seeing it." Stacie smiled and handed the camera to him.

Ben bent over his bag, fussing with the cameras to give himself time to recover. His hands shook. *What the hell just happened?*

"So how did you get into photography?" Stacie asked in a normal tone of voice.

Ben took a breath and closed his bag.

"It was kind of an accident," he said, straightening up. "When I was in middle school, we went on a field trip to the Norton Simon Museum up in Pasadena."

He looked at Stacie. Nothing strange about her. Just a beautiful woman listening to him.

"I was kind of a Philistine. Thought the painting was boring."

Stacie gave him a small smile. There was a buzz in Ben's chest somewhere near his heart.

He lost his train of thought. All he could see were the serious green eyes surrounded by long dark lashes. All he could think of was kissing the lovely shape of her mouth.

"And?" she prodded.

"Oh. Well." Ben rushed to gather his thoughts. "We happened to pass a room with photographs—all black and white." He shrugged. "For some reason, it caught my attention and I detoured in. I didn't detour back out." He laughed. "The bus left without me. My dad had to drive to Pasadena and get me."

Stacie looked at him quizzically. "What were the photos?"

He smiled. "I'd like to say they were something classic, like Edward Weston or Ansel Adams. Frankly, I can't remember the photographer's name, if I even looked at it. They were pictures of trash."

"Trash?"

"Umm," he said. "Plastic bags on the beach. Beer cans in a field of wildflowers. He—or she—was telling a story of environmental destruction. Even at twelve I could see that. It was something I'd never thought about until I saw those images."

Remembering the impact those photos had had on him, Ben didn't notice Stacie's face soften. "I'd never thought about how photographs tell stories. I didn't know people took pictures without other people in them. I was a kid. I thought pictures were all about family and friends and dopey poses."

She was listening, head slightly cocked, like she'd listened that morning in the Heritage Park. The breeze flicked the leaves in the shrubbery around them and the shadows on her face danced. Small wrinkles at the corners of her eyes suggested she was about to smile.

"So, when your dad picked you up at the museum, were there threats and groundings?" she asked.

"No," Ben laughed. "My dad's pretty great. When we got home, he dug out an old SLR..."

"SLR?"

"Sorry. Single lens reflex camera. Non-digital. I got a book from the library," he went on, "and I started to learn how to use it. I started taking pictures for the school newspaper and, in high school, the yearbook. But I really didn't like taking pictures of people. I liked taking pictures of things that told stories about the people."

"For instance?" she asked.

"For instance," he repeated, "we had a fire drill one day. I grabbed my camera because I wasn't leaving it behind to get burned up if it wasn't a drill. Or stolen. But as we went by the empty classrooms, I was struck by the books on the floor, the papers on the desks, things half written on the blackboard."

He grinned and raised his eyebrows at her. "So I dodged my teacher—easy to do in the mob—and cut into an empty room. While everyone was outside, I took pictures."

"Were you caught?"

He laughed. "Oh, yeah! Vice-principal was going through the rooms to make sure no one was left behind and he found me. Detention for a week."

Stacie laughed with him. "Here, you being a cop, I thought you'd be a rule follower."

He grinned and shook his head. "Not always."

"So, what kind of stories are you telling with the manzanita?" She nodded to the stand of trees.

Ben hesitated.

"Time," he said. He gestured to the manzanitas. "The old wood and the shiny new bark. The curls graying in the dust."

"The lizard?"

Ben frowned slightly.

"Wasn't it a lizard that day up in the park? I thought I heard it dash off."

"Ah, yes. It was." Ben smiled at her. "I'd forgotten. He was shedding. Most of the old skin was pretty tattered, but there was one large flake on his tail. I had to wait for the light to be just right to show it. Thank you again for waiting."

Stacie lifted her chin slightly in acknowledgement.

"I'm surprised you didn't become a photojournalist. Sounds like it would have been a perfect career."

Ben looked back to the manzanita grouping, not really seeing it. "I intended to," he said finally. "You know. Be on the cover of *National Geographic*." He shook his head sadly and paused again. Stacie waited.

"Then I went to Iraq."

He heard her take a deep breath. "Ah," she said quietly.

Ben turned and saw her looking at the manzanitas, too.

"But you knew that, didn't you?" he surprised himself by asking her.

She turned, and he looked deep into eyes filled with compassion.

"Not that you'd been to Iraq, no," she said, not pretending she didn't know what he was talking about. "I only had the sense you'd been through something very…" She paused, searching for the right word. "Disorienting," was what she finally said. "Something haunting."

"What made you think that?"

Stacie made a face and turned to watch the shadows under the manzanitas.

Ben waited.

239

"You looked tired, I guess," she said finally. "Pinched around the eyes. Like maybe you didn't sleep well. It seemed like you'd lost some level of...joy...from your life. Like a stream that was once buoyant, but is now filled with debris." She paused. "That day up in the Heritage Park? I surprised you on the trail. You put up a wall around yourself when you knew I was there. Not angry, so much as..." Another hesitation. "As private. Protective."

Nothing that would have told me *that someone had gone through hell,* thought Ben. He was astonished at her perceptiveness.

"You're in the wrong business," he told her. "You should be a cop."

She gave him a small smile, then looked away.

He leaned back onto one hip, reached in his pocket and pulled out the smoky quartz.

"Is that why you gave me this?"

Stacie turned back, saw the crystal in his hand, looked up at him in surprise. "Yes," she said.

"People say your aunt could look into people, see what they thought, how they felt. If they were ill."

"That's true," Stacie said without hesitation, her eyes holding his. "She could. She had a gift."

She's testing me, Ben thought.

"Some say you have that ability, too."

"I know they do." She looked away, neither agreeing nor disagreeing.

Ben touched her lightly on the wrist, noticed how warm her skin was. A shock of longing flooded through him.

Stacie turned at the touch. Ben lifted his hand.

"You said this was mine." He raised the hand holding the quartz. "What did you mean?"

240

She dipped her head, looked at the ground. Ben let her think it through.

"What do you know about quartz?" she asked, turning back to him.

He shrugged, frowned. "Not much, I guess. It's a rock." He gave her a small smile. "Sorry. A mineral. A friend told me. Not much beyond that."

"Your friend is right. Quartz is the most common mineral on earth. Granite contains quartz. Sand is quartz." She paused. "But, in my opinion, quartz is also the purest stone on earth."

"I thought diamonds were the purest. Aren't they just graphite or carbon or something?"

"Just carbon." She smiled. "I still say it's quartz. Let the diamond people sue me.

"Anyway, there are lots of kinds of quartz. When it's pure, it's colorless. When it's purple, it's amethyst. Yellow or golden or orangish brown, it's citrine. The smoky is just that." She nodded at the crystal in his hand. "Smoky colored. Sometimes very dark, sometimes less so."

Heavy footsteps sounded on the trail above them. They both glanced up to see a trio of young male hikers come into view.

"Morning!" called one of them.

"How's the view today?" Stacie asked them.

"Gorgeous! Clear out to Catalina. You should go up." One of the hikers smiled at Stacie as they passed.

"Maybe we will."

Then they were gone.

"What's up there?" Ben asked.

"As he said. A great view. It's a popular destination, but it's pretty steep." She nodded at his heavy camera bag.

Ben rose to the challenge. "Let's try it."

"Okay." She grinned. "Just remember, it was your idea." She pulled her ball cap back on, swung her bag around to her back, and they headed up.

It *was* very steep. Ben found himself leaning on his knees to pull himself past the steepest sections.

They were both breathing hard when they reached the top.

"Wow!" was all Ben could manage when they'd hauled themselves to a large flat rock under an old oak. In its worn and stained surface, the boulder showed it was commonly used as a resting spot.

He slipped his bag to the ground, untied the flannel shirt from his waist and dropped it. The warm breeze began to dry the sweat gluing his T-shirt to his back.

Stacie had been right. The view was amazing. He could see up the coast to the curve of the bay at Eden Beach, out to Catalina which was as sharp as a cutout on the horizon. To the south, the coast curved down toward Cabrillo Point where it faded into haze.

Stacie sat down on the rock, pulled off her messenger bag and dropped it next to her. She slipped out of her flannel shirt. "I should have done that before we started climbing," she said, leaning back on one hand and taking off her ball cap to fan herself.

Ben dropped down next to her and became aware of the smell of her hair and skin mingling with that of the dust, the eucalyptus and chaparral. The breeze lifted her hair except where damp tendrils curled on her forehead. The sun flickered through the shadows and ricocheted from the auburn strands, sending out flashes of gold. There was a sheen of sweat on her chest, a tiny drop sliding down between the swell of her breasts.

Ben realized he was staring. He looked up.

Stacie was looking back. She stopped fanning.

Ben's gaze dropped to her mouth. He leaned toward her as if pulled by gravity. She didn't move. Her lips parted slightly.

From beyond them, two pre-teen girls came running out of the chaparral, shrieking, "Race you!"

Stacie's gaze was torn away suddenly.

For Ben, the world dimmed. The moment broke.

A group of girls pounded out of the shrubs, hard on the heels of the first two. They didn't even glance at Ben and Stacie as they passed, intent on the head of the path the two of them had just climbed.

"Slow down!" called a woman coming down the path behind the girls. "It's too steep for running! If you break a leg, I'm feeding you to the coyotes!"

"Hey, Bev."

The woman looked surprised.

"Hi, Stacie." She glanced at Ben. "Are you working today?"

Stacie shook her head. "Just enjoying the day. Your Brownie troop?" She nodded to where the voices were arguing on the trail.

"I thought the climb would wear them out. I shouldn't have brought cookies." There was a shriek from the trail. "Gotta go."

Bev hurried off.

Stacie grinned after her friend. "I can't believe she got them to climb all the way up here."

"You got *me* to come up here," Ben answered.

"No, no. This was your idea remember?" Stacie wagged a finger at him.

Ben smiled as he leaned back on his hands, his eyes on the ocean in the distance.

They sat in companionable silence for a while before he spoke.

"So, what else makes quartz special, besides its purity?"

Stacie looked at him. "You sure you want to get me started on this?"

Ben lifted a shoulder. "Gives me a chance to catch my breath."

She grinned. "Wuss."

"You can be arrested for that, you know. Contempt of cop."

She laughed out loud. Ben grinned, savoring the sound.

"Just for that," she told him finally, "I'm going to give you the two-dollar lecture instead of the fifty-cent one."

"Fire away."

"Okay. First, quartz is piezoelectric."

"It's what?" Ben jerked a glance at her. "You're making that up."

"Nope," she assured him, grinning. "It means quartz responds to pressure by producing electric current. And vice versa. Electric current can make it pulse. That's why they use it for timing in quartz watches."

"There's really quartz in them?" Ben asked, surprised. "I thought it was just something the manufacturers called them to make them sound, I don't know, scientific or mystical or something."

"No. There's really quartz in there. Mostly man-made quartz, to eliminate any impurities, but it's quartz, none-theless.

"During World War II, though," she went on, "they didn't have man-made quartz. They used the real thing in radios."

He frowned. "Like in crystal radio sets? My dad built one as a kid."

"Like that," said Stacie, "Quartz was very important

during the war. I watched an old video online about it. I guess at the time, it would have been a newsreel. Now it's on YouTube. Anyway, they cut the quartz to different thicknesses to tune it to different frequencies."

"Seriously?" Ben lifted an eyebrow.

"Seriously."

"Who knew?" said Ben.

She smiled, and Ben thought she hesitated.

"You asked why I gave you the crystal." She paused again, choosing her words carefully. "People put out electrical impulses, too. When they're angry, sad, happy. Scared. Sometimes those impulses naturally match those of a crystal. The crystal calls to them or they call to the crystal, I'm not sure which."

She's not joking, Ben thought. And weird though it was, it made a kind of sense.

He looked at her steadily. "You're saying I'm like a radio?"

Stacie didn't laugh.

"Exactly," she said, the shade of the oak flickering across her face. "We all are."

"And you can tell when a crystal has the same frequency as a person?"

She hesitated, then looked him straight in the eyes. "Yes. Sometimes."

Ben pulled his smoky quartz out of his pocket again. "So, this one is singing my song?" He smiled slightly.

"Yes." She paused for only a moment, reached into her jeans' pocket and pulled out a crystal. "This one sings mine."

The stone lay on her palm like nothing he'd ever seen before. It was perfectly colorless, except for the small white and green crystals that clung to it at one end. It was as clear as water. Clearer than water, if that were possible. Like air and light condensed into a small, perfect crystal. The sun flashed from the surface.

"This one came to me almost twenty years ago," Stacie was saying. "I was at a gem show in Pasadena with my Aunt Me." Stacie stroked it with her thumb. "I picked it up and couldn't put it down. Aunt Me bought it for me. I've had it ever since."

"It's amazing," said Ben, and it was. He looked at the one in his hand as Stacie slipped hers back into her pocket.

"I know you think I'm crazy," said Stacie, matter-of-factly, turning back to the view. "Most people would. In fact, I don't tell most people."

Ben rolled the smoky crystal in his hand, seeing the color shift in its depths. He felt Stacie's eyes on him.

"That day in the shop? I just knew that one was yours. That…you needed it for some reason. I didn't know why. Only that it was important." She shrugged.

"That it would heal me?" he asked after a moment.

"No," said Stacie firmly. "Crystals can't heal."

"But some people think they do, you said. Like your assistant."

Stacie sighed, then scrubbed her face with her hands. "I will never understand why people want to give credit to something outside themselves when a change comes from within them."

"What do you mean?"

Stacie waved her hands in frustration. "Mir was in her last year of high school. She was having a hard time in a couple classes. Her folks were stressing college. She wasn't getting the grades and wasn't sure she wanted to go anyway. She was in love with someone who didn't love her back. She had just started working for me. It was her first job and she was very unsure of herself. If all the stress wasn't enough by itself, she started eating a lot of comfort food, junk food, in response to the stress. Of course, she broke out. And gained weight. Which caused more stress."

Stacie sighed again. "I recommended a touchstone for her. As it happens, it was a smoky quartz, too."

"For grounding," said Ben.

"Yes," said Stacie, surprised. She looked at him questioningly.

"A friend told me."

"Ah. So anyway. What I hoped was that it would remind her to stay calm. Center. Focus on what was important to her. And it did. She stopped worrying about exams. Blew the guy off. Stopped eating all the crap. Lost weight. The acne went away." She smiled. "Now you've seen her. She exhales confidence with every breath."

They sat for a while in silence.

"Ben." Stacie put a hand on his arm, and her eyes captured his. "It wasn't the stone that 'healed' her. It was her change in attitude. Her change in the way she looked at herself. All that came from within her. All the stone did was give her permission to open that channel. That's all the stones do. Give people a place to focus. To remind them to be still, to listen inside. To see what they need to see. To make room to make whatever changes they need to make."

Was she trying to tell him something? Ben didn't know. Looking into eyes like a shallow sea lit by the sun, he couldn't tell.

He only knew he wished there were some place private, where he could feel her hands on him. Touch her. Kiss her throat, her breasts. Make love to her, maybe for hours.

Ben felt something—darkness, fear, anger—slide away. For the first time in a long time, all the pieces that were him clicked into place to make a whole.

She misunderstood his silence. She lifted her hand, sat back, and a light went out in her eyes. "You *do* think I'm crazy."

"No," he said slowly. He was having a hard time catching his breath. He wanted her hand back on his arm. "I don't think so. I don't understand, Stacie, but no, I … no."

He saw the doubt in her eyes. She turned to look out to the ocean, her face withdrawn.

"Stacie. Look. I don't think you're crazy, but really… I mean... Really? Believing that crystals can affect us or we can affect them? I know you believe that, but…" Ben stumbled to a halt as Stacie turned back toward him. "It does make some sense. But it would take some getting used to for me."

She gazed at him silently for a moment, then sighed. Ben knew that what she was about to say she'd said dozens of times.

"Ben. Go back four hundred years to the Puritans in New England. Now imagine telling one of them you had a device that let you hear voices from across the ocean. No, better, from outer space. Or tell them you could take the heart from a dead man, put it into a dying man, and the dying man would live. What would happen?"

"Well, yeah, but that's medicine and science…"

Stacie interrupted him. "You know as well as I do they'd send the kids out to gather wood for a witch barbecue."

"Well, yeah…" Ben started to say again.

"Okay, now go forward four hundred years into the future. Will we have colonies on other planets? Will we have destroyed the world? Or maybe we'll have learned to communicate with our minds augmented by crystals. Can you say for sure we won't have?"

Ben scrambled for an answer.

"Ben. Those Puritans were no different from the people

today who called my aunt a witch because she had the ability to see things they couldn't," she said with quiet intensity.

Her eyes held him, waiting for an answer. High above them, a hawk called.

"I see your point..." he said finally, simply to be saying something.

"Do you really?" she asked quietly.

"You said mine was for grounding," he said suddenly. "What does yours do?"

Stacie turned back to stare at the ocean in the distance. Ben recognized the gesture from talking to many people who'd been involved in a crime. She was trying to decide whether to tell him the truth or not.

She took a breath. Looked at him. "It helps me see things clearly," she said, watching him steadily.

Ben frowned a bit, feeling uncomfortable. "What things?"

Stacie pursed her lips and rocked her head back and forth. Deciding how much truth to tell, Ben thought.

"People things," she said. "The things we all see and often ignore. If someone is lying. If someone is in pain. Those things."

Ben waited. The red-tailed hawk sailed from over their heads down toward the coast.

"What do you see when your stalker approaches you?" Ben asked quietly.

Stacie's eyes went wide, startled. "Where did *that* come from?" she asked, echoing the question Ben was asking himself.

I'm as crazy as she is, he thought. *Thank God Cruz isn't here.*

Stacie was watching him, looking for signs of mockery, he thought, but he wasn't mocking her. He really wanted to know.

249

He could almost see her decide to give him half an answer. He read distrust or maybe just caution, in her eyes.

"Darkness. Static," was what she said. "He interferes with my radio reception."

"That's all?"

She looked at him steadily. "For now."

Ben felt as if a door had been closed softly in his face. He wanted to open it again, but wasn't sure how. He couldn't say he believed in the crystal communication thing, when he didn't. The radio thing was a good argument, but people being electric? Sending impulses into the world and receiving them?

He wasn't ready to buy that.

Though looking into that beautiful face, he thought he'd be willing to believe anything she told him. Longing, like a magnetic pull, tugged him toward her.

Suddenly, his stomach growled. Loudly.

Stacie laughed. "I guess that means it's near lunch time," she said.

"Always lunchtime somewhere in the world." Ben stood and pulled Stacie up. He held her hand for a moment. She didn't pull free.

His stomach growled again. Louder this time.

Stacie snorted.

"We'd better head down before you starve to death," she said.

"Yeah," he said, puffing his chest out. "It wouldn't be good for my manly image to faint from hunger."

She released his hand, stepped back, and smiled up at him, forgiving him, he thought, for his reluctance to believe.

She picked up her messenger bag from where it lay on the ground, stuffed her flannel shirt into it, lifted the strap of the bag over her head, and pulled the Cubs cap on.

"Down is easier than up," she said.

"After you."

Ben was grateful for the steep descent. It meant they both had to concentrate on keeping their footing, rather than talking.

Too quickly they were at the interpretive center.

Stacie stopped and turned to him, catching him in the middle of thoughts he realized he probably shouldn't be thinking. He hoped she couldn't see *those* clearly.

She seemed to intuit his discomfort.

Well, she would, wouldn't she? Ben thought.

She smiled. Relaxed. All awkwardness from the mountain gone.

"There's a café over there," she said, pointing, "if you want to feed the beast. And if you plan to stay longer."

"You're not?"

She shook her head. "I need to get some work done today. But if you wouldn't mind, maybe you'd walk me to my car? They'll let you back in."

"Of course."

At the car, Stacie pulled her keys out of a pocket.

"Thanks," she said, giving him a quick smile before turning to put the key in the lock.

Ben paused. An hour ago the idea had not been in his head, but now it seemed obvious.

"Stacie?"

"Yes?" She turned back.

"If you're hungry, too, maybe we could have lunch together."

Her slow, delighted smile was a gift to him.

"Yeah," she said. "Yeah, I'd like that a lot."

"How about I follow you to the Eden Beach Hotel. The restaurant on the deck?"

"I'd love it."

"I'll meet you at the front of the parking lot and follow you," Ben said. "It's a battered old gray Camry."

Stacie nodded, tossed her messenger bag into the passenger seat, and slipped behind the wheel. Ben waited until she'd locked the doors, waved through the window, and headed slowly to the front.

Ben jogged to his car, the camera bag bouncing on his hip.

He didn't notice. Joy sang through him. Contentment. Warmth, as if sunlight were moving though his body.

He laughed for no reason.

His mind on lunch and what else might lie ahead, Ben didn't notice a nondescript pickup slip out of the shadows at the back of the parking lot and follow them out the gate.

NINETEEN

THE SKY BEYOND THE TOPS OF THE HILLS WAS STARTING TO lighten, but it was still dark where Stacie waited with Bananas at the top of the stairs. Ben had texted to say he was on his way up. The darkness and fog made her nervous, but she had Mir's pepper spray in her pocket. Bananas, seated at her feet, was completely relaxed.

The dog got up and began wagging his majestic tail. A moment later, Stacie heard the car. She smiled and relaxed, too.

It was her second day out with Ben. They had ended up spending three hours in the sun and ocean air on the hotel deck the previous day. They'd talked about everything. How Eden Beach was changing, with all the home building and the new office centers near the freeway. The Academy Award winners and losers. Music.

The time had passed in a flash, and Stacie had been reluctant to call a halt to it so that she could get to the office to work. When Ben had asked her to go for an early walk at Marsh Creek Beach, about ten miles down the coast, she'd immediately said yes. Not only could she get in an early morning walk, with the tide out, Bananas could have a long run. Best of all, it meant more time with Ben.

The sound of his car coming up the hill brought a thrill of anticipation. Still. She was trying hard not to imagine these as *dates*. Maybe more like a friendship starting.

Maybe more than that. She tried not to hope too hard.

Ben rolled up and turned onto the short apron by the garage. Bananas' tail was practically rotating off.

Ben got out, grinning, and Bananas grinned back. "Hey, boy!" Ben bent down and took the dog's great head in his hands, ruffling the big ears and rubbing his nose. "Ready to run?" If possible, the black dog's tail moved harder.

Stacie studied Ben. He hadn't shaved yet and the stubble was dark along his square jaw. Somehow it made his eyes a brighter blue. He was wearing a red cotton sweater over a button-down blue shirt under his corduroy jacket. He still needed a haircut.

The desire to touch that face, to run her hands though his hair, rushed through her. She only just stopped her hand from reaching out.

"Well, come on, then!" Ben straightened and opened the back door of the Camry. Bananas shot into the seat, turned and sat down, facing the front. Ben laughed.

He turned back to Stacie and acted surprised. "Oh. You, too, Stacie," he said.

"Thanks," she said wryly, grateful the banter gave her heart a chance to slow. "I see how I rate."

Ben walked her around the car, opened the door, and she slipped in, tossing a couple old beach towels into the back seat with the dog.

"Planning on swimming?" he asked as he got behind the wheel.

Stacie held up a thumb. "Large dog." Her index finger followed. "Water." Her middle finger. "Sand."

"Ah." Ben grinned and turned the car downhill toward Tamarind.

"Coffee?" Ben asked, pointing at the cups in the console holder.

"Love it!"

"Sugar and creamer are in the bag, if you want. I brought breakfast, too."

Stacie opened the bag and found a couple scones.

"Well," she said, smiling at him, "when I review this little tour company online, I'll have to mention all the amenities."

"Thank you, ma'am," he said seriously, then grinned.

"Shall I doctor your coffee for you?"

"No. Black. If you're a cop, cream and sugar are the mark of a wuss."

"Good!" She laughed. "Then I can use yours."

"And welcome to it." Ben flicked his blinker on and turned south onto the Coast Highway. Close to the water, the fog pulled in more closely. Outside of town, the ocean on their right was invisible.

Stacie sipped the coffee and it warmed her. "Umm. Good." She shrugged deeper into her pea coat, glad she'd grabbed the bright teal-colored merino cowl Eileen had knitted for her.

"You warm enough?" Ben had seen her pull the cowl up closer to her chin. "You can put the heater on."

"Umm," she said. "I'm good. Coffee is perfect. I'll warm up once Bananas starts walking me."

"By the way," Ben gestured to the floor at her feet where there was a new can of tennis balls, "I brought him a present."

"Oh, you will be his friend for life!" laughed Stacie.

Ben smiled as he reached for his own cup.

As they left Eden Beach behind, Ben asked her, "No more notes?"

Stacie shivered. "No."

The one dark spot the previous day was when Stacie had arrived at the office to find a torn piece of paper wedged into the door. *I warned you*, was all it said. She'd immediately called Ben, who had told her to report it to Meissner.

"I got a text from Detective Meissner yesterday afternoon. She's coming by later today to pick up the last one."

"Did she say anything else about it?"

"No. Just that." Stacie didn't tell him how much Meissner's lack of comment had worried her.

When they pulled into the parking lot for the beach, there were a couple cars and a van already there.

"Surfers, I guess," said Stacie.

"Possibly," said Ben, opening his door. "We're getting a lot more homeless people living in their cars, though."

Ben came around the car and opened the door for Bananas as Stacie got out. The car rocked as the dog catapulted onto the gravel of the lot. He danced in place as Stacie put his leash on him.

"He really is a big dog," Ben chuckled as he reached into the car and pulled out the cylinder of tennis balls.

"Yeah," said Stacie. "Who knew? He was so cute and cuddly when my friend gave him to me. I had no idea he'd get to weigh almost as much as I do."

"What kind of mix is he?"

"Vet originally thought poodle and Labrador, but as Bananas got bigger, he thought something like a poodle/Newfoundland mix, maybe. Personally, I think he's part gorilla."

Ben laughed as the three of them crossed the lot and went through the tunnel under the highway. "How old is he?"

"Six, seven-ish. Syl works in the shelter in town. She thought I needed company after my aunt died." She smiled down at the dog trotting happily at her side. "Turned out he was the best medicine I could have been given."

When they came out and hit the breeze off the water, Stacie buttoned her pea coat, flipped the collar up, and pulled the cowl up so it partially covered her head.

To their left, a necklace of tide pools was strung around the base of the bluff, wet where the waves had pounded it overnight. The bluff above the tide pools was covered with coastal shrubs and stunted pines. The condos at the edge of the bluff lay hidden in the fog that had thickened as they had driven south. Off to the right, the long, flat curve of the beach disappeared into the thick, gray mist. The waves rolled in from nowhere.

As Ben reached to button his corduroy jacket, the wind caught the corner and flipped it up. Stacie was startled to see his holster before he pulled the jacket closed.

She frowned, uneasy. "You brought your gun today?"

Ben nodded, casually. "Normally, I don't carry it when I'm off duty, but I'd like not to be surprised." He turned to face her and saw the worried look. "I don't expect he'll approach, not when you're with me, but stalkers are unpredictable. And after the last note…"

A distant warning buzzed deep in her mind, chilling her.

"Ben."

"Umm?" He looked up from the buttons.

"There isn't anything you're not telling me, is there? You wouldn't be using me as bait to catch this guy."

There was no mistaking the surprise on his face. "No. Of course not. I wouldn't put you at risk like that. I just want to be sure I can keep you safe." He waved a hand to the empty

257

beach. "Especially when we're somewhere as deserted as this."

She kept her eyes on his face. "But there's something else, isn't there?"

"There's always something." He evaded her question.

"You know something about this guy?"

"No," he said firmly. "I don't know anything about this guy. There have just been some...complex things happening. They've got us all on edge. They're being investigated." He smile briefly. "But not by me."

That was, she sensed, at least part of the truth.

She took a deep breath and let it out slowly. She nodded. "I keep thinking I can have a normal life." She looked at Ben. "But I can't, can I?"

"Not until we can get a handle on him," said Ben apologetically.

He held her eyes for a moment. Stacie took in the creases at the corner of his eyes, the slight puffiness under them.

"You look tired."

He made a face. "Restless night," was all he said and turned toward the water.

Stacie let it go.

They walked down to the firm, water-packed sand at the ocean's edge. Bananas yanked on his leash, breaking into Stacie's thoughts. "Okay! Ben brought you a present and you're gonna love it." She released the catch on the leash, and Ben popped the top on the tennis ball canister. At the sound, Bananas raised up on his hind feet and his front feet waved. It was only brief, but then he did it again.

Ben laughed out loud, and Stacie realized she'd never heard him sound so carefree. "What was that?" he asked Stacie as he hurled the ball down the beach. Bananas spun and raced after it, ears flying.

"It's his bananas dance," Stacie told him. "It's how he got his name. When I first got him, he would do that and turn in a circle when the squirrels came through the yard. I used to call him my bananas dog. The name just stuck."

"Well, it suits him." Ben grinned as Bananas came galloping back up the beach, pink tennis ball in his mouth.

Ben reached for it and Bananas danced backward. "Oh, so that's how you want to play." Ben shook his head. "Can't outsmart this cop, dog." He pulled another ball from the canister. Bananas spat out the one he was holding and backed up. Ben tossed the new ball and Bananas kicked up sand as he raced off. Ben snagged the ball the dog had dropped, and he and Stacie began to walk down the beach after him.

"Not much of a picture day," said Stacie, nodding to the bag over Ben's shoulder.

"Not now, but…" He shrugged. "Could burn off. I never know." They watched Bananas galloping back toward them, unmindful of the waves that washed in over his feet. He spat the ball out and pranced backward.

Stacie bent to grab it. "We should take turns." She pitched the ball outward. Bananas trotted over to where it landed a short distance away. He came back and, rather pointedly, dropped the ball at Ben's feet.

They both laughed as Ben bent down. "Okay," said Stacie, tucking her hands into her pockets. "I guess we don't take turns!"

They walked for a while on the hard-packed sand, dodging incoming waves, punctuating their amble with Ben tossing the ball for Bananas who sometimes spat the ball out, and sometimes tried to get Ben to chase him. Stacie's hand curled around the crystal in her pocket. She was content. Safe. Warmed by the coffee, the brisk walking. Even the amethyst felt warm against her heart.

"Thank you, Ben," Stacie said finally.

He looked surprised. "For what?"

"For giving me a bit of my life back." She pulled her hand out of her pocket and waved at the beach. "Helping me get out. To feel like I'm not caged or trapped." A few more steps and she added, "For not treating me like I'm a charlatan."

"About the intuition, you mean?"

She nodded.

"Doesn't mean the jury isn't still out."

"I know." She smiled. "But you were nice about it."

Ben hesitated. "I knew a guy in Iraq. Used to talk about listening to the little voice. To stay out of trouble." He shrugged. "Saved his butt a number of times. Maybe saved mine."

"Smart guy," said Stacie. "Too many people ignore their intuition. Their little voice."

"Well, yeah," said Ben. "We all say that. 'I knew that would happen.' But do we? And how do you know when it's right?"

"Practice," she said. "Even then, it's not always dependable." *Unless you're Amelia*, she did not say. "Sometimes it won't warn you. Sometimes you think it's warning you and it's nothing. Sometimes it's saying something you don't want to hear.

"Bananas, no!" she called as the dog thundered down the beach through the water after a flock of seagulls. The birds lifted off, screeching as the dog spun in circles in the water beneath them. "Come!" Stacie shouted.

Bananas, unable to reach the birds, gave the canine equivalent of a shrug, and trotted up the beach, picking up the ball where he'd dropped it.

"He doesn't bark."

"Not often," says Stacie. "Mr. Mellow. The world is his

friend. He must be more Lab or Newfie than poodle. When he does bark, though, I pay attention."

Ben chuckled as the dog spat the ball at his feet and danced backward. "Relentless, aren't you?" Dog and ball flew down the beach again.

They watched Bananas, tail up, ears flapping as he dove into the sand after the ball. He turned, sat, then flopped on his front paws, watching them walk toward him.

"Great. Wet *and* sandy. Lazy!" Stacie called. Bananas just thumped his tail in the sand.

"I can't believe you've never been here," Ben said. "You've lived in Eden Beach all your life."

"That's true," said Stacie. "But the times I go to the beach, I usually just walk along the boardwalk on Main Beach or up through Bayview Park over to the Point." She shrugged. "I was never a big sunbather." She pointed to her pale face. "Like I said the other day: sunburn, freckles."

She glanced at him as he bent to retrieve the ball and tucked it in his pocket. "So how do you know about this? Were you a surfer growing up?" she teased him.

"Nope. I was born in southern Louisiana. No surfing in the bayous." He gave her a lopsided smile.

Looking at his smile, Stacie wondered how she ever could have thought him closed or guarded. His look was open, relaxed today.

"New Orleans?"

The smile broadened. "No, though most people assume that's where we came from. No, I was born in Lafayette, smack dab in the center of Cajun country."

"Really?" said Stacie, surprised. "My Aunt Me had a friend who's Cajun. Her grandmother was…" She stopped talking and walking and stared. Ben, who'd kept going, stopped a couple steps beyond her and turned back.

"Robard!" said Stacie. "You're Emmie Robard's son?"

The large, very wet and very sandy dog charged up, dropped his ball and punched Ben in the leg with his nose. Ben laughed as he bent to get the ball, saying, "Yes. She said she knew you."

Stacie's world shifted. She'd been dreaming—wishing— since the day at the Heritage Park that Ben was a man who would understand and accept her gift.

If anyone could, it would be the great-grandson of a *traiteuse*.

Why then, she wondered, *does he say the jury is still out about believing in intuition?*

Perhaps, she thought, *he's always wanted a normal life, too.*

Stacie nodded, keeping her thoughts to herself. "I met your mom several times at the tea shop. She's a delightful lady."

Ben laughed again. "Yes, she is. Crazy, but delightful." The ball went flying.

Ah, thought Stacie. *Maybe the jury has been out a long time.*

"She said she consulted your aunt once," added Ben. "Maybe more than once."

"Oh," said Stacie as they continued down the beach. "I didn't know that. Amelia always kept readings to herself."

She nodded at Bananas digging at something near the base of the bluff.

"I hope he isn't into something that's going to perfume your car." Stacie shook her head.

"Can't be worse than it already is."

"Is your dad Cajun, too?"

Ben shook his head. "Not to my knowledge. Or to his. In

fact, there was a big blow up in the family when Mom agreed to marry him."

"Why?" Stacie was puzzled.

"Not Catholic," said Ben. "In Mom's family, Catholicism is a birthright. Lot of the family wouldn't speak to her afterward."

"That's a shame."

"Yeah, well." Ben gave a small grin. "Family is even more important. When I was born, and Dad said he was fine having me baptized a Catholic, all was forgiven." He glanced at her. "My dad's a great guy. I'm pretty sure they were already looking for a reason to forgive Mom and accept him." He grinned more. "Didn't hurt that it was obvious Dad thought the sun rose and set in my mom, either."

"So what are you all doing in California?"

"We moved to the Valley when I was about eight, and my dad started working at the hospital there. He changed to the South Coast Medical Center when I was in my early teens."

"Your dad's a doctor?"

"Umm. Surgeon."

Bananas had flopped on the sand again, near a large rock at the base of the bluff. But as they passed him, he leaped up and came galloping after them, sand flying, pink ball in his mouth.

"You come down here to swim? Is that how you know this place?" Stacie asked as Bananas spat the ball at Ben and danced backward.

"Yeah." Ben grunted as he bent for the ball. "It's one of my favorite places. Usually not a lot of people here this time of morning."

"You never said. Were you a swimmer in school?"

Ben shook his head. "No. Not really interested in compet-ing. Or pools. But I like being beyond the breakers. It's quiet out there, surprisingly." He paused, threw the ball for the dog and took a few more steps before he added, "I started swimming after I came back from Iraq."

Stacie wondered for a brief moment if he'd contemplated suicide. A guy she'd gone to high school with had done just that after returning from a stint in the military. Had killed his wife and then swum out to sea.

"Because of the quiet?" was what she finally asked him.

He looked at her in surprise, then turned back to the dog charging toward them. "Exactly that," he said. "For the quiet."

Ben grabbed the dog's big head and ruffled his ears before he bent to grab the ball and throw. Stacie stayed silent.

"The sea," Ben continued, "is unambiguous. It is what it is. It doesn't have any agenda. It's not manipulative. It simply exists." He took a deep breath as Bananas came running back, dropping the ball.

"Heel, Bananas. Sit," said Stacie. The dog hesitated a moment, uncertain, then did as she commanded. Stacie looked up at Ben.

"No darkness?" she asked quietly.

"Oh, it can be dark," Ben said turning to look at the water. "Powerful. Dangerous." He looked back at her. "But not malicious. Vindictive."

"Easier to deal with than people?"

He didn't smile. "In many ways, much easier."

He'd given her a gift, letting her in so far. She nodded. "I can't say I understand," she said. "I've never gone through what you have. But I can try."

"Thanks," said Ben. "I appreciate that." He gave her a ghost of a smile. "And if you ever tell Cruz this, I'll deny it."

She smiled in response. "What's that?"

He drew a deep breath. "Your crystal helps," he said,

gesturing toward the ocean. "It's like looking into the sea. Light becoming dark. No uncertainty. It's itself. It's like the ocean in my pocket. It's quiet."

"I'm glad," she said simply.

He glanced down at the big, wet, curly-haired dog wagging his tail slowly in the sand. He frowned slightly and reached for his camera bag. "Don't move," he said. "Don't let Bananas move."

Surprised, Stacie took a grip on the dog's collar. "Stay," she told him.

Stepping away from them and in front, Ben pulled the small digital camera from his bag. Stacie realized it was the dog's ball on the hard-packed sand Ben was looking at, and the paw prints around it.

"Shall I step back?"

"No." He framed a shot, moved, took another. He worked from different angles, different distances. Then he smiled.

"Here." He pulled an image up on the small screen.

The dog's paw prints, the ball, her boots, and the dog's wet paws told the story of what they'd been doing.

Teasing she said, "You don't shoot people."

"Boots don't count." He smiled.

"We can move?"

Ben nodded. "You can move."

Stacie bent, snagged the ball and tossed it back the way they had come. She could almost hear Bananas sigh with disgust as he sauntered over to get it.

"Complain all you want," she told the dog. "We need to head back."

"Breakfast first?" Ben asked, pulling the bakery bag out of his pocket.

"I'd forgotten," laughed Stacie. "Yes."

They ploughed up into the loose sand, then sat down on a

piece of beach to share the scones. Bananas plopped next to Ben. When they were done eating, Ben grabbed the ball from between Bananas' paws, put it and the one from his pocket back into the canister.

When he put a hand out to her, Stacie didn't hesitate to take it. He pulled her to her feet.

Neither one of them moved to release their hands.

"Okay?" asked Ben, raising their joined hand slightly.

"Very okay," she said. Her fears of the last weeks slid away, and happiness rose in her like a tide.

The van was gone when they got back to the parking lot, replaced by two more cars and a pickup, although they'd seen no one else on the beach.

"Bananas, stay," Stacie said as she reluctantly let go of Ben's hand so he could unlock the car. He grabbed the towels from the back and, handing one to Stacie, they rubbed Bananas down, getting him partially dry and leaving a lot of the sand in the parking lot. Stacie shook the towels out and laid them on the back seat.

"Not necessary," said Ben. "He can't do a lot of damage."

"Still." Stacie pointed the dog into the car. "Might as well do what I can."

Ben closed the door as the dog settled down, lying across the seat, head on his paws. Stacie reached for the handle on the passenger door and was startled when Ben laid his warm hand gently on hers.

She raised her eyes to his, puzzled.

Time paused. The wind fell. Sound moved away. Stacie smelled the sea on his jacket, his skin.

Saw the look on his face. Soft. Serious.

Hesitating. Asking permission.

He didn't have to ask twice.

Stacie slipped her fingers between his and lifted her face.

Leaned closer. Ben raised his free hand, stroked her chin with his thumb, then slipped his hand behind her head, cupping the nape of her neck. The warmth of his hand slid all the way down Stacie's body, and she went slack. As Ben bent his head, she closed her eyes. His mouth found hers unerringly.

His mouth was soft, warm. He tasted of coffee and chocolate from the scone. His unshaven chin rubbed against her face. He sucked gently at her lips, tugging, tasting, finding how they fit together.

Stacie felt herself falling, her past rushing by her or up to her, filling this moment. The world rocked.

It really does that, she thought wildly.

Stacie heard a soft sound from the back of her throat.

So did Ben.

His hand dropped hers, slipped around her waist. He pulled her closer.

Stacie lifted on her toes, her arms slipping up around broad shoulders. She parted her lips, and Ben's tongue gently reached inside.

Stacie lost herself in the smell and taste of him. The feel of his hard body against hers.

She moved closer, stepping one foot between his, and slid a hand into his hair. It curled thickly over her fingers as she tugged him, unresisting, down to her. His tongue teased her.

They might have stayed there for minutes, hours.

The sound of gravel spitting under tires broke them apart. Stacie felt lost, confused as Ben broke the kiss. She turned her head in his hand in time to catch a glimpse of the pickup sliding down the drive to the entrance of the lot, skidding onto the highway.

She turned back to Ben, his eyes, deep blue, soft and liquid. His thumb stroked her check.

"I'd do that again," he said quietly. "But sometime today, Cruz expects me to show up at work."

"Oh, cripes. Work," said Stacie. The world crashed back.

Ben held her for a moment more, then lightly kissed her again, as if to prove he'd meant it.

He opened the car door. Dazed, Stacie got in. After the warmth of Ben's arms, she felt suddenly cold.

She shivered as Ben got in behind the wheel.

"Cold?"

"A little," she said.

He leaned to the dashboard and flipped the heater on high. It blasted them with cold air.

He made an apologetic face at her. "Well, that didn't help."

Stacie laughed. "It'll warm up in a bit. But would you mind stopping at In A Minute on our way back?"

"That coffee place just up the coast?"

"Yes. They make a terrific hot chocolate."

"Done."

They chatted quietly—mostly about Bananas—on the drive, but Stacie was still really wrapped in Ben's arms, in the moment in the parking lot. She hadn't felt this happy in a long time.

After the quiet of the beach and the soothing sound of the waves, the noise in the small coffee shop hit them almost physically. A number of tables were filled with friends chatting. In a corner, there was a cluster of close-packed women knitting.

When Ben and Stacie reached the counter, the barista smiled.

"Stacie! You don't usually come in during the week."

"Beach walking this morning. We're half frozen."

"The usual?"

"Yes, Sue. Two?" Stacie looked at Ben who nodded. "Two," she said turning back to the barista.

"In a minute!" Sue said. She grinned and turned to make their drinks.

"You come here a lot," Ben said.

Stacie nodded. "Usually on my way to the Becker." She pointed at Sue steaming the milk at the other end of the counter. "I'm addicted. If they were in town, I'd be in serious trouble."

He smiled.

Stacie raised her voice to Sue. "How's the house hunting going? You and Kerry find anything worth fixing up yet?"

A light went out in Sue's face. "Oh, still looking."

"Problems?" asked Stacie.

"Not really."

Another barista was just finishing a sale near Stacie and Ben. "Her brother doesn't like the new boyfriend," she told Stacie, quietly. With a glance at Sue, she whispered, "Neither do we."

"Oh?" said Stacie. "I didn't know she was seeing someone."

"He's new. Some customer. He jerks her around." The barista wrinkled her nose. "We're all hoping she figures it out and drops him soon. Or he drops her. For her sake. Kerry says he won't buy the house with her if the new guy is in the picture."

She stepped away to help a new customer.

A moment later, Sue was back with the hot chocolates and a genuine smile. "Guaranteed to unfreeze the most frozen of customers."

"Exactly what I need," Stacie told her as Ben paid for their drinks.

Stacie was quiet on the way back to the car. As Ben

unlocked the door, she gazed vacantly at the coffee shop, a small frown between her eyes.

"Something wrong?" asked Ben, holding the door.

Stacie blinked, looked up at him, then back at the coffee shop. She frowned again. "No, not really." She hesitated, then shook her head slightly. "Maybe a bit of a headache," she said.

"It was noisy in there."

"It was," she agreed uncertainly. She shook her head again.

Ben closed the door as she got in the car. Bananas barely opened an eye as Ben slammed his door. Stacie cupped her hands around the warmth of the cup.

"Thank you for this," she said. "And for the morning."

Ben paused, hand on the ignition and looked at her. "The first of many, I hope," he said.

Stacie felt warm. And not from the hot chocolate.

TWENTY

STACIE WAS BUSY ALL MORNING WITH CLIENTS IN HER OFFICE.
There were moments, though, when her mind slipped back to
the previous morning at the beach. Ben's arms around her.
His kiss. "First of many," he'd said. She kept fantasizing
about the next time. More than once she had to drag her attention back to numbers.

It was a glorious day, too, which made staying focused
difficult. The early morning fog had burned off, although
Catalina was still hidden, as it often was, in haze. It was
sunny and warm, the sky above brilliant and blue. A light
breeze kept things feeling like spring.

The beautiful weather had gotten into everyone. Occasionally, Stacie could hear Mir talking brightly with
customers or laughing with Eileen. As Stacie walked her
clients out, she'd see Bananas dozing on the back patio,
wandering in the open door to munch kibble, or lying at
Eileen's feet.

The protesters were absent, though she suspected they'd
be back. Stacie hoped they weren't annoying other businesses, but was glad they were gone for today. She knew

Troy was still out there, too, but for the first time in weeks, Stacie was at peace.

She came downstairs a little after noon. Her 1:30 p.m. appointment had cancelled, and Stacie was grateful for a bit of a break.

"Where's Mir?" she asked Eileen, a flutter of fear in her heart when she realized the young woman wasn't there.

"She went to get lunch and walk the critter," said Eileen, as Stacie realized Bananas was gone, too.

"Good. He was disappointed that Ben wasn't waiting for us this morning," said Stacie, dropping into the chair next to Eileen.

"He likes your policeman, then," said Eileen, eyes on her yarn.

"I don't think he's *my* policeman. It's Bananas he likes." Stacie smiled, then paused.

The amethyst was heavy and warm next to Stacie's heart.

Was it warmer than usual?

Don't be silly, she told herself.

She smiled, remembering her nine-year-old self hoping the stone really was magic.

What would Ben think of that? she wondered. Would she ever tell him?

Eileen was looking at her.

"He was kind to get me out walking again, though. I certainly need the stress relief right now. And I feel safe with him."

"Umm," was all Eileen said.

"I know what you're thinking," said Stacie as she got up.

Eileen just smiled, eyes on her work.

"Mir should be back shortly," Stacie told her. "I made iced tea this morning. Would you like some of that?"

"Yes, that sounds..." Eileen glanced up and froze. Stacie spun toward the door as Eileen reached into her knitting bag.

Troy was stepping into the shop.

A gun? Stacie thought irrationally and frantically as Eileen rose to her feet. *Does she have a gun?*

Her heart hammering, Stacie fumbled in her pocket for her phone. *Ben. Ben. Ben,* was the refrain in her head.

She was dragging the phone out when the newcomer pulled off his sunglasses.

Same blond hair. Same arrogant stance.

Hazel eyes. Different nose.

Not Troy.

The relief almost brought her to tears.

But I know him, she thought. *I've seen him. Where?*

Stacie tried to find a smile.

"Hello," she said. "Can I help you?"

"I hope so," he said, and adopted a worried look. "I'm looking for my sister. Well, my sister to be." He feigned embarrassment. "She's actually my fiancé's sister. But we're so close, she's like my little sister already." He smiled.

And Stacie knew who he was.

The adrenalin from fear flashed into anger that almost consumed her.

How dare he come here?

"Oh?" was all she said, her voice steady despite the rage shaking her.

"Yes. Her name is Ginny?"

Behind her, Eileen took a sharp breath.

He looked at Stacie, trying to read her face, but Stacie betrayed nothing.

"Sorry," she said evenly. "I don't know anyone by that name."

"Maybe she didn't give you her name. Small, blond, very thin. Shy. She would have been looking for, well, help."

Stacie produced a bland look and lifted her hands slightly as much as to say, *Sorry. No help here.*

The imitation smile faltered a bit.

"Well. Well, this is a bit difficult. I hate to speak ill of her, but I hope you'll understand. Ginny is a bit rash, and she's young and, well, she's gotten herself...well, into trouble, if you understand me. She's understandably upset. She's been raving about getting rid of the baby. And, well..." Here he paused to give a nervous laugh. "I'm afraid she talked about coming here, coming to you. For help." He put heavy emphasis on the last word.

"You'd better leave," said Stacie, amazed at the coldness in her own voice.

"Look, I certainly won't tell anyone. I just need to find Ginny. My fiancé is worried about her."

Does your fiancé know you raped a fifteen-year-old girl? She remembered the bruises on Ginny's throat. This guy was dangerous. Stacie had to get him out of the shop.

"I'm just trying to help her..."

Stacie lifted the hand holding the phone. She had already thumbed in 911. She needed only to connect.

"If you don't leave, I'm calling the police."

The blond man dropped the friendly pretense and stepped toward her menacingly.

"Not without the girl," he said.

"No girls here," she said, lifting the phone and dialing. "Now go."

"Don't play games." He took another menacing step toward Stacie.

"911," said a voice. "What is the nature of your emergency?"

"My name is Stacie Cappella. I own The Bell, Book and Crystal on Glen Eden near Tamarind. There is a man in my store threatening me. I need the police immediately."

She didn't hear the dispatcher's response.

"You bitch," said the man. "I know what you are. I know what you've done. You're a murderer! You'll burn for this, you know. You'll burn! God will burn you!"

He spun around, stopped short of the door and turned back, his face blotched red and white. He flung an accusatory finger toward her. "God will not suffer a witch to live!" he shouted. He turned, almost knocking Mir down as he shoved out the door. Bananas whirled, growling, and snapped at him as he passed. The man didn't appear to notice as he trotted, stiff-legged, down the steps and across the street.

Bananas wagged his tail as if nothing had happened as Mir, wide-eyed, closed the door behind her.

"What on earth was that about?" she asked.

"Ma'am?" the dispatcher was saying in Stacie's ear.

"He's gone," she said. "He's just stormed out."

"Do you still require police assistance?"

"No," said Stacie. *What I need is another life*, she thought. *Or a freaking gun permit.* "No, I'll call them later and put in a report. Thank you."

"Yes, ma'am." The dispatcher rang off. Stacie slipped the phone back into her pocket.

Mir looked pale. She licked her lips. "That wasn't...him, was it? Your stalker?" she managed to say.

"No. It was the guy who got little Ginny pregnant."

"He's a piece of work and no mistake," said Eileen, turning to sit down. Stacie turned and saw what the older woman was holding. Not a gun. A pair of long, wicked-looking, large-gauge wooden knitting needles. "I'm too old for this."

275

Another time, Stacie might have laughed. But now, she breathed out a gust of air and collapsed next to her friend. "I am so ready for all this...bullshit...insanity to *end*!" she announced to the ceiling. She brought her gaze back down and scrubbed her face with her hands. "I don't suppose, Mir, that you got some tequila with lunch."

"I can go back," said Mir, trying to smile.

Stacie laughed and heard the sound of tears in her voice. Mir placed the bag with the food on the counter and knelt to put her arms around Stacie. Bananas poked his nose into her side. Stacie put her arms around both of them.

Eileen got back to her feet. "In lieu of tequila, chamomile all around, don't you think? Or some of that iced tea?"

She was heading toward the kitchen when Colin bounded in.

"I thought I saw Mir with a Cabos bag," he said. "I hope you planned enough for me, too?"

Then he saw the looks on everyone's face. "What happened?" he said seriously.

"Nothing," said Stacie. "We just had a scare."

She scratched Bananas' ears.

"And you," she said to the dog. "Did you have a psychotic break? You never growl, much less try to bite anyone."

Bananas wagged his tail as if he had no idea what she was talking about. Satisfied with his ear scratching, he went out onto the patio and dropped into a shady spot.

"So what just happened?" Colin looked between Mir and Stacie.

Stacie told him briefly about Ginny's visit and now Jer's.

"What a bastard," said Colin.

"Tea," called Eileen from the kitchen.

Colin and Mir helped Eileen share out the nachos, salads

and enchiladas while Stacie called the Crisis Center to tell them about Jer's visit.

"Thanks," Danielle told her. "We know how to handle it."

"Is she okay?" asked Stacie. "Ginny? I know you can't tell me anything, I just want to know she's okay."

"She is. She's safe."

"Thank you," said Stacie. "As long as he can't find her, that's all I need to know."

They tried to talk about inconsequential things while they ate, but they kept coming back to Jer, the vandalism, the protesters, the stalker. She didn't tell them about the note she'd found Sunday. There was only so much she could expect her friends to handle.

"Do you need me to follow you home tonight?" asked Colin as he headed back to his studio.

"I hate to ask, but yes," Stacie told him. "I'll be working late, and Stan and Betty are not night owls. I hate to ask them to stay up to watch for me." Colin was usually up past midnight.

He nodded. "Call when you're ready to lock up. I'll come over."

He looked at Eileen. "Dessert?" he asked hopefully.

The three women laughed.

TWENTY-ONE

BEN WAS INTO HIS RHYTHM. THREE OVERHAND STROKES, A breath, three more, a breath. The gray-green sea rose and fell, like a great, primal beast breathing. Fog curled over the water. Off to his right, he heard the waves crashing on the beach, a syncopated beat to the smooth rolling of the ocean. Off to his left, there was only the sea.

His mind was empty, calm, but deep inside he was filled with happiness, pure and glowing. And peace. As if, finally, he could see a future he could love.

A woman he could love.

Smiling to himself, Ben turned and stroked toward shore, bodysurfing the breakers into the sand.

He was warm, loose. Shaking the water from his fingertips, he shoved his hair out of his face. *Maybe time to get a haircut*, he thought. *I'm beginning to look like Hayes*. He grinned at the thought. If he had time, he'd get one before he had to go to court today. Make a better impression on the judge, not to mention the lieutenant.

His stride slowed as he moved from hard-packed to loose sand. He stepped into his flip flops as he passed the spot where he'd dropped them and trudged up the stony, inclined path that led to the shoulder of the highway where he always parked. The road was busier now than when he'd arrived at first light.

As the Camry appeared from the fog, Ben stopped. The right rear tire was flat.

"Oh, crap."

After a few more steps, he realized it was worse than that. The car was sitting on all four rims.

"What the hell?"

A quick look told him all he needed to know. Someone had slashed his tires.

"Damn him!"

Swearing creatively, Ben stripped off his wet suit and plucked the car key from the pocket of his swim suit. Tossing the wet suit into the trunk, he grabbed his towel and dried off. He pulled on his sweats, snagged his phone and dialed.

Cruz is going to kill me, he thought as the phone rang. *I don't have time for this.* Fortunately, he didn't have to be in court until the afternoon. *So much for the haircut,* he thought.

"What the hell are you calling for this early?" asked Tucker by way of greeting.

"Like you're not up."

"Didn't say I wasn't up. Just figured you'd be out wrestling sharks at this time of day."

"Yeah, well. While I was doing that, some asshole slashed my tires."

"Tires, as in plural?"

"Tires, as in all four."

Tucker laughed. "Wow. Whose wife you been sleeping with?"

"Not funny! It was that shit-for-brains, Todd Huff."

"You see him?"

"No. If I'd seen him, I'd probably have shot him."

"I'm guessing you need a ride?"

"You're guessing right. Bring the truck. With luck, I can get four new tires and we can get them put on before noon."

"So, you're telling me you don't have triple A?"

"Triple A is for wusses," said Ben, grinning. "I have you."

"Yeah, yeah. Maureen tells me I'm a pushover."

"Maureen is right. Now get off the phone and get down here. I'm freezing my ass off."

Ben told Tucker where to find him, hung up and got in the car. He sighed, then called Cruz.

STACIE'S LAST CLIENT, Deidre Duncan, finally left about 9:30 p.m. Trying not to show her nervousness, she scanned the street closely as she let DeeDee out the front door. She hadn't seen Troy, but she'd been edgy all day, like she was being watched. As far as she could see, the street was quiet. Nonetheless, Stacie locked up quickly and went back upstairs, Bananas padding after her.

Stacie rolled up to her desk with a sigh. She would have preferred to go home, light the fire to take the chill off the air, snuggle up with Bananas and read. But that would be pretty much impossible for another month or so. Tax season was always an endurance race, but it felt longer this year. Yesterday morning she'd found the front of her store egged *again*. After Jer's visit, she was pretty sure he was responsible. She was just glad it was eggs, not rocks, he was throwing. At least not yet. It was cheaper to wash the siding than to replace the windows.

For a moment, Stacie thought wistfully about Ben. She hadn't been able to see him again, though he'd called almost every day to check on her. He'd had a crazy week, too.

Someone had slashed his tires while he was at the beach. He'd sounded grim when he'd told her.

Thinking about Ben was not getting her work done. She turned to her monitor and spent the next hour or so working on the Duncans' return.

Normally she'd send a client like this to a CPA because of the return's complexity. But after heart surgery left him frightened and confused, Parker Duncan had found a touchstone at The Bell, Book and Crystal. He swore the stone kept him calm and cleared his mind. DeeDee wasn't sure, but Parker wouldn't take his taxes to anyone else. It helped that the Duncans were meticulous in their files and records. However, Stacie had made it clear that, if she were over her head at any point, she'd call in a CPA.

She was finishing up about quarter to eleven, when Bananas, lying in the hall at the top of the stairs, suddenly sat up. His tail lay flat and unmoving on the floor. A low growl came from his throat.

Stacie froze, hand hovering over the keyboard, heart pounding. She felt disoriented.

Troy. The sense of him was so strong, it was as if he were in the room.

She stood, flipped off the lights, and went to stand in the office door. Bananas rumbled again. Stacie put a hand on his neck. She didn't hear anything, but the big black dog was rigid.

The security lights in the garden flashed on.

Bananas' rumbling got more determined. He stood up, moved out from under Stacie's hand and padded into the darkened room at the back of the house. Stacie followed. Standing to the side of the window, she carefully lifted the edge of the curtain. A shadow moved at the side of the house out of range of the lights.

She slipped her hand into her pocket, curling her fingers around her crystal. She didn't need the sense of razors slicing her palm to know he was there. She could almost see his eyes searching for her in the dark.

Panic chilled her blood. All the doors and windows were secure, but as surely as he was locked out, she was locked in. She couldn't get out the back and didn't dare go out the front. If he broke a window, she'd be trapped inside with him.

She pulled out her phone and hit the call button.

"Stacie?" Ben's voice calmed her immediately.

"He's here, Ben. In the backyard."

"You're sure?"

A flash of anger stabbed her. "Of course, I'm sure!" she said. "Bananas is growling. He never growls."

"I'm just down the block," he said, calmly, making her regret snapping at him. "I'll check the back."

"The gate's locked."

"I'll manage. Keep the dog with you." He disconnected.

She laid a hand on Banana's collar. She didn't want him bolting downstairs.

A car stopped in front.

Oh, God, she thought. *What if Ben runs into him?* Panic filled her throat again.

The lights in the yard went out.

Her phone pinged. Colin.

"Warning!!! Outside!!" read the text.

"Ben," she texted back. She could practically see Colin's eyebrows go up.

She heard a noise at the gate. The lights flashed on. Her hand tightened on the dog's collar, but she was afraid to look out.

Her heart jerked erratically. All she could think about was the danger she'd put Ben in.

Bananas relaxed, and his tail wagged. The world righted itself.

A few minutes later, her phone rang.

"I can't see the whole yard from the gate," said Ben. "You're upstairs?"

"Yes."

"I'm coming to the front door. Bring the dog with you and let me in. Don't open up until you see me there."

Holding tight to the dog's collar, Stacie navigated the narrow stairs, Bananas trotting happily next to her, tail wagging wildly. It was as if the last ten minutes had never happened.

Stacie stopped at the bottom of the steps. The bathroom door was closed as always, and from here she couldn't see into the kitchen. She didn't sense Troy anywhere nearby. She reached for her crystal. The razors were gone. Her palm still burned, but she knew he was moving away.

Through the glass panel in the front door, she saw Ben standing in the glow of the security light. She let go of Bananas and opened the door.

Ben slipped in. His gun was in his hand. "Lock it behind me. Keep the dog here and wait until I come back."

"He's gone," Stacie told him.

Ben simply nodded. "Stay here," he repeated.

He opened the bathroom door, went into the kitchen and out the back door. The lights in the back flashed on again. Stacie saw him cross the patio.

Her phone rang. Eileen.

"Stacie! Someone's behind the store!"

"It's okay, Eileen. It's Ben. There was someone there a while ago. Ben's checking now. I'm okay."

She heard Eileen's sigh of relief. "I will sleep so much

better when that creep is in jail. Call me when you're home and locked in. I'll be up."

"I will," Stacie promised.

Ben was locking the back door. She looked at him questioningly. He nodded.

"Someone was there. I heard him go over the back fence. Some things look out of place. You'll have to check tomorrow. I don't want you going out there now. I'm not sure where he might be. There are too many shrubs on the north side for me to see clearly." Ben holstered his gun. "You should consider clearing them out."

"They belong to the building next door. I talked to the management company after the alarm people were here. Their technician complained about them, too. The rental agent said the owner wasn't willing to cut them back or have me do it."

Ben frowned. "He knows why you're asking?"

"Yes."

Ben shook his head. "Are you about finished for the night?"

"Yes, I was just shutting down."

"Go ahead and finish. I'll wait here."

Stacie hesitated. Troy was gone, but she didn't want to give up the sense of safety she had with Ben nearby. "You can come up."

"Lead on."

Stacie led the way upstairs, or rather, Bananas did, bouncing up ahead of them and waiting, wagging, at the top of the stairs.

"I'm sorry I snapped at you before," Stacie told Ben, as she shut down her computer. "I was just scared out of my mind."

"No problem," said Ben with a small smile. "I spend all day with Cruz. I'm used to being snapped at."

Stacie locked her desk. Ben checked the windows in the office, the back bedroom and the bathroom. They headed down stairs, and Stacie locked the door at the bottom.

Bananas was already at the front door with Ben, but Stacie hesitated.

"Stacie?"

She waved her hands helplessly. "I know he's gone," she said. "I just don't know *where* he's gone." She gave a tiny shrug that was meant to be braver than she felt. "I guess I'm still a bit spooked."

"I'm going to follow you home," said Ben. "Though I'm not comfortable with you being on your own tonight."

She laughed without humor. "You're not the only one. But it's too late to go to my friends in Costa Mesa.

"Colin's?" Stacie thought Ben was reluctant to ask.

"Oh! Colin." She pulled out her phone and dialed. "I hate to endanger him. He's done so much already."

Colin picked up on the first ring. "All okay, girlfriend?"

"Yes. You can stand down tonight. Ben's going to see me home and locked up."

"I seeee," said Colin, loading the word with innuendo.

"No, you don't," Stacie told him and hung up, leaving Colin laughing.

She clipped the leash on Bananas, armed the alarm, locked the door and walked with Ben across the street to the lot where her car was parked. She had no doubt Colin was watching from his apartment. She flicked a wave. His porch light flashed off, then on.

As she slid behind the wheel, Ben leaned on the door. "Lock the door. Don't leave until I'm behind you. I just have to turn around. When you get to the house, don't get out of the car until after I do."

Stacie nodded. She watched Ben walk out of the lot, his

eyes constantly moving, especially watching the oleanders at the side of the building next to the parking lot. Stacie had never noticed them before. But she noticed them now. She eased the car up to the sidewalk where she could watch Ben.

When he'd swung around and stopped by the driveway, Stacie pulled out and headed up the hill, keeping Ben on her bumper.

At the house, she pulled into the garage, and waited in the car until Ben had swung around, pulled up behind her, and gotten out of the car. She let the dog out, leashed him and closed the garage door.

"He has to make a pit stop," she told Ben, walking Bananas to the stretch of weeds across from her house. Ben stayed with her, eyes moving constantly.

"Do you know your neighbors?" he asked.

"Yes," she replied. "Most of them anyway." She pointed to the left of her house. "Betty and Stan Kaufman over there. Elena and Robin Locke up the hill." She motioned to the roadside the dog was watering. "The Friedmans, Nelsons, and Margot Somerset," she gestured around the cul-de-sac at the end of the road. "I know most of the others to say hello to."

When the dog had made his rounds, Stacie unlocked the gate and unclipped Bananas' leash. The dog bounded down the stairs. The security lights flashed on.

"Do you know who lives behind you?" Ben asked, as they walked down the steps.

Stacie smiled. "Fred Langley. Nice guy. Used to be sweet on Amelia after his wife died."

"Who could you go to at night if you needed help?"

"Any of them. They all know what's happening. Fred, if I had to go out the back. The Kaufmans," she pointed south, "or the Lockes, if I had to go out the front."

"Good. You've thought about this."

"Oh, believe me. I've thought about it."

"Are any of them armed?"

Stacie hesitated.

"I'm not taking notes," said Ben, and she thought she heard a smile in his voice.

"Yes," she said. "The Lockes, almost certainly. Robin is very protective of the neighborhood. Stan and Fred, probably. Margot, absolutely. She had an attempted break in a few years ago and she lives alone."

"Have you thought about it? A gun?" They reached the bottom of the steps. Bananas was already waiting by the door.

"No."

He looked at her, surprised by her vehemence. "Why?"

She sighed. "Having a gun is like inviting trouble. I've taken a few self-defense classes. That's prudent. But getting a gun." She shook her head. "No."

She unlocked the door.

"I'll see you inside and walk through," Ben told her.

Stacie opened the door. Bananas barged in and galloped to his bed in the dining room, circled and dropped, head on his paws.

Ben's phone rang as Stacie locked the doors. "Robard." He listened. "Okay. Thanks. I'll wait until they get here."

Stacie looked at him puzzled.

"Just for tonight, I've asked for the patrol to sit outside as much as possible. They can't be here all the time. They'll have to answer other calls," he said. "But hopefully, it will be enough to deter anyone from trying to disturb you."

"Thank you," she said. The wave of relief almost made her weak.

"I'll wait until they can come. Shouldn't be too long."

"I'm going to make some tea," said Stacie. "Try to settle

my nerves. Would you like coffee?" She smiled. "Or try your luck with chamomile tea?"

Ben made a face. Stacie laughed. "Coffee it is."

He walked with her into the kitchen and dining room. Stacie noticed that, although he hadn't taken his gun out, his jacket was open and the holster was unlatched.

Seeing the kitchen was clear, and all the windows locked and covered, he turned to her. "I'll check that everything is secure while you do that." He gave her a look, asking her permission.

She gestured to the back of the house. "Please. And I'd better call Eileen."

Once Eileen was assured she was home safe, and that the police would be outside, Stacie reached for the kettle to fill it.

Ben called from the back bedroom. "Stacie? Do you know this window is broken?"

She smiled to herself, put the kettle on the burner and walked back to join him.

"Yes," she said, going into the room that had been her aunt's. There were two small bay windows, both with window seats. One looked toward the garage apartment. Ben was standing in front of the one that looked onto the patio. He raised an eyebrow.

"As you are aware," she said archly, "my pitching arm is not what it should be. I was throwing a ball for Bananas when he was a puppy and," she gestured to the crack running across one of the pair of casement windows, "it went awry."

"You must have hit it just right."

"Or not," she said. "Like everything else in this house, the windows are old."

Ben shook his head. "That's what, five, six years ago?"

"About."

"And you never got it replaced?"

"I like the old glass. And…" Her throat tightened with memories.

"And?"

Stacie stared at the glass for a moment. Ben waited.

"When Syl first brought Bananas from the shelter… Amelia and I had been so close… I was… I guess I was angry. That she thought a dog could replace Aunt Me. But he was such a ridiculous looking puppy. And somehow…" She stopped. Sniffed. Cleared her throat.

In the dining room, dog tags rattled as Bananas lunged to his feet. Nails clicked across the wood floor in the living room, hallway, and into the bedroom. Bananas nudged her hand.

Stacie looked down into his brown eyes and rubbed the big curly-haired head.

"Somehow he knew I needed him." She darted a glance at Ben. "I didn't know. But he did." She looked down at the dog. "He still does."

Her gaze went back to the broken window as she stroked the dog's head. "I was playing with him. I was throwing the ball against the house as hard as I could. I was so angry to lose her. Missing her so much. Angry with Syl, giving me this new responsibility." A glance at the dog, who gave a slow wag. "Bananas thought it was great. He was galloping all over the patio retrieving the ball and spitting it out. Then I missed the wall. And hit the window." Another glance at Ben. "Not for the first time."

She looked down. "It's your fault." Bananas wagged his tail more enthusiastically as if he knew she was teasing him.

Stacie looked at Ben, blinking tears. "It was the last straw. This was my aunt's room. I'd broken her window. I just plopped on the ground and started bawling. This big mutt," another look down as she ruffled the dog's ears, "started jumping all over me, licking me, wagging that ridiculous thing he calls a tail. And I started laughing. And crying.

"It was like a dam broke," she said, looking up at Ben again. "I'd always admired Amelia. Standing on her own. I thought she was so strong. But at that moment, I could almost hear her telling me not to be an idiot. That she had never been alone. That she'd always had friends. To talk to. To give her advice. To help her. That I had friends. Who sometimes could see what I needed even when I couldn't."

Bananas sneezed. They both laughed.

Stacie smiled at Ben. "And before you ask, no, I didn't actually hear her."

He grinned, and the corners of his eyes crinkled. "It *was* in my mind."

Stacie's heart cracked open.

"I could tell."

She gestured at the books, the reading light wedged into one of the bookshelves. "I come in here to read, sometimes, when I want to be close to her. The window reminds me of that…" She studied the long break in the glass. "That moment of clarity. Of gratitude. To her." She looked at Bananas and flipped his ears. "To Syl." She looked up into Ben's brilliant blue eyes. "To all my friends."

Time took a long inhale. The air around Stacie grew warm, heavy. She heard her aunt's voice clearly: "He will make you so happy."

"It isn't secure, Stacie," Ben told her gently.

The atmospheric charge vanished.

"No," she said, disoriented. "I suppose it isn't." She sighed and the weight of fear settled over her again. "I'll get someone out to replace it."

Ben looked at the books in the cases lining the little nook. "Her books or yours?"

"Mostly hers. She liked mysteries."

He gave her a sidelong look. "Did she always know the ending?"

Stacie laughed out loud. "No," she told him, grinning. "She always complained about that."

The kettle in the kitchen gave a shriek.

"That's for me," she said. "Out of the way, you." Bananas, who'd sat down, jumped to his feet, turned as tightly as he could and trotted out.

Stacie went into the kitchen. She heard Ben pause in the living room.

"That is one big crystal."

Stacie turned the burner off and poured water into her mug and into the single filter for Ben's coffee. She looked over her shoulder as Ben came into the kitchen.

"Yes." She hesitated. She had to know where Ben stood, now, before this went further.

Is it going further?

She took a deep breath and tried to sound off hand. "It was my aunt's scrying crystal."

Ben frowned. "Crying crystal? What does that mean?"

Stacie shook her head. "Scrying. With an s in front of it. It's the practice of 'seeing,' or divination."

"Telling fortunes?"

"If you like." Stacie shrugged a shoulder. "There are a few especially gifted people who can use crystals—or a bowl of water or a mirror—to look into the future. Mostly, anyone with the skill simply looks into the human heart."

"Do you use it," Ben gestured toward the other room, "like that?"

"No," said Stacie firmly. "That was my aunt. And my great, great grandmother, Anastasia. The crystal was origi-nally hers, but it had been in her family a long time." She shrugged a bit again, her eyes on the water moving slowly through the coffee grounds. "Supposedly, Anastasia foresaw her husband's death."

She looked up at Ben's questioning eyes.

"Didn't you do the same thing, the day the church folks threatened you on your doorstep? Didn't you say you would predict someone's death?"

So he did hear me, she thought as she turned back to the coffee filter. What could she say?

She remembered Colin's suggestion: Lie.

"They wanted a witch, I gave them a witch," she said. "Maybe not too smart, but at the time, I wasn't thinking clearly." *Not exactly a lie*, she thought. Hopefully, there would be time—and understanding enough between them—for her to explain some day.

If I ever understand it, she thought.

She turned to face him again.

"Even if I did have the ability to see the future, I'm not sure I would use it.

"Why?"

"People didn't always want to hear what Aunt Me told them." She thought about Amelia warning Pamela about Chuck.

"Not even if they came to her, asking?"

Stacie shook her head. "Especially then."

"I don't get it."

She leaned on the counter, crossing her arms. "People go to a reader, a seer, when they fear the worst and want to hear the best. If she confirms their fears, they blame the seer." She shook her head again. "Even if it's good news, they're never happy."

"Why?" asked Ben, surprised. "Good news is, like, good, right?" He gave her a lopsided grin and frowned.

Stacie sighed.

"You'd think. But everyone has expectations of what their lives should be like. They're excited when they hear their kids will marry or be successful. Or their husband—it's mostly women who come to seers—their husband will get a new job he loves.

"They're not so thrilled, though, when the marriage is to a same sex partner. Or the kids *are* successful—as a screaming rock musician or street mime. Or when their husband's dream job is ministering to people in the back country of New Guinea."

"I see what you mean."

"You've seen the kind of trouble I have at the store already, with just rumors that I can 'heal.'" Her fingers carved air quotes. "I don't need more."

"Didn't it cause trouble for your aunt?"

Stacie sighed again, feeling the emptiness inside where her aunt had been. "Yes. But she was a good person. She always wanted to help."

"You do, too."

"In a smaller way." Stacie turned and dunked her tea bag in the mug. "I try to make things available that people can use to discover their intuition on their own. Crystals, Tarot, music, water. You have to trust your own heart. Some people lean on the intuition of others too much and are disappointed when it doesn't work out."

"Like believing false prophets."

She looked up at him, surprised.

"Exactly. Even people who say they want to encourage their own intuition, really don't. They want happy answers, a way to avoid pain. Following intuition isn't always easy. Not everyone wants to follow the signposts, even when they're right there."

The coffee finished brewing. Stacie pulled the filter off, set it on a plate and handed the mug to Ben.

Stacie gestured to the other room. "Shall we sit down? Not you," she told Bananas as he got up from his bed. His tail stopped wagging. "Bed."

As they passed the crystal, Ben glanced at it, stopped, then looked puzzled. "Do I see a bubble in there?"

Stacie stopped next to him. "Yes. It's called an enhydro. Occasionally quartz traps liquid in it when it's forming. Gas bubbles can get trapped in the liquid."

"Like a spirit level?"

She grinned. "Exactly like that. I used to love playing with this one, watching it move from end to end. This crystal is especially rare because the enhydro is inside *another* crystal trapped in the larger one." She looked at him. "My aunt thought that's why this one was particularly useful in scrying."

"She told my mom I'd come back safely from Iraq, you know."

Again Stacie was surprised. "Aunt Me didn't often do that," she told him, as she moved to sit on one end of the sofa. "She tried to avoid prophesying deaths—or, in your case, not. It's too tricky. Even if you're right, you're wrong." She leaned back and blew on her tea. "She must have been very sure you'd come back. And trusted Emmie."

Ben moved toward the wing chair. He ran his hand over the mantelpiece, a long slab of rough-edged oak as he passed. "I know Mom trusted her," he said absently. "This is a remarkable house," he added, as he sat and looked around.

Changing the subject, thought Stacie.

"How on earth did you find a jewel like this?"

"My great grandfather built it," she told him.

His eyebrows lifted high in surprise. "Your family's been here that long?"

"Yep," she said. "Since the 1920s. Almost lost it a few times in fires. But we cling on. Stubborn."

"That's why the glass in the windows is old."

"Yes. My great grandfather scavenged most of the lumber." She pointed at the manzanita trunk framing the archway to the bedrooms. "Found wood in the canyons. Got some of the windows from old houses that were being torn down. My dad laid the flagstones in the patio. Had the sliding doors installed. My grandmother re-designed the kitchen."

"And you?" Ben smiled.

"Painted. Built the fountain outside. The garden was Aunt Amelia's project until I took it over."

"Did your great grandfather make that gorgeous rocker, too?" Ben nodded to the chair by the sliding glass doors.

Stacie smiled. "No. My great, great grandfather, Tomasz, made it for his wife, Anastasia."

"You're named after her?"

"Yes," said Stacie, curling her hands around her mug. "I prefer Stacie. Aunt Me used to call me Stasha."

"You said she predicted his death?"

"That's the story Amelia told me Anastasia had told her."

"Okay. I'm listening," said Ben when Stacie stopped.

"Are you sure?"

"Are you kidding? I love stories like this. I was raised hearing them."

Stacie smiled. "Okay then." She took a sip of tea. "Tomasz—my great, great grandfather—was the leader of a group of local nationalists in Bohemia when it was part of the Austro-Hungarian Empire. He was executed as a revolutionary. Anastasia warned him not to go to a partisan meeting. She thought it was a trap. But he went anyway.

Anastasia knew the moment he died. Or so Me said." Stacie was suddenly very aware of the amethyst warm against her skin.

"But they didn't arrest her?"

Stacie shook her head. "She fled to her family in Russia.

"Ben, she was pregnant. She had a nine-year-old daughter. It was winter. She loaded the rocker and a few other things onto a pushcart. A pushcart! And they walked into Russia. Along with a couple goats. Anastasia told Amelia she would have died rather than leave the rocker behind." She glanced over her shoulder. "I think of her every time I sit in that chair. Think of them all."

"She sounds like a fearless lady," said Ben, looking at her. "I see where you get it."

"I'm not fearless," said Stacie, wondering if she'd have been brave enough to strike out into the unknown in the winter. "I'm scared to death." Chilled, she pulled the afghan off the back of the couch and draped it over her lap. "But I always feel safe here. Protected. Surrounded by family."

Stacie found herself looking at Ben. The solid sureness of him. The warm, blue gaze. Safety. Protection.

Time stretched. The ticking of the clock slowed and faded. Stacie looked back down the river of time into a small, snow-bound cabin. She heard the rocker creak, the fire snap. "*Stasha*," she heard someone say.

Bananas murmured in his sleep.

"Stacie."

Stacie blinked. The bubble of time popped. The flow rushed on.

Ben was staring into his coffee, turning the mug in his hands.

"Stacie. I don't want you to take this the wrong way. I know your aunt raised you, that you were really close. But is it *really* possible? That some people can see the future? That you—or anyone—can just *know* things about people?"

She stared at Ben blankly. For a moment, she didn't know where she was. When she was.

"I'm sorry. What?"

Ben looked up at her. "I know we talked about crystals and how people can be connected to their particular...vibrations or frequency. And that makes a kind of sense. But do you *believe* the rest of it?"

Stacie pulled herself back, focused on his question, the question she always tried to avoid answering directly. She was about to sidestep it now. But something stopped her. Maybe it was her own intuition. Or maybe it was the amethyst crystal near her heart, feeling warm, almost liquid.

Maybe it was just the beating of her heart telling her she had to trust someone, sometime.

"Yes," she said. "Yes."

"Like a sixth sense?"

"Exactly," she said.

"Intuition is the heart whispering," Amelia had told her. "Even when we're deaf to it, the heart hears whispers of danger or love, truth or lies. It tells us to go or stay. Most people don't listen. They think their minds know everything, their brains. Their intellect. But it's the heart. The heart hears. The heart knows. We must listen when the heart speaks."

Amelia's voice was so clear, Stacie could hear her.

Ben was looking at her strangely.

He gave her a strange smile. "So rocks sing, and the heart talks?"

With a jolt, Stacie realized it hadn't been her aunt's voice, but hers.

Oh, no, she thought. *Oh, no.*

Don't be afraid, she heard Amelia whisper. *It's your gift.*

No! It was your gift. I don't want it! Stacie thought desperately.

She tried to backpedal. "We all have intuition, Ben. For some of us, it's stronger than for others. Some of us ignore it when we should listen to it. You said it yourself. We all say 'I knew I should or shouldn't have done something.'" That's intuition. Most of us can only access it for ourselves. Some people—like my aunt and my great, great grandmother—had an ability so strong they could use it for others."

"And you?" he asked quietly.

Yes, Amelia, she thought, panic rising. *What about me?*

"I get...hunches," she finally said. She was surprised to see Ben react oddly. "Sometimes I act on them."

She saw his slight smile. "Like betting on Johnny Boy to win the fifth at Santa Anita?"

"Well," she said, smiling. "I guess calling it a hunch depends on whether Johnny Boy wins or not."

He watched her for a moment as if waiting for more. She wasn't sure she was ready to say more.

"But it's more than hunches for you, isn't it?" he finally said.

"Not really," she said evasively. Not long before, she would have said that with confidence. Now, she wasn't so sure anymore.

She reached for her tea.

"Stacie."

She took a sip, then looked up at him. "Umm?"

"You said you gave me the smoky crystal because I looked tired. That's not enough—at least in my book—to decide someone needs grounding." Then, as if someone were dragging the question out of him, he asked quietly, "What did you see?"

There it was. The challenge. Someone asking her to "see"

for them. Even Colin never asked her that.

I don't want this, she thought vehemently. *I just want to be normal.*

"I don't..." Stacie started to deny she saw anything, but Ben's face stopped her. He had opened himself to her by asking. She couldn't refuse to tell him the truth.

Because she *had* seen. Oh, not in images that most people would recognize. But in flashes of insight so intense, a truth so powerful, it must be spoken.

If this...whatever it was...with Ben were to go anywhere, her insight told her that he would never forgive a lie. Even if he couldn't believe the truth.

"You'd been badly hurt. Not physically," she said quietly. "But your soul was damaged. You were doubting yourself, afraid to trust your judgement. It was as if your spirit was bleeding."

Ben took a breath so deep, it was as if he hadn't really breathed for a long time. He closed his eyes briefly, nodded once.

"How did you know it was Troy outside your office tonight?"

A chill washed over her, remembering.

"Bananas was growling..." she hedged, but Ben shook his head.

"You didn't say *someone* was outside. You said *he's* outside. You didn't say you'd seen him. Later, you said 'he's gone,' before I'd searched the yard."

Stacie hesitated. His steady blue eyes watched her.

Truth, her intuition whispered. *It has to be the truth.*

She took a breath. "Troy's like...like a change in barometric pressure. There's a pressure in my ears, or a stabbing here." She pointed to her forehead. "It's like..." she paused searching for words.

"Like a disturbance in the Force?" Ben asked, referring to *Star Wars*.

"Don't laugh," she said, a smile touching her lips. "That was probably as close a description of what happens as I've heard. I just don't get the cool sword."

She sipped her tea. Ben waited, as if he knew she wanted to say more. Stacie was surprised to discover he was right. Now that she'd started, she did want to say more.

"When Troy is close, I feel a...a void." She closed her eyes and reached for words. "It's like I'm in a dark house, and suddenly I pass the opening to the cellar. I can sense the extra darkness. The emptiness. The depth. Like passing an open grave, I suppose they would say in a ghost story." *An open grave*, echoed in her head. She shivered and opened her eyes. "Talk about a disturbance in the Force."

She looked into dark blue eyes that were taking her very seriously.

There was a long silence in which they simply looked at each other, dark blue eyes into green. Then Stacie saw something else very clearly.

"But you know what it's like," she said quietly. "You get them, too."

Ben opened his mouth, but Stacie went on.

"Tonight," she said. "Why were you outside my shop tonight?"

"I just...wanted to be sure you were safe," he said, after a pause. "I was at my folks' house down the coast, and I just thought I'd roll by to see if everything was quiet."

"But you don't do it every night."

"No. Of course not. I was just on my way home."

"It was just coincidence."

"Yes," he said, but Stacie could see he was trying to convince himself.

Suddenly Stacie knew something else.

"You have a hunch that Troy isn't just a stalker," she said. A chill raised the hair on her arms. "That he's something more. That's why you wore your gun when we were out walking."

"Hunches don't mean anything," protested Ben.

"They mean a great deal," said Stacie seriously. "What is it, Ben?"

An emotionless mask slipped into place on Ben's face. His cop mode. Whatever he knew or suspected, he couldn't tell her.

Fear slid into her belly. Her hands went cold.

Bananas' dog tags rattled loudly in the silence as the dog lifted his head. A moment later, Stacie heard the sound of a powerful engine climbing the hill above the house. It passed, came back and stopped.

"The cavalry." Ben looked down at his mug, lifted it, and finished the coffee. Only then did Stacie realize they'd been staring at each other.

He rose. Stacie set her mug on the table and got up, too, dropping the afghan onto the sofa.

Bananas trotted in, going to Ben, who scratched the dog's ears.

"He did you proud tonight," Ben told her.

"Yes, he did," she said. "Most of the time, he's a big goof. Mr. Hail-Fellow-Well-Met. But I'm beginning to see that when the chips are down, he can be a protective goof."

"He makes me feel a bit better, leaving you alone like this," said Ben.

I wish you wouldn't leave me alone, thought Stacie, and flushed, wondering if she'd spoken aloud again.

Stacie didn't need intuition to know that Ben didn't want to leave, either. It was written clearly on his face.

She reached automatically for Bananas and touched Ben's hand where it rested on the dog's head.

He lifted his hand and laid it over hers. His fingers curled around hers. Tightened.

He bent toward her. She lifted her chin to receive his kiss.

His lips grazed hers.

The fear slid away. Her chill gave way to warmth. And desire.

The gate creaked. Heavy footsteps pounded down the stairs outside.

Ben pulled back and drew a deep breath.

"The cavalry," he said again, quietly, and smiled ruefully. He hadn't let go of her hand.

"To your rescue."

"I wish they'd waited a few minutes."

"So do I."

There was a knock at the door.

Ben let go of her hand.

"Stay safe. Don't hesitate to call 911 if you need them," he said, turning toward the door.

"Ben."

He looked back.

"I'm very grateful you came by the store tonight."

The smile he gave her was warm, intimate. He nodded and opened the door to the patrol officer. They exchanged greetings, then the officer went back up the stairs.

Stacie followed Ben out.

"Go inside. Lock up. I'll lock the gate," he said.

"Good night," she said and did as he asked.

But she watched him cross the patio and climb the stairs. She watched until his car drove away, and the security lights went out.

TWENTY-TWO

BEN'S CHAIR CREAKED AS HE REACHED FOR THE FILE. *I'd better talk to Cruz about this*, he thought as he moved toward her desk.

Closer to her cubicle, he walked into a wall of unpleasantly strong perfume and heard his partner talking to someone. A very loud, demanding someone. He stopped.

"I insist you do something!" said a shrill woman's voice. "Why is that woman still allowed to run that...that...business? She's dangerous! Why don't the police shut her down? She could kill someone!"

"Now she's dangerous. Last time she was a fraud."

"You sound like Andrew. Demeaning. Belittling. I know what I know, and I demand you take me seriously! She put a hex on me! I know she did."

"Celia," he heard Cruz say, in a tone of voice that Ben knew well, "There is no such thing as a witch."

Not again. Ben closed his eyes.

"Well, you explain my accident, then," the furious voice responded. "I could have been killed!"

"You could have been drunk!" snapped Cruz.

"How dare you!" said Celia Byers, angry to the point of hysteria. "You forget who Andrew is. When he's mayor, I'll see that you're fired. You're not as special as you think!"

Briefly, Ben thought about stepping in, giving Cruz a hand. Then, smiling to himself, he backed away.

"Celia, I have real work to do. If you want to talk to Andrew, be my guest," Cruz was saying.

A heavy-set, heavily made up woman, in yards of flowing magenta material, lurched to the opening of Cruz's cubicle. She turned clumsily to glare at Cruz, out of sight behind the cubicle wall.

"You haven't heard the last of this. If you won't take care of it, I'll find a way to take care of it myself!"

Celia turned and steamed out of the office toward the parking lot.

Ben waited a beat, then went back toward Cruz's desk and the hanging cloud of scent.

He dropped into the chair Byers had just vacated. Cruz was rubbing her forehead.

"Nice chat with auntie?" he asked, trying to look innocent.

Cruz glared at him.

Ben laughed. "Kids are filing for divorce from their parents now. Maybe you should see if you can divorce your husband's relatives."

"Crap," said Cruz. She opened a drawer, pulled out her purse and dropped it on her desk. "This isn't going to be good for my home life. Paul actually likes Andrew." She sighed. "I suspect I'm going to hear about this from the lieutenant, too."

"So what was auntie's complaint this time? I heard her say something about an accident?"

Cruz held up a hand and made a face of disgust.

"She drove off the road, up in the canyon. Lucky for her

she only went into the ditch and didn't hit oncoming traffic. She's an alcoholic. I could smell it on her even now."

"It's 10:30 in the morning. Are you sure it wasn't that horrible perfume?"

"No. Andrew's complained to Paul. He wants her to go for treatment. If she gets arrested for drunk driving, it isn't going to help his mayoral campaign. But he can't get her to agree."

Ben frowned. "Didn't Stacie say alcoholism was why auntie went to her for healing?"

"I wish you'd stop calling her that," said Cruz irritably.

Ben grinned.

"But yeah. That's what she said. And that was strange."

"Why strange?"

"Celia doesn't admit she has a problem. Why would she tell someone like Stacie—no offense, but someone on the fringe—that she has a drinking problem?"

Before Ben could respond, Mike Breckenridge pulled up at the opening of Cruz's cubicle. "Robard," he said.

Breckenridge had been with EBPD far longer than Ben or Cruz and had worked Crimes Against Persons for most of that time. In his late fifties, he was still in decent shape, though the desk was taking its toll on his waistline and jowls, and painting dark circles in the mahogany skin under his eyes. His years tracking the perpetrators of violent crime had forced his short-cropped, salt-and-pepper hair into full retreat from his forehead. Though his faded brown eyes might look tired, there was nothing tired about Breckenridge's mind.

"Mike." Ben looked up.

"Wasn't sure you were in today," said Breckenridge and grinned. "Didn't see the white horse tied up outside."

"Pardon?"

"Isn't that the transportation choice of heroes?"

"Hero?" Cruz gave Breckenridge a puzzled look.

"You didn't know? Your partner rode to the Cappella woman's rescue last night." Breckenridge's eyebrows twitched meaningfully. "Had the patrols sitting outside her door, too, guarding the drawbridge."

Ben flushed. Cruz looked from Breckenridge to him. Her face didn't change, but he knew that mentally she had both eyebrows raised to her hairline.

"Yes, I did," said Ben, answering her look. "Someone got into the yard behind her store. She was scared. She called me. I checked it out and followed her home."

"She called *you*." Breckenridge put heavy emphasis on the last word.

"Yeah."

Breckenridge sighed. "And we waste all this money on 911 dispatchers."

Color rose in Ben's face. He knew he was being ragged, but his feelings about Stacie were too new and unsettled for him to take the ribbing well.

"We've become friends," he said, too defensively. He saw Cruz grab her coffee and bury her face in it, hiding her grin.

Breckenridge held up his hands in front of him.

"Hey! I got no beef with it," he told Ben. "Frankly, I'm glad you're assigning yourself the stalker. I've got more assault, murder, mayhem, and lost women than Danner and I can handle." His smile disappeared and he rolled his shoulders. "How long before I can retire, again?"

"More?" asked Cruz.

"Oh, yeah. The fun never stops. While your partner was playing the 'knight in shining armor,' a guy got stabbed right in front of the Cappella woman's store."

"What?" said Cruz.

The blood drained from Ben's face. "It wasn't Colin was it?"

"Who the hell is Colin?"

"Friend of Stacie's. Lives across the street. He's protective of her."

Breckenridge lifted an eyebrow. "*He's* protective of her?"

Ben ignored the dig. "Who was hurt?"

Breckenridge shook his head. "The moron trying to set up a big cross in front of the store."

"Are you serious?" asked Cruz.

"Yeah. Can you believe it?" Breckenridge shook his head. "There was even a gas can. Don't know if he was planning to burn the cross or the store. Guy at the restaurant at the corner was locking up, saw him and called it in. When the patrol got there, there was a struggle going on, and they saw the guy fall. They were fast enough to save his life."

"Who stabbed him?" asked Ben, puzzled.

"No idea," said Breckenridge, heaving a sigh. "The attacker blasted off, and the patrol could only get a partial on the truck. They were busy stopping the bleeding."

"That doesn't make any sense," said Cruz.

"Tell me about it," said Breckenridge.

Cruz looked at Ben. "You think the cross burning thing makes any sense if it's the folks vandalizing the store taking it up a notch?"

Ben gave a small shrug. "Awful big notch, going from throwing eggs to burning a cross and possibly the store. It seems like a weird thing for church people to do. That's more KKK, hate crimes stuff, isn't it?"

"They don't even do that much anymore," said Breckenridge. "They get tiki torches at Walmart. Lighter weight."

"Could the cross burner be the stalker?" asked Cruz.

"He was there. Or had been," said Ben, half to himself.

"That's why Stacie called. But I can't see why the stalker would burn her out." He looked at Breckenridge. "You?"

The older detective shook his head. "I've never heard of it happening before, but," he shrugged, "psychos aren't one-size-fits-all."

"Why would a Good Samaritan stab somebody setting up a burning cross, then run away?" asked Ben. "Wouldn't they do what the restaurant owner did? Call 911?"

"You'd think," said Breckenridge.

"Your victim didn't say anything?"

"No, he was down a few pints and not talking when the patrol reached him," said Breckenridge. "He went into surgery last night, but we haven't been able to talk to him. Not about what the hell he thought he was doing. Not about who stabbed him."

"You're sure it's the victim who intended the cross burning? He's not a passerby who tried to stop it and got stabbed for his trouble?" asked Cruz.

Breckenridge nodded. "Patrol said they smelled the gas on him."

The three veteran cops chewed on the puzzle for a few moments. Suddenly Cruz sucked in a quick breath that was not quite a gasp.

"You have an idea?" asked Ben.

She nodded staring into the middle distance between the two men. "Suppose," she said thoughtfully, drawing out the word. "Just suppose, for the sake of argument, that the victim is the vandal, and he decided to burn a cross. For whatever reason. Cappella's stalker was there. She calls Ben. He sees Ben answer her call. Then Ben takes her home. The stalker can't get to Cappella. The vandal, with awful timing shows up. And the stalker takes his frustration out on him."

"Cruz, that makes less sense..." started Ben.

Cruz held up a hand, stopping him. She looked up at Breckenridge.

"Would it make sense, Mike, in your experience... Would it make sense that the stalker, in some dark twisted way, might have interpreted the vandal as a rival? Trying to get Cappella's attention? Or that the cross burner was taking attention from him, the stalker?"

Breckenridge frowned, put his hands in his pockets and leaned against the edge of the cubicle. "Highly unlikely," he said after a minute, "but not impossible, I guess. Like I said, not all psychos are alike."

Ben started to say something but Cruz stopped him again.

"You remember the phone call Stacie said she got?" she asked him.

Ben nodded. "Yeah. I think so."

"I remember," said Cruz. "He told her to get rid of her *boyfriends*—plural—or he would."

"Yeah, but..."

Cruz rolled over him. "When he confronted Stacie and Colin in the coffee shop, he accused her of cheating on him with her boyfriend."

Ben was still puzzled. He made a rotating motion with his hand: And, so?

"Something Meissner mentioned. Someone smashed all the ceramic planters on Colin's steps a few nights ago. Maybe he's moving from vandalism to assault." She kept her eyes on Ben.

Ben suddenly saw where she was going, and it chilled him.

"You're thinking that if vandalism doesn't work, this guy is willing to kill someone who threatens a relationship with the woman he's staked out as 'his.'"

Cruz looked at him steadily and nodded.

"You think I'm a target."

She nodded again.

"Not Huff."

"We don't know," said Cruz. "We both just assumed. We never checked it out."

"You're talking about your car getting keyed, and someone slashing your tires?" asked Breckenridge. "Heard about that."

"The whole department did," said Ben, looking at Cruz. She gave him a wide-eyed stare.

"Guy'd be a moron to target a cop," said Breckenridge.

"Maybe he doesn't know I'm a cop," said Ben.

Now it was Breckenridge's turn to gaze into space. He slowly shifted his weight back and forth, rubbing the edge of the cubicle between his shoulder blades as if to scratch an itch he couldn't reach.

Finally, he nodded. "Yeah. It makes a kind of pattern. It'd be weird as hell, but not impossible. Marking his territory. Threats first, trying to scare you and these other guys off. When that doesn't work, he moves it closer to home with the cut-up car and the tires. Then he loses it and tries to kill one of them. Shit. You're giving me a headache, Robard." He rubbed his forehead.

"While you're listening, I'll give you another one." Ben hesitated for a moment, then plunged. "Could this atypical stalker be your serial killer? Could Stacie be his next target?" It had been sitting in the back of his mind for weeks now, but saying the words out loud made Ben go cold.

Cruz shot him a warning look and shook her head ever so slightly.

They were both surprised to see worry increase in Breckenridge's face. His shoulders dropped.

"No," he said tiredly. "Unfortunately, we may have a couple other candidates for that honor."

"Shit. No," said Cruz.

"Yeah. One could be the missing girl you talked to Steve about a couple days ago," he said.

Ben shot Cruz a look. She glanced back and raised her fingers from her desk to stop him saying anything. She'd tell him later.

"But we got another report of a missing girl last night," Breckenridge continued. "Neither, as far as we know, have been stalked, though we can certainly ask. But right now, I'd say we're dealing with a different crazy there."

"Why do you think one or both girls might not have just run off?" asked Cruz.

"Your girl," he nodded at Cruz, "fits the description of the killer's last victim. Blond, early twenties, shy, bit of an outsider, no close family."

"She's got a sister, though, hasn't she?" asked Cruz, frowning.

"Yeah. But apparently not close. Danner's going to try to talk to her today."

"The other?" asked Ben.

"The other one." Breckenridge sighed. "She worries me. She doesn't fit the pattern, what little we know of it. Very dependable. Family close by. Large circle of friends. She works. But she's blond, too. Early twenties. I'm following up on her today. She may not be a new victim, but she shouldn't have gone missing either."

Not Stacie's description, thought Ben. So why wasn't he relieved?

"Yeah, but there are lot of blonds in their twenties," said Cruz. "And girls go missing for other reasons."

"True," said Breckenridge, scrubbing his face with a

hand. "And I don't really have any reason to suspect they're victims. But since we started looking at all the missing women and unsolved murders of women in Orange and San Diego counties, we've started seeing a pattern. At least we think so. Right now it's cluttered with women who went missing for other reasons. We're trying to sort all those out. But the consensus between departments is that he kills more frequently than we originally thought. And he may have a circuit."

"A circuit? You mean, he hits the same areas on a regular basis?"

Breckenridge nodded.

Ben caught Cruz's eye. He could tell she felt as sick as he did.

"Wouldn't that be incredibly stupid?" asked Ben.

"I hope so, Robard," Breckenridge told him. "Unless the bastard gets stupid, we might never catch him."

He looked at Ben. "One of those missing girls was last seen at your girlfriend's store. We'll be talking to her about the girl." He heaved himself off the cubicle wall. "Either of you have any more thoughts, let me know," he said. "And you." He lifted his chin toward Ben. "You watch your back. If this son of a bitch *is* targeting guys he sees as rivals, I don't want to be scraping you off the pavement."

"Thanks," said Ben.

With a last nod, Breckenridge was gone.

Cruz blew out a large, gusty breath. "Well, shit."

She leaned forward, drew her cigarettes from the bag and pulled one out, along with a lighter. "I need a smoke. Join me?"

"Sure."

She grinned. "Lover boy."

Ben rolled his eyes.

They walked out to the benches in front of the civic center. The sun was warm, but a cool breeze blowing off the ocean reminded them summer was still a couple months away.

Cruz lit up, pulled on the cigarette, blew out a cloud of smoke, then sat down. A few people were heading past the plaza on their way down to the shops near the beach.

She took another drag on her cigarette. "You know what pisses me off?" she said, suddenly. "Celia can wear that sickening perfume and poison the air everywhere, but people complain about this." She lifted her cigarette.

"Perfume won't kill you," said Ben mildly.

Cruz snorted. "Stay in a room with that," she gestured vaguely back to the police department, "for an hour or two and tell me that again."

"You may have a point." Ben smiled slightly and waited.

Cruz took another pull at her cigarette. "So. You had patrols sitting outside your girlfriend's house last night."

"She is not my girlfriend." *Not yet*, he thought. "The stalker had been circling her office. She was pretty shaken. I just checked things out and made sure she got home safely."

"And called the patrols."

"Asked and answered, counselor."

"But she's not your girlfriend."

"Cruz," said Ben darkly.

Cruz lifted a shoulder. "If you say so." Ben was sure he saw her smile before her lips wrapped around the cigarette. She took a last puff and rubbed the butt out in a tray of sand nearby.

She rose. "Well, Casanova, even if it puts a crimp in your love life, we have to go out there again."

"What? Why?" asked Ben, getting up. "Because of your batty aunt?"

313

"*Paul's* aunt," she said. "No. Another complaint. While you were getting new tires put on your car the other morning, a guy came in to file another fraud allegation against her. Said Ms Cappella is selling herbal abortion aids."

"*What*?" Ben threw his hands out palms up. "Are you kidding me?"

"'Fraid not," she told him. "Said his fiancé's sister supposedly went to the 'witch,'" Cruz flicked her fingers in air quotes, "his words, not mine," she added, "to get herbs or spells for an abortion."

"That's ridiculous," said Ben angrily. "Stacie doesn't do that."

His partner shrugged. "We gotta ask, Robard."

"Cruz, did you see any herbs there? A pot boiling in the corner of the room? Hear any cackling? This is stupid." Ben took two steps away then came back. "The woman is being stalked and is scared to death. We've got some kind of killer in the region, women going missing, and we're taking 'witch' talk seriously?"

Cruz raised a hand in a "stop" gesture. "I don't disagree with you. I'm just saying…"

"Why is the sister's fiancé coming to us anyway? Why not the sister? Or the girl? She should be the one to come in with a fraud complaint." Ben went on in a high voice, "She said these herbs would work but I'm still pregnant."

"Apparently the girl has disappeared, like Breckenridge said. No one's seen her since she went to the shop."

"Then why not a missing persons? And why not the girl's family? And why am I just hearing about this?"

Cruz glared. "Like we didn't have anything else going on this week?"

Ben knew she was right. They'd both had to be in court. They'd been scrambling, too, trying to salvage not one, but two cases they'd worked on for months. Both were starting to unravel.

"Fair enough," said Ben.

Cruz went on. "I asked him why he wasn't filing a missing persons report. He says the girl's eighteen. She's an adult. She can go where she wants. But for exactly the same reasons you heard Breckenridge say he's worried, I filled Danner in.

"As for the family, he claims the sister is the only relative nearby, and she breaks down crying whenever she talks about it."

"Breckenridge said they weren't close."

She shrugged. "All I know is what the boyfriend told me. He said he wanted us to be aware that Ms Cappella is selling drugs for abortions without a license. He did say he and the sister are worried that the girl might be in trouble somewhere."

"This is bullshit, you know that."

"Ben," Cruz was using her soothe-the-angry-partner voice, "I don't want to say this, but the guy said 'everyone' knows she helps girls get rid of babies."

"Everyone? Who the hell is everyone? Oh, wait, some bozo on Twitter, right?"

"Sarcasm will not help."

Ben rubbed his forehead.

"Breckenridge is right, Ben. You're getting too close. Maybe I should handle this alone."

"No," he told her. "Stacie's going to be livid as it is. I don't want her to think I'm a coward as well."

"Okay," said Cruz. "But don't screw this up, no matter how bullshit it is."

"Fine," he said. "But this is yours. You lead."

. . .

TWENTY MINUTES LATER, they walked into The Bell, Book and Crystal. Bananas, lying at Eileen's feet, bounced up, his mouth open in a grin. He trotted over and butted Ben's hand.

Ben scratched his ears.

"Hi!" said Mir, smiling as she recognized them.

Eileen, who had headphones on and her tablet on her lap, glanced up when the dog got up. She paused whatever she was playing, took the headphones off and smiled, too. Cruz nodded.

"Do you need to see Stacie?" Mir asked.

"Please," said Cruz.

Mir picked up the phone. "Stacie, the police are here for you. No, the same ones." She set the phone down. "She's coming."

They heard footsteps on the stairs, and a moment later Stacie stepped into the room. Ben's heart turned over. He hated being here for this.

She smiled at Ben, but he saw fear in her eyes. She knew that, with the two of them here, this wasn't social.

"Detectives," she said, nodding slightly. "What is it?"

Ben looked pointedly at his partner. Stacie, surprised, turned her glance to Cruz.

"Ms Cappella," she began, and Ben could sense her reluctance. Cruz knew this was as ridiculous as Ben did. "I'm afraid we've had a complaint. From a Jeremiah Hammond. The complaint is that you're providing materials for herbal abortions."

Stacie became absolutely still, not even moving when Bananas went over and touched her hand with his cold nose. Her face blanched in anger, her freckles suddenly stood out starkly against her pale skin. Two red patches appeared on her cheeks.

"Excuse me?" she said quietly. "I do what?"

316

Cruz went on doggedly. "He alleges that his fiancé's sister, Virginia Barker, came to you for help to end a pregnancy."

"Jer," said Stacie.

"Yes," said Cruz. "You know him, then?"

"Did he tell you he was the one who got her pregnant? Did he tell you *he* was the one who sent her in here, terrified and alone, to ask for herbs to abort the baby?" asked Stacie, almost conversationally. "Did he tell you she's just fifteen?"

"He said she was eighteen," Cruz told her.

"She isn't," said Stacie. "He raped her, Detective Cruz. The poor girl was so alone she came to *me* for help, a total stranger. Not the police. Not her parents. She's as afraid of them as of Jer. So I helped her."

"What kind of help?"

"What do you think?" snapped Stacie. "The first time, I offered to take her to the Women's Crisis Center. She was so terrified they'd take the baby away from her, she ran out of here like all the demons of hell were after her."

"Mr. Hammond said he hasn't seen Ms Barker since she visited your shop."

"Not after the second time she was here, I'm glad to say," Stacie told the detective. "The people from the Women's Crisis Center came to get her. But he sure as hell saw her after the first time she was here!"

"What do you mean?"

"Oh? Didn't Mr. Good Citizen tell you that when Ginny refused to have an abortion, and tried to get him to marry her, he tried to kill her?"

"What?" said Cruz.

"No? Guess he forgot that," said Stacie, her bitterness and anger burning the air. "She had to crawl out a window and walk here."

Eileen got up, came over and put her hand on Stacie's back.

"Stacie," she said quietly. "We're all angry. There's no need to get nasty. Detective Cruz is doing what she has to."

Stacie rubbed her forehead. "I know. I'm just getting so tired of these bogus accusations. All I'm doing is running my business. I'm being vandalized. Threatened. Slandered. Stalked. The protests are driving some of my customers away. I'm told nothing can be done about any of that. The only things the police continue to investigate are charges that half-baked crackpots keep making."

She paused and glanced toward the front window.

"Stacie," Ben began.

"No, Ben, I'm tired," she said, turning back to him. Ben saw Cruz raise an eyebrow as she looked at him. "I know you're busy. I know you have to follow up on complaints. But what about me? My life has been put on hold. I can't go out on my own. I'm afraid in my own shop and my own home. My friends," she gestured at Eileen and Mir, "are now at risk. You heard about what happened to Colin?"

They both nodded.

"Frankly, I see no end in sight. What will happen? Case closed when I'm finally driven out of my business and out of my home and have to go live in hiding somewhere?

"I'm tired of it," she said for the third time. Bananas, who had been looking up at her bumped her hand. Stacie smiled at him. "Yes, you big hairball. I know you're there." She laid her hand on his head, petting him and stroking his ears. The dog thumped his tail on the floor.

Stacie took a deep breath and blew it out in a gust.

"Detective Cruz. I'm sorry. Eileen is right. I know you're doing your job. But I'm angry. Angry about what he did to that poor child, and really angry that he would accuse me of something like this.

"I told you before. I'm not a healer or a medical person. I don't know the first thing about herbs that cause abortions."

"The herbs in your backyard?" Cruz nodded toward the sunlit garden visible out the back windows.

"They're all cooking herbs. Oregano. Thyme. Peppermint. Nothing that would hurt anyone. They're there for fragrance, color and bees."

Stacie suddenly looked exhausted.

I'll bet she didn't sleep much last night, thought Ben.

"Mr. Hammond showed me a book on herbs they found in Ms Barker's room. It had a sticker on the back from your store," Cruz told her.

"Yes, it probably did," said Stacie, glancing out the front window. She told Cruz about Ginny coming in on that busy Saturday, going through the book, and how she'd clutched the book to her as she had run from the store. "There is not one book —not one, Detective—on those shelves that recommends herbs for abortions. I do not keep those kinds of things here. They're dangerous. For exactly the reason you're here. If an author *does* mention that an herb has *historically*," she emphasized the word, "been used as an abortifacient, that's all it is. Historical information. And all of them include a warning not to use any herb for medical purposes unless under the care of a doctor."

Stacie was getting angry again and caught herself. She took a deep breath. Cruz let her get some of her equilibrium back.

"Eileen and Mir were both here when Ginny came in the second time," she finally said, her voice calmer. "We all saw the bruises on her throat." Stacie's voice had started to shake. Ben saw tears come into her eyes. She stopped talking.

"Why did she come to you?" asked Cruz.

Eileen answered for her.

"She said Stacie was the only one who'd been kind to her," said Eileen. "Isn't that a sad thing?"

"And you saw the bruises?" asked Cruz.

"I did. She was scared to death, Detective. She was telling the truth."

"He threatened Stacie, you know."

All eyes swiveled to Mir.

"He came in here and he threatened her."

"Did he?" Cruz turned back to Stacie.

"With hellfire, yes," said Stacie. "But after I'd seen Ginny's throat, and he was so very...menacing, I called 911. As soon as I did, he left."

"He threatened to burn her," said Mir. Ben heard the anger in her voice, too. "That's what he said. He said God burns witches."

"That's not exactly a threat..." Cruz started to say.

"I didn't think so either," interrupted Stacie, "until he tried to burn my shop down last night."

Ben and Cruz looked at her in puzzlement for a moment.

Cruz put it together first. "You're telling me that Jeremiah Hammond was the person stabbed outside last night?"

"Yes," said Stacie, surprised. "Detective Meissner called this morning to tell me he was in the hospital. That she thought he'd planned to burn the store. I thought you knew. That's why I was so angry. That you'd come here taking his story seriously after he planned to burn me out."

"No, we didn't know," Cruz told her. "We just learned about the assault this morning. But Detective Breckenridge didn't mention his name."

"Just to be clear, Stacie. Hammond isn't the man who's been stalking you, is he?" asked Ben.

"No. He isn't. When he first came in the other day, though, I thought it was Troy. They have similar build and hair color. But Hammond has hazel eyes, and his nose and face shape are different."

"Hammond," said Ben suddenly. "He's not related to Obadiah Hammond, the preacher for the Holy Star?"

"I don't know if they're related," said Stacie, "but Jer was here in the crowd the day that preacher led them in their chants."

"And he got a fifteen year old pregnant," said Cruz.

"Yes," Stacie told her. "Then tried to kill her."

"Breckenridge is going to love this," said Cruz.

"By the way," Stacie said to Ben. "Troy was back again last night."

Ben started. "How do you know?

"This morning, when I went out to fill the birdfeeders, I noticed the bulbs were all gone from the security lights. And the statues were all knocked down again."

"I feel guilty about that," said Eileen. "After Stacie told me she was home and secure last night, I went to bed and I'm afraid I didn't hear or see a thing."

"Not your fault, Eileen. Please don't blame yourself." Stacie patted her friend's hand where it rested on Stacie's arm.

Suddenly she looked at Ben, her face white again. "He came back," she said. "Did he attack Jer because Jer interrupted him?"

"It's a possibility," Ben admitted.

Stacie went still, shoved her hand into her pocket and looked outside again.

The crystal, thought Ben. *She said she was never without it. That it helped her see things clearly.*

What was she seeing now?

Crap. I'm not believing this, am I?

Still. He had to ask.

"Stacie?"

She dragged her attention back to Ben.

"That's the third time you've looked out the window since we arrived. Are you expecting someone?"

Eileen stiffened and looked at Stacie sharply.

Stacie looked at Ben for a long time. He could almost see her trying to decide what to say.

"No one I want to see," she said finally. "I think Troy's out there."

Cruz raised an eyebrow.

"A change in barometric pressure?" asked Ben. He felt Cruz's incredulous look on him.

Stacie looked steadily at Ben.

"Yes," she finally said.

"I'll take a look," said Ben. "Stay here," he said to Cruz, and had only a moment to see her what-the-hell look.

Ben went out on the front porch and looked up and down the street. A dog walker. A couple joggers. Customers coming out of the restaurant at the corner. Someone across the way parking a car. No single blond men.

He scanned the building across the street. The blinds in the upstairs office for lease looked more open than they had a week or so ago, but Ben wasn't sure.

He checked the heavy shrubs on the north side of the bungalow, then went around the other side, up the path that went into the backyard of Eileen's apartment building. The gate was open, and he went through. No one was there, but Ben had the sense that someone *had* been there. It irritated him that he couldn't spot the irregularity that told him that. He went around the entire backyard. In a couple spots, he leaped up to grab the top of a fence or wall, then walked his way up it enough that he could see over the top. Nothing.

Ben went back to the front and over to the lot across the street. There was no one sitting in any of the cars.

"Trouble?" called a voice. Ben looked up and was surprised to see Colin standing on a small balcony that overlooked the lot. "I saw you searching across the street."

"You see anyone hanging out here in the last hour or so?"

"No," said Colin. "My computer is right here," he pointed to the window to the left of the balcony. Ben noticed it was open a few inches. "I keep a pretty close eye on Stacie while I'm working. I hear the cars come in and go out. Did she see him?"

Ben shook his head. "No. Just checking while we're here."

"Good." Colin nodded and went back into his apartment.

Ben walked around the back of the office building, came out on the other side and circled back to The Bell, Book and Crystal.

Stacie looked up when he came back in.

"No one there," he said, "that I could spot. Colin hasn't seen anyone."

"I appreciate you checking, Ben," she said.

"Sure," he said. He could just imagine what Cruz was thinking and would soon be saying.

She was looking at him now.

"I think we're done here," he said to her.

"Yes," said Cruz, giving him a bland look that did not bode well. "We are."

Cruz turned to Stacie. "Detective Breckenridge is going to talk to Hammond later. We'll tell him what you've told us. We'll also tell him that Virginia is at the Crisis Center. He was worried about her. He'll be relieved to hear it. And

Detective Meissner will probably want to talk to you about pressing charges against Hammond for vandalism. Possibly attempted arson."

"Yes," said Stacie. "She's already told me as much. But I'd much rather he went to prison for rape. And attempted murder. Ginny deserves that."

"I'll check with the Women's Crisis Center, see if we can get a statement from the girl," Cruz told her.

"Thanks," said Stacie, as they left.

Ben glanced back, before he closed the door, hoping to catch her eye. Stacie was staring, unsmiling, out the front window, arms crossed, rubbing her shoulders. She looked so alone.

TWENTY-THREE

As Steve Toleffson locked the big, iron gate behind her, Stacie turned to her tour group. "This has been a lot of fun," she said. "You had really great questions. I would never have thought to ask some of the things you did. I'm glad Frances' notes were so good that I could answer them, though I'm sure your family and friends are nervous about your enthusiasm about poisons."

"Makes dinner parties interesting," said one woman.

There was a ripple of light laughter, and Stacie joined in. "Thank you for coming. Come again, soon."

They began to disperse. A few of the women in the group of mystery writers, who called themselves The Gruesome Sisters, came over to offer their thanks and to chat a bit more. The amethyst pendant under Stacie's shirt began to warm noticeably. She glanced around and saw Ben standing not far away. Her heart began to race, and she smiled at him with happiness.

He didn't smile back.

She didn't have a moment to wonder why as one of the women was asking her to identify one of the plant images on her phone. Stacie gave her the name, they talked about its properties again, the woman thanked her, and the remaining writers moved off.

"All locked up tight, Steve?" Stacie asked the security guard.

He nodded. "All secure."

They turned to head down to the interpretive center, their heavy boots crunching on the gravel. Ben walked toward them. Stacie smiled again, but Ben was closed up, shuttered.

"Good morning," she said to him, her smile fading. "Detective Robard, you remember Steve Toleffson?"

Ben nodded and reached out to take Steve's hand. "If you don't mind," he said, "I'd like to talk to Ms Cappella."

"Sure. See you, Stace." He lifted a hand, nodded at Ben and walked off.

Stacie watched Steve go, then turned back to Ben.

Cop mode. *Angry*, she thought. *Why?*

"So," she said, lightly, gesturing at the bag on his shoulder, "more photos? Good day for it." She looked up at the clear blue sky. Although cool in the shade where they were standing, the warmth of the sun in clear patches was summer-like.

"I thought you weren't volunteering here anymore."

She was surprised by his almost accusatory tone, and frowned. "I normally wouldn't be. I'm covering for another docent who couldn't be here. A new grandbaby."

When Ben didn't respond, Stacie found herself babbling into the heavy silence.

"By rights, I really shouldn't have agreed to cover. With all the upheaval," she waved her hands to cover the vandalism, the stalking, the false accusations, "I'm really, and I mean *really* behind. But Frances has covered for me so often when I get jammed up, I really couldn't say no. I'm heading straight to the office from here to get a bunch of files and my laptop. I'll probably work most of the night."

It was as if Ben didn't hear her. He glanced over her shoulder and lifted his chin to indicate the fenced garden she'd just left. "I thought you said you didn't know about herbs for abortions."

Stacie blinked, startled. That was definitely an accusation. She followed his look toward the poison garden behind her.

And flushed with anger.

"I don't," she said firmly. "I only know what's in Frances' notes." Stacie reached into her messenger bag, pulled out the carefully written note cards and held them out. "Only what's here."

Ben barely looked at the cards in her hand.

"So you do know about them."

"I told you. I only know what's here. And there is nothing, *nothing*, here on abortion.

Ben looked at her woodenly. In his eyes, she read doubt and betrayal.

"You don't believe me." Slowly, Stacie lowered the hand holding the notes. "Well. Thank you for the vote of confidence."

"Look at it from my standpoint," Ben started to say.

"Oh, I am looking at it," said Stacie, her voice tight. "And what I see is that someone I thought was a friend can believe I'd recommend poison to a fifteen-year-old child."

"I'm not saying that."

"Of course, you are."

"You said you didn't know anything about herbal abortions." Ben pointed at the gate to the poison garden. "Now here you are, teaching people about the very plants you said you knew nothing about."

"I told you. I'm working from Frances' notes." She

327

shoved the notes back at him. "Here. This is all I know about the poison garden. See if you can find anything about herbal abortifacients in here."

Ben didn't reach for them.

"Take them, Ben," she insisted angrily. "You think I'm such a liar. Look at them!"

"And what was that performance the other day at your store?" Ben asked, ignoring the cards in her extended hand.

Stacie went white in the face of Ben's bitterness.

"What are you talking about?"

"The little show. Acting like you 'felt' someone outside. The one that sent me running around obligingly, looking for a killer."

Stacie drew a sharp breath. She hardly heard Ben continue.

Ben shook his head in disgust. "A change in barometric pressure."

"Killer," she breathed.

The garden went out of focus.

"Come, my little dove. We must hurry. Can you walk?"

The snow was so cold it burned her cheeks. They would kill her, kill her daughters. Like they killed Tomasz.

She closed the door behind her. They walked into the darkness.

"Cruz thought I was a fool," said Ben, unheeding. "Maybe she was right."

"Women. He's killed women," she murmured to herself as Ben went on.

The lack of aura. The void around Troy. The razors. The blood on her hands.

"Blood on his hands," she whispered.

Suddenly, as if she were transported there, she saw a girl, blond, lying in a shallow grave, her neck at an odd angle.

Her hand went to her throat.

She was going to be sick.

In a Minute. Sue wasn't there this morning. Just the darkness.

"Sue," she croaked.

"What?" Ben stopped in mid-tirade.

"The barista. Sue. She's dead. Troy killed her."

"Stop it, Stacie!"

Stacie didn't hear him.

"That's what you haven't been telling me. He's a serial killer."

Ben stepped back, as if she'd slapped him.

"Where did you hear...?"

"I didn't want to see," she said. "That day at the coffee shop. I knew what he was. But I didn't want to see it. I didn't want to think about him...about him..." She took a deep, shaky breath and looked at Ben. "About him trying to kill me."

"That's enough!" he snapped.

Stacie jolted back to the present. Fear shifted to anger.

"That's enough?" Stacie threw his words back at him. "I'm being stalked by a serial killer, and you don't think I have the right to know just what kind of danger I'm in? What kind of danger you've let me put my friends in?"

"I did not say he was a serial killer."

For the first time in her life, power moved in Stacie like warm electricity, sparkling as it flowed through her body. She felt light, surer than she'd ever been.

"You didn't have to," she said, surprised at the quiet authority in her voice, anger gone. "I knew it the moment I met him. I just didn't realize what I knew. No," she corrected herself. "I was afraid to see. I didn't want to see."

"Oh, please."

For the moment, Stacie didn't even feel his cynicism. "He's killed again," she said. "The barista at In a Minute. That's where I first saw him. The morning he approached me at the preserve. He was there. Flirting with Sue behind the counter. Rather, she was flirting with him." She closed her eyes, sadness rising. "She's dead. He's broken her neck."

Ben was looking at her strangely, but Stacie was impervious to his doubt.

"She's buried in a yard. Someone's yard." The image returned. "There's a bougainvillea nearby. Water." She looked into Ben's blue eyes, and in a distant part of her mind, watched her heart breaking. "Bougainvillea doesn't grow wild," she told him gently. "Find her. She has family. They need to know."

She turned away from Ben and headed downhill toward the front gate, absently jamming Frances' notes into her messenger bag.

"Stacie," Ben called. She didn't turn. There was no reason to.

She moved, unseeing, through the garden, through the gate. She reached into her bag as she got to the car, her hands automatically seeking her car keys.

As she pulled out of the parking lot, the power that had been sustaining her began to ebb. Tears she didn't know she'd been hoarding began filling her eyes. She didn't know if they were for herself or for the poor girl she barely knew.

She spent the drive to the shop pushing away unwanted images: the dead girl trying to get Troy's attention. Her broken neck. Her vacant eyes.

Ben, laughing at Bananas.

Ben's face, filled with what she had hoped was the beginning of love.

Ben's angry face, filled with distrust.

She pulled into her usual spot in the parking lot across from the shop, got out, locked the car and crossed the street to the shop. As she locked the front door behind her, one of the wind chimes rang once. Her self-control failed.

She hurled her keys across the room. They crashed into the door leading to her office.

"I don't want this!" she shouted into the empty room. "Do you hear me, Amelia? I don't want it!"

Like a scene from a nightmare, a memory flashed in her mind.

"Stasha," her aunt had asked one day when she'd come to pick up Stacie, a sophomore, outside her high school. "Who is that girl? The one with the long blond hair? In the pink shirt?"

Stacie stuck out her tongue. "Mariana Kelso. She's a model," Stacie said, in the condescending sing-song tone teenagers use when they envy something. "Or going to be. She and her mom are always going to beauty pageants. All the boys are gaga over her."

Amelia didn't hear her. "Is that her mother there?" Her aunt nodded toward the woman standing near a BMW wearing a suede designer bomber jacket, jeans, and red heels.

"Yeah. She's pretty stuck up, too."

"Wait for me here, please."

"Sure," Stacie said, frowning in puzzlement at her aunt's retreating back.

Amelia went to Mrs. Kelso, spoke softly to her after drawing her aside. Stacie watched their faces. Her aunt's sad, but earnest. Mrs. Kelso, at first smiling tolerantly at the plain woman with a hand on her arm. But very quickly the smile failed, her face became hard. She snatched her arm from Amelia angrily.

"You're mad!" Stacie heard her say. She wasn't shouting,

but her voice was loud enough to arrest the attention of everyone nearby. "Don't you ever come near me or my daughter again. Ever!"

She threw herself into the Beemer where Mariana was already waiting. She pulled out so fast, she almost drove over the curb around the school's front lawn.

Weeks later, Mariana stopped coming to school. Not long after that, the whispers started.

"Your aunt is a witch."

"She put a curse on Mariana."

"She wanted a million dollars. When Mrs. Kelso wouldn't give it to her, your evil aunt told her Mariana would die."

Then Stacie's date for the prom had stood her up, left her standing mortified in the living room in her new dress and gloves as the clock ticked far past the time he should have picked her up. The hazing and shunning at school had gotten so bad after that, her aunt had taken her out, and Stacie had studied at home for her GED.

When the pretty teenager *did* die, even the few friends who'd stood by Stacie stopped talking to her.

Naturally there'd been police with endless questions. How did you know the child would die? Did you ask for money? Have you done this before?

In the face of their interrogation, her aunt's quiet dignity had been impressive, but Stacie had burned with a combination of pride and shame. Finally, the cops had stopped coming, and that had been the end of it.

It was the only fight she'd had with Amelia. "Why did you say anything? She was going to die anyway!" Stacie had shouted.

"Her parents deserved to know," her aunt had said quietly. "They needed time to come to terms with it. To say good-bye. The child had to be given time to come to terms."

"But what about me?" Stacie had railed. "What about *me*? I want to go to parties. I want to go out on dates. I want a boyfriend! I'm tired of being the weirdo. Nobody will ever love me!"

"My gift is a responsibility, Stasha," her aunt had told her, her face drawn and sad. "It can be a heavy burden at times like this, too. But not to use it..." Amelia shook her head. "You'll understand that someday."

"I won't," Stacie had told her. "I won't. I'm not a weirdo like you. I'm normal. I'm normal!"

Now, her chest was hollow. She'd been right, young as she'd been. She'd known. Known she'd always be alone. Like Amelia. Witches were always alone. No one loved them. No one would ever love her.

For a brief few days, she'd thought...she'd *hoped*...it might be Ben.

She shook her head. How stupid was that. He was just like the cops who'd come to the house after Marianna died. Unimaginative. Suspicious. Anything they didn't understand, sheer craziness.

Ben thought she was a liar.

"I just wanted to be normal," she said out loud, in a shaky voice. She placed her hand on the large smoky crystal on the counter and felt the emotional tug as the big crystal drew away the anger, the fear, the sadness, the grief.

"But I'm not." She closed her eyes, as the stark truth washed through her. "And I never will be."

The weight of the conviction was almost too much to carry. She looked around the shop. So often it gave her comfort. Now it was alien, something apart from her. Or maybe, as her aunt had said, a burden.

Because who was she trying to kid? All the double talk—it's just intuition, everyone has intuition, the shop is just something I do for fun—was just that. An effort to deny the gift that had now forced itself into the open.

Everyone talked about Stacie like they talked about her aunt. Look at that Byers woman. Even Mir.

And they didn't even know about this.

Now Ben. Her Ben.

Her lost Ben.

Her heart lay like a weight under the warm amethyst.

Stacie heaved a great, shuddering sigh, reached under the counter for the tissues, wiped her eyes, blew her nose. Tax season was no time for drama, she thought. She didn't have time for it.

She plucked her bag off the counter, walked across the room to pick her keys off the floor, unlocked the door and went tiredly upstairs to get her work.

TWENTY-FOUR

"Shit."

Ben spun around and marched up the trail. He felt like a goddamn fool. Cruz had been sure of it. She'd reamed him out after their last visit to Stacie's shop.

"What the hell was that all about?" she'd demanded almost the moment they'd walked out the door. "Like you two were on a special wavelength and the rest of us didn't tune in? A change in barometric pressure? Are you becoming nuts?"

"It was something she said…"

"Oh? When? Never while I've been with you. You *are* sleeping with her, aren't you?"

"No, of course not."

"Because of course, you'd tell me if you were doing something that stupid? You'd tell me if your judgement was so fucked up you're useless to me."

Ben had exploded. "You're the one who wanted to match make the first day we were here!"

"I was joking!" She looked at his face. "But you're not."

"Cruz…"

"Don't you dare 'Cruz' me. Get in the damn car."

It had been tense between them for days. *She'll kill me when she learns this*, Ben thought, *that Stacie does know about poisons.*

He realized he was climbing the trail he'd walked with Stacie.

No. He was *not* going to walk up memory lane.

And he was not in the mood now, for pictures.

He turned on his heel and headed back down. He'd go home, grab his wetsuit and go for a swim.

As he stepped out the entry gate, he noticed an old truck racing toward the front of the parking lot. It almost collided with a car turning out of one of the lanes. *Asshole*, thought Ben darkly. *The world's full of them.*

And idiots claiming to be cops. He jerked the car door open. *I can name one in particular.*

He fumed to himself as he drove down to the highway, letting anger take over his emotions.

She'd played him for a royal fool. Sucked him in. But isn't that what con men did? *And women*, he thought bitterly. This was his business, fraud. He should have seen this coming. Was he so damn desperate he'd let a pretty face blind him?

Classic. What a moron I am. What a mess I've made. Cruz will never trust me again. Great.

To think I'd actually begun to believe all this woo-woo stuff, he thought derisively. *Telepathic crystals. Fortune telling. Mumbo jumbo. Voodoo. What would it be next? Vampires and werewolves?*

His stupidity sickened him.

The loss of Stacie sickened him.

He felt a kick in his chest.

Stacie.

As the anger flowed away, grief filled the void.

He loved her. He knew it with every cell in his body. Smart, funny, courageous, loving, beautiful.

A con artist.

Is she? Could you be that far wrong? asked a small voice that sounded a lot like his mom's.

Stop it, he told himself. *Yes, you can be that far wrong. Remember Dania.*

Dania was different, and Ben knew it. His mom was right. He'd loved Dania—correction, *wanted* Dania—with his gonads. Stacie… Stacie…

Ben hurt. His chest hurt in the way his leg sometimes hurt where he'd caught shrapnel in Iraq. Stacie was everything he hadn't known he'd wanted. Everything he admired in Cruz, in his mom. Everything Dania had not been. Everything Dania would never have thought to be.

"Shit!" he shouted, slamming his fist into the steering wheel.

It didn't matter. Con artist or not. Fortune-telling kook or not. He loved her. It was going to take a long time, maybe forever, to forget her.

It might be time to find some place other than Eden Beach to work.

In a Minute came up on his right and almost without thinking, Ben pulled in. He sat in the car a moment arguing with himself.

He needed coffee, he told himself.

Bullshit, he responded.

He got out and went in.

It was moderately busy inside. He took a quick look for the blond who'd helped them the day he and Stacie had stopped by.

The day he'd first kissed her.

Stop it.

The blond wasn't there.

It doesn't mean she's buried somewhere, he thought. *Her day off.*

But as he looked around, he thought the counter staff was subdued.

Robard, don't be an ass.

When it was his turn, Ben gave the barista his order. "You're short-handed today," he said. Opening the conversation.

You're really not going to pursue this, his serious cop self said.

But apparently his woo-woo self *was* going to pursue it.

"Yeah. We may be hiring, if you know someone who's looking," the barista said.

Ben pulled out his wallet. "Did that small blond leave?" he asked. "Can't remember her name. She helped my lady friend and me the other day. She was great. Funny. Fast."

"Sue," the barista told him. "Yeah, she is great." He shrugged. "Just didn't come in last Wednesday. Hasn't been in since."

Ben chilled.

Coincidence, his serious cop self said.

You really don't believe that, his woo-woo self retorted.

"Maybe she ran away with a boyfriend?"

Another shrug from the barista. "Maybe."

"What do the police say?" asked Ben.

"She's over twenty-one. It's only been few days. Her parents and her brother are really freaking."

She has family, Stacie had said. *They need to know.*

Ben felt sick.

The barista handed Ben his coffee.

"Thanks for coming in."

Ben nodded and left.

He sat in the car arguing with himself.

This isn't real, he thought. *People really don't have visions. There is no such thing as Second Sight.*

Or healing by touch? How can I come from the family I do and not believe this?

There's a rational explanation.

Is there?

Is Stacie right?

Finally Ben pulled out and headed home.

He was just coming up on Canyon when his cell rang. Ben glanced down.

Cruz.

He almost didn't answer it. His head was not in the game.

Don't be an ass, Roburd. She's your partner. Get your head in the game.

He thumb-swiped the phone.

"'S'up, partner?"

"Hey, Ben. Sorry about this on the weekend. But Kelly called me. I'm at one of her bankruptcy houses. I'm going to give you all the I-told-you-so's you want. But you and your hunches might be right."

Ben accelerated sharply onto Canyon on the red, cutting off a driver making a left from the southbound highway, and jerked the car to the curb. The driver blasted the horn and flipped Ben a single-digit salute.

Ben didn't notice.

"Talk to me," he told Cruz.

"House is bank owned. They sent a realtor in to check the place. See what it needs to get it ready for market. She came in, took one look, backed out, threw up and called us. Kelly came out first, then called Breckenridge and Danner. Then she called me.

"Ben, this is sick. There are scalps. Ten of them. Pinned to a sheet on the wall in the living room. The whole house smells of bleach, and the crime scene guys have blood in the bathroom. But it's the scalps. They're all red and blond. Even the dyed one. Freaked the realtor. Hell, it's freaking me."

As clearly as if he'd already heard the answer, he asked her, "Why did Kelly call you, Lauren?"

She paused. "The house, Ben? It's on Milton Drive."

"Yeah?" Ben scrambled to find the street on the road map in his head. But he already knew where this was going.

"The deck looks right onto Fern Dell. Right into your lady friend's yard."

Ben felt like he was floating outside his body. "Is there a bougainvillea in the backyard?"

There was dead silence on the phone. "Wait," she said finally. Thirty seconds later she came back. "It's right by the pool. How the hell did you know that? I didn't even know that and I've been here twenty minutes."

Bougainvillea. Water, Stacie had said.

Several images flashed through Ben's mind.

Breckenridge telling him they had a partial plate on a truck.

The truck at the beach the morning he had kissed Stacie.

The truck he'd seen on the street across from Stacie's store.

The truck he'd seen racing out of the preserve parking lot half an hour ago.

The goddamn truck!

"Two things, Cruz." Ben spun the wheel hard left and squealed into traffic, swearing fluently to himself. Horns blared. He accelerated. "Have the crime scene guys look for a grave in the back. But I need you at the crystal shop now. And I mean *now*, Cruz. Stacie's there. She's on her own. I'm pretty sure I saw him following her. Tell Breckenridge he's driving the truck. The one they saw the night that guy was stabbed. I'm on my way."

"What? Ben wait…"

Ben tossed the phone down. He briefly heard Cruz shouting before she cut off.

Ben cut to the left around a slow moving car, darting briefly into oncoming traffic, then he swung right, narrowly missing another car. Ice-cream-eating pedestrians jumped back to the curb as he drove hard onto Third.

When he hit the top of the Third Street hill, he was momentarily air borne, the Camry protesting when he crashed down. Ben didn't hesitate. He flew through the stop sign, skidding right onto Parker, cursing the street layouts in Eden Beach. He swung left onto Glen Eden. Leaning on the horn, he blew through two signs and a light, covering the mile and a half in no time.

From several blocks away, he caught sight of Stacie crossing the street to the parking lot.

His heart hitched. The adrenaline peaked and began to flow away.

He lifted his foot from the accelerator.

She was okay. Stacie was okay.

He was going to look like a fool again, but in light of what Cruz had told him, he didn't much care.

Stacie wasn't going to want to talk to him. But he was going to fix that. Whatever it took, he was going to fix it.

WITH HER LAPTOP in one hand and her messenger bag stuffed with files, Stacie crossed Glen Eden to her car. She glanced up and saw Colin's apartment door standing open. There was water on the steps where he'd tended his new plants. For a moment, she thought about going up. Crying on his shoulder.

No, she told herself. *That will have to wait. These clients can't.*

And it wouldn't change anything.

She unlocked the Honda's door, popped the locks and set the computer on the floor in the back seat. She pulled the messenger bag over her head and dropped it on the seat.

The world dimmed. The sound of traffic moved away, as if she'd been dropped down a well.

Stacie's heart slammed her chest once, twice. She straightened quickly and scanned the parking lot across the roof of the car.

Nothing.

She started to turn.

Her head jerked backward as someone grabbed her hair. Twisted.

"You bitch," he hissed in her ear. "You fucking bitch. You're just like her. I told you, you whore. But no." His fist twisted tighter. Her hair was pulling out at the roots. "You wouldn't listen. But I'll teach you. You don't fuck with me!"

Fear melted her knees and Stacie almost fell. But Troy jerked her head up, pulling her to her feet. She yelped.

"Shut up bitch. You can scream later." His voice dropped to a whisper. "Oh yes, you'll scream." He licked the side of her neck.

He yanked her backward, kicked the back door closed. He bent her head back, and pushed her toward the front seat of the car.

He was going to kill her. He would rape her, then kill her. She would end up in a grave. Like Sue.

A tsunami of terror and anger-driven adrenaline surged

through her. She dug her boots into the ground and tried to twist into the angle of her neck.

Troy jerked her head harder. There was a knife at her throat. She gasped.

"Beg, bitch. Beg me not to kill you."

Never, thought Stacie. *I will die here, now, in this parking lot, before I do that.*

She lashed out hard with her heavily booted foot and was deeply satisfied when she connected with his shin.

"Fuck!" For a split second, he loosened his grip.

Stacie twisted away from the knife point and ducked. Troy yanked on her hair and Stacie didn't fight it. She straightened her knees and pushed hard, driving her head into his face.

The crack of bone on bone made her see stars.

"Fuck!" shouted Troy, as he grabbed at his nose.

Stacie spun, stumbled and staggered toward Colin's stairway. "Colin! Colin!" she screamed.

Before she'd gone three steps, Troy grabbed her arm and spun her around. There was a blow to her cheek. She fell, her temple crashing into the ground. Her wrist twisted under her.

No pain, she thought distantly. *I don't feel anything.*

Then Troy was on her. Before she could ward him off, he'd grabbed the front of her shirt and flipped her over, straddled her legs and squeezed her throat with one hand. Her hands came up automatically, grabbing his wrist.

"Oh, yeah, bitch. That's what I like. Fight." He reached down and shoved his other hand between her legs. He leered. "Hot pussy. I like that, too."

Stacie stopped thinking.

Her hands, curved into claws, shot up to gouge, tear at his face. Surprised, his head jerked back, and the grip on her throat loosened.

Growls came from her throat as she lashed at him, bucked to throw him off. Her only thought was *Kill him*.

Troy hit her, a hard fist to her face. Stacie saw it coming and managed to twist her face away. The blow hit her ear. She lunged up snapping at his face, trying to bite him. She flailed at him as he tried to catch her wrists. Her fist hit him hard in the mouth.

Somewhere in the distance, there was yelling. A door slammed. Feet pounded stairs.

Troy looked up as brakes squealed.

Stacie heaved upward, hitting, tearing, snarling. Troy caught at her hair again, slammed her head on the ground. The world dimmed then brightened. Suddenly, there was only fear.

He grabbed her shirt front and yanked her close. She could smell his breath. Mad eyes burned in his face.

"We're not done, bitch. We're not done."

He shoved her head back to the ground, leaped up, kicked her once in the ribs and was gone.

She rolled over, holding her side.

She saw feet as Colin ran by her yelling incoherently. An engine caught, gunned. Tires squealed and a car crashed over a curb.

A hand touched her shoulder. A reserve of adrenaline kicked in. Stacie lashed out, her hand connecting with a cheek bone.

"Shit!" said Ben, jumping back. "Stacie, it's okay. It's me. It's Ben. I'm here. He's gone."

For a moment, Stacie stared up into brilliant blue eyes in incomprehension, her lips peeled back from her teeth in a snarl.

"Honey. It's me," Ben said quietly.

Recognition dawned slowly.

"Ben? Ben!" she gasped.

"Yes." Kneeling he reached for her again.

Ben. *Her* Ben. He had come. Like a miracle, he had come.

Her fingers curled in his shirt.

"Troy," she croaked. "It was Troy."

"Yes. Don't talk."

The parking lot was suddenly full of police cars, lights flashing, sirens suddenly going silent. Voices yelling. Heavy engines roaring back to life, squealing tires. The sound of tortured springs as the cars went over the curb. Sirens again.

Stacie heard it only as background noise. Her gaze was locked on Ben's face as he helped her to sit. She clung to him, leaving blood on his shirt. "He's going to kill me. He told me…"

"Don't talk. You're safe now." He looked up. "Cruz!" he shouted, and Stacie heard her reply. "I need an ambulance!"

"No, I'm okay," she said.

"No, you're not. You can't see yourself." His voice was tight with fury. "You're bleeding."

"I'm okay. I don't… I just want to go home. I don't want an ambulance."

"You're getting one." His voice was curt.

The last of the adrenaline receded. Weak and shaky, Stacie let herself relax into the arm around her.

"You're bossy," she said.

Ben looked at her surprised. She saw fear fade from his eyes.

"I'm a cop," he said gruffly, trying to hide a smile. "Get used to it."

Tears rushed up and, with a sob, overflowed. Ben crushed her to his chest. Sitting on the asphalt, bleeding all over his shirt, Stacie clung to him and cried.

All the while, Ben murmured into her hair. "I've got you. I've got you. You're safe."

"She okay?" Stacie heard Colin ask, his voice shaking.

Stacie tried to nod into Ben's shirt.

"She will be, I think," said Ben. "She's hurt, though."

"He was sitting on her. He was..." Colin stopped as his voice broke. "I'd like to kill him."

"I'm a cop," said Ben "I didn't hear that."

"Just as well," said Colin. Stacie heard Colin move, heard the scratch of jeans on a smooth surface. "She put up a hell of a fight," Colin continued. "The son of a bitch was bleeding like a pig."

"Are you okay?" Ben asked Colin, concern in his voice.

"Adrenaline is *such* a bitch," said Colin. "Leaves you flat."

Hearing Colin, Stacie's ebbing sobs turned into something like a laugh. She looked up. Her friend was half sitting on the bumper of her car, looking exhausted. His right hand rested on a baseball bat.

Ben looked down at her. "How do you feel? Can you stand? I'd like to get you out of this parking lot."

She wasn't sure, but Stacie nodded. Ben rose from his knees and helped her wobble to her feet. Dizziness passed over her like a premonition. Her stomach heaved.

He's coming back. Troy's coming back.

She clutched Ben's shirt.

"You need to sit down."

"My apartment," said Colin.

"No," said Stacie. "The shop."

"The apartment is closer."

"I need to go to the shop," Stacie insisted. "I just, I just need to be there. I'm safe there."

Ben glanced at Colin as Cruz walked up.

"We've got the plate and two cruisers are after him now. He's headed down the coast. We've put the word out. We should get him before he's gone too far."

"He's dyed his hair..." Stacie started.

"Don't talk, Stacie. Not yet." Ben turned to his partner. "Lauren, Stacie wants to go to her store while we wait for the paramedics. We can ask questions there."

He paused and looked at Colin.

"Colin needs to sit, too."

"I wouldn't say no," said Colin. Stacie suddenly realized how pale her friend was.

"I can't believe you went after a stone cold killer with a baseball bat," said Ben.

"You what?" said Stacie and Cruz at the same time.

"Yeah," said Colin. "Maybe not my finest hour."

"Yes," said Ben, "It was. You got him off her before he could do more damage. Thanks."

"Let's get you both inside," said Cruz. She took Colin's arm while Ben supported Stacie.

Stacie stopped. "My files. My client's files. They're in my car. I can't leave them there."

"I'll get them," said Cruz.

Once in the shop, all Stacie's strength vanished. She collapsed into a chair. Colin sat a bit more gracefully, but his enormous sigh told Stacie how drained he was.

Ben went to the kitchen and came back with a damp cloth. He wiped Stacie's forehead where she'd hit the asphalt. She hissed when he touched it. All the pain she hadn't felt while she was struggling with Troy now arrived. She noticed her ear was ringing.

"You're going to have a goose egg there," Ben told her.

"Do you have anything to bandage it with?" asked Cruz.

They heard the warble of the paramedics in the distance. "Never mind. I know some folks who will have."

A moment later the shop was full—too full—of people, voices, questions, lights in her eyes, fingers prodding. Through it all, Stacie, now shaking, kept her eyes on Ben. Ben talking to officers. Ben talking to Cruz. Ben with the paramedics. At some point, she became aware of someone putting a hot mug into her hand.

She looked up to see Eileen.

"What are you doing here?" Stacie asked dumbly.

"I just got back from church. I saw the commotion." She put her hand on her chest. "My heart about stopped," she said, tears in her voice.

Eileen cleared her throat. "The detective recognized me and let me in." She nodded toward Cruz, talking to a tall black man with a receding hairline who, Stacie suspected, was another detective. "She told me the short version of what happened. I'm sure they'll have lots of questions, and I'm underfoot. I won't stay. But I knew you would want this." She gestured at the cup. "Colin, too." She nodded at their friend sitting close by. Colin raised his mug in a toast. "But honestly? I wanted to be sure myself that you were okay."

Stacie inhaled the fragrance and her heart almost broke with memories of her aunt. "Chamomile," she said.

"Of course," said Eileen and patted her hand. "I'll call you later to check on you. But if you need me for anything, just call me. Any time."

"Thank you, Eileen," said Stacie. Eileen squeezed her arm and disappeared into the crush.

"Colin." She reached toward him with her free hand. "I can never thank you enough…"

"Oh, please, girlfriend," he said, brushing away her words with an airy hand. "Don't mention it. And I mean *don't* mention it. I should never have missed the SOB. If any of the Jays had seen me I'd never live it down. *Completely* ruined my batting average. Not to mention my rep."

Stacie tried to laugh, but it turned into tears. Ben materialized, taking the mug from her and replacing it with his warm touch.

Fortunately, the crying bout was short because Cruz was suddenly there with the new detectives. "Ms Cappella, this is Detective Steve Danner and Detective Mike Breckinridge. They're with Crimes Against Persons. They have questions for you."

It was then that Stacie learned that Troy—or the man calling himself Troy—had been watching her from one of the streets above her house. Something shriveled inside at the thought of him watching as she pottered in the garden, played with Bananas, talked to her neighbors.

"He's probably the one who cut up my car. And slashed my tires," Ben told her.

"Ben!" Stacie interrupted before he could go on. "I thought that was random. You never said Troy had targeted you."

"It was only conjecture," Ben told her. He turned to Breckenridge. "I told you I didn't think he knew I was a cop," he said. "But I got a good look at him out there." He tipped his head toward the street. "He was at a meeting of vets at the hospital. I met him there. Fowler was the name he was using. Carson Fowler. Claimed to be an Iraq vet. But he didn't act like one. My guess now is that he followed me."

"Fowler isn't his real name," said Stacie, knowing it was true as she said it. "He may not even remember his real name. He's been hiding so long."

"What do you mean?" asked Ben quietly.

The insight she'd so feared answered for her. She spoke directly to Ben.

"He's been hiding since he was a child. Lying. Pretending to be something he wasn't. Someone he wasn't. It's just…" How could she describe the powerful sense of illusion that hung around Troy? "He's insubstantial. As if he doesn't really exist. I'm sorry, Detective," she said turning back to Breckenridge. "I can't be any clearer than that."

Skepticism was written all over Breckenridge's and Danner's faces.

Even Ben, Stacie could tell, was struggling to accept it.

But he was trying.

Stacie squeezed his hand in gratitude.

"Ms Cappella, you told Detective Robard where to find a young woman's body. How did you know where it was?"

"I didn't know where it was, Detective. I only knew that Sue was buried near a bougainvillea."

"Sue?"

Stacie nodded. "She's… She was…a barista at the coffee shop I stop at almost every week." She nodded at Ben. "I told Detective Robard that I remembered seeing Troy there the first morning he targeted me."

Detective Breckenridge didn't openly scoff, but doubt could not have been clearer on his face.

Stacie knew she could no longer deny her Sight. She had to claim what was hers. No matter the cost.

She remembered her aunt's quiet dignity so many years before.

"I have a gift, Detective. Sometimes, I'm not sure that's the right thing to call it. Not when I see a nightmare like this. I know you don't believe me." She looked at him directly. "But that doesn't mean my gift isn't real. Excuse me."

She reached for her tea. Her throat was starting to hurt.

The tea was starting to cool, but the fragrance still soothed her.

"Sometimes I see things," she continued as she put the tea down again. "I feel things. I don't always know what they mean." Ben's hand tightened in hers. She'd never told him this. Never admitted it to herself. She knew he would have questions later. "But this time I knew what it meant. I saw who and where she was."

"You told Detective Robard that this guy, Fowler, was a serial killer. Why did you say that?" asked the other detective, Danner, she thought Cruz had said.

From the corner of her eye, she saw Colin go rigid.

"Because he is. I've known it from the first day. I just was too afraid to even think that. I didn't know the extent of it until today, though."

She saw the raised eyebrow as the detective shot a look at Ben.

"I know you don't believe me," Stacie told him again. "I've had many years to come to terms with this, and I'm not sure I can believe it sometimes."

They had more questions. Some she could answer. Some she couldn't. It was Cruz, surprisingly, who finally drove them off.

She came back to Stacie. "Ms Cappella…"

"Stacie, please, Detective."

She saw an amused look on Ben's face as Lauren Cruz tried to adjust to this new level of familiarity. "Stacie," she said finally. "I'm not sure how you do what you do, or how you knew about this… But I don't suppose you know of any others? Mike won't ask," she added hurriedly, nodding to the black detective talking near the door. "But…if you know…?

Stacie shuddered. "No, Lauren. I don't. I only hope there aren't any more. Someone said there were…ten?"

"Merciful heaven," Colin muttered.

"Yeah. That's what we think." Cruz paused.

Suddenly Stacie was hurting from her head, to her ribs, to the twisted wrist, and ankle. "Lauren, can I go home? Please? I just want a hot bath and my dog." Her hand squeezed Ben's. *And you*, she told him silently. *Please, come with me.*

Ben responded by tightening his grip.

The paramedics argued. They thought Stacie had a light concussion and bruised ribs that might be cracked. She should go to the hospital for x-rays. She refused. Ben tried to order her. She refused. She was terrified to be alone in some place strange. She just wanted to be home. It had always been her safe haven, her sanctuary.

Seeing she would not change her mind, Ben told the paramedics he'd look after her and that, if there was any change, he'd see she got to the hospital.

They finally let her go with assurances she would check in with her doctor the next day, and turned to pack up their things.

Cruz came back. "We're about done. But you'll have to come into the department tomorrow to get those injuries documented," said Cruz.

"Documented?" asked Stacie.

"You'll have to have your injuries photographed, Stacie," said Ben. "For court. When we catch him."

Stacie felt sick. Take her clothes off for a stranger and let him photograph her like this. Hadn't she been through enough?

She turned to Ben. "Can you do it?" she asked. "Could we do it at my house instead?"

He and Cruz exchanged a look. "That shouldn't be a problem," Cruz told Stacie. "I'll double check and call Ben later." She turned to Ben. "I'll get the camera out of the car."

Stacie reached for her tea. It was cold. She set it back on the table. She really, really wanted it hot. She was chilled to her bones.

She closed her eyes for a moment. When she opened them, the shop was almost completely empty. Ben was locking the door behind Cruz. He had a digital camera in his hand.

"Colin," said Stacie, turning to her friend. "Are you okay? Really?"

"Between us girls?" he asked lightly.

"Colin."

He sighed. "Yeah. I'm okay. Pissed that he got away. I wanted so badly to kill him." A nod to Ben. "Sorry, but that's the way I feel. Though maybe that was more likely in the heat of the moment, rather than now."

"Glad to hear it," said Ben wryly.

"But, yeah, Stacie. I'm okay."

"He knows where you live," she said.

"He also knows I swing a mean bat."

Ben chuckled. "Cruz said you took a piece out of the truck. There's broken tail light all over the parking lot."

"All I could get."

"If you'd connected, he'd be in the hospital right now," said Ben.

"I tried my best," said Colin. "I have no idea how I missed."

"Thank you."

"No need, Stace," said Colin, reaching out to squeeze her hand. He produced a lopsided grin. "Though really, I'm not sure you needed help. Another minute, you would have killed him yourself."

Stacie looked at him seriously. "I was trying to."

Colin nodded. "We're on the same page."

He sipped his tea, made a face. "Except now. Chamomile tea has its place, but I'm going home to get a stiff drink. Or four."

"I'd rather you weren't alone in your apartment tonight. Can you... Isn't there somewhere you can go? Someone you can go to?"

Colin gave her a bright smile. "Yeah," he said. "Happens there is someone. Maybe you're right." The color came back to his face.

"Good," she said.

Colin got up stiffly, then bent down to kiss her forehead.

"Gently..." she said.

"Oh. Sorry."

"Then I'm off." He looked at Ben. Looked back at Stacie. "I leave you in good hands." He gave her a theatrical leer. "Literally," he said and grinned.

Stacie blushed.

A moment later, it was just Ben and Stacie.

Ben gave her a look.

"A hot bath and your *dog*?"

"Bananas can be very comforting."

"You might be impressed with *my* comforting skills."

"Umm," she said doubtfully. "You don't have soft, silky ears."

"You don't know that for sure. You've never tried them."

Stacie laughed. An honest, heart-felt laugh that made her face and ribs hurt.

"You're going to have a beautiful black eye," he told her.

"But you'll kiss it and make it better?"

His eyes darkened, and he touched her on the cheek gently. "That's not all I plan to kiss."

Warmth surged from Stacie's scalp to her toes, settling in dark, intimate places.

She still felt the bruises, but discovered she didn't care. She was with Ben. *Her* Ben.

Ben collected her things, then came back to help her get up.

"Ben," she said as he extended his hand. "Will he come back? He knows where I live. He knows my friends..."

We're not done, bitch. We're not done.

"No," said Ben. "He's on the run. He has no place to hide. We have a description of him and of the truck. We have a plate number. We'll get prints from the house. We'll find him.

"Besides. I'm not going to leave you alone." He took her hand and pulled her gently to her feet.

"Now let me take you home," he said and grinned. "To your dog."

Stacie smiled at him. Despite it all, she felt happy. Happier than she'd been in...forever, she thought.

Ben tugged her to him and put his arm around her very carefully. "But first," he said, "let me demonstrate my comforting skills." He bent to kiss her.

TWENTY-FIVE

BEN INSISTED SHE LEAVE HER CAR IN THE LOT AND LET HIM drive her home. Stacie resisted, but by time they had made the short drive up the hill, she was glad. Shock was setting in. She was cold and fighting off tears.

She also hurt. Every place on her body—from her ankle to her temple—throbbed. The extra-strength pain relievers the paramedics had given her were helping, but they only dulled the aches. Limping down the long staircase to her front door took forever. She clung to the handrail with a shaking hand and was grateful for Ben's warm hand under her elbow.

She sighed with relief when they reached the patio. Bananas' grinning face waited on the other side of the glass as Ben took her keys and unlocked the door. The big dog leaped onto the flagstones almost knocking Stacie down.

"Easy, big guy," Ben told him, reaching for his collar. "She's had a rough day."

Stacie fell to her knees, threw her arms around the dog's neck, buried her face and sobbed. Bananas' stood rock solid. His tail slowed its beat, and he snuffled her ears. Ben stroked her hair gently.

As the storm of sobbing slowed, Ben took her arm. "Stacie. Love. Let's get you inside." He helped her to her feet and guided her inside. "You," he said, turning to the dog. "Go do what you need to do."

Understanding he was no longer needed, Bananas went off at a run toward the back of the house.

"Do you want me to make some tea for you?"

"No." Stacie wiped tears from her face and shook her head. "I just need to get clean. I need to get him off me. I keep smelling him on me."

Ben nodded. "Let me get your boots for you."

Stacie sank gratefully into the sofa. Ben knelt in front of her to undo the knots in the laces. Without thinking, Stacie reached out to touch his hair.

Ben looked up, and Stacie's fingers trailed down his temple to his cheek. "Thank you," she said. She tried a smile. "I guess I'm not as tough as I thought."

"Don't kid yourself," he said, blue eyes serious. "You're damn tough."

She produced the whisper of a laugh as her head dropped back against the couch. "Doesn't feel much like it."

"Like Colin said, adrenaline is a bitch."

This time her short laugh was genuine. She raised her head to Ben's smile.

"That's better," he said and bent to tug the boots off.

"Bath or shower?" he asked.

"Bath is the only option."

"Stay here while I fill the tub." Ben touched her face. A moment later he called out in amazement. "You have a claw foot tub?"

"Umm," was all she could manage. She was suddenly exhausted. She closed her eyes as she heard the water gush into the tub.

When she opened them again, she was lying on the couch, pillow under her head, afghan over her. Ben was in the wing chair, book in one hand, the scent of fresh coffee rising with the steam from the mug in his other. Outside, it was almost completely dark.

Stacie took a deep breath as she came fully awake. Dog tags rattled as Bananas lifted his head from his paws to look over the edge of the sofa and sniff her face.

"I thought you needed the sleep more than the bath," said Ben.

She reached out to pet the big dog. She was stiff and sore.

"How long was I out?"

He glanced at his watch. "Just over four hours. It did you good. The color is back in your face."

Stacie smiled, then winced. "I'm sure it's very colorful," she said.

Ben did not laugh.

Stacie pushed the afghan aside, swung her legs over the edge of the couch and sat up. As she did, she noticed her shirt, torn and bloodied. The horror of the afternoon crashed back. She felt sick.

"Okay, color went away again," said Ben, putting his coffee down and getting up. "Do you need help to the bathroom?" He put a hand on her arm. "Concussion can sometimes make you puke."

"No," she said as the nausea passed. "I'm okay." She looked up. "It was just suddenly...remembering everything."

"Yeah, I know," said Ben grimly. "Been there." He massaged her shoulder gently. "Before lights out, your plan was to get clean. Still want to do that?"

"Yes," she said. "That will help."

"Okay. I'll refill the tub."

A short while later, Ben came back, handed her a glass of

water and a couple pills. "You're probably going to start to hurt again."

"I don't doubt that," she said, and swallowed the pills.

Ben took the glass, helped her up and guided her into the bathroom.

"You'll be all right?"

Stacie nodded.

"Okay. But if I hear gurgling, I'm going to bust down the door."

Stacie smiled weakly.

"Just remember. I'm right here," he said seriously.

She nodded again. Ben closed the door.

Stacie hissed as she folded carefully onto the small chair in the corner and began pulling off her socks. When she started unbuttoning her shirt, she found three buttons had been torn off, and the right sleeve was ripped away at the seam. Anger and disgust washed through her. She ripped the shirt open, popping off the remaining buttons, and tossed the shirt into a corner. Her bra followed. She never wanted to see any of these clothes again.

It took immense effort to get up and slide her torn jeans and underpants down. She kicked them to the corner as well.

As she turned, she caught her reflection in the mirror. A dark purple bruise, almost the shade of the amethyst crystal around her neck, showed at the edges of the bandage at her temple and darkened the orbit of her left eye. Her cut lip was swollen. There was a dark blackish bruise across her right-side ribs. Bruises blued her legs. The knuckles of both hands were grazed and the nails were broken and torn. Her neck hurt, her head throbbed, her wrist was sore when she moved it.

I'm a mess, she thought, the tears trembling in her eyes.

Bits of the fight flashed through her mind. Her hair being twisted. Troy's colorless eyes so close, so insane.

His awful strength.

We're not done, bitch. We're not done.

Fear cramped her stomach. Her heart seized with panic.

Ben's in the living room. The police will catch him. They have him already.

She repeated it like a mantra. It calmed her down.

She turned from the mirror and climbed stiffly into the tub. Ben had made it blissfully hot. Slowly she lowered herself down, the wet heat slowing her heart rate. Between the warmth and the medication, the pain began to melt away. Unbidden, tears began to flow, quietly this time. Stacie didn't know if it was from fear, reaction, or relief that it was over. She let them fall.

She took a breath and slid down and under, the hot water stinging her face and scalp. As she sat up again, she pulled the forgotten bandage off her temple, hissing as it caught a bit on dried blood.

As her muscles warmed, Stacie reached for a wash cloth and the lavender soap, its fragrance soothing her. She scrubbed every inch of her body, lathered her hair and washed it twice. The hot stream from the bath spray felt wonderful, and Stacie realized how the bath water had cooled.

It was easier to get out of the tub than it had been to get in. She pulled the plug and listened to the water drain away as she toweled dry. She turbaned a towel around her damp hair and caught a glimpse of her body in the mirror just before she pulled a purple robe off the back of the door.

We're not done bitch. We're not done.

Stacie shivered. Pulling a tube of arnica gel from a drawer, she spread it generously on the bruises she could reach, her neck and her wrist. She lapped the robe high around her neck and cinched the belt tightly around her waist.

Using the sprayer, she rinsed the tub. She eyed the pile of filthy, bloodied clothes in the corner with distaste.

Had to be done some time. She took a deep breath, gathered the clothes into a ball and tucked them under her arm. A cloud of steam surrounded her as she opened the door.

In the living room, Ben was lying on the couch, pillow folded under his neck, stockinged feet crossed at the ankles. He was deep into the book she now recognized as one of her aunt's novels. The cup of coffee, empty, sat on the table next to him.

Stacie was caught off guard. He'd made himself at home. In her house. Her kitchen. And he looked like he belonged. Like he'd always been there.

She was surprised to see him rolling the smoky quartz in one hand as he read, but the sight filled her with warmth.

Bananas filled the floor space between the couch and the table. He lifted his head and his tail thumped, but he didn't move.

"Traitor," Stacie told the big dog.

"It's my animal appeal," Ben told her, dropping the book onto his chest and tilting his head backward to grin at her over the couch arm.

"That would explain it."

"You look better. How do you feel? " asked Ben, as Stacie started to move toward the kitchen.

"Stiff. Achy. But the bath and the pain killers help a lot."

"Anything I can do?"

She shook her head. "No. It just has to heal, with a lot of help from arnica."

"Arnica?"

"Umm. For the bruises. And the muscles."

"Never heard of it."

She paused by the back of the couch and frowned. "You look like you could use some, too," she said, reaching down to touch the bruise on his face. "What happened to you?"

"You don't remember?"

"I'm afraid I don't remember very much," she told him. "And what I remember, I'd rather forget."

"You slugged me."

"*I* slugged you?" she asked incredulously.

Ben grinned. "Yeah. You weren't in your right mind. You probably thought I was Troy. When I touched you, you belted me." Ben raised a hand and rubbed his cheek. "You pack a hell of a wallop. I'm tempted to agree with Colin. We should have just let you finish him off."

Stacie's stomach curled.

"No," she said seriously. "Maybe I'll joke about that someday. But not today. Not now."

"Sorry," said Ben, his smile falling away. "You're right. I shouldn't have said that."

Ben put the novel, face down on the back of the couch and pulled himself up to a sitting position. As he swung his legs over to the floor, his feet encountered dog.

"Move, you," he said, nudging Bananas with a foot.

The dog sighed and lurched to his feet.

Ben got up. "Here. I'll take those." He reached for the clothes in Stacie's hands.

"Put them in the garbage. I never want to see them again."

"I'll bag them. We have to take them into the police department tomorrow."

"Why?" asked Stacie, stunned.

"Evidence."

Stacie closed her eyes a moment. "Does this never stop?" she asked him.

Ben hesitated. "When we catch him, it'll go to trial. You'll have to testify. So no. For a while, it won't stop. But it can stop for now." He leaned in and kissed her gently on the undamaged temple. "Where are your trash bags?"

"Under the sink."

Ben headed to the kitchen. Stacie heard rustling as he stuffed the clothes in a bag.

She went to the scrying crystal, reached a hand toward it. Paused, her heart beating fast.

What would it tell her? Did she want to know?

Frightened, she withdrew her hand.

"Wondering what the future holds?" Ben asked quietly. Stacie hadn't heard him come back to the living room.

"No," she lied.

"Did your aunt ever tell your future?"

Stacie looked at him surprised. "That's a personal question."

"It is," he said, but didn't withdraw it.

"No," she said. Then realized Amelia had.

The hospice nurse had just left. Stacie was sitting by Amelia's bedside reading to her.

"Stasha, bring me my crystal, please," Amelia had interrupted her.

"Aunt Me, just rest..."

"Please, Stasha."

Stacie had brought the crystal in from the living room. Amelia, too weak to hold the heavy stone, asked Stacie to lay it on her chest, next to her heart." She folded her hands over the beautiful quartz and closed her eyes. Her face got the soft distant look Stacie knew so well.

When Amelia opened her green eyes, pale now with age, she smiled brilliantly as she looked up at Stacie. "He'll make you so happy," she'd said. "I'm so glad."

Amelia had been unable to lift the crystal off her chest. Stacie had taken it from her and placed it back in the fountain in the living room. When she'd returned to her aunt's side, her dearest friend was gone.

The amethyst next to Stacie's heart was warm, silky, pulsing gently. A second heartbeat next to hers.

It hadn't been her imagination. From the moment she'd met him in the Heritage Park, the amethyst crystal had responded to Ben.

It was Ben her aunt had seen. Stacie knew it as clearly as if Amelia had spoken his name.

It was Ben. It would always be Ben.

"What is it?" Ben asked her. "You look like you've seen a ghost."

Stacie realized she'd been staring at him.

"Nothing," she stammered. "I just…it's nothing."

Ben didn't push it. He went to the patio door and set the trash bag of clothes next to it.

Bananas' toenails clicked as he made his way to the kitchen. They heard the sound of kibble crunching.

"That makes me think," said Ben. "Are you hungry? Can I get you something to eat?"

Stacie realized suddenly that she was starved.

"You cook?"

"No," he said, "I dial."

She smiled at him, making her face hurt. "Then dial. I'm going to get dressed."

She started toward the bedroom, but hesitated in the manzanita arch.

Had Ben murmured, "Too bad?"

She looked back. Ben's dark head was bent over his phone as he scrolled through phone numbers. The image of him on the trail at the Heritage Park, wind ruffling his hair, came to her mind. The memory of the day on the beach, his face serious as he told her about Iraq. The warmth of his body next to hers. His kisses.

Warmth and desire rushed through her. The aches in her ribs, her ankle, her wrist, her face all washed away. All she had room for was Ben.

She didn't think any further. She went back to where he sat on the couch and put her hand on his as he lifted the phone to his ear.

"Hang up," she said.

Startled, Ben looked up. Paused.

Stacie knew what he saw on her face. She saw it reflected in his.

A distant voice was speaking on the phone.

Ben disconnected without taking his dark blue eyes off her face.

Holding his gaze, Stacie stepped across his knees, her robe parting below the waist.

Ben inhaled sharply, shot a quick glance downward, then looked back up. His eyes softened and his pupils dilated as he leaned back. The tiniest of smiles played at the corners of his mouth. His hand fell to the side as he dropped the phone on the couch.

Stacie lifted her robe and settled one knee on either side of his thighs. Various muscles protested, but not so loudly she couldn't ignore them. She was in no mood to listen anyway.

She leaned toward him, resting her hands on the back of the couch, one on either side of Ben's head, and lowered herself to his lap. The heavy crystal on its chain dropped out of her robe and hung down to touch Ben's chest, just over his heart. He sighed.

"Stace, are you sure...?

"Shut up," she whispered.

Holding his gaze until the last moment, Stacie bent slowly toward his mouth. She flicked her tongue out to wet her lips. His eyes widened and his lips parted in response. Her mouth touched his, soft, responsive. She closed her eyes.

Ben's hand slid up her thigh. She felt herself opening.

She kissed him gently, first one lip, then the other, working her way around his mouth. There would be no one pounding at her door, no inconvenient interruptions. They had all the time in the world. Stacie intended to use it.

Ben responded to her kisses in kind, tugging gently at her mouth with his teeth.

"Careful," she murmured into his lips. "A bit tender there."

"Sorry," he said, softening the kiss.

Her robe belt loosened as he slid his hand farther up her thigh, his thumb caressing the crease where her thigh folded into her abdomen.

Softly, she lifted her face from his, caught his eyes. Quickly and playfully, she bent to kiss his nose and pulled away, smiling. He chuckled.

If I hadn't been in love before, she thought, *I would be now*.

Not taking his eyes off hers, Ben stroked her triangle of hair. Stacie inhaled sharply and deeply. She bent to touch his bottom lip with her tongue and tasted coffee as he opened his mouth to touch his tongue to hers. She moaned softly in the back of her throat. She pushed one hand behind his head, tangling her fingers in his hair, pulling him carefully deeper into the kiss. Her other hand dropped to his side and began to work his T-shirt up, fingers searching for his skin.

Now both of Ben's hands were at the tops of her thighs, massaging, teasing. Now he pushed her robe aside, and slid his hands around to cup her ass, toned by walking and yoga.

He pulled her firmly closer to him. Stacie felt him harden as she settled more deeply into his lap.

She slipped her hand between them and began to work his belt buckle. She fumbled with it briefly, then Ben's hand slid over hers and expertly released the buckle.

She lifted her mouth from his and smiled into his eyes.

"You've done this before," she murmured.

He raised an eyebrow. "Not like this."

Stacie lifted up in front of him, pulled the robe's belt free and dropped it to the floor. She leaned toward him, offering him her breasts. He smiled up at her briefly and bent his head.

The tug of his lips on her nipple shivered all the way to the tangle of hair between her thighs. Ben knew it. He moved a hand between her legs to stroke her gently.

Stacie leaned farther into him, pulling his head closer. Never moving his mouth, he reached behind her to shift her robe above her hips. Sliding her knees deeper into the couch, Stacie lifted herself from Ben's knees, rocking deep into his lap.

She yelped and jumped free of Ben's lap to land on the couch next to him.

"I'm sorry," said Ben, his eyes unfocused. "Did I hu...?"

But Stacie was laughing hysterically, collapsed helplessly against the sofa back. Bananas stood in front of her, grinning, tail waving.

"What...?"

"Bad dog!" Stacie gasped, tears running down her face. "Bad, bad dog!"

Bananas' tail slowed, but didn't stop. Bad dog, he understood. Laughter, he understood. But the two together had him confused.

Ben was confused, too.

"Bananas?" he said, looking from the dog to Stacie.

"He goosed me!" Stacie told him almost unable to speak for laughing. "I'm deep in the moment, and suddenly I had a great big, wet, cold nose right where I was expecting something very much warmer!"

Ben looked down at Bananas' happy face. "Thanks, pal. Whose side are you on?" He tried to pull his face into a frown, but was grinning too widely. "Stacie's right. Bad dog!" But Bananas was now in on the joke. His tail wagged harder.

Stacie was wiping tears from her eyes as she caught her breath.

"Gives new meaning to the phrase *ménage a trois*," said Ben as he turned toward her.

"Talk about a moment killer." She pulled her robe together as she got up off the couch.

"We need more privacy," she said, holding a hand out to Ben. He took it and let her pull him toward the bedroom.

Nails clicked on the floor behind them.

As they stepped into the bedroom, Stacie turned. "Definitely not you," she said to the dog and closed the door firmly in his face.

STACIE DIDN'T KNOW she'd fallen asleep until she found herself waking up. The soft bedside light was on. Outside, the dark sky was pitch black speckled with stars. The lights on the oil derricks shimmered like fireflies.

Her head was pillowed on Ben's shoulder, her left arm across his chest, her leg across his. He'd pulled a quilt over them both. He was reading the book she'd left on the nightstand.

He looked down at her as she shifted, laying the book on his chest.

"Oh, wow," she said.

"I told you. Now what do you think of my comforting skills?" Ben leaned sideways and kissed her injured temple gently. "And my silky ears," he whispered.

Stacie smiled as she reached up to stroke the lobe of the ear closest to her. She was carefree for the first time in weeks and happy down to her bones.

"Those are worth a wow, too," she said, "but I'm afraid it's the soreness everywhere I was moaning about. Those meds are wearing off.

"If you think that's bad, you'll want to stay away from a mirror for a few days. Your colors are intensifying. You're black and blue," he kissed her temple again, "and green and yellow," his fingers traced the bruise on her ribs, sending a delicious shiver over Stacie's skin, "everywhere, too." He kissed her ear gently and breathed, "Almost everywhere."

Stacie giggled and nestled closer to him.

"This is an amethyst, isn't it?" he asked, touching the deep violet crystal that lay between them.

"Umm."

"I've never seen you wear it."

"I wear it all the time. I just don't make it public."

Ben looked at her curiously. "Why?"

How much should I tell him?

"I'm not sure I should tell you," she said finally.

"Why?"

"Technically, it's stolen property."

"Excuse me?" Ben's eyebrows shot up, and Stacie grinned.

"A many-times-great grandfather smuggled it out of a mine that belonged to the tsar. It's been in my family for centuries."

"That was quite a risk, wasn't it?"

She nodded. "It was." She glanced down at the crystal. "Considering its value, especially at that time, and considering that it belonged to the tsar, he probably would have been executed if he'd been caught."

"If it was that valuable, why didn't he sell it?"

"That wasn't why he took it," Stacie told him. "He claimed that when he touched it, he saw the face of the woman he would marry. He believed that made the stone his. And hers."

"Did he marry her?"

Stacie nodded. "According to family legend, he met her a few days later at a market."

"Great story."

"That's not all." Stacie lifted the crystal and held it in her hand. It was warm. That could have been from their bodies, but Stacie had learned more about her gift now. This warmth was coming from inside the stone, not from outside. And there was a distant... pulsing...so slight she wasn't really sure she could feel it. Perhaps like a mother would feel her baby's heartbeat while it was still in the womb.

"Since then, it's predicted love for a number of family members."

Ben tried not to look skeptical.

"You're looking skeptical," she said.

"Yes, well, Stacie. Do you blame me?"

"No," she said, and didn't. She decided to leave the rest of the story for another time. He needed to get used to this a little at a time.

She ran her hand down his chest and onto his side. Curiously, she pushed the quilt lower, exposing his abdomen.

"No tattoos?" She glanced up at him. "I thought guys in the military were so bored they inked each other."

"Disappointed?"

Stacie shook her head. "Surprised is all. Why not?"

Ben shrugged with his free shoulder.

"What?" she said. "What's that look?"

"No look."

She pointed to his face. "*That* look," she said, smiling. "You look like a kid busted with his hand in the cookie jar." She looked closer. "And you're blushing?"

Ben looked away, the sheepish grin still on his face.

He looked back at her. "Truth?"

She gave a slight nod, wondering what the deep secret was.

"I don't like needles."

Stacie dropped her head back and laughed. And laughed.

"Sorry," she said, when she'd caught her breath. "I'm not laughing at you. I just didn't expect that." She was happy to find that Ben was grinning at her.

"How on earth did you get into the Army? I thought military inductees got tons of inoculations."

Ben rolled his eyes. "You have no idea. I swear we got jabbed every day at breakfast and twice on Sundays. I'll take a suicidal insurgent with an AK-47 over that any day."

Stacie laughed again.

Ben stroked her, running his hand over the tattoo lying just outside her right hip bone.

"You obviously don't have the same fear."

"Umm. It's not that big a deal."

"A galaxy," he said, his finger tracing the spirals.

"Umm."

"Why a galaxy?"

"The infinite. The unknowable." She smiled up at him. "I was seventeen. I was thinking deep thoughts."

"And now?" asked Ben.

"Definitely thinking deep thoughts."

"Of?"

She rested her hand on his stubbled chin, and ran her thumb over the bruise she'd left on his cheek. "Thinking of infinite, unknowable possibilities."

Ben slid his hand up across her belly, trailing his fingers along her sternum between her breasts. His index finger came to rest at the hollow of her throat.

"Not everything is unknowable," he said huskily, his eyes dark.

Stacie slipped her hand behind his head, stroking the nape of his neck before burying her hand in his hair.

"All knowledge worth having comes at a price," she said.

He raised an eyebrow as Stacie bent forward to kiss him.

TWENTY-SIX

When Stacie woke the next morning, the other side of the bed was empty.

A man was talking softly in the other room.

She panicked, fear sending icy knives through her abdomen.

We're not done bitch. We're not done.

Then she heard the crunch of kibble, the rattle of dog tags. Ben.

With the relief, came tears. She laid her hand over her heart and waited until it slowed to a normal beat and the tears stopped.

Moving slowly, she crawled out of bed and pulled her robe around her. She glanced out the deck windows as she passed through the living room. Heavy fog dripped from the leaves of the huge ceanothus that overhung the railing. The trees at the back of her lot were faint in the mist. She could not see the roof of Fred Langley's house just twenty-five feet down the slope.

"Thanks. Keep me posted," Ben was saying as Stacie

walked into the kitchen. He disconnected and looked up, his face grim.

"You didn't get him," Stacie said flatly.

Ben shook his head. "This," he said, tipping his chin up to the fog outside, "had already rolled in down the coast. The patrol lost him. All the departments up and down the highway are watching for him, and the Highway Patrol is looking. But the fog is dense all along the coast and it's inland pretty much up to the foothills. Weather reports say it doesn't look like it will burn off today, either."

"So no one knows where he is." Stacie couldn't breathe. Her heart was pounding so hard her ears were ringing. She tried to sense if Troy was anywhere close, but her intuition was blocked by fear. She reached into her pocket and realized her crystal was on her dresser.

Ben saw the gesture. He shoved his phone in his jeans pocket, crossed the kitchen in two strides and put his arms around her rigid body. With her head against his bare chest, his heart beating in her ear, Stacie's heartbeat slowed, but an icy current of fear still flowed through her.

I'll never be safe again, she thought. *I'll never be safe.*

"We'll get him, Stacie," said Ben firmly, as he stroked her hair.

Stacie nodded stiffly, not trusting her voice.

She wasn't so sure.

THE WEEK that followed was a nightmare for Stacie. She jumped every time her phone rang or someone came into the shop. Concentrating on work was impossible. She snapped at Bananas when he nudged her and was ashamed of herself when his wagging tail slowed and drooped sadly.

The story about Troy's killings had captured national

press. Local reporters had quickly connected Stacie's assault to the serial killings. They stationed themselves outside the shop, and some found their way to her home. Surprisingly, Mir declared herself Stacie's spokesperson and handled the interviews on the sidewalk in front of The Bell, Book and Crystal with grace and gravity.

At her home, as the news trucks and reporters filled the narrow cul-de-sac, the neighbors systematically called police to have them removed or ticketed. Fred Langley, stony face in place, stationed himself in a deck chair at the top of her stairs so no one could get to her front door. He stared down anyone with questions.

The only plus side to the exposure was that she no longer had to hide the situation from her clients. They now understood why she was so far behind in her day-to-day book work, and accepted that she'd hired another bookkeeper to help. Her tax clients were understandably concerned about her ability to concentrate under the circumstances. Stacie, too, worried that her accuracy would suffer. Fortunately, Eileen knew a retired certified public accountant who agreed to double check Stacie's returns for a reasonable fee, which eased her clients' concerns.

To top it off, fog and low temperatures were keeping tourists away. However, local residents, driven by curiosity, discovered the store, and a number of them made purchases. It wasn't enough to off-set the extra expenses, but it helped.

If all that weren't enough, when Stacie returned to the store on Tuesday after the attack, she found "witch" painted on the picket fence in front. Mir and Ace painted it out that afternoon, but not before pictures of it appeared in the news. Stacie wanted to scream.

She ranted to Ben and Lauren when they stopped by later that day, as they'd started doing whenever they were in the area. Stacie had come to like Lauren Cruz a great deal, and had begun to trust the detective as much as she trusted Ben.

"I thought it was Jer!" she almost shouted, her voice verging on hysteria. "Didn't you say he'd admitted it? Isn't he in the hospital or jail or some place?"

"He did, and he is," Cruz told her. "And Ginny's statement will keep him there. This has to be someone else, possibly someone who's seen the news stories and is acting on his own."

"*Madre santa e tutti gli angeli*," said Stacie, scrubbing her face with her hands. "Is this *never* going to end?"

If it weren't for Ben, she thought, she'd go crazy.

Ben stayed with her every night. He took her home, brought her to the office. He'd printed, framed, and given her the image she'd liked so much from the day at the manzanitas and one of the lizard shedding—one of the shots he'd taken the day they'd first met on the trail. She hung the manzanitas in the living room, between the fireplace and the patio doors. But the other was in her office above the shop, where she could see it for hours every day. They anchored her, reminding her of days that seemed a lifetime ago.

Worried for her safety, Ben had asked a couple patrol officers to station themselves at The Bell, Book and Crystal on their days off, and paid them for their time. Stacie chafed at the surveillance, but was grateful, too. It meant Eileen did not have to come to the shop, and Mir was protected. Stacie worried about both of them, afraid Troy would hurt one of them if he couldn't get to her. At the same time, she felt caged by all the good intentions. Every day that passed, she was more angry and resentful. She wanted Troy caught. Jailed.

Forever.

Longer if possible.

Then came one bright spot. Colin, looking out his office window just before dawn the Monday following what had been an impossibly long week, saw someone at Stacie's fence. Grabbing his phone, he padded down his stairway barefoot and in sweat pants and trotted across to the shop.

"Good morning, Sunshine!" he called out, and was rewarded when a startled Celia Byers looked up. He got a clear shot of her with paintbrush in hand, and "WI..." clearly painted on the fence.

She lunged at him. But Colin danced backward, taking video and laughing as she lumbered after him.

"You can't do that!" she screamed at him. "I'll sue you!"

Colin called Stacie moments later to tell her.

"Sorry to wake you," he said, still laughing, "but it was too perfect!"

"Would you send it to Detective Meissner?" she asked.

"Already done."

When Stacie told Ben, he couldn't stop laughing. "Have him send it to Cruz," he spluttered. "It will make her day."

When the partners stopped by the next day, Lauren was grinning ear to ear. "Her husband called me yesterday to ask me to drop the charges," Stacie told Ben's partner.

"Are you going to?" asked Lauren.

"I'm considering it, though I'm really angry. He said she's going to a clinic in Arizona for treatment."

"That's what Paul told me, too," said Lauren. "I wouldn't be surprised if she doesn't come back."

"Too bad." Ben grinned at his partner. "Family dinners won't be nearly as interesting anymore."

"Andrew was more upset when he found out Colin was going to the papers," said Lauren.

Colin had called a friend at *The South Coast Record* and given him the scoop—and the video. The story was due out later in the week. The video was already posted on the newspaper's website. "He was threatening to sue."

"You explained to him about freedom of the press? The public's right to know? All that?" asked Ben.

Lauren grinned. "I sure did."

"Won't help his run for mayor."

"Yeah. Ain't it a shame," she said.

Then Cruz got serious. "I'm afraid that's the good news," she told Stacie. "Steve Danner asked us to stop by."

Stacie felt a chill. She laid a hand on Bananas' head.

"Some wildcat miners found Troy's truck off a dirt road in the desert north of Vegas, near the Utah border." Cruz told her. "It had been totally gutted by fire."

"Is it too much to hope he was in it?" asked Stacie.

Ben stepped closer and took her hand. "There *was* a body in it, Stacie. But not his. There's a young woman missing from the town of Ely. The Nevada State Police think it may be her."

For a moment, the room faded. Her skin went cold as the blood drained from her face.

We're not done, bitch. We're not done.

"Stacie? Stace?" Ben was saying.

Cruz took her other arm. "You need to sit down," she said, as she guided her to a chair. "You've gone white."

"The good news is that he's running. And he's running away," Cruz told her, once she had some color back in her face.

"The bad news is that no one's caught him. And he's still killing women," said Stacie faintly. "Poor, poor girl. Her poor family."

"The Nevada police have some leads," said Ben. "They're following up. The FBI is also looking for him. They'll find him, Stacie," he added firmly.

"How many more women will die, though?" she asked. She saw the answer in Ben's face.

"Stacie," said Lauren tentatively. "Stacie, what do *you* think?" She shook her head. "Jeez. I can't believe I'm asking this."

Stacie smiled wanly. "Detective Cruz," she said, "are you asking me to use my witchy sense to find him?"

"Okay, fine," said Cruz, throwing up her hands. "Call me a doubting Tomasina, but... Can you?"

Stacie shook her head. "No, Lauren. I'm sorry. As much as it makes me sick to my stomach, I've tried to sense him because I want him caught. But he's either too far away, or too fixated on someone else. Or I'm simply too frightened." She shook her head again. "I've never been able to control this. I'm really very sorry."

As the days passed, the police seemed to get closer. In Provo, a woman who'd seen the artist sketches on the news tried to take a picture when someone she thought was Troy tried to pick up a friend of hers. He'd spooked and left them quickly. They'd reported it to the police. Detective Danner brought the blurry photo to the shop, but Stacie couldn't give him a firm identification. The sickness in her stomach made her think it was Troy, but she was honest enough to admit to herself it could just be fear.

There was a possible sighting in a small town in Kansas. Then in the Texas panhandle. Troy was running. He was getting farther away. Even better, as far as the police knew, there had been no more killings.

By the first week in April, Stacie was comfortable enough to return to her yoga class with Colin and Mir. She asked Ben to stop posting police in the shop.

"Ace is starting to get jealous," she told him jokingly when he and his partner stopped by one afternoon. "And

Colin's whining about the cookies Eileen is making for them."

"If Eileen isn't going to be making cookies, I guess there is no reason for Lauren and I to stop by anymore," said Ben.

"Bumped out of first place by a cookie. Jeez."

"Never bumped out of first place," said Ben, grinning as he leaned in to kiss her.

Lauren rolled her eyes. "I'm beginning to think I liked your monastic period better," she said. "Besides, doesn't your dog think three's a crowd?

"What?" she asked when Ben and Stacie started howling with laughter. "What am I missing?"

Ben breathlessly waved a hand indicating he was never going to tell her.

"Fine," said Lauren. "Be that way." She looked around, suddenly realizing there was a big dog-shaped empty spot in the shop. "Where is the dog anyway?"

"At the groomer's," said Stacie when she could talk again. "Second time. Idiot tried to make friends with a skunk the other night."

"I'm guessing it didn't go well."

"No!" said Ben and Stacie together.

"He's been exiled to a dog house on the patio," said Stacie. "Even that is too close. The groomer is still trying to get the smell off of him, but the last time this happened, it took almost a month and four washings. I have few enough customers right now. I don't dare bring him here and lose more."

"And there is no way I'm staying anywhere near a skunk-stink dog," Mir added. She put two fingers to her mouth. "Gag me." All of them laughed.

Now that she could stop worrying about Troy, Stacie

focused on her life and her future. On Ben's future. Very specifically, her future with Ben.

Stacie had been surprised when her neighbor and gallery owner Margot Somerset had negotiated all the steps to Stacie's house one evening.

"I've seen the news," she told Stacie. "I wanted to see how you're doing. I'm sorry I haven't come by sooner."

"That's okay. Come in, and I'll tell you about it."

They'd had a glass of wine while Stacie told Margot what hadn't been in the paper. As she was leaving, Margot had seen Ben's photo.

"This is beautiful! Where did you get it?"

Stacie told her.

"Does he have more?"

"Yes, he does," Stacie told her. Stacie had spent an evening with Ben at his apartment—with a pre-skunk Bananas taking up half the floor space—looking through his files of photos. "He has lots more."

"Who represents him?"

"No one. He doesn't think he's good enough, though I keep trying to convince him he is."

"If all his work is this quality, he definitely is. Send him to me. I want to see more."

After some arm twisting—and some significant pushing from Tucker and Maureen—Ben reluctantly agreed to show Margot some of his photos. Highly persuasive, Margot talked to a skeptical Ben about what made his images unique, how to make them stronger, and explained what "body of work" meant. She finally succeeded in talking him into joining a group show at her gallery in August.

With tax season finally winding down, Stacie and a still-reluctant-but-willing Ben were planning a ten-day picture-taking excursion to the Sierra Nevada. Stacie was looking forward to it almost more than Ben.

Finally, it was done. The April fifteenth tax deadline had passed. Everyone who needed to be was on extension. Life could go back—mostly—to normal.

The next night, Ben took her to dinner to celebrate surviving another tax season and surviving the previous two months. Later that night, they lay curled together in bed.

"Ben."

"Umm?" was the sleepy reply.

"You're going to be developing a lot of pictures for the show, aren't you?"

"That remains to be seen," he said. Stacie heard the smile in his voice. "I may not get anything worth developing." He bent and kissed her head. "I may chicken out," he whispered.

She laughed. "Will Tucker let you?"

"I'm more worried about Maureen."

She tipped her head back to look at him and poked him in the side. "*I'm* not the one you have to fear?"

"Nah. You're a novice compared to Maureen," he grinned. "She's been handling Tucker for years now."

"I see. I'll have to take lessons from her."

"Oh, lord," said Ben shaking his head. "I'm in trouble now."

Stacie rolled up on an elbow to face him and pulled the quilt around her. "Your bathroom is awful small to do a lot of work, isn't it?"

"Well, it's not large." He looked at her strangely. "What are you getting at?"

Stacie hesitated, afraid she was about to cross a line.

"It's just that... The apartment under the garage is empty. There's water. It's larger than your bathroom." She stopped, not sure what to say next.

Ben smiled faintly. He was hesitating, too.

"Stacie," he said finally. "Are you asking me to move in?"

She took a deep breath. "Yes," she said. "Yes. I guess I am. Though I thought I was only asking your darkroom to move in."

"I go where my enlarger goes," he said, grinning. He reached up to draw her into a kiss.

Stacie let the quilt fall away and ran her free hand down Ben's chest, stomach, abdomen.

"Speaking of enlarging," she said.

ALTHOUGH THE DECISION had been made lightly, Ben and Stacie talked a lot over the next few days about what his moving in would mean.

"As long as it's understood that I control the remote," Ben told her seriously.

"Neither of us has a TV, Ben."

"Only because I don't have space," he countered. "Here," he waved an arm around her small living room, "there's room for a good-sized flat screen."

Stacie raised an eyebrow. "That's why there are sports bars."

Ben grinned.

There were more serious discussions, too, about the demands and risks of Ben's career as a police officer, and the even thornier issue of Stacie's gift.

"Stacie," said Ben Sunday morning as they sat on the patio, hummingbirds darting around them. A still somewhat-fragrant Bananas sprawled on the bricks in the sunshine a safe distance away. The remnants of Ben's breakfast specialty —pancakes and bacon—were spread on the table. Stacie was half-asleep on a nearby chaise longue. Ben had been watching the sun flash and flare from the golden needles in the rutilated quartz pillar near her.

Stacie lifted her head and squinted at him.

"The day Breckenridge talked to you about your gift," he said, not having to specify what day that had been, "you told him you see things, know things sometimes. Sometimes you don't know what they mean."

He paused. She simply waited.

"I didn't think you meant just now. Just recently. That this had happened all your life."

"Yes."

"Like with my crystal."

"Yes."

"You said it was just intuition."

"It is," she said firmly. "Except when it's something…more."

"Like when?"

Stacie swung her legs off the chaise and came over to sit next to Ben in the shade. She didn't touch him. She told him about the episodes from her childhood. About the state senator. About Celia Byers' heart condition.

"She has a heart condition?"

"Yes. She's living on borrowed time."

"Shouldn't you tell Cruz?"

"No," said Stacie. "It's Celia's condition to disclose."

"Did you tell Celia?"

"No. And I worried about that. But first, she wouldn't believe me. And even if she did..." She glanced away. "I really don't want to start the whole 'mystical healer' thing." She shook her head. "I still don't know what I want to do about this. Or how I'm going to handle it." She looked at him. "I should have listened better to Amelia. She tried to teach me."

Ben put a hand over hers.

They sat silently for a while, long enough for Bananas to whine and shift in his sleep, long enough for a big black and yellow bumble bee to visit almost all the blossoms on a nearby lupine.

Stacie waited. He had to ask it or it would fester between them. And he had to believe her when she told him the answer.

"What do you know about...us?" he finally said.

"Our future?"

"Yes."

"Nothing."

"Nothing?"

She shook her head. "Besides the fact that you're going to do the dishes, nope."

"You've got that wrong. I cooked."

She smiled at him.

"So we could be like any other couple in the world and fall apart next week."

"No," she told him.

"You know this? Or you simply want it to be true?"

"I've known from the moment I met you that we were destined to be together for the rest of our lives," she said quietly.

"Sounds like a bad romance novel."

Stacie laughed. "It does. But it's true."

"How do you know?" he asked seriously.

Stacie reached up, pulled the amethyst crystal out of her shirt, and lifted the chain over her head. "This," she said, laying it in his palm. The red heart in the depths of the violet crystal glowed against his hand.

Ben lifted an eyebrow.

"I will tell you a story," said Stacie. Now she told him all of it.

She told him how, since her many-times-great grandfather found it, the stone had always identified a love match as it passed through her family, how that knowledge had sometimes been ignored or thwarted, how the crystal had broken when her great, great grandfather had been murdered. "It never called to anyone for Amelia," said Stacie. "She thought the power of the stone had been lost when it broke. She was so sure, that when it started signaling to me I didn't recognize it."

Ben rolled the crystal in his hand, then grinned as he handed it back to her. "It's a great story," he said. "I expect you'll tell our daughter some day."

The crystal was there, warm, captured between their two palms. It pulsed twice, sending a shivering current through her.

"Daughter," she said a bit breathlessly. Hesitantly she asked, "Do you want children?"

"Yes, of course," Ben told her. "Don't you?"

"Absolutely," she said and smiled. The amethyst tickled her palm. She smiled more broadly, then laughed. "Oh! Very absolutely."

TWENTY-SEVEN

OVER THE NEXT COUPLE WEEKS, BEN, AIDED BY TUCKER, moved his things into Stacie's—"now it's *ours,*" Stacie insisted—house. They cleaned and painted the garden apartment and hit garage sales for a few pieces of furniture to flesh out the studio.

Stacie smiled as she watched Ben settle in.

"You're like a kid on Christmas morning," she said as she helped him shove a garage sale table into place. "Oof," she said. "How did you and Tucker ever get this thing down the stairs?"

Ben grinned. "Beer power."

"You're getting used to thinking of yourself as a photographer," she said.

"I wouldn't go that far," he said cautiously. "It will depend on what happens after this trip. And after August. But I *am* getting excited about this trip." They spent most evenings pouring over maps and making campground reservations online. "I've never been up to the Sierra Nevada."

"Intimidated by Ansel Adams?"

"You'd better believe it!" he told her.

"Will everything fit in the car? Or will we need a trailer for Bananas?"

Ben had sold the Camry to a surfer who didn't mind the mildew smell, and bought a used midnight-blue Honda Pilot. He was sure everything would fit—cameras, camping gear and dog. Stacie wasn't so sure until he came home with a rooftop cargo carrier fitted to the car.

She laughed and patted Bananas' head. "You get to ride inside after all, fella."

"But," Ben shook a finger at the dog, "If you try making friends with a skunk again, *you* will be the cargo we're carrying on the roof."

Things had settled down at the office, now that the tax deadline was past. Warming temperatures drew tourists who filled the streets and The Bell, Book and Crystal after the marine layer had burned off. While some of those visitors became new customers, an uncomfortable number came in because of the notoriety. They asked questions about Troy and what it was like to be stalked by a serial killer. Ben suggested they tell the curious they couldn't talk about it because it was an ongoing investigation.

"Is that true?" Stacie asked him.

"Does it matter?"

"No," she said. "If they're really determined, I'll refer them to Detective Breckenridge."

Mir was working full time as Stacie scrambled to get all the bookkeeping work done before she and Ben left. She was looking forward to covering the shop for Stacie while the couple were gone.

Eileen promised Stacie she would check on the younger woman. "It's been a long time since I've worked in a store, but I'm willing to lend a hand, if needed," she told Mir.

"I'll be happy to come over, too," said Colin as he

munched one of Eileen's cookies. "As long as there's food, that is."

Mir simply rolled her eyes.

By working long hours and having Ben dial dinner four nights out of seven, Stacie managed to get all but one job finished the day before their departure. The last client—who had no sense of time or deadlines—had kept changing and delaying their appointment. Stacie had finally nailed her down for six in the evening.

"Sorry, Ben," she told him over the phone. "I'd hoped we could have an early night. Try to remember what we've forgotten."

"If it's forgotten, it's going to have to stay forgotten. There's barely enough room left in the car for the Hound of the Baskervilles." Stacie laughed. "Don't worry about it. Do what you need to. I'm running late, too. Cruz decided all the paperwork has to be done before I go."

"Ah. She figured out your clever ploy to get out of town and leave it all on her desk, did she?"

"That's why she's the detective," said Ben. Stacie laughed again. Love felt so good. She'd never realized how it would transform her life.

"Look," he said. "Why don't you grab something to eat there, and I'll do the same. I'll bring home some kind of deadly dessert to start our vacation right."

"Now that is an idea I can second! Remember to put it on the top of the fridge or He-Who-Must-Not-Be-Named will get it."

"By the way, the stink dog's last shampoo appears to have gotten rid of the last of the skunk. I put him in the house when I brought him home from the groomer's. Taking no chances," Ben told her.

"Wise man. That's why I love you."

"I love you, too."

AFTER SHE SAW MIR OFF, Stacie locked up and walked down to the Italian restaurant at the corner.

"No fiancé tonight?" asked Peter as he bagged up her to-go order. His family owned the popular dinner spot, and Stacie had been coming in for years.

"No. We're both stuck working late," she said.

"Don't make it a habit," said Monica, Peter's wife, as she rang up the sale. "It's too easy to lose touch if you don't spend the evenings together."

"*We* don't spend evenings together," said Peter.

Monica gave him a look. "What do you call this?" she asked waving a hand between the two of them.

Stacie laughed and waved as she left.

The sky above was still clear and blue, but darkening to violet over the hills in the north and east of Eden Beach. Out toward the ocean, though, fog was rising, dimming the blue to gray and cooling the air as the sun dipped into the mist. Stacie shivered as she walked back to the shop. *Should have brought my sweater.* No matter how warm the days were, evenings were still chilly along the coast.

The smell of tomato sauce, oregano and basil rose from the sack in her hand, and Stacie's stomach grumbled. *Good thing Colin didn't spot me*, she smiled to herself as she let herself back into the shop, *or I'd be sharing*. She ate at the tiny table in the kitchen and tidied up. Glancing at the clock, she realized there was still a lot of time before Heidi arrived. *Especially if she's late, as usual*, thought Stacie.

Mir had dusted and cleaned all the cases before she'd left, so Stacie pottered around the store rearranging displays, straightening the books. She pulled on her sweater and picked up several boxes of new wind chimes. Whenever the weather started to get nice, they started to sell and she wanted to fill in some gaps in the garden.

She glanced up as she unlocked the sliding doors to the garden and stepped out. The sky had darkened further. A few stars managed to penetrate the glow of the city lights refracted by the thickening fog. In a few minutes, they'd be completely hidden. As she stepped out, the security lights flashed on. One immediately winked back out. She sighed. The lightbulbs burned out almost before she finished changing them. She hoped they still had some in the kitchen.

She set the chimes on the table outside. Leaving the sliding door open behind her, she went into the kitchen to look. Yes, there were two bulbs left. She'd have to leave a note for Mir, have her get more while she and Ben were gone. She snagged the step stool by the kitchen door and carried it and the bulb outside.

With the new bulb to illuminate the yard, it didn't take fifteen minutes to get the clanging, ringing chimes unboxed and hung. Now she was ready for summer.

She carried the boxes back in, checked the clock and sighed. A quarter after six. She shook her head as she locked the glass door behind her.

Stacie didn't think she showed her impatience, too badly at least, when Heidi turned up at 6:35, trailing excuses, as usual. Their escape to the mountains couldn't come soon enough.

THE ARMY and the police department, thought Ben as he walked across the parking lot, had one thing in common: paperwork. He was a lot later than he'd thought he'd be partly because everyone had come by to make jokes about him living in his car, or about going off to be a mountain man. Only Cruz knew he was headed to the mountains to take pictures. Thankfully, she'd kept quiet, though there were times he knew she'd been dying to say something.

He couldn't complain. She'd finally chased him out, offering to finish the last half hour or so of work before she headed home. She hadn't had to offer twice. It had taken him ten seconds to lock his gun in a drawer, drop a few remaining files on her desk and head out the door.

Ben thumbed Stacie's number on his phone as he got into the laden Pilot. Voice mail. Must still be with her client. He glanced at his watch. 7:30. He hoped she'd be home soon. He'd split a pizza with Cruz, but he was already hungry again.

At the tone, he told the digital recorder, "Hey, sweetheart. I'm just finished and heading home now. Cruz ate most of the pizza. So if you're not home in the next half hour, I will not be held accountable for making these two slices of red velvet cake disappear before you get there. See you soon."

Ben grinned as he started the car. Going home had a richer meaning now that he had someone to go home to. And he didn't mean the dog.

He drove through the thickening fog past The Bell, Book and Crystal. Through the front window, he saw Stacie talking to a small dark-haired woman who was gesticulating wildly. Stacie was smiling. The fullness in his heart whenever he saw her still surprised him. He'd never thought he'd feel like this. Celia Byers was an alcoholic pain in the ass, he thought, but he'd always be grateful she'd put in a fraud report about Stacie. There was no way Ben would have met her otherwise.

Maybe Stacie's right, he thought. *Maybe we are meant to be together forever*. He smiled at the thought.

Ben looked out to the coast as he turned around in the cul-de-sac, but there was nothing to see. The village down in the curve of the bay, the coast, even Fred Langley's house behind theirs had vanished in the heavy fog.

His phone vibrated in his pocket as he pulled the car into the garage. Stacie, probably, telling him she was on her way.

He snatched up the bakery bag, sidled out of the garage and closed the door. At the top of the steps, he paused. Bananas was barking frantically.

Thank God I locked him in, thought Ben. *The skunks must be going through the backyard again.* The idea of driving for ten days with a skunk-drenched dog in the car did not bear thinking about.

He shook his head. The idiot.

He unlatched the gate and headed down the steps. He paused a moment halfway down.

"Crap," he said under his breath. The security lights were out. He had just replaced them a few weeks ago. He was going to see if there was another brand that lasted longer. Stacie said the bulbs at the store burned out overly quickly, too.

He was familiar enough with the steep stairs that the darkness didn't slow him down, and there was enough city light reflected from the fog to be sure of his footing. Once he was on the patio, the lights by the back door would come on.

Bananas was still going crazy. He took a deep breath, but couldn't smell skunk. Raccoon?

He shrugged. He'd leash the beast when he got inside and walk him. That would help settle him down.

He was annoyed when the lights by the door did not come on as he stepped onto the flagstone patio. Then his foot hit something solid that rolled away.

One of Stacie's spheres?

He barely registered the thought when his brain screamed, *No!*

Ben dove toward the ground.

Too slow.

The blow caught him, spun him across the patio. His head hit the fountain's stone base and consciousness winked out.

FINALLY, thought Stacie. Heaven knew she liked Heidi, and the woman had a wicked sense of humor, but her sense of time! Or rather her lack of a sense of time. Stacie had expected to be gone long before now.

She pulled out her phone out and laughed when she heard Ben's message. She called back, but got *his* voice mail. No matter. She'd be home in a few minutes. *And that chocolate cake better still be there*, she thought smiling as she dropped the phone back into her pocket.

Stacie locked the door to the shop, set the alarm and, with a light step, crossed the street, pulling on the welcome warmth of her pea coat. It was the first night in a long time that she wasn't carrying her briefcase, taking work home. She almost felt guilty. But it was all done. When she got back, she'd work on the returns for everyone on extension. Despite being away for ten days, the work load would still be manageable.

The fog was so thick she could barely make out the outline of Colin's apartment building across the lot. She'd have to watch the curves on the way home. Some idiot was always coming down faster than was safe. Bad enough on a clear day. Doubly dangerous in a dense fog at night.

Stacie paused by the car and laid a gentle hand on her abdomen and thought about Ben. So many reasons to get home safely. A crackling fire on a foggy night, a warm heart beating next to hers. *Make that two warm hearts*, she thought and smiled again.

She pulled the car door open and gasped as the amethyst went cold, like a shard of ice driven into her heart. For a split second, she was frozen in place.

Hurling her purse into the passenger seat with one hand, she yanked the amethyst crystal out of her shirt with the other. It wasn't her imagination. The crystal was like ice in her hand.

The world tilted. Sound receded. The fog was full of whisper-soft voices that called her name. Time went out of rhythm, twisted. Past and present collided, merged. She felt Ben's body was hers, and their body was growing cold, too cold, on the ground.

For a heartbeat, she thought she'd died.

"Ben," she whispered. "No!"

Dropping the necklace, Stacie dove into the car. With a shaking hand as icy as the crystal, she drove the keys into the ignition. She almost screamed in frustration when the car sluggishly refused to move. Sobbing and swearing, she kicked the emergency brake free and the car leaped forward.

Stacie paid no attention to the seat belt warning chirping as she tore toward the exit. She clawed in her jacket pocket for her phone, her left hand on the wheel as the rear tire went over the curb bouncing the car sideways.

Barely aware of the road, Stacie scrolled for a number she'd never used.

"Pick up. Pick up," she chanted as the phone on the other end rang repeatedly.

"Cruz."

Stacie almost cried.

"Lauren! It's Stacie," she almost shouted as she ran the

stop sign at the intersection and hauled the car into a tight left turn.

"Stac...?"

"Lauren. Ben's..." He's *not* dead. *He's not dead!* her mind screamed at her. "Ben's in trouble."

"What? What do you..."

"It's Troy. He's back. He... He has Ben. He's at the house."

"Stacie, how can you..."

"I just know, Lauren! I just know! Please! You have to come now. Now!"

"Stacie..."

A tight right curve sprang out of the fog. Stacie grabbed at the wheel with her right hand to drag the car around. Her phone flew out of her grip, hit the dashboard and dropped into the darkness under her feet.

"Help me, Lauren!" Stacie shouted at the phone, praying it hadn't turned off. "Help us, now!"

Believe me, she pleaded in her thoughts. *Don't doubt me now.*

It was all she could do. Her hands were full with the twists in the road.

It was six minutes from the shop to the house, but every minute stretched and bent. She knew every turn in the road, yet every one of them was a surprise and a terror in the fog that swirled around her, trying to lure her off the road and into disaster. It was every nightmare she'd ever had.

When her garage loomed out of the fog, Stacie almost drove by it. She slammed on the brakes, stopping the car almost in the middle of the road.

"*Ben!*" she screamed as she threw open the car door. He was here. She knew he was here. She heard Bananas' hysterical barking in the house.

She threw open the gate and ran down the fog-shrouded stairs, knowing he was waiting for her. Halfway down, she saw a dark form lying on the ground near the fountain. "*Ben!*" she called again, fear making her voice unrecognizable.

Almost before she took the last step, he lunged out of the dark, grabbing her arm, throwing her off balance and spinning her around. In a moment he had her backed against him, his left arm pinning her left arm against her side. His fingers were jammed under her jacket, digging painfully into her right breast. She began to pull away. Felt the knife at her throat. Stopped.

"That's right, bitch. Things are a little different now, aren't they?"

Stacie's pounding heart was shaking her whole body, but at the sound of his hated voice, something inside her shifted, became calm, centered and yet...other. As if someone else occupied her mind.

He had killed her Ben. Even if she died, she would make him *pay*.

"I *said*," said Troy, clawing fingers deep into her breast, "things are different now, aren't they?" Stacie gasped and jerked her head back as the knife point pushed in under her chin. Blood ran along her skin. Her blood? Ben's?

"No little faggot. No pretty boyfriend. No fucking *cops*!" He spit the word out. The spray hit the side of her face, and she flinched.

"Too bad, so sad," Troy went on in a sing-song voice. "Poor pretty boyfriend. Ran right into my knife. Pretty blood. All over."

Troy leaned into Stacie, ran his tongue up the side of her face and stuck it into her ear. Every muscle in her body went rigid.

"Yeah, you like that, don't you? Wait until we play with my knife," he whispered, and she thought he was giggling. "It will be much more fun. Oh, yeah."

The familiar part of Stacie's self moved farther away. Looking back, as if from outside, she didn't recognize the person left behind: cold, calculating, and very, very angry.

She was sharply aware of everything around her. Bananas barking, his voice going from loud to distant as he ran from one end of the house to the other, slamming his big body into the patio doors. The reek of Troy's body. The sound of sirens far away on the highway. The damp fog thinning slightly as a breeze flowed down into the garden. Light glinting on the mineral pillars standing like sentinels at the edge of the patio.

"Now bitch. Let's *play*." His knife slid down to her breast, and he grabbed her ear in his teeth.

Glass exploded onto the patio.

"What the fu...?"

Bananas, barking and snarling, plunged through Amelia's window. He barreled straight toward Troy.

Troy shoved Stacie away, knocking her to her knees against the stones at the edge of the patio. He turned to meet the attack as the big dog leaped.

He screamed as Bananas' jaws closed on his upraised arm. There was a terrible yelp and squeal of pain as the dog dove into the knife in Troy's other hand. Bananas twisted away in mid-air taking Troy down with him.

Stacie wrenched a stone pillar from the ground as Troy staggered to his feet, intent on finishing the dog.

"You filthy bastard!" Stacie screamed as she lurched to her feet and went after Troy.

He spun around, knife in hand as she charged him. Stacie was already swinging with all her strength as he came at her. He swung his knife, but her arm on the down stroke drove the stone pillar into the side of his head. He crashed to the ground, his head cracking loudly on the flagstones.

Stacie's rage put her beyond thought. She raised the pillar and stepped toward Troy's body. She wanted him dead. He'd killed her Ben. He'd killed her dog. She wanted him *dead.*

"Stacie! No! Don't!"

Stasha, no, don't, whispered a voice in her mind.

"Stacie, honey. Don't. He's out. Put it down. Sweetheart. Please. Put it down."

The calmness of the voice got through. A cool trickle of sanity slipped into her mind. She hesitated. Looked up.

The world came into back into focus.

Ben was in front of her, one hand held up toward her. Blood darkened his temple and ran on the side of his face. The right sleeve of his jacket was also dark with blood. A knee of his pants was torn out.

An illusion. He was dead. She'd felt him die.

"Stacie. Please. Put it down," said Ben softly. "He's not getting up. It's okay. It's over. Put it down, sweetheart. Please." Ben's eyes watched her warily.

Stacie blinked. Not dead?

"Ben?" she whispered. The world tilted. Stacie felt herself snap whole again.

Not dead!

"*Ben!*" The stone pillar smashed onto the patio.

She stepped toward him, and between one breath and the next, he was crushing her to him with his good arm.

"You were dead. You were dead," she muttered into his chest over and over as the sound of sirens washed up the canyon.

"I'm right here. I'm here," he told her.

"Oh, Ben," she said finally and stopped.

"Oh, Ben, what?" he asked into her hair.

"Just 'Oh, Ben.'"

Suddenly the street above was filled with shrill, pulsing sirens, red and blue strobe lights and the sound of doors crashing. The sirens cut off, leaving the silence echoing.

"Robard!" Cruz yelled. "Robard! Where the fuck are you? Give me some goddamn light down here!" Feet pounded on the stairs, and the beams of flashlights moved wildly across the patio.

"Here, Lauren," Ben called as his partner hit the bottom of the steps. "We need an ambulance."

"Get an ambulance up here!" shouted Cruz to the officers up on the street.

A powerful search light suddenly flashed on from above, its merciless light showing Cruz, gun drawn, the look on her face promising retribution. Ben bloody. Troy lying on the ground bleeding. Bananas lying a few feet away.

There was a weak whimper.

"Bananas! Oh, Bananas!" In an eye blink, Stacie was out of Ben's arms and on her knees by her dog. His coat was matted with blood and there was a puddle of it on the ground next to his chest. Stacie reached out to pet his big head. His tongue flicked out to lick her hand and his tail moved weakly. "My big beautiful boy. My sweet, brave, beautiful boy," Stacie murmured. She stroked his ears as tears ran down her face.

Ben knelt painfully at Stacie's side. "He'll make it, Stacie."

Cruz took one look and shouted up to the street. "Gunderson!"

"Yeah, Detective?"

"Call Warren Chen and get him out here now."

"The K-9 vet?"

"Yes! The vet. Tell him we have a big dog needs emergency care *now*."

"He's probably not on duty."

"Now!" Cruz shouted with an edge to her voice. Gunderson raised a hand placatingly and reached for his radio.

"And somebody get some First-Aid kits down here. Now!"

"Right here, Detective," said an officer at her elbow.

"See to Ben and Stacie," she said, nodding toward them with her head. "And see if you can stop the bleeding on the dog."

The officer nodded. "What about him?" He gestured at Troy.

"When you've seen to them first," she said, her voice hard.

He moved away and Cruz went down on a knee next to Troy. She put a hand to his neck. "Too bad," she muttered after a moment. She checked the dog bite on his arm, then hauled her cuffs out. "We need a second ambulance," she called up to Gunderson.

"For the dog?" Gunderson asked, unwisely.

"No, not for the dog," Cruz told him as if she were speaking to her ten-year-old. "We've got a killer here who is, unfortunately, not dead. Make sure they've got restraints." She shook her head and dragged Troy's wrists around to cuff him.

TWENTY-EIGHT

STACIE LOWERED HERSELF SLOWLY, CAREFULLY TO THE chaise longue on the patio and sank back against the cushions. The sounds of a quiet jazz trio floated out of the open French doors. It was Ace's combo's new CD. She'd be playing it a lot in the shop in the future.

She closed her eyes and let the hot sun seep into her skin. The turquoise blue shorts exposed her torn knees, scabbed over. The white tank top showed off the bruises on her arms and the bandage at her throat. It did little to cover the bulky bandage on her ribs where Troy's knife had cut through the heavy pea coat and gouged her ribs.

She didn't care. The nightmare was finished. Troy was locked up. He would never hurt anyone again. Now, she just needed to feel the sun and breeze on her skin. She was lucky to be alive. Everyone said that. She wanted to savor that life.

The life she was going to have with Ben. The life they were going to have together.

"You all right?" Alain called as he came out with a plate of hamburgers and headed toward the grill behind her. He and Emmie both looked much more rested than they had the night

402

at the hospital where they'd appeared after someone on the ER staff had called them.

"Very much all right. Thanks."

Voices floated out of the open window behind her. She'd been thrown out of her own kitchen by their friends. She heard Tucker's deep rumble, heard Maureen, Eileen and Emmie laugh. Colin made a tart retort, which brought more laughter. Stacie smiled at the sounds.

It was good to relax in the sun and smile. Four nights earlier, as she'd waited at the vet's surgery, she'd thought she'd never smile again.

When the vet, Warren Chen, had arrived at the chaos on her patio that night, she'd thought, from the worried look on his face, that Bananas would die. There was a vicious cut across his ribs pouring blood onto the patio, and he was bleeding on one shoulder and the insides of his legs from the glass of the window. Chen had sedated him, and two officers had carried the big dog up to Chen's van to be whisked away to surgery. Stacie would have gone in the van with Bananas, but Ben and the EMTs had insisted she go to the hospital to be stitched herself. Until then, Stacie hadn't even realized she was bleeding.

Dog tags rattled as Bananas limped out of his spot in the shade near the fountain, eased awkwardly to the flagstones near Stacie's chair and rested his big head on her thigh. She laid a hand on his head and stroked his ears. His tail thumped.

"You're a mess," she told him fondly. "You big dope." Large patches of his coat had been shaved away so that Chen could remove shards of glass and stitch him up. The dog had been lucky. Troy's knife had slid across his ribs and the glass fragments had missed major arteries in his legs. He'd come close to losing an eye as well. When Chen had told her Bananas would be okay, Stacie had sobbed uncontrollably in

Ben's arms. It was then that the shock of the whole night had finally set in and she'd begun to shake. The hospital had wanted to keep them both overnight but Alain had overruled them. He and Emmie had taken the couple home with them.

Ben stepped out of the French doors, thumbing his phone off and sliding it into a back pocket of his jeans. His right arm was bandaged where he'd taken fifteen stitches in the cut from Troy's knife. His right temple was turning green around the three stitches it had taken to close the cut from where he'd hit the fountain. He was limping slightly, his knee stiff and bruised where he'd torn it open on the flagstones. At the hospital he'd tried to joke that he'd taken less damage in Iraq, but Stacie hadn't been able to laugh. When he'd repeated the joke to friends a short while earlier, she'd managed a smile, but she'd slipped her arms around Ben, far too aware of what she'd almost lost.

"I see you're fawning over your hero again," he said, sitting on the chaise longue on the other side from the dog. Bananas rolled his eyes toward Ben, as if to say it was only what he deserved.

"*Our* hero," Stacie told him, setting a hand on her abdomen. "I'll never malign his protective abilities again."

Ben laid his hand over hers, and his eyes softened. "I've already promised him filet mignon at least once a week."

Now Stacie did smile. "He won't let you off that lightly. I already told him you'd promised it to him twice a week."

Ben snorted. "I see that's how it's going to be. Two against one." He tapped a finger lightly on the back of her hand. "At least for the next seven and a half months."

Stacie lifted her hand and twined her fingers with his.

"Well, one thing is sure," said Ben. "There's no putting off replacing that glass now." He nodded to the spot where plywood covered the shattered window in Amelia's room.

"All right, you two. Enough of that." Colin waltzed out the door carrying a tray of glasses. Matt Harrelson followed him with pitchers of iced tea and lemonade. Emmie and Eileen were right behind them with bowls of salads and chips. "You'll have plenty of time to be alone."

"At least for a few months," said Alain. "Then that little boy will keep them up at night. I remember those days."

"Girl," said Stacie.

"And their *grandmère* will be here, oh, at least every day or so," said Emmie, smiling.

Startled, Stacie looked up suddenly at Emmie. A jolt of electricity seemed to jump between them. Emmie gave her a slight smile and raised an eyebrow.

"They," whispered Stacie glancing down at her hand joined with Ben's. Ben, trading remarks with Colin, didn't hear her.

Stacie rubbed Bananas' forehead. "*Three* times a week," she told him quietly.

"Oh, Stacie!" said Mir as she set silverware and paper napkins on the table nearby. "Where did you get this darling statue? It looks just like Bananas!"

"It is Bananas," said Maureen. "Ben e-mailed some photos the other night and asked me to do it. It came out of the kiln this morning."

"She worked day *and* night. Neglected me and everything," Tucker said. "I even had to make the cookies today."

Ben feigned choking on his iced tea. "Last time I checked you didn't even know the house *had* a kitchen," he said as a car door slammed on the road above.

Tucker laid a hand on his heart. "I'm hurt. Truly wounded."

"He did help," said Maureen with a straight face. "He went to the store for chocolate chips."

405

"*Et tu?*" said Tucker. "I thought wives were supposed to cover for their husbands."

Maureen shook her head. "I keep telling him to stop reading the fables published in the women's magazines at the newsstand," she said to no one in particular as everyone laughed.

There were footsteps on the stairs. Ben raised a hand as Lauren and her husband came down.

"Detective. Good to see you in an unofficial capacity," called Eileen.

"Who said it was unofficial? Last time I let Robard out of my sight, he almost got himself killed. I do not want to break in a new partner." She turned to her husband as she got to the bottom of the steps. "For those who don't know—which is about all of you—this is my long-suffering husband, Paul Eilers." Paul raised a finger to a non-existent hat.

"Colin, what are you doing?" Stacie asked her friend who was going back and forth across the patio examining the flagstones with an imaginary magnifying glass.

"Looking for blood," he said.

"Colin!" Eileen protested.

"You ghoul!" Mir slapped him on the shoulder.

"What? Everyone's thinking the same thing," said Colin. "Right, Ace?"

Ace choked on his lemonade and looked incredibly guilty.

Ben was looking at Stacie with worry in his eyes, but she smiled. "Proves my point. Some men never graduate middle school."

"I certainly never saw any reason to," said Colin. "So who cleaned it up?"

"No idea," said Stacie. "When we got home yesterday, the flags were wet, the window was boarded up, and all signs of...that night were gone. I assumed the crime scene guys cleaned it up."

"I told her we're not that considerate. It's more likely that a friend cleaned it up." Ben looked pointedly at Cruz.

"Not me," Lauren lied unconvincingly. "I would have called in a crew. I'm afraid I've seen more than my share of blood in the last week. Some of it leaking from people I care about." She winced suddenly, realizing what she'd said and who she'd said it to. "Sorry. That was thoughtless."

Her remark sobered everyone up. There was a pause as they all thought about why they were here. To celebrate Stacie and Ben's—and Bananas'—survival, their wedding announcement, and the announcement that Stacie was pregnant. It could so easily have been a triple funeral.

In the silence, the hamburgers sizzled as Alain flipped them.

"So what's happening with this bottom feeder?" asked Tucker finally. "That's what I want to know." He looked at Cruz, who turned to Ben, and asked if he wanted to fill everyone in, or if he wanted her to.

"I just talked to Steve Danner," said Ben. Cruz looked relieved. "The killer formerly known as Troy," he said, trying to lighten a dark moment, "appears not to exist."

"What?" said Eileen.

"So far, they can't find his prints on file, though they're still looking. The Army—no surprise there—doesn't have a Carson Fowler on record as having served in Iraq, at least not one that matches this guy. Stacie was right. The names he was giving were not his own. The IDs we've found so far are all faked. Some of them are pretty good.

"They have his prints all over the house where he was squatting, so he can't disclaim the body buried in the backyard or the...souvenirs...he had there. But he doesn't want to.

Danner said he woke up this morning screaming about his 'things.'"

Stacie shuddered.

Ben didn't tell them that Troy kept screaming about killing the "red-haired bitch" for ruining everything. He didn't plan to ever tell Stacie that.

"They're beginning to take DNA samples from..." Ben glanced at Stacie. She squeezed his hand tightly. "From the hair he had collected," Ben continued. "There are a number of police departments trying to match those with missing women and those we suspect he's killed." He paused again. "It will be a long process, but he's not going anywhere. Ever again."

It was a relief to hear Troy would die in prison, but Stacie knew she'd always remember the women he'd killed. Especially Sue. Their deaths would keep her awake at night for a long time into the future.

"I was lucky," said Stacie quietly.

"We all were," said Ben.

"And you can never again question the strength of my crystals," said Stacie, deciding it was time to lighten the mood.

Tucker guffawed. Ben looked at her in astonishment for a moment, then chuckled, too.

"What about that young girl?" Mir asked Stacie. "The one that came to you for help? Do you know what's happening with her?"

"I called the shelter yesterday," said Eileen, answering her. "They can't tell me where she is, of course, but the director did tell me she's safe with a family who will help her finish school and help her care for the baby."

"She's decided to keep the child, then?" asked Stacie.

Eileen nodded. "I gather she was adamant about it."

"What about the guy who tried to strangle her?"

"Oh, he's denying it," said Cruz. "But Ginny's agreed to testify against him. And after Steve talked to the church people about him, he got calls from two other women about Jer's violence. Including from his alleged 'fiancée,' who, it turns out, isn't related to Ginny at all. He'll be charged with statutory rape and multiple counts of assault and vandalism. Stacie's new surveillance cameras and," she nodded toward Matt, "Mr. Harrelson's caught him in the act."

"And Praise Be To Jesus," exclaimed Colin throwing his hands in the air, "the Holy Star Evangelical Church is gone!"

"Really?" said Stacie.

Cruz nodded. "You haven't seen the news?"

"Not since I've been starring in it," said Stacie.

"Well, with the news of the preacher's son assaulting young women and vandalizing businesses—that bit with the cross made him very unpopular—they decided to pull up stakes. One of the reporters got onto stories about Hammond having multiple families and stolen funds from two previous churches, too."

"It's been a busy week in Lake Woebegone," said Stacie.

"Jeez, Robard," said Tucker. "You may have to go back on active duty just to get some peace and quiet."

"Burgers are done," said Alain.

There was a clatter of chairs and a shuffling of plates as everyone got up and headed toward the grill.

Ben started to stand, but Stacie tugged his hand slightly, and he settled back down.

"Ben, maybe now with...now that I'm pregnant, is it still a good idea to resign?"

Ben glanced toward Lauren, but she was laughing with Emmie.

"I've been wondering the same thing. I may stay for

another year or so, until we can build up some savings, see if the shows pan out. But I think, in the end, I'll leave."

"Are you okay with staying?"

He nodded. "Yeah. I am. Cruz will hate me though, when I do leave. She was serious about not wanting to train a replacement."

Stacie laughed. The amethyst crystal lay warm against her heart.

"She'll hate me, too," she said. "But maybe we could name one of the girls after her."

"She'd like that," said Ben, then did a double take. "Wait. One of them?"

Stacie just smiled.

READ ON FOR A SAMPLE OF SING ME THE RAIN. BUT FIRST, A THANK YOU...

Dear Reader,

Thank you for reading *Dangerous Visions*, part of my Eden Beach Crime series. I hope you enjoyed it. I'd love to know what you think of Stacie, Ben, Bananas and the rest of the cast. Drop me a line at LizHartleyAuthor@hotmail.com.

If this is the first of my books that you've read, I'm truly grateful you took a chance and gave it a try. I hope you enjoyed visiting Eden Beach so much that you'll come back again.

Whether you're a new reader or a returning reader, I'd like to ask a favor. If you're comfortable with it, I'd love you to review *Dangerous Visions*. Honest reviews—what you liked, what you didn't—help other readers discover a new book or author. If you have the time, here's a link to my author page at Amazon, where you can find all my books and post your review.

If you freeze at the thought of doing a review, I've posted some guidelines on my website that can help you get started, whether you're reviewing my books or anyone else's. All authors will be grateful you took the time. I know I will be.

To learn more about Eden Beach and the quirky people living there, visit www.LizHartleyAuthor.com. You can follow me on my blog or subscribe to my quarterly newsletter.

If Facebook is where you keep up with friends, family, and favorite authors, you can follow me there, at https://www.facebook.com/LizHartleyEdenBeachNovels.

Again, thank you for reading *Dangerous Visions*. I hope to meet you again in Eden Beach.

Now, read on for a sample of my upcoming Eden Beach Main Street Novel, *Sing Me the Rain*.

Gratefully,

Liz Hartley

SING ME THE RAIN

DAVID WOKE SLOWLY FROM A HEAVY SLEEP, RISING LIKE A SEA creature ascending from the depths of a lost ocean. He listened to the sound of his breathing, felt the weight of his body, warm and content, pressing into the bed. He was helpless to move even if he had wanted to. At the moment, he didn't want to. He didn't want to remember the waking world. There was pain there, he knew, and sorrow. Just for a few moments more, he wanted to enjoy this lovely lethargy, the strange sense of contentment, of life finally being right.

Slowly he became aware that his mouth felt glued shut and tasted like he'd licked the sidewalks around Pershing Square in Los Angeles where the homeless sat and wandered, talking to themselves. In the distant reaches of his mind, tiny flashes of pain sparkled, threatening to gather into a headache. A headache he was sure would spread to the rest of his body. Soon.

It had been a long time since he'd drunk enough to warrant a hangover, but the signs were unmistakable. He'd planned to have a drink, but he hadn't planned on getting drunk. He only hoped he hadn't done or said anything stupid enough to give the staff—or worse, the customers—grist for gossip.

On that thought, he became sharply aware of several things.

One, the sound of quiet breathing was not his own.

Two, his left arm was wrapped tightly around a tidy female waist, snugly caught between a generously curving hip and a rising rib cage, while his left hand was filled with the delicious soft weight of a generous, warm breast, his thumb pressed against a nipple relaxed in sleep.

Three, a nicely rounded bottom was tucked close against his genitals which were doing their best to get him to wake up and pay attention.

Over it all hung the fragrance of a beautiful woman.

And sex.

David's eyes snapped open. A thin blade of yellow light from the parking lot outside sliced through the gap in the hotel blackout curtains and stabbed him through the forehead. The distant shards of dispersed pain in his head crashed and splintered across the bridge of his nose.

Squinting against the pain, David lowered his gaze to the woman nestled next to him.

Tucked just under his chin was a head full of soft, tawny curls moving gently to the rhythm of his breath. In the dim light of the digital readout on the bedside clock, he saw the delicate whorls of a lovely ear and the soft, smooth curve of a cheek along which lay long, dark eyelashes that framed an eye which, when open, was the soft green-blue of fine aquamarine.

A face he knew well.

The breast in his hand he'd come to know very well indeed.

His eyes slammed shut.

Oh no, he thought. *Oh no, oh no, oh no.*

He couldn't have.

Not with Sarah.

That couldn't happen.

That *mustn't* happen.

But it had.

The condolences had been killing him. For two days, a steady stream of dealers, retailers and industry reporters had flowed by the convention show booth to give him their heartfelt sympathy, to tell him how unique Sam had been, that he would be missed. To say they were glad David was back at SMK, Inc., the colored gemstone company everyone called Kellerman's.

Then there were those who hadn't heard. Who had come to the booth expecting to see, looking forward to seeing, Sam. Some of them had broken down into tears when David or one of the others had told them about Sam's death just after Christmas.

David hadn't known that grief could be so exhausting.

He'd taken it stoically for two days, but last night he'd gone into the hotel bar. *Just one drink,* he'd thought. *It'll help me sleep.* But the first drink had opened the sluice of memories, and David had taken another to try to close it again.

He'd seen Sarah walk by the big windows facing the lobby, seen her spot him, hesitate. Then she'd walked in and sat down next to him. She was not very sober herself, and he'd been almost shocked. Sarah Barton was the epitome of self-control. Never a hair out of place. Carefully, conservatively, perfectly dressed.

She'd asked how he was doing. Said how sorry she was. Laid a gentle hand on his arm.

But when her eyes—those beautiful blue-green eyes—had

welled with tears, so had his. She'd loved Sam as much as he had, David knew. His father's loss was an enormous hole between them.

It was the tears that had undone them both.

They'd had another drink, this one together.

Things were hazy after that, except that they'd ended up here. In her room. In her bed. They'd made love not once, but twice. That part he remembered with absolute clarity. He also remembered that it had been...remarkable. Miraculous. He had been astonished at how perfect she had felt, at how perfect they had felt together. They had laughed like children, touching foreheads.

Laura never laughed in bed.

He had never had a night like this one.

A dangerous thought.

Oh, Sarah, he thought. *What have we done?*

From the day she'd started working at Kellerman's, ten years before, Sarah had never been less than professional. In the six weeks since Sam's death, nothing had changed. She and David had had only polite, business conversations. *He's a potential new client who's requested a call from one of the principals,* she might say. *Have you had time to check the new shipment of emeralds?* he might ask.

What would she think of him now? What *could* she think? Would she sue for harassment? Or worse, charge him with assault?

Oh, God. The talk. There had been enough of that when Sam brought Maurice into the business.

What if she quit?

He felt Sarah's warmth against him. Memories of the night flashed back to him.

With a rush of emotion that twisted his heart, David realized that it wasn't the business or the gossip that worried him as much as the thought of never seeing Sarah again. Suddenly, deeply, he knew he couldn't bear that.

He couldn't think about that right now, not least because of the throbbing pain in his head.

David couldn't see the clock over Sarah's shoulder, but the sliver of sky visible through the gap in the curtains was getting lighter. He had to face this, and soon. They had to get to the convention hall floor, get ready for the day's business. As it was for other gemstone dealers from around the world, the Tucson Gem and Mineral Show was Kellerman's biggest show, their once-a-year chance to talk to customers face-to-face and to develop new customers. David had to be on top of his game, or as on top of it as he could be with only a few hours sleep. He had to show their customers that the business was solid, stable, even with Sam gone.

Sam.

Grief hit him in the chest so hard he couldn't breathe.

What would Sam have said about this?

David's gut shriveled imagining his father's face if he'd been alive to know his son had slept with Sarah, the woman Sam considered the daughter he'd never had. David had never forgotten the sadness and deep disappointment that had furrowed Sam's face the day David had told him he was leaving the colored stone business to teach.

He closed his eyes against the memory. His father's face. So sad. So old.

Ten years I could have worked with him and made him happy, thought David. Now it was too late.

This was no time to think about what ifs. He had to get up. *They* had to get up. They had a show to do.

David was reluctant to break contact with Sarah, but there was no choice.

Slowly, oh, so slowly, he drew his hand out from under Sarah's breast and gently lifted his arm, rustling the sheet.

His right arm was bent under the pillow beneath her head. As he carefully pulled it out, gently sliding her head and pillow off his numb hand, Sarah stirred. David froze.

"Kyle?" she murmured.

Kyle?

David waited, heart pounding in time with his head.

Who's Kyle? he wondered. He'd known Sarah for ten years, but he realized he really knew nothing about her.

Sarah seemed to slide softly back into sleep.

With his left hand, David worked the tangled sheets out from under his backside, and finally free, slipped out of the bed.

As he stood upright, his stomach revolted. He felt dinner and drinks rising. Rising…

He stumbled unsteadily across the room, ramming his shoulder painfully into the corner of the wall by the bathroom.

Despite his sense of urgency, David tried to close the door quietly. He dropped to his knees just in time to deliver the previous night into the toilet.

When there was nothing left to throw up, he unthinkingly turned on the tub faucet. The thundering noise in that small area drove more arrows of pain into David's head.

If Sarah hadn't been awake before, she would be now, he thought.

He wet a washcloth and scrubbed his face. Cupped water to his mouth, spat, turned off the tap.

Cold and sweaty, he stood shakily and wrapped the poor excuse for a towel around his waist. He sat on the edge of the tub and lifted the cool, wet cloth to his aching eyes.

Now what? he thought. *Now what?*

How was he—how were *they*—going to get through the rest of the week?

How could he have been this stupid?

He dropped the washcloth on the side of the tub and stood up, massaging his temples. Reluctantly, he opened the door, catching a look at his reflection in the mirror over the sink. Tousled medium-brown hair, dark eyes shadowed with pain, stubble shadowing his chin.

Mouth that felt like dirty asphalt.

He felt like hell. He looked so much worse.

It did nothing for his self-confidence.

He tightened the towel and turned the corner into the hotel room.

Light poured into the room from the open window along with chilly dawn air. David winced. Another brilliant winter day in the desert.

Wrapped in his shirt—his shirt!—Sarah stood at the open sliding door, looking out across the desert city. Her hair fell around her shoulders in tangled curls. Until last night, David had never seen it loose. Sarah was always armored in heels, some kind of tailored slack suit, a high-collared blouse, and a take-no-bullshit attitude.

With a shock, he saw how tiny she was. At 5'8", David wasn't a tall man, but Sarah couldn't be five feet.

She turned, and David caught his breath.

It was impossible not to notice how beautiful she was. Her hair, a mix of blond, brown, and gold, her pale skin flushed with rose. Her face was like an elf's—pointed chin, tiny nose, widow's peak—except the smudged make-up gave her a sultriness he didn't connect with elves. David felt himself hardening again. For a moment, all he could think of was getting back into bed with her.

Then he saw her aqua eyes, almost glowing in the morning light.

She was furious.

It made her seem taller.

ACKNOWLEDGMENTS

BOOKS ARE NEVER A SOLO EFFORT, AND *DANGEROUS VISIONS* is no different. I am sincerely grateful to my beta readers who read the first draft with care and enthusiasm. Their suggestions were invaluable.

Mary E. DeGuelle, Senior Forensic Specialist, retired, Orange County Sheriff's Department (OCSD), California, saved me from forensic gaffes. Cindy Wall, author of six YA novels featuring ham radio operators Kim Stafford and Marc Lawrence, urged me to expand Colin's role. Lauri Martin wanted to see more of Ben (figuratively speaking). Julie Walsh insisted I steam things up.

Eileen Hicks, Lana Gerber, and Helen Lewis provided proofreading assistance. Darcie Preuitt read the manuscript with her English teacher's eagle eyes and saved me from a number of cringe-worthy mistakes. However, in the end, all errors are mine.

The gorgeously suspenseful cover is the work of Kim Killion at Killion Publishing. Thank you, Kim, for giving me goosebumps with this one.

As I have before and no doubt will again, I depended on

Devon Monk, author of more than twenty urban fantasy novels, for her ability to see deep inside the structure of a story to what is missing. She is almost always right. She suggested that I remove the prologue, which I did, and kill the dog, which I did not.

Thank you, all.

Liz

ABOUT THE AUTHOR

LIZ HARTLEY IS THE AUTHOR OF TWO SERIES SET IN THE SMALL TOWN OF Eden Beach, California: The Eden Beach Main Street Novels, and The Eden Beach Crime Novels.

Liz has worn jewelry and picked up rocks since she was old enough to stand. She was probably fated to spend more than twenty-five years writing about jewelry and gemstones. She has both Graduate Gemologist (GG) and Fellow of the Gemmological Association of Great Britain (FGA) diplomas. So it's no wonder that birthstones play a prominent role in her novels.

An enthusiastic traveler, Liz has lived and studied in Japan, traveled with gem and mineral enthusiasts to Brazil, journeyed to southern Africa with members of the Los Angeles Zoo (where she was a docent for five years), and made two "grand tours" in Europe.

She does not own a TV, but loves movies and will read just about anything that doesn't get out of her way.

ALSO BY LIZ HARTLEY

Trust Not the Heart: An Eden Beach Main Street Novel

www.ingramcontent.com/pod-product-compliance
Lightning Source LLC
Chambersburg PA
CBHW072002110726
47910CB00005B/1627